Caryl McAdoo

Vow Unbroken

HOWARD BOOKS
A Division of Simon & Schuster, Inc.
New York Nashville London Toronto Sydney New Delhi

Howard Books
A Division of Simon & Schuster, Inc.
1230 Avenue of the Americas
New York, NY 10020

This book is a work of fiction. Any references to historical events, real people, or real places are used fictitiously. Other names, characters, places, and events are products of the author's imagination, and any resemblance to actual events or places or persons, living or dead, is entirely coincidental.

First Howard Books trade paperback edition March 2014

HOWARD and colophon are trademarks of Simon & Schuster, Inc.

For information about special discounts for bulk purchases, please contact Simon & Schuster Special Sales at 1-866-506-1949 or business@simonandschuster.com

The Simon & Schuster Speakers Bureau can bring authors to your live event. For more information or to book an event contact the Simon & Schuster Speakers Bureau at 1-866-248-3049 or visit our website at www.simonspeakers.com.

Interior design by Davina Mock-Maniscalco

Manufactured in the United States of America

10 9 8 7 6 5 4 3 2 1

Library of Congress Cataloging-in-Publication Data
McAdoo, Caryl.
Vow Unbroken / Caryl McAdoo.—First Howard Books trade paperback edition.
pages cm
ISBN 978-1-4767-3551-1—ISBN 978-1-4767-3552-8 (ebook) 1. Widows—Fiction. 2. Texas—History—19th century—Fiction. 3. Christian fiction. 4. Love stories. I. Title.
PS3613.C26V69 2014
813'.6—dc23
2013022673

ISBN 978-1-4767-3551-1
ISBN 978-1-4767-3552-8 (ebook)

Without my beloved, humble, and supportive husband
of forty-five years, this story would certainly never have
been penned. So much more than my inspiration
and encourager, Ron completes me and makes me whole.
He leads me and is devoted to our triune relationship
with Father God through His Son.
Thank you, sweetheart. I love you more than yesterday,
but less than tomorrow.

And to all the handmaidens of the Lord
who have made and kept their vows—God has not
forgotten you. He loves you deeply and rejoices over you
with singing. Hold fast to your vision and do not give up,
not ever, for He is your faithful Father whose Word
never returns void, but always accomplishes its purpose,
His good plan for you.

For You, O God, have heard my vows; You have given *me* the heritage of those who fear Your name.

Psalm 61:5 NKJV

CHAPTER

ONE

He took the pinch of cotton Sue offered and rubbed it between his short, pudgy fingers. "I'm truly sorry, Mis'ess Baylor. Two cents is all I can pay."

She seethed but forced at least a show of civility. "Mister Littlejohn." She spoke in a stiff staccato. "A week ago. Before everyone left. You promised three and a half to four cents a pound! You said depending on the quality. That is the main reason. The biggest reason. That I didn't go with the others."

The man smiled. "Oh, I might have said two and a half or maybe even three, but things change. You know that."

She couldn't stand being talked down to, especially by such a lying loafer.

"I wish I could help you, but two cents it is. I mean, besides, anyone can see." He held the sample up. "It's shoddy lint." He shook his head. "Pardon me for saying, Mis'ess Baylor, but a granger you are not."

"Anyone can see its excellent quality, you mean."

A bit of breeze, a very little bit, stirred the top layer of dust from the street; it cooled her skin, but her insides still steamed.

He stuck out his bottom lip. "I'd advise you to take my offer. I can pay half now, the rest when I return."

Sue studied his face while a hundred calculations ran through her mind. He certainly didn't look like the weasel he'd turned out to be. Her cotton was as good as, if not better than, any of the loads that left last Thursday. She reached up and massaged her neck, then lifted her braid to let some air dry her sweat.

She glanced over at her wagons. Levi had Becky laughing hard. The children would be so disappointed. Maybe if—

No. She would not allow this thief to take advantage of her family. How could he even think to? The loathsome, immoral oaf! She'd worked too hard getting her crop in. Everyone had, even her nine-year-old, Becky. Why, at two cents, she'd hardly realize any profit after the extra seed and what she paid the pickers.

She squared her shoulders and, determined anew, faced him again. "I'll accept three and a half cents per pound. All cash. Not a fraction less."

"Two cents, ma'am. Half now, half when I get back." He jingled the coins in his vest pocket.

Perspiration trickled down to the small of her back. The sun, though its climb had barely begun, already shone bright on the eastern horizon and heated the mid-September air so that every breath scorched her throat. Much like Jack Littlejohn, it offered no mercy. And like the air, her throat held no moisture, though she needed to swallow.

"You're wasting my time. Good day, Mister Littlejohn." She whirled and headed toward her wagons. Her face burned, and she knew full well that it had turned red. How dare that man! A grubby hand grabbed her arm and, whirling her around, jerked her to an abrupt stop. She yanked away from his grasp and glared; she wished the fire inside her would somehow leap forward and set the despicable excuse of a human being ablaze.

"Keep your cheating hands off me."

He almost looked apologetic. "Be reasonable, Mis'ess Baylor. Two cents is a right fair price. Besides, who else you going to sell to?"

She swatted at a fly buzzing about and adjusted her hat, never taking her eyes from the man's. "I'll burn my cotton before I sell it to the likes of you." She stopped next to her first wagon and faced the second one. "Levi, we're going."

"But, Aunt Sue—"

Doing everything in her power to keep from bursting into angry tears, she glared. Never, never, never would she give that horrible man the satisfaction of seeing her lose control. She kept her voice calm and steady. "Levi, now!"

"Yes, ma'am."

She climbed aboard and probably struck the reins against her mules' backs a bit too forcefully. The poor animals hadn't lied to her. She made a point to sound sweet. "Get up, now, Dex." She clucked. "Hey, now, Daisy."

She wanted to scream, but held it all in.

The wooden wheels creaked under the load. Metal clanged against metal. The harnesses strained as the four animals snorted and urged the two wagons, heavy with all her hopes and dreams, into motion. Plans had been to camp out, spend a night under the Texas stars in the heart of the small community she called home. Plans had been to order the children a pair of new shoes each and a bolt or two of fabric for some new clothes. But as she knew all too well, plans often changed.

One more time. Why did this keep happening? One more

time a man had tried to take advantage of her, bilk her because she was alone. Her father the judge would tell her that she should have insisted on a contract, or at least a deposit; she had absolutely no legal recourse against the charlatan. Should have paid to have it hauled like last year, but no. Well, that wasn't an option now. How glad she was that her daddy lived so far away and would never know about her stupidity. She'd disappointed him enough for one lifetime.

What could she do now? She had to sell the crop. It represented all her savings, and if she didn't get a fair price, she'd have to sell off some of her land—her husband's and his brother's legacy to the children. That no-good Littlejohn! Why had she taken him at his word?

She closed her eyes a moment and whispered, "Help me, Lord."

God willing, maybe she could catch up to the cotton train, then make the trip with the Foglesongs and Howletts and the rest. Maybe only two wagons could travel farther each day; start earlier of a morning, and stay after it until dark. Those Jefferson buyers were big guns, too; paid in gold coin on the barrelhead.

Ideas and options raced through her mind as she steered the team out of the Sulphur Fork Prairie settlement toward her farm four or five miles south. A few she dismissed as crazy. Her blood still boiled. What a waste; all that way for nothing.

"Ooooogh!" She was glad her daughter was riding with Levi and didn't witness her outburst.

She simply had to get her cotton to Jefferson, and do it before the rains set in. The question was, Could she go alone? Levi would certainly be a help, but could he pull enough weight? Be responsible for such a long hard haul? Her nephew was a good boy and strong for fourteen, but— Who? Who else could she ask? The answer came like a bolt of lightning—Elaine!

She'd see if her best friend would go. Larry could look after their kids. The baby had turned four her last birthday, and the oldest girl was sixteen. He shouldn't mind all that much. Pulling to the right, she waved the reins on the mules' backs again and turned toward the Dawsons' place.

Anyway, the unexpected visit would bless the whole bunch, even Levi and Becky. They'd love having the children to play with for a while. That would give her the opportunity to propose her plan. She stopped the team on the shady side of the barn and climbed down. She went back to help her daughter off the second wagon before heading to the house.

"Mama, I'm not a baby." Becky thrust her fists on her hips and frowned. "I can get down by myself."

"Fine, little girl, but you had better watch your tone."

Joseph, one of the middle Dawson boys, ran out. "Mama, Mama! Miss Sue's here with Becky and Levi!"

A passel of children came from several directions, and laughter and greetings were shouted all around. Her friend waited on the porch, smiling. Sue so admired Elaine's wisdom and appreciated her advice. As long as she'd known her, Elaine Dawson had never jumped into anything or made one snap decision. Instead, everything she did, every move, had been well thought out.

Sue wished she could be more like that. She needed Elaine's cool head now. Her friend would just have to agree to help. Besides, with her along, the journey would even be fun. Once seated on the porch, with tea served and the children playing, Sue explained her predicament and asked Elaine to go with her.

"Are you crazy, Susannah Baylor?"

"No, I am not. You tell me, what choice do I have?" Sue hated the desperation dripping from her words. She sipped the tea Elaine had poured and watched the children playing, her mind spinning. How could she talk her friend into it? She'd used almost everything she could think of, but not one argument she'd offered had budged Elaine.

Finally, Sue surrendered. "Oh, fine, then. If you won't go and help me, what do you think about Rebecca staying here? The trace would be so hard on her. The round trip is liable to take me a month or better."

Elaine shook her head. "You simply cannot go. Listen to me! You and Levi cannot do this alone." She leaned forward and held Sue's eyes. "Now pay attention. It's too dangerous. Anything could happen. There's the Indians, thieves, and wild animals; the wagons or mules might break down. You'll have the Sulphur River to cross, not to mention the White Oak Creek bottoms. What if you got stuck? What would you do then?"

"How about Larry going? I wouldn't ask, but—"

"Please don't, honey. You know he's got way too much to do around here to be gone a month. We've already bought wheat seed, and our fields need a lot of work before they're ready to plant."

"Maybe I could hire someone in Cuthand, before I have to cross the river."

"And you'd leave on that possibility. Come on, Sue." Her friend's eyebrows both went up, and her eyes, troubled only moments ago, suddenly sparkled. "I know! What about Henry Buckmeyer? I'm pretty certain he's still around."

"That layabout heathen?"

"No, wait a minute. You shouldn't judge him on the gossip.

I've known his mother for years, and she's a wonderful Christian woman. Everyone speaks highly of her. I can't imagine she didn't raise her son in the faith. He could be the perfect one to help you."

"So what if his mother's a Christian? You'd really suggest I spend a month on the trace with a single man? What about abstaining from all appearances of evil?"

"What about Doug Howlett?"

"He and Shannan went with the others, and took Samuel and the girls along with them."

Elaine looked off toward where the kids played and sighed. "What about Hershel Massey?"

Sue drew back and pursed her lips. "Now who's crazy? He's at least eighty years old!"

"Really? He sure doesn't look it." Elaine tucked a loose strand of hair back into her bun. "Well, what I know for certain, without any doubt, is that you cannot go alone."

"But you refuse, and I have to get my cotton to the buyers. It'll be the first time in all these years that we won't be living on the razor's edge. The first time since Andy passed that I'll have coin enough to actually buy more than just the bare necessities." Sue angrily swiped at a stupid tear threatening to run down her cheek. "And if I don't, and I can't make any profits, I'll have to start selling off the land. I just can't do that, Elaine. So what do you suggest?" Elbows on the table, she hung her head, holding her face with both hands a minute, then looked back up. "Everyone I could've asked to help has already gone."

The older woman dipped the fancy tea infuser that her mother had sent from back east in her cup. "There's got to be someone. Let me think a minute."

"Even if you thought of anyone, who would be willing to pack up and light a shuck on such short notice?"

"Nothing says that you have to leave today."

"Elaine! Don't you understand? I've got to get my lint to Jefferson. Before the buyers leave, before the rains set in. I can't waste any more time if I'm ever going to catch up. Not when the train already has a four-day lead on me!"

"Well then, it looks to me like we're back to Henry. Surely he'd be a help if he's free to go. And since when do you care about what people think anyway?"

Sue finished her tea in one gulp. This wouldn't be the first time she'd disagreed with her friend, even though Elaine did usually sound the voice of reason. "Well, I'm just sorry. He's been nothing but a lazy, old . . . hermit, mama's boy."

"He isn't old, Sue. He's in his early thirties at most."

"Well, I don't think he would be any help at all. Probably more of a burden who'd only slow me down."

"He'd be a man with a gun, and he was with Jackson in New Orleans." Elaine reached across and captured her hand. "Susannah! What you're considering is too dangerous! It's a long way to Jefferson, and a hard trail." She stood and turned her back with her fists on her hips. "You cannot go alone. And I'm sorry, but I won't keep Becky. I'll not play any part in this idiotic scheme of yours." She faced her again. "Please, at least go see Henry."

Sue shook her head and sighed.

"Just go ask him; see if he'd even be willing to go. Leave your wagons and the kids here for the day, take Larry's bay, and go out to the Buckmeyer place right now. Won't you?"

She didn't like her hands being tied behind her back, and that's exactly how she saw the impossible situation. But maybe her friend had a point, though she hated to admit it. She probably did need help, but Patrick Henry Buckmeyer? If she was a betting lady, she'd give odds that he'd never worked an honest day in his life.

Succumbing to Elaine's pleas, she heard herself agree to go, and her friend leapt into action. "Larry!" she hollered. "Would you please saddle up your horse? Sue's going to need to borrow him for a little ride this morning."

Becky's high-pitched screams pulled Sue's attention to the children. On the ground, her daughter squealed and giggled at Levi's tickling. The Dawson children all scurried away from them. She jumped up and ran after her best friend, shrieking with delight. She stretched out her arm and touched Sophia Belle, only a year older. "You're it!"

For their sake, Sue told herself. She couldn't let them down. Life had been too hard already on ones so young. Her thoughts wandered to their fathers, and the vision appeared full force again, starting to replay in her mind for the thousandth time. But she shook it away, refusing to allow it to paralyze her as it usually did. Not now, not today.

"Sue?" Her friend's husband stood beside his horse at the bottom of the porch steps. "Got him all ready for you."

She came back to the present and rose, reaching for the reins. The man was top-notch, a hard worker and good provider. "Thank you, Larry. I'll be doing my best to get back before dark."

"No trouble. Be safe."

Elaine walked up and slipped an arm around his waist. "We'll keep some supper out for you and Henry."

Sue huffed, shook her head, swung into the saddle, and then straightened her bothersome dress. She should have worn

Andy's trousers, but since she'd been going to town . . . "We'll see."

Elaine laughed. One thing Sue loved about her friend was her carefree, boisterous laugh. "Sue Baylor, if you're crazy enough to head off on the Jefferson Trace with eight thousand pounds of cotton by yourself, then you're absolutely right. We will see."

Setting her heels against the gelding's flanks, Sue clicked her tongue. Levi and Becky waved, obviously thrilled over their extra time at the Dawsons'. She decided to head home first, then loop around to the Buckmeyer place. The layabout probably was either gone or drunk, and it would be a wasted trip. Maybe she could hire some help along the way.

The bay moved into a comfortable lope. She arrived at her house well before high noon. She had made a mental list on the way, and the first thing she did was to change into her dead husband's trousers—she wouldn't be trying to impress anyone. Then she hurried about gathering her few remaining coins and collected a change of clothes for herself and each of the children. She rolled her skirt and stuck it in the bag, too, just in case.

From the back of the dresser drawer, she pulled out Andy's pistol and stuck it into her waistband, then put all the extra powder and shot in her bag. She preferred shooting the flintlock, but figured she might need all the firepower she could muster on the trace. Levi was a decent shot, but having another gun could be a lifesaver. Elaine was definitely right about that at least.

Outside, she opened the barn gate. "You take care of your calf, Bess, and stay out of the bottoms." She watched her old cow amble off, then looked around with a strange foreboding. A notion swept over her that she'd never see the place again.

Did it mean the journey would go bad? Was the Lord trying to tell her not to go? If something happened to her, what would Levi and Becky do? Take no thought for tomorrow played through her head. She couldn't think about it. She wouldn't. She would only think about getting her cotton to market and trust the good Lord to help her.

She packed everything on the horse and mounted, hardly able to believe it had come to this. That very morning when she'd set out before sunup, she and the children had been so excited, full of hope and expectation. She shook her head. No matter. She'd chosen the only logical course. What else could she do? She clucked her tongue.

On the ride toward the Buckmeyers' place, she considered what she knew of the lazy mama's boy known to all by his middle name. Henry Buckmeyer, indeed. Everyone on the prairie knew all about his war stories as well as his drunken brawls, but the tales of him serving with Andrew Jackson certainly didn't fit with her picture of a soft, indolent sloth who mooched off his poor old mother. There was no promise he'd even be there.

A part of her hoped he wasn't.

CHAPTER

TWO

HENRY REARRANGED THE STRETCHED HIDES around the fire pit to catch the best of the smoke, then went back to the bois d'arc seeds. He loved the smell of burning hardwood, especially red oak. After spreading the last batch of cleaned seeds out on the wooden planks he'd lined up, he went to washing the next bunch. He sure didn't enjoy the sticky green things, or the ache in his back either.

Blue Dog rose and growled once. Not expecting anyone, Henry slipped over to where his musket rested, lifted it, and let it balance in the crook of his arm. He readjusted the pistol in his waistband and waited.

"Hello to the house," a female hollered on approach.

The dog growled again, this time louder. Henry silenced the mutt with a look and then shouted back, "Hello to you. Come on ahead."

A woman? What could a woman want with him? Maybe she was lost, had followed his smoke in. When she rode around the cedar into sight, he could hardly believe his eyes. The beautiful widow Baylor, wearing a straw hat instead of the usual cloth bonnet, rode up, sitting astride Larry Dawson's bay gelding—wearing trousers no less. He would've thought the lady would ride sidesaddle and wear a skirt.

He smiled. His mother always said any woman immodest enough to strut around in britches should be hung up by her thumbs. Still, britches or skirt, she was every bit as beautiful as that day when he first saw her on the porch of the Sulphur Fork Trading Post four years ago.

He removed his hat and nodded. "Welcome, ma'am. To what do I owe this pleasure?"

She surveyed his work, then looked to him. "Good day, Mister Buckmeyer. I've come with a business proposition for you."

Returning the musket to its rest, he caught the horse's headstall and then offered his hand toward her. She ignored it and swung out of the saddle without benefit of stirrups.

Immodest, rude, and a bit of a show-off. "Business you say?"

She dusted her hands on her pants, looked around the yard again, then faced him. "I'll come right to the point, sir. I'm looking for some assistance and would like to speak with you about the possibility of providing the help I need."

"Doing what?"

"I've got two wagons full of cotton that I must get to Jefferson. They're already loaded and waiting."

"Didn't everyone leave a few days ago?"

"Yes, they did. Four days to be exact."

"Why didn't you go with them?"

She stiffened. "If it's any of your business, I had my crop sold." She looked away. "Or at least, I thought I did." She met his eyes again. "A businessman had offered four cents a pound, a fair price, but when I took my cotton in this morning for the agreed delivery, the scoundrel tried to bilk me."

She removed her hat. "So, I've decided I must take my cotton to market myself. I need someone to help me haul my lint south to Jefferson, where I can sell it for gold coin. I am prepared to pay you a fair wage once it's sold, sir, if you're up to an honest day's work."

He laughed. She appeared so blue at the mizzen with her chin in the air, acting all high and mighty; it didn't much fit her asking for his help. Her face turned red, and she glared. He smiled and waved off his social gaff. "Sorry, ma'am. I didn't mean to laugh at you, but honest work is all I know. You've been listening to those old busybodies' scuttlebutt, haven't you?"

"Well, I, er, uh; I suppose, but I truly . . ."

He let the lady—who obviously listened to and believed gossipmongers—stammer on, not offering her pride any salve. While she chattered her apologies, he considered her proposition. This could be the opportunity he'd been looking for. Maybe not the exact order he'd planned, but the widow definitely needed someone to go with her; she'd never get to Jefferson without help. He should be able to sell his seeds there; it would save him the trip to St. Louis.

He finally interrupted her. "I'll go on one condition, Mis'ess Baylor."

She stopped abruptly and stared. "What did you say?"

"I said I'll go on one condition."

She took the haughty posture again. "And what, may I ask, is your condition, sir?"

"I get to carry my own wares along."

She shifted her weight. "How much room would you need? My wagons are pretty well loaded."

"I have fifty hides and over a hundred pounds of seed. Plus, fifty or so pounds of tobacco. And, of course, my own tucker."

She looked to the side, then to the ground. "Before we come to agreement, there is something I'd like to ask."

"What's that?"

She faced him. "Are you a believer, Mister Buckmeyer?"

"Don't talk to me about God."

"But why not? Mis'ess Dawson said your mother's a devoted Christian. Didn't she teach you from the Good Book?"

"Mother taught me to read from the Bible, ma'am." He could hardly believe the woman's audacity. "And she was a believer to be sure, but I wonder if you might tell me where your God was when she lay in bed for a month suffering, hurting so bad she could barely stand it?"

Sue looked around as if searching for an answer. "I'm sorry, sir, I'm certain that the Lord was right there with her." The volume of her voice lowered. "After all, He promises never to leave or forsake us."

He shook his head. "Sure seemed to me that He forsook my mother. Anyway, I consider the state of one's soul a personal topic, wholly inappropriate for open scrutiny. So why do you ask anyway?"

"Sir, it's a matter of trust. The journey will be long, and you and I will be traveling together alone. I don't know you all that well personally and am concerned about appearances, of course, but, well, if I knew you were a Christian, I could believe you are an honorable man. Certainly, you get my gist."

"I can assure you, ma'am." He took his hat off and wiped his brow with the back of his hand. "On my mother's grave, I have never acted inappropriately with any woman in my life."

She stepped toward him and took his hand. Hers seemed so small around his. "Oh, Mister Buckmeyer! Your mother didn't recover? I had no idea. How could it be that I hadn't heard a word of it? When did she—"

"Three weeks now." He pulled his hand away. No need for her to be acting like she cared. "Don't fuss about it, she's gone."

"But I do feel so bad for being ignorant of that horrible news."

"Don't." He cleared his throat and stared at the woman, looking past her handsome features; maybe he was wrong about her after all. "She's gone and that's that."

"But—"

He held his hand up. "Please, I don't want to talk about her."

She stiffened, almost like he'd slapped her. "Of course."

"So, do you have the room?"

Her shoulders relaxed a bit, and her face softened. "What is it you have again?"

"A hundred pounds of bois d'arc seed, fifty pounds of tobacco, and fifty or so hides." He stroked his chin and wished he'd shaved that morning. "Past that, provisions."

"Yes. Yes, of course." She held up a finger and smiled. It brightened her face. No one could deny she was a handsome woman, even in trousers. "And I also have a condition, if you please."

"Tell me."

"My stipulation is that we can sleep on your furs at night. Would that be agreeable?"

"No problem, unless the rains set in."

"Of course." She nodded.

"And when were you planning on leaving, ma'am?"

"As I said, my wagons are loaded and waiting. I'd like to leave this afternoon. How long will you take to get ready?"

He laughed again. "Mercy, Widow, no grass grows under your feet, does it?" He looked around. "Will in the morning do?"

She dipped her head slightly, bouncing her hat against her leg in a quick rhythm. "My name is Susannah, sir; friends call me Sue. You may call me Mis'ess Baylor. My wagons are at the Dawsons' and ready to go. I've borrowed Larry's horse to come here and thought to leave as soon as I've returned the animal. I realize this is short notice, but—"

"Ma'am, it's going to take me the better part of the day to get ready." Was he making a mistake? She for sure was a powerful demanding woman. "Mule needs packin', got to gather up some things, then walk to the Dawsons' place to meet up with you."

She looked him square in the eye. "Walk? Why in Heaven's name would you do that? Where's your horse?"

"Smokehouse."

She looked puzzled.

"Broke his leg; had to shoot him."

"Why that's terrible. But he's in the smokehouse?"

"Made jerky."

Her face soured.

"One never knows about needing meat, Mis'ess Baylor. Why should the buzzards get my horse?"

"Well, I suppose you wouldn't really need him on the trace anyway." She glanced toward the smokehouse. "You'll be driving one of my wagons, but I'll thank you not to be offering any of your jerky along the way. To me or my children."

"Children?" Her kids hadn't crossed his mind. "You're not thinking of hauling them to Jefferson, are you? Thought you said we'd be alone."

"I did, I did, but I meant as the only adults—we'd be the

only adults traveling. Certainly, I intend to take my children. For Heaven's sake, what else would I do with them?"

Henry exhaled, considering all the trouble youngsters could conjure up. "Don't have someone who you can leave them with? Like Mis'ess Dawson?"

"Levi is fourteen now and will be fifteen come December, so he'll be a big help. And Rebecca. She won't be any trouble. She's a wonderful little girl."

"I'm certain that's true if you say so, but—"

"They'll be fine, I assure you." Her expression told him the matter had been settled—at least in her mind. Independent and stubborn. "Now, I really don't want to have to wait for you to walk all the way to Larry and Elaine's."

He shrugged. "I don't see another option."

She rubbed her brow and sighed. "We'll just have to ride double. Now how can I help you get ready? I do not like wasting time, and we are burning daylight."

He walked to the shed and retrieved his saddlebag. He held it out toward her. "Go rummage the kitchen for whatever you think we should take." Before she reached the cabin, he hollered after her, "You'll find two brown jars of honey under my bed. Be sure to grab both of those."

She turned toward him with raised eyebrows. "Have a sweet tooth, do we, Mister Buckmeyer?"

He removed his hat, ran his fingers through his hair, then replaced it and grinned. "Doesn't everyone?"

He watched her hips sway until she disappeared inside. Maybe that's why his mama thought women shouldn't wear trousers. He turned and set about getting Brown Mule packed. A month's worth of jerky got stowed in whether the widow wanted to eat it or not. He'd definitely not be saying more about it to her. After his animal stood loaded and waiting, he did offer half the beans and corn bread that he'd warmed for dinner earlier and shared his first meal with his new boss lady.

With his drying seeds stored out of the weather and the unwashed ones in the shed along with his unfinished furs, he raked the fire embers. He checked on his honey jars' packing—wouldn't want them to break—and smiled to himself. If only she knew what hid inside, she for sure wouldn't have made that honest-day's-work comment.

He tied his mule's lead loosely around the bay's saddle horn and then climbed aboard, noting the sun. Should be enough light to get to the Dawsons', but no way would he agree to set out this evening.

He lowered his hand toward her. She caught his arm below his elbow; he grabbed hers, then pulled her aboard. He pressed the gelding with his knees, and his new, most unexpected adventure began. Sure had been one strange day, and even though he'd been up all night checking his traps and fishing, and it'd been more than thirty hours since he slept, he'd never been more awake.

"Come on, Blue Dog." The canine barked and ran ahead of the bay.

"You're not planning on taking that mangy creature all the way to Jefferson, are you? Wouldn't you be better served leaving him here to guard your place?"

"No, Blue Dog is the best I ever had, ma'am." He urged the bay to an easy trot. "He'll carry his weight on the trace, but don't worry. I wasn't planning on charging you any extra for his services."

The widow very obviously did her best to hold herself away from him as far as she possibly could. She talked nineteen to the dozen, telling him what she expected and the route she wanted to take, Cuthand to Pleasant Mound to Captain Daingerfield's Springs; same way he'd have gone. She spoke of pushing ahead, traveling every possible extra hour of the day. They'd be following behind the wagon train in the hope of catching up and joining the larger group. The brim of her hat poked the back of his neck now and again.

She suddenly fell quiet; he felt her press more and more into him. The hat's brim rode up his neck to rest against his own. Before the ride was half over, she snuggled in close, leaning all her weight against him. Her small arms encircled his waist. He figured she had fallen asleep and was thankful her prattle had ceased.

But the whole time, he couldn't help thinking what a fine-figured woman rode against his back. Even if she did wear men's clothes.

He decided the best thing to do was set his mind on what all he would need for the journey on the trace.

CHAPTER

THREE

ONCE THE DAWSONS' PLACE came into sight, he leaned back, moving her slightly away from him. "Mis'ess Baylor?" He raised his voice a notch and rocked. "Mis'ess Baylor! We're almost there."

She immediately pushed away, avoiding all contact except for her hands on the saddle. With no mention of her little nap, she cleared her throat. "Well, looks like we've made very good time. I pray that becomes our habit on the Jefferson Trace."

A little girl came running toward the horse. He slowed the gelding to a walk.

"Mama! Mama!" She ran with both arms stretched out as though wanting to be picked up. "You're back! Aunt Elaine helped me and Sophia Belle make tea cakes for dessert, but we had to wait for you to eat one." The child was a miniature of her mother, with a halo of curls around her dirty face.

He stopped the horse and offered his hand. Sue took it this time and slid off the side against his leg. The little girl leapt into her arms. She seemed too big to be carried, but what did he know? Her mama went to giving the child's smudged cheeks a spit bath. He remembered how much he'd hated those.

A gangly, half-grown boy followed a few feet back, eyeing him with a look of suspicion.

The young lady had only curiosity in her eyes. "Who's he, Mama?"

Sue sat her daughter down and kneeled beside her, looking up. "Rebecca, Levi." She gestured toward the boy. "I'd like you to meet Mister Patrick Henry Buckmeyer. He's hired on to help us get our cotton to Jefferson. We'll be leaving tonight." She stood, still holding the girl's hand. "Mister Buckmeyer, this is my daughter, Rebecca, but we call her Becky. As you might know, Levi is my nephew."

He tipped his hat. "Miss Rebecca, very nice to meet you." Then he nodded to the boy. "You, too, Mister Levi."

The girl laughed and smiled the same bright smile he'd seen earlier on her mother's face. "You're funny."

"Well, thank you. I consider that a compliment, little miss." He backed the horse a few steps. "Why don't you and Miss Rebecca go on up to the house, ma'am; I'll see to the animal." The boy had started walking away. "Hey, Levi, you interested in helping to rub down Mister Dawson's gelding?"

Levi turned and stopped, but gave no verbal answer. Instead, he stared with a hint of disgust. The kid must have a burr under his saddle.

Sue waved the boy toward the barn. "That'd be wonderful. Thank you, sir." She smiled again. She might be bossy, but he sure enjoyed that smile, and she seemed rather stingy with them. "And thank you, Levi." The widow nodded to the youngster, obviously urging him to go and help, then turned back to Henry. "Elaine said she would save us some supper, but I don't intend to stay too long. We can get a few miles head start on tomorrow, so don't be lollygagging in the barn, please."

Larry walked out, passing her on her way to the house. "Did I hear you say something about leaving tonight?"

"Sure did. I'm more than anxious to get on the way. I do appreciate the use of your horse, Larry. Mules still hooked to the wagons?"

"Heavens no, Sue. Me and Levi unhitched 'em soon as you left this morning. They're out grazin'. It's getting pretty nigh onto dark; you don't need to be leaving tonight anyways." He walked on and tipped his hat brim as he approached. "Henry, good to see you. The wife'll sure be greatly relieved that you agreed to accompany our Sue." He took the gelding's headstall. "How's things been out your way? Any bear?"

Henry dismounted. "Fine. Haven't seen any bear, but I took a couple of big cats last month. Mated pair, I figure."

Larry shook his head. "How's your mama doing?"

"She passed three weeks ago."

"Oh, no. Sorry to hear that. Sister Buckmeyer was one fine lady."

"Thank you." Henry held the reins up. "I'm happy to cool the bay down and get him settled."

"No. You go on in and get some supper. Levi can help me."

Henry chuckled. "Sure am proud you gave Mis'ess Baylor's animals a good day of rest."

"Yeah, I figure they'll be needing it all right."

He headed on up to the house. The women were in the middle of a conversation as he stepped onto the porch. He didn't mean to eavesdrop, but he hesitated.

"Well, I wanted to leave tonight."

"Too late now, I guess."

"Bosh! Henry wanted to wait till tomorrow, too, and now

he's getting his way. I sure hope he won't have any trouble taking orders from a woman after we leave."

"That why you put those britches on? I hope you'll at least try not to be too bossy." Mis'ess Dawson sat Sue's plate on the table. "Either way, he's a godsend."

Henry didn't know about being sent, seemed to him it was his decision to come along. He knocked with one knuckle. Mis'ess Dawson looked up and smiled. "Come in, come in, Mister Buckmeyer. I'm fixin' you a plate right now."

He removed his hat. The wonderful scent of corned beef and cabbage filled the kitchen. "Thank you, ma'am."

His new boss lady gave him a nervous smile, then forked another bite.

Mis'ess Dawson set a loaded plate in front of him.

"Looks delicious. Thank you, ma'am."

"My pleasure, believe me." She smiled and went back to the washtub and supper dishes. "Susannah had me mortified, planning to head out on her own. I love her, but sometimes she's stubborn as any of those mules out there."

Sue held her fork midair. Her face reddened. "Excuse me, Elaine! Stubborn? As a mule?" She turned to him. "I planned to leave tonight, but can't fight you all. Just remember, I'm the one paying your wages." She scooped a bite of creamed potatoes, then added, "I'll expect to pull out of here at first light."

"Then that's when we leave, ma'am." He swallowed his bite, then faced her. "I been thinking, ma'am, do we have everything we need for the trace? Extra iron, hobbles for each animal?"

"My mules are tamed and good mannered." She looked over at her friend as though the woman would support her statement. "They won't be wandering off."

"I don't doubt that they're good mules, as you say, but after three or four days of pulling, any animal would be hunting a way to escape those loads. Doesn't mean they're bad or ill mannered; it's only natural." He pressed. "Do you have any with you?"

She shifted her weight and put her fork down. "No, sir, I do not. I've never used them before. Maybe the Dawsons have a set we can borrow." She looked to her friend.

"I've no idea what all he's got out there. You can ask Larry when he comes in."

"And what about extra shot? And powder?"

Sue seemed relieved. "Yes, I have both. Packed it all and brought my husband's pistol should we need an extra gun. If there's any trouble, I mean."

"Very wise." He nodded and did his best not to sound patronizing. "What about iron? With five, one of those mules is bound to throw a shoe along the way."

She looked over once again at her friend, then back. "Uh, well, I didn't bring any extra. The farrier came out the beginning of the month, so they've been recently trimmed and shod. Perhaps Larry might have some shoes, too." She looked again to Mis'ess Dawson. "I'll buy replacements after I sell the cotton. Or pay for it."

"Oh, if we have some, you know you're welcome to 'em."

"Grain?" he asked.

"I'm carrying about thirty pounds."

"We'll need more; we can buy some along the way. Flour and salt pork? What about grease for those axles? And when were they last greased?"

She looked like a trapped animal. "Thirty pounds of flour, and enough salt pork. Levi greased the axles the day before we loaded the cotton. I didn't carry any extra, of course. Wasn't planning a long trip. As you're aware, I thought I had my crop sold."

"Yes, ma'am." He nodded. "That low-down scoundrel who backed out is definitely to blame. I'm only trying to think of everything. Extra leather for the harnesses and leather tools I can use to repair them if need be? And what about axes?"

She glared and scooted her chair back from the table, then stood.

The door slammed, and Rebecca busted in with another little girl on her heels. "Are you done yet, Mama? Can we have a tea cake now, Aunt Elaine?"

Mis'ess Dawson nodded, and the second girl retrieved a plate covered by a dish towel. She placed it carefully on the table. The two little ladies were giddy.

Larry came in. "Looks like I timed this about perfect. I'm ready for one of those sweet cakies if you gals are ready to pass 'em out."

Clearing her throat, Sue took the soft, not-too-sweet cookie that Rebecca held out to her. "Thank you, sweetheart. Larry, Mister Buckmeyer has pointed out several things that we might need on our journey, and I'm hoping you might have some of them so that we won't be delayed further. I'll either replace it when we return or pay for it, your pleasure."

He hesitated to ask, but thought it worthy of mention. "That's one more thing, since you brought it up. How much cash are you carrying, ma'am? Don't mean to pry or be too personal, but I'm wondering if it is enough for, say, four more mules. Or oxen maybe? They'd be a good bit cheaper."

"But not as sure-footed. I won't have any oxen pulling my cotton." Sue folded her tea cake in a handkerchief she pulled out, then tucked the treat away in her pocket. "I'm certain my coin will be sufficient. You might not know, the Good Book says God will provide all our needs. I'm comfortable with that."

"Yes, ma'am." Henry smiled, glad she hadn't pulled her Bible out and gone to thumping it at him. "Didn't mean to offend."

"No offense taken. Please go over your list with Larry, won't you? Unprepared for a long journey, I obviously overlooked a few things. I'm grateful for your thoroughness, sir."

"You're most welcome, ma'am, and I'll gladly do that." He stood, taking a tea cake Rebecca offered with one hand and putting his hat back on with the other. "Oh, and something else—sorry to keep bringing more up—what about wax and oil?"

She made a face and huffed.

Her friend's husband spoke up. "I have plenty you can load."

"Thank you, Larry." Sue nodded. "Since we won't be leaving tonight, I'll take Becky to bed now." She started out, but turned back. "First light, Mister Buckmeyer."

"Yes, ma'am."

Mis'ess Dawson faced him, too. "How about a pallet near the stove?"

"Oh, no, ma'am. I'll be fine in the barn. But thank you for the kindness, and the supper. It was delicious."

"Why, thank you, sir."

He faced the man of the house. "If you've got a minute, we can see what you might be able to spare." He started toward the door, and Larry followed. Before stepping out, he turned and tipped his hat. "Ladies, a good night's sleep to you both." On his way to the barn, he noted the location of the privy.

Henry made himself roll out before the first rooster crowed, even though he felt like he'd hardly slept. Once he saw to the necessaries, he lathered his face and pulled out his knife, working in the moonlight. Directly, he had all the extra supplies from Larry packed and the mules hitched. With sufficient grease, wax, and oil, leather and tools to work it, two more sets of hobbles, and some extra iron, he was comfortable to set out even if it wasn't everything he thought they needed.

Only thing that bothered him was those loads. He counted sixteen bales, eight per wagon. At five hundred pounds each, that was twice what a wagon usually carried.

Wasn't long before Larry came out with two steaming cups of coffee. He handed one to Henry. "Thank you, sir."

Larry snorted. "No need callin' me sir, Henry."

"Hey, I want to ask you about something. I'm a bit concerned she's got the wagons overloaded."

The man shook his head. "Naw, don't worry none about that. Andy, her late husband, and his brother were loggers. Had these wagons specially built for haulin' timber."

"Proud to hear that." He sipped his coffee.

"Yeah, no need to worry." Larry motioned toward an iron pot. "What you got there?"

"Put on a pound of beans to soak last night. Figured we'd eat them for our first evening on the trace."

"Well, I hope you'll have room for all the food my wife packed up for you. She and the girls cooked morning to night yesterday."

"Even if there wasn't, I'd make room. She's one great cook. Hadn't had such a good meal since Mother took sick." Henry extended his hand, then shook Larry's. "Thanks for all your help, sir."

"There you go sirring me again."

"Oh, that's Mother's upbringing showing out. Taught me to say sir to every man and ma'am to all the ladies. Claimed it never hurt to show another human being a little respect."

"Yep, like I said, she was a good woman. Suppose that's why you never married, huh? Couldn't find one like her?"

Henry laughed. "Maybe so."

CHAPTER

FOUR

SUE SNUGGLED INTO THE COVERS and smiled, relishing the feel of her husband's back against her chest. Holding on tight with her arms wrapped around him, she squeezed. "I love you, Andrew." She sensed him turning and puckered, but the man wore the face of Henry Buckmeyer! She screamed and pushed him away. "You!"

Her eyes opened to a dark, quiet, unfamiliar room with her exclamation reverberating in the stillness. Thank the Lord. It was only a dream. Her heart still pounded against her chest. She looked around, trying to get her bearings, and soon remembered where she was. Becky lay in the bed beside her. She swung her legs off the feather mattress and buttoned her shoes on. Quickly dressing in the dark, she headed out to wake her new employee so she could finally be on her way.

As soon as she opened the door, the aroma of coffee greeted her and brought a smile. That Elaine was some kind of lady. She didn't see her friend, but poured herself a cup of the brew and headed outside. In the moonlight, she distinguished the shadowy figures of Larry and Henry speaking by the barn. Well, he was already up—a good sign.

She moseyed on out toward the men. “Good morning, gentlemen. Room for a lady here, or is this a private conversation?”

Henry smiled broadly, and his teeth shone in the light of the moon. “Morning, boss. Always room for you.” He gestured toward the back side of the barn. The harnessed mules stood in front of the wagons. She’d know Daisy’s snort anywhere. “We’re ready to pull out as soon as you and the children are.”

“Have the animals been fed and watered?”

“Yes, ma’am.”

“Did Larry have everything you needed?”

“No, ma’am, but most of it. He’s lending me his post maul axe. Should be able to pick up the rest along the way.” He smiled.

She returned the gesture with a genuine one of her own as her insides bubbled with glee. Her cotton would actually leave for market that morning. Her hope and anticipation for a brighter day returned. “That’s grand news, sir. I’ll go wake Becky and see what Elaine’s packed for us.”

The difference in the statures of the two men in front of her caught her attention. Henry stood a good four or five inches taller than Larry, and his expansive shoulders made quite the contrast to the smaller man’s narrow frame. She shook her head, disgusted and surprised at herself that she stood there comparing the two in such a manner. What was she doing?

She turned toward the house, but made a full circle, facing the men again. “What about Levi?”

At the mention of his name, her nephew appeared in the shadows of the barn door. “Over here. I’m up, Aunt Sue. Your man Buckmeyer had me cleaning the mules’ hooves ’fore the crack of dawn.”

“Excellent!” Her enthusiasm rode over the boy’s sarcasm

and paid it no nevermind. He disappeared into the barn. Sue whirled and almost trotted back inside and tiptoed up to her sleeping daughter. "Becky?" She shook her little girl's shoulder, trying not to wake the whole house. "Rebecca." She bent and kissed her baby's cheek. "Come on, sleepyhead. Get up and get dressed. We're ready to go."

Elaine came out, tying her apron on. "Let me get y'all's breakfast. I made it for the road because I knew you wouldn't think of sittin' down at the table of a morning to eat it." She smiled her big ol' I-love-you smile.

Sue went over and wrapped her arms around her friend. "Sorry I got upset last night. I just love you so much, and I'm thankful for you." She leaned back from the hug and looked Elaine square in those deep brown eyes. "Sure will be amissing you while I'm gone."

"Well, I didn't mean to upset you either. Those sentiments are mutual, my dear Susannah." Elaine pushed a flour sack into her arms. "Here's some vittles the girls and I cooked up yesterday for the road." She pulled Sue into another embrace and patted her back. "I'm going to be praying for you and your little caravan every day until I see you again."

"Thank you. No doubt we'll need all the prayers we can get."

Becky came out rubbing her eyes.

"Get a move on, missy; we're waiting on you to leave."

"Mama." The girl made no effort to move, just stood there with her eyes closed. "I don't want to wake up. I'm sleepy."

Sue sat the sack of food on the table, then went and gently took her daughter's hand. "Come on, now. I'll help you, but we have to hurry. Mister Henry is ready to leave."

"He can go by his self, I don't want to go."

"Rebecca Ruth, do not use that tone of voice to your mother, do you hear me?"

"Yes, ma'am, Auntie." She nodded and turned back to the bedroom.

"And you apologize to her, too."

"Sorry, Mama."

"It's all right, baby. Let's hurry now." She mouthed a thank-you, then guided her daughter away. She really should scold Becky more, but disciplining her baby soured her stomach. Besides Rebecca being her only child, the poor little thing had to grow up without her daddy, and that was all Sue's fault.

By false dawn, she waved good-bye to her friends. Her chest practically burst with the excitement of beginning the journey, but Elaine's words kept ringing in her ears like water sprinkling a fire's embers.

Until I see you again.

Would she ever see her best friend again? She had another moment of foreboding. Was taking her cotton on the Jefferson Trace a mistake?

Until I see you again.

She sighed and turned her attention back to the team. "Come on, Daisy. Get up, Dex."

Elaine waved one more time. "Y'all be careful now. Send news if you get a chance."

"We will."

The wagons groaned, and the mules strained to get them moving. Mil pulled with Brown Mule, and Mabel got the day off, tied to the second wagon. They snorted and pawed the earth, and the big wheels rolled.

"Take care of yourselves."

Henry walked up beside her wagon. His dog wagged its tail following close on his heels.

"You sure are going to be getting tired, Mister Buckmeyer." Sue glanced down. "I see no reason in the world why you shouldn't ride."

"For the mules' sake, ma'am. I figure we should save 'em best we can. Every pound they don't have to pull will help." He didn't look up. "We'll take turns, driving and walking."

She didn't rightly care for him telling her how it was going to be, but his reasoning was sound and should definitely be implemented. "Of course, we'll all walk a turn. Give us a chance to stretch our legs, too. Would you tell Levi that I'd like him to walk the next hour? Tell him that I said it's to save the mules, please." Just because she was paying him didn't mean she shouldn't use her manners.

"My pleasure, ma'am."

After some time passed, her nephew suddenly appeared afoot beside her seat. She didn't know when he'd gotten down and Henry had climbed aboard; they must have accomplished the switch without ever stopping the team.

"It ain't right, Aunt Sue." Levi looked back.

"Isn't, Levi, there's no such word as *ain't*." That he ignored his grammar peeved her to no end. "What isn't right?"

"Your man Buckmeyer. He's letting that mangy dog of his ride in the wagon. Invited him up as a matter of fact. Thought you said we needed to save the mules from pulling any more weight than they had to."

"Yes, that's right." She tried to look back, but couldn't even see the wagon, much less its driver or his wrongly encouraged passenger. A sudden jolt bumped her hard. "Mercy! I hate those stupid, huge cracks in the ground! Oh, but I don't want it to rain either, not until we get this cotton to market."

"Yes, ma'am. Dry as it's been, I seen a few could swallow up a newborn calf."

"Have seen, Levi. You have seen a few."

Becky leaned over across her. "Can't you ever learn to talk right?"

"You're treading on thin ice, Bitty Beck."

"You two stop it." Sue pushed her little girl back to her own side of the bench, then looked down at her nephew. "You say he called Blue Dog up into the wagon?"

"Yes, ma'am. He sure did."

"Hey, Levi!" Becky leaned across her again. "Mama's walking next, then I get a turn."

"You don't need to be walking at all, little girl. You wouldn't even be able to keep up."

"Can too! I can even keep up skipping. That's what I'll do. I'll skip, and I'll show you!" She sour-puckered her whole face at him, then plopped back down. "Tell him I do get to walk a turn, Mama."

Sue smiled down at the boy. "Guess we'll have to give her a chance, don't you think?"

He waved her off and ran ahead, then turned around and trotted backward. "It ain't right. You always give in to her, Auntie."

"I don't like boys, Mama."

Sue grinned at her daughter. "Well, no one said you had to, but Levi's family. He's not just a boy; he's like your brother. You might get upset with him now and then, but you shouldn't stop liking him. Anyway, how could you? You love him."

Becky looked up from under her bonnet's brim with a

dreadful serious expression. "Well, he's my cousin and not my brother. And he's mean, too. Loving don't mean you have to like."

Sue sighed. "Doesn't, Becky. It doesn't mean."

"Oh." She looked up and giggled. "Sorry. Don't tell Levi."

Flicking the reins, Sue looked ahead. Her nephew ducked into the edge of the woods holding on to his hat. "Levi," she called. "When your time's over, you can take this wagon with Becky."

He popped back into sight and nodded. "Sure."

"I'd like to speak with Mister Buckmeyer."

He grinned. "Yes, ma'am." Then he disappeared again.

"Where's he going, Mama?"

"Oh, off exploring a little, I guess. You sure do ask a heap of questions."

"It's how I got so smart. Didn't you know that?"

"I suppose." She rode in silence a distance, and Sue appreciated hearing a crow call to its friends. "Do you know what I have in my pocket?"

"What? A surprise for me? Will I like it?"

"Oh, I'm sure of it." She pulled out the wrapped tea cake Becky and Sophia had baked. "Break it in half, and we'll share it."

Her daughter broke it and handed the smaller half to her, but Sue didn't say anything. "Thank you for sharing, Mama."

"Thank you for using your manners, my sweet love."

After eating her tea cake, Becky interlocked her fingers and twiddled her thumbs. "Are we almost to Jefferson yet?"

"No, dear. It will take many days to get there. Why don't you practice your ABCs and your multiplication tables while we ride?"

"Where are we going to sleep? Did we bring beds?"

"Mister Henry has some soft furs he said we could sleep on. We'll spread them under the wagon."

Her inquisitive mind obviously—and finally—sated, the girl started saying the alphabet, giving a word that started with each letter. Sue studied the trail ahead. What a blessing that the wagon train had cleared it well. The sun almost peeked over the tops of the pines and oaks along the trace. Soon enough, the open prairie would give it a good opportunity to shine down bright and heat things up.

She could hardly wait for the cool weather to come again. First cold front should blow in by the time she headed back home with her pockets filled with coin. It was going to be so wonderful. The wagon bumped her hard again, rolling into and over another crack in the dry black earth.

Her daughter was on *K* and used *crack* for her word.

"C-r-a-c-k." Sue looked straight ahead, correcting her matter-of-factly. "It's a *C,* not a *K,* baby, although they do sound the same. For a *K* word, what about *kangaroo*? Or *king*?"

Becky gave her one of her I-can-do-it-myself looks. "How. About. Castle?"

"No, that's a *C,* too. And watch your tone."

"Fine then, *kiss;* that's a *K*."

She smiled at her precocious daughter. "It certainly is."

It would be a long day.

Anxious to get down and stretch her legs, Sue started anticipating Levi's return, but the boy hadn't come back into sight since darting into the woods. "Leee-vi." No response, so she hollered a little louder. "Levi!"

He came running up beside the wagon. "Yes, Aunt Sue?"

"I was wondering. How hard was it changing places without stopping the wagon?"

"Simple enough. Buckmeyer climbed aboard and took the reins. I jumped off. Weren't nothing hard about it at all."

"There wasn't anything hard," she corrected. "So do you figure your hour is up yet? I'm ready to walk a bit."

"Sure. Already took care of my necessaries, so now's fine with me." He extended a hand toward the wagon and timed the rhythmic turn of the wheels, jumping aboard without a hitch. He climbed up beside her. "Now you; jump on down."

She carefully half crawled around Becky, holding on, then stood off the seat and teetered on the edge of the sideboard. She examined the terrain ahead. It seemed a long way down; sure didn't look as easy as it sounded.

"Jump. You'll be fine. Bend your knees a little when you land."

She leapt off. A short muffled scream escaped before she hit hard, losing her balance. She rolled onto the ground, then scrambled up to a sitting position as quickly as possible, flat on her behind with her legs extended out in front. She looked up in time to see Henry trying to hide a smile.

She stretched—as though sitting was exactly what she'd planned all along—until after the second wagon passed, then she rolled over to her hands and knees and pushed herself off the hot, hard-packed ground. Good thing she had on Andy's trousers, even though she knew it wasn't fittin'. She didn't care; a skirt flying up over her head could have been even more embarrassing.

For a long while, she walked behind the wagons. Keeping up was no problem. She wanted to speak with her employee, but waited until she could try and forget him hiding that grin.

Finally, she mustered her courage and hurried her step to walk beside his seat. Sure enough, the dog stretched out on the buckboard, sound asleep, tongue lolling. "Mister Buckmeyer, I thought we discussed the wisdom in saving the mules from pulling every pound possible."

"Yes, ma'am. We sure did."

"In that light, I can't see how you think it's fine for that dog of yours to ride in the wagon. After all, I imagine he weighs forty or fifty pounds."

"Good guess. Forty-five last I weighed him."

A thorned ivy caught her trouser leg. She twirled to keep from tearing the material. She quickly unsnagged the nasty vine, then pivoted and hurried to catch up with him again. "So then why is that lazy mutt riding?"

"Tonight, when we're sleeping, Blue Dog will be awake and working. After a night or two, you'll not begrudge him a nap or a ride."

She looked away. Well, no one, not even a mangy old blue dog, should have to work day and night. "So what kind of time do you think we're making?"

"Maybe a mile, no more than a mile and a quarter, an hour."

"And how much farther do you think it is to Cuthand?"

"Nine mile or so."

"Will it all be pretty flat?"

"Oh, there's some rolling hills, but nothing too steep. We'll be coming up on the Aikin place around noon. Thought we'd give the mules a rest there, let 'em get a drink, and we can eat some dinner."

"Good idea." She shaded her eyes and smiled up at him. "Becky insists that she wants a turn to walk, too."

He grinned. "I'll keep an eye out."

Sue sped up and took longer strides until she reached the first wagon. Levi and Becky were singing "Blow, Ye Winds, Blow." She sang the lead, belting out, "My father's got an acre of land." Then harmonized to his melody on "Blow, blow, blow, ye winds, blow." Her daughter had a beautiful voice like her daddy, and Levi did, too. "An' you must dig it with a goose quill. Blow, blow, blow, ye winds, blow."

Had to be a Baylor trait.

Seemed she'd been walking at least three hours before her turn finally ended. The sun shone mercilessly, and she'd soaked the bodice of her cotton shirt. "Levi, I'm coming up. Think I can get aboard without stopping? I'm afraid I didn't do so great getting down."

"It's easier getting up, Aunt Sue. I promise."

"So tell me what to do, and I'll try it. I hate to stop the team, as getting the load moving is the hardest."

"Yes, ma'am, that's what Buckmeyer said."

"I don't think it sounds proper you calling Mister Buckmeyer by his last name alone. I don't mind you using his first name, Mister Henry, but a respectful Mister is due as I see it."

"Yes, ma'am."

His claim proved true, and she boarded without incident. She wasn't so sure about letting Becky jump, but the girl carried a powerful stubborn streak and usually got her way.

"When you get down, you have to stay in my sight now, or Mister Henry's, at all times. You hear me?"

"Yes, ma'am. But first thing, I've got to find me a tree or a bush because I gotta go."

"Well, keep the wagon in sight then, and the rest of your turn, you have to be able to see me or Mister Henry, too. If you can't see either one of us, then we can't see you. Are you big enough to do that? Look at me, Rebecca Ruth." She waited. "I will not be able to see you the whole time. The wagons will be moving. You cannot run off and forget to keep either me or Mister Henry in your sight."

Becky stood on the edge of the sideboard with her hands on her hips. "Yes, ma'am, I said!" She leapt into the air. "Whoopee!" Skipping alongside the wagon, she smiled. "I'm going to go find me a spot, Mama. I'll be back directly."

"I'll count and see how long it takes you." Her daughter disappeared, and Sue started counting. She didn't like Becky being out of view, but she understood. Besides, she was nine years old, and would be ten next summer. Sue could hardly believe almost a decade had passed since she was born. She shook her head. Double digits; where had the time gone? Ten years.

She rested her eyes a moment.

CHAPTER

FIVE

BECKY SKIPPED NEXT TO THE WAGON AGAIN, and an uneasy tightness lifted that Sue hadn't noticed before. The dog trotted beside her daughter. "Hey, Mama, look. Blue Dog is my new friend." She petted the animal's shoulder, and he barked and ran a bit ahead. "Mister Henry says my time is up, and he wants Levi to come back there."

"But how are we going to do this?" Sue turned to her nephew. "Think you could jump down and help her up?"

"Here I come!" Excitement filled the little girl's voice.

Sue turned in time to see her daughter step onto one spoke, catch hold of another, then ride the wheel up to the sideboard, where she jumped off and teetered a moment before Sue grabbed her arm. "Rebecca Ruth Baylor! Don't you ever let me see you do that again! Do you hear me? You could have been killed. What were you thinking?"

The little girl threw both arms around her. "I'm fine, Mama." She leaned back. "It wasn't hard to do, and I didn't get hurt at all. It was fun!"

"It was dangerous! And you scared me half to death!"

Becky rolled her eyes. "Sorry, I never meant to scare you."

She put her hand on Sue's cheek and patted softly. "Sorry, I really am. Will you forgive me?"

She hugged her child tight. "Of course I will."

Levi shook his head. "Bitty Beck, you're going to have to do better than that." He jumped down. "Since your man wants me, guess I'll go back and relieve Henry."

Sue shook her head. "Levi—Mister Henry, and please don't be snitty."

He rolled his eyes at her, too.

She couldn't get any respect out of these two. "Thank you, Nephew."

In no time, her hired hand appeared alongside her wagon. "We should be coming up on the Aikin place directly. It'll be on a little hill on the right." Blue Dog showed up wagging his tail by Henry's side. He reached down and scruffed the mutt's neck.

"Oh, I didn't realize it would be so soon. I thought you said noonish. Are you certain we can't go on a little longer before we stop? What have we come, four or five miles?"

"The Aikins' place will be five. If you want to kill a mule our first day out, we could press on." He smiled, but she didn't appreciate his poor attempt at humor. "They're nice folks. You'll enjoy Martha."

She glared down at him. That man! She'd never known anyone who could get her so riled up so quickly. Maybe asking him along was nothing but a big mistake after all. He evidently could not remember who the boss was, because he kept demanding things and making decisions like he had all the authority. "You overstate a bit, don't you?"

"Listen, you've got good animals, ma'am, but how long has it been since they pulled two tons all day? And in such heat. If I was a betting man, I'd bet never."

She hadn't thought of that. Humph. He acted like it killed him to explain anything, like she should instantly accept everything he dreamed up as if it was the greatest idea she'd ever heard. He could've just said something.

"I know you want to beat the devil around the stump, Mis'ess Baylor, but sooner or later, we've got to stop and rest these animals. The Aikins' would be a good place in my estimation, if you're of a like mind."

In one respect, she hated his logic and how right he always seemed. In another, she definitely did not want to hurt one of her mules. All four had been with her these past ten years; she couldn't stand the thought of causing any harm to come to any of them. So in that respect, she had to appreciate his wisdom. Even if she didn't want to or like it.

She faced front, purposely dismissing him. "I'll be watching for the Aikins'."

Henry took the point and quickly distanced himself out in front of the wagons. She studied his walk. He certainly was all sure of himself. His words rolled over her again regarding the mules and how they'd probably never pulled such a load all day. She hadn't even thought of such a thing. He would definitely win his bet. So why did she feel so much animosity when he was only helping? She sighed; probably because of him always acting like he controlled the world.

Before the sun rose to its highest mark in the bright blue, cloudless sky, the home he'd told her about came into view. A small pond sat off to the left of the house. He pointed toward it. "Take the mules to water. I'll let the family know we're here." He trotted ahead, then hollered over his shoulder, "I'll be back to help unhitch the teams. Ask Levi to get started."

Sir, yes, sir, she thought, then stood. "I hadn't planned on unhitching them." Her volume dwindled as she sat back down. He'd either run out of earshot or purposely ignored her. Here the trip had barely begun, and he persisted in making every decision, like it was his job to tell her how things were going to be and issue orders as though someone had crowned him king.

Well, she was not going to unhitch the mules. He would grain them, and they could drink, but she intended to get back on the trail in short time. She turned the team, and Dex threw his head; probably smelled the water. She was parched herself. A man came onto the porch, and Henry waved.

"Becky, we're going to stop here for a while. Would you please get Mama a drink out of the barrel?"

"Yes, ma'am." The girl stood and jumped off the wagon before Sue could grab her.

"Rebecca! I didn't say get off before we stopped. I told you we were going to stop. You scare me plum to death, girl. Think about things before you just go off and do them."

Becky ran alongside. "Oh, Mama, it wasn't nothing."

"Wasn't anything."

"I didn't hurt myself." Blue Dog left Henry's side and raced back to the girl. She kneeled, and he ran into her arms. "He likes me. See, Mama?"

"I see, I see. Hope you don't get any fleas." She had often contemplated a dog for the children, but never could justify feeding one. She wished now she had bought that nickel pup at the last camp meeting. Her darling girl had so few pleasures, and she sure had cottoned up to Henry's mongrel.

Sue pulled the team to a stop short of the pool and climbed down. Levi stopped Mil and the brown mule next to her wagon. The animals stomped and snorted. He went straight to pulling their harnesses off.

"Stop! Stop that, Levi. What are you doing?"

"Mister Buckmeyer." He accentuated the *Mister,* obviously for her benefit. "Said we'd be resting the animals and told me to unhitch 'em."

"Well, you just wait one minute." She headed off toward the house with nary a sip of water.

Before she reached the rough-hewn dwelling, a young woman came out and stood to the right of the owner. She almost touched Henry and seemed unable to take her eyes off him. Humph. If she was the woman of the house, Aikin had certainly robbed the cradle. Five stair-stepped children rushed out, running past their pa and hollering like a wild herd of little scallywags.

A woman with graying hair appeared as Sue neared the porch. A chubby baby straddled her hip. The mother nodded, giving Sue's trousers a once-over. "Good day, Mis'ess Buckmeyer, and welcome."

"Oh!" She shook her head. "No, ma'am. He's not my— We aren't— I'm sorry, where are my manners?" She extended her hand and tried to laugh, but knew it sounded forced. "I'm Susannah Baylor, Mis'ess Aikin. I have a place a little west and south of here out on the prairie. Not too far actually. So pleased to meet you, ma'am."

The woman laughed heartily. "Well, we sure hadn't heard our Henry got married, but I knew it'd take a beauty like you to catch him." She winked. "If he ever gets caught, that is. Sorry for the misunderstandin', dear. Come on in now, Mis'ess Baylor, and get out of this sun. Imagine you're in need of a cool drink." She faced Henry. "You been getting along all right? Eatin' enough?"

"Yes, ma'am, doing fine. I do miss Mother's cookin' though."

The woman nodded and headed inside, holding the door open behind her. "You'll have to excuse the mess, Mis'ess Baylor. I've been tryin' to get a new quilt done, teaching the girls, you know. They're all helping."

Sue stepped forward to follow her. "Oh, don't fret one bit about that. I understand. That drink sounds heavenly, Mis'ess Aikin, and please, my friends call me Sue."

"Well, mine call me Martha." She turned to the moonstruck girl. "Lizbeth, pull up a bucket of fresh water for our guests, please."

"Yes, Ma." The young woman's staring was downright embarrassing. The object of her foolishness flashed a dazzling smile every now and again. He was handsome in a rugged sort of way, Sue guessed. Why hadn't she noticed before? Well, he shouldn't encourage the girl like that. But then, maybe, that's exactly what this stop was all about. After all, he obviously knew the family well. Lizbeth squeezed by her pa and blatantly brushed Henry on her way to the well.

For no reason, Sue's breath caught in her throat, and her face suddenly burned.

"Now come on in and rest a spell. It's been ages since I had another woman to visit with." Martha turned and ducked back into the shadows of the house.

Sue glanced over at Henry. Why hadn't she noticed how blue his eyes were before? She followed the older woman inside, leaving her hired man to be tempted by the wiles of that shameless girl. Made her uncomfortable for some reason, but it would have been rude not to accept the invitation inside.

He opened the door for Lizbeth on her return. She sloshed water from a wooden pail, grinning up at him her whole way through the door. "Thank you, Henry."

Oh, dear, did she bat her lashes? Did sparkles twinkle in the girl's eyes, or was Sue only seeing things?

Lizbeth poured two cups of water, handing one to her mother and the other to Sue, who gulped it down without a breath. A drop escaped and ran down her chin. She wiped it, closed her eyes, and smiled. "Thank you so much. That's the sweetest water I've drank in a long time."

Martha adjusted the baby and opened her blouse. As the little one latched on, she threw an apron corner over its head and laughed. "Oh, you's probably extra thirsty like my sweet little Maggie here. I'll get her fed, then we'll see to dinner for all the rest."

The daughter refilled Sue's cup, then sat the bucket in the washtub. She skedaddled back out without another word. Martha chatted on about the heat, her goats, baby Maggie, and the Methodist circuit rider who came through last month, but Sue found she had trouble concentrating. Standing to fill her cup again, she peeked out the window.

The men had the mules unhitched and jawed beside one of the wagons; the children played kick the can with Blue Dog on Becky's heels, and Lizbeth shadowed Henry like a lovesick puppy.

"He buried Sister Buckmeyer and baptized my Lizbeth all in the same day. If only she could have lived to see her son saved."

Aha! So she was right. "Sister Buckmeyer? So Henry isn't saved?"

"I'm afeared not."

"I wasn't sure. I asked, and he sounded a bit angry at God over his mother's suffering, but he never did give me an answer really."

"His mother sure prayed hard enough, but— Oh well, there's still time yet, I suppose. I always wondered—"

"Excuse me, Martha, I'm sorry for interrupting, but I need to tell Henry something real quick. Be back directly."

"Oh sure, you go ahead." She gestured at little Maggie. "Baby girl's asleep. I'll go put her down, and we can start dinner."

Sue hurried out and trotted toward the wagons. She walked straight up to Henry, blocking the younger woman's access. She spoke in a low tone meant only for him. "Mister Buckmeyer, I thought I made myself clear."

"About what?"

"Not unhitching those mules."

"Did you?" He leaned over, almost touching her ear with his lips. "I don't mean any disrespect, ma'am, and I am not trying to usurp your authority, but either these animals rest, or they're goners, and we'll never get your cotton to Jefferson."

She stood there, blood boiling under the blazing sun. Unfamiliar butterflies fluttered in her stomach. She wiped her forehead on her sleeve and bought herself a few extra seconds to settle the blood and the butterflies. "Is it ever going to be cool again?"

Making a spectacle would only serve to embarrass her—and him as well. The animals were already unhitched, so she caved and nodded. "Fine, we'll stay, but not for long. Please tell me now that you do not plan on spending the night here."

He smiled. "I'm not planning on spending the night here." He raised one eyebrow. "But it wouldn't be a bad idea either."

"Mister Buckmeyer."

He held his hands up. "Only joshing. An hour, two at most."

She didn't smile. "One hour. Were you going to graze them, too?"

He gave her one nod and an aggravated expression. "Figured to after I grain 'em."

"Fine then. I'll help get dinner ready." She turned to her nephew. "Would you please fetch the flour sack Aunt Elaine sent along? We don't want to be a burden to the Aikins."

"Yes, ma'am."

Sue turned toward the house and hollered without looking back. "Give it to Miss Lizbeth to bring in, Levi."

The young woman protested. "But, but—"

Sue kept walking. "We'll get dinner ready, sweetie. Your mama's caring for the baby."

Many stories and hearty laughs later, Sue settled on the shaded quilt in the yard with her plate in her lap. Becky squatted cross-legged beside her. Blue Dog came onto the pallet and tried to lie by her daughter, but she shooed him off. The eldest Aikin daughter hovered, obviously waiting for Henry to sit so she could position herself as close as possible to him.

The sought-after man sauntered up, laughing with the girl's daddy. "Sue, William here had an extra set of hobbles and a few other things we might need. Told him we'd settle up before we leave—if that suits you."

"And I told your man if you agreed, I'd gladly take a bolt of good cloth for these gals of mine to make some purty new dresses. If you was of a mind to be obliged for the shopping, that is. I figure you'd be a good un to pick something out they'd really like. Purty hard for Mama to get away, and I ain't much good at it." He laughed and took a place in the grass just off the pallet and smiled at his wife. "That suit you, Martha mine?"

She grinned and looked like she might blush. After handing

him the plate she'd piled high with pork ribs, corn on the cob, purple hull peas, carrots, and corn bread, she stroked his cheek. "You're too good to me, my darlin' dear."

They were so cute, even after being together all those years. Sue wondered: had Andy lived . . . ? No. That train of thought served no good purpose. Pointless dreaming about how things might have been. She hurried back to the present.

"It would be my pleasure if that will cover the cost of everything, Mister Aikin. Maybe I should pick out two?" She turned to her new friend. "What color do you cotton to, Martha?"

"Well, I've always been a mite partial to blue, and it draws out my girls' sky blue eyes."

"I'm fond of purples, most all shades," Lizbeth offered. "You like purple, Henry?"

He shrugged. "Well enough."

Another one of the girls frowned. "Well, red's my favorite."

And the one who'd taken up with Becky, she looked to be about five or six, swatted at her sister. "Yellow's best." She faced Sue, nodding. "Get yellow, bright, shiny, happy yellow." She giggled.

Sue joined her, laughing. "Sounds to me like a rainbow fabric would work to please everyone." She smiled at Martha. "Perhaps a delicate floral print?"

"Whatever you find would be perfect, I'm sure."

She turned to the man of the house. "All right then, you have yourself a deal. Thank you, sir, I'll gladly shop for you, but I'm afraid I could never repay you for all your hospitality and the good company of your family. Especially since it looks like we're about to eat you out of house and home." She looked back to Martha. "It's been a true pleasure."

"Oh, dear, the pleasure's all mine. You're such a blessing."

"Blessings all around, I'd say." Aikin patted Henry's shoulder and bowed his head. "Lord, thank You for the grub. Help it keep us strong and healthy to do Your will. Amen."

Henry finally lighted and took his hat off, sitting with his back against a tree, and just as Sue figured, the young woman settled next to him where their knees almost touched. Sue tried not to notice but she kept losing Martha's conversation for paying too much attention to the girl and the man's reaction to her flirtatious goings-on. Once Lizbeth burst out laughing at something he must have said and slapped his bicep.

It seemed she just had to keep touching him. Sue glanced at Martha, who appeared oblivious to her daughter's shameful behavior. Lizbeth got up once to get Henry more ribs, and when she sat back down, she put herself even closer. Sue couldn't believe it and willed herself to look away. Why should it bother her?

Only a few minutes passed before Henry's laughing drew her attention back. He leaned into the young girl leaning into him. He caught Sue looking at him, and held her eye too long before she was able to glance away. He cleared his throat, and, in her peripheral vision, she saw him sit back fully against the tree again.

A short time later, not a morsel remained, but it didn't matter because Sue couldn't take one more bite even if she wanted. While she had insisted on including their tucker, Martha proved equally insistent on throwing their own part into the midday feast. The hilarious yarns spun and sweet fellowship offered lifted her spirits more than she could ever have imagined.

Even Lizbeth's outrageous flirting failed to spoil the day, although Sue thought Henry certainly might have egged her on a little less. But maybe he liked her. That might be the biggest reason he wanted to spend so much time there. Maybe he considered her a prospect for marryin'—even if he was almost old enough to be her father. What difference could it possibly make to her?

Sue shook her head and brought herself back to the day. Any attraction Henry Buckmeyer had to the young woman shouldn't bother her in the least, but for some reason, it made her feel a bit old and tired all of a sudden. Comfortable, though; she was quite comfortable, even in her britches.

She rose. "I hate to bring this wonderful time to an end, I do, and I truly look forward to when we can visit again, but we're burning daylight, and we really should be getting back on the trace."

Martha jumped up, came over, and hugged her tight. "Absolutely. I don't want you to lift a finger with these dishes either. Just do whatever you need to get back on the road."

"No, no. I didn't mean— I'll help."

"Won't hear it." Martha looked at Henry, who stood. "Now you fellows get those mules hitched up so y'all can get back on your way."

"Come on, Henry, ain't no reason to argue with her." William handed his empty plate to Lizbeth.

She held her hand out for Henry's, too. "It was so good to see you, Henry. Hope you'll come back through once Mis'ess Baylor's cotton is delivered."

Levi and the two oldest Aikin boys jumped up as well and headed for the barn.

Henry tipped his hat to Lizbeth before putting it back on. "Can't never get enough of good people and good food." He held Lizbeth's eye. "I'll be back, but some handsome young man will probably have you wed in no time." He grinned at

Sue, then Martha. "You and William have a fine family, ma'am. Thank you for all your hospitality." He turned and went after the boys.

The girl started to follow, but her mama spoke up. "Lizbeth, gather up these dishes now and get 'em to the kitchen while I say my good-bye to my neighbor and new friend."

"Yes, Mama."

The woman then turned to Sue. "Want you to know I'll be remembering you in prayer every day until you come again."

"Why, thank you, Martha. Can't ever have too many prayers going up. And I'll surely be back, as I have some fabric to deliver." She winked at the six-year-old.

It pleased her that no one objected to leaving, and that in no time the men and boys had hitched the mules and her cotton was back on the trail. The midday rest seemed to have revived the mules; it looked like they pulled the load with less strain. Perhaps that the terrain steadily fell toward the Sulphur bottoms helped. Whatever the reason, the pace elated Sue.

The second hour, when her turn came to walk, she fell back to speak with Henry. "Aren't we moving along at a much better clip? Won't we make Cuthand today at this rate?"

He nodded. "I figure upwards to a mile and a half, maybe two an hour, but I still plan to stop and make camp in the next hour or so. We'll put into Cuthand midmorning tomorrow."

"What? Why? Why would you think of quitting so early when we're making such good time?"

"We'll have almost eleven miles behind us for the day, and that's a good mark. It'll be best to make camp this side of the trading post."

She stared up at him, but he never looked down.

Who did he think he was? "Mister Buckmeyer, I'd count it a privilege to know why you think that you're the one making all the decisions around here." He looked down, but didn't say a word. "Why is it that you act like you're king of the world or something when I'm the one paying your wages?"

He looked hurt and a bit shocked, then his eyebrows furrowed and he shook his head. He appeared to steam, and she had no doubt he held his tongue for what seemed like an hour, though it was most likely only seconds. When he finally spoke, it was forced. "I apologize if I've offended you."

Without another word, she stopped in her tracks and let his wagon pull ahead. It was like the time when she was six years old and Daddy caught her playing with her mother's face powder. Foolish and stupid and wrong! But Henry wasn't supposed to be making the decisions. She was the boss, so how did he do it?

The cotton belonged to her, and this trip—her trip—was all about taking her crop to market. She'd hired him to help, not take over. She clearly remembered saying she needed help.

The more she dwelt on his blatant egotism, the more her face burned with anger. Or was it shame? The earlier peace had slipped easily away, replaced by a desire to slap Mister Patrick Henry Buckmeyer right across his arrogant face.

By the time he hollered "Ho" to the mules, she was the one steaming and fit to be tied.

Had she been driving the front wagon, she never would have stopped it until dark. Then Mister High-and-Mighty would have had to keep going and keep up. Why hadn't she thought of that and relieved Levi when the self-appointed czar first said something? Royalty, indeed! Did he think he was in Russia?

And why did she always come up with the good ideas when it was too late to put them into motion? Stopping after barely more than two more hours on the trail! Ridiculous!

"Levi, you get the mules hobbled, I'll start a fire for supper." Henry began scouting for wood. "Hey, Rebecca, you and Blue Dog can help me gather some kindling." He noticed her coming around the corner. "If that's fine with your mother."

And still he gives orders! Well! At least he didn't bark any chores at her. She fumed inside. Men! Why did they automatically think that everything had to be done their way? Did they not think a woman ever had an intelligent thought?

Did he not realize that she had plowed her field, planted the seed, chopped the cotton until her blisters had blisters, then helped to pick it in a timely manner, see to it that it got ginned and baled, then loaded into her wagons? Who did he think had carried it to the Sulphur Fork Trading Post, where she supposedly already had a buyer? She clenched both her fists.

She went to the back of the wagon and laid her forehead against it. Pictures flashed across her mind's eye of the lovely Miss Lizbeth and Henry laughing together. "Oh, stop it, Sue Baylor." She took deep breaths. "Help me, Lord. Help me."

She remained there until her heartbeat slowed and her face cooled. Who wanted to start a big argument on their first day? And after such a sweet time at the Aikins'. There was a long trip ahead. Why had she said anything at all?

Men. She was certainly glad she lived by herself and took care of her own business without the constant rule of a man.

She went to the larder and fished out the cornmeal and fatback, grabbed her Dutch oven, then made her way to where Henry nursed the fire. A pot already hung from a limb held over it by a sturdy forked branch on either side. He looked up.

She pointed to her pot. "What's that?"

"Beans. Shouldn't take too long. Already soaked 'em overnight at the Dawsons'."

"Well, of course you did." She busied herself making corn bread, then sat the oven on the coals and scooted a couple of bigger ones onto the lid. "Mister Buckmeyer?"

He looked up from stirring the beans.

"I do not intend to be at odds with you the whole way." She took a deep breath and shook her head slowly. "Eleven miles a day is unacceptable. We'll never catch our neighbors, my friends, stopping midafternoon for two-hour dinners or making camp hours before sundown."

He shrugged. "With only five mules, we'll do good to make eight or nine mile tomorrow."

She studied his face. Why did he have to be so stubborn?

"Second day's likely to be their worst, ma'am."

"I don't understand why you would say that. The mules did fine today. We should've kept going! We could've easily made Cuthand."

"You ever been to the Cuthand Trading Post at night?"

"No, but what's that got to do with anything?"

He glanced over to where Becky and Blue Dog played chase the stick, then sighed. "I have. Trust me. You don't want to be anywhere near that place after dark."

She wanted to protest, make him understand that she had to get her cotton to Jefferson, but her aversion to exposing the children to a den of iniquity stopped her short. One more time, he was right. But why couldn't he just have told her that the first time he said he wanted to stop early?

"Fine, but tomorrow we have to pick up the pace. It's absolutely imperative that I get my cotton to market before the buyers leave."

He nodded, then glanced again at the little girl and his dog. He loved simple, and Widow Baylor was anything but. What a contrast she was, so beautiful, yet so hardheaded—downright stubborn to a fault. He looked back and stared into her eyes; she met his gaze.

"I'll get us there. It's just as imperative to me that I get my own goods to market, but, Mis'ess Baylor, not at all costs."

CHAPTER

SIX

THE NIGHT SONGS the crickets and locusts and frogs sang soothed Henry's troubled soul. Been a long, hard day. He yawned and pondered what he had gotten himself into. He liked life on the trail: the crackling embers' warmth, the night breeze in the trees, sleeping under the stars, working days like normal people.

A hoot owl called, answered by a nightingale. The camp's rhythmic sleep sounds settled over his heart, and he closed his eyes.

A series of thumps shook the ground ever so slightly. Blue Dog crawled forward and licked his hand. Henry raised his head and scanned the darkness. Holding one ear closed, he turned his head. A twig snapped out in the trees. The foul odor of alcohol, sweat, and stale tobacco floated on the still night air.

The breaking of more small branches fractured the silence. Plodding horse hooves sounded an easy rhythm, getter louder by the step. Henry quietly rolled to his knees, lifted his musket, then soundlessly stood on the dark side of the wagon.

Blue Dog's throat rumbled. Levi looked around, then spoke too loud into the darkness. "What, you mangy dog?"

Henry gave Blue Dog the stay signal and then moved out into the woods. From the shadows, he glanced at the other wagon, where the two females slept.

A strange man's voice erupted in the night. "Ho the camp!"

Blue Dog's throat rumbled, but he stayed put. He stared intently toward the sound.

Levi rolled and crawled from beneath the wagon on the fire side, facing the unwelcome visitor. Blue Dog joined the young man with the hair on his neck bristled. He stood, shoulders squared. "We're bedded. You have no business here."

An unshaven drunk rode into camp. "Well, if you ain't 'tween the hay and the grass, I ain't soaked." He slapped his knee and laughed, dismounting. "Speakin' of being soaked, you got any shine, boy?"

Blue Dog growled a soft warning.

Henry circled around the drunk's nag, searching the shadows between quick looks back to the camp. Seemed the man rode alone, but best to make sure.

Sue's head rose slightly.

"You the man of the camp? Where's your ma, boy?"

Levi glanced at the other wagon and betrayed the location of the girls. Blue Dog moved to stand between them and the stranger. He bared his fangs and stared at the interloper.

"Ha! There you are." The man tried to whirl and awkwardly bent at his waist while removing his hat, but he got balled up and almost fell over. "Good evenin', my lady. All you got's this boy here? Hmm." He staggered toward her. "Well, ain't I the lucky one tonight? Guess I done got dealt the high ace!" He smiled, but Henry knew full well without even seeing them that the stranger had wickedness in his eyes.

Blue Dog took a step toward him, daring him. The man had best take care, or Henry's dog would rip his throat out.

"Call off your dog, my lady, so as we can get t'know each other a bit bedder." At first, he grinned, then got louder. "Go ahead, I said! Call him off."

In an instant, she moved out from under the wagon with her flintlock pointed at the man. "You are not welcome here, sir. Now get back on your horse and ride out while you're still able. I'll not hesitate for one breath to blow your head from here to kingdom come."

The little girl screamed, then scurried out and hugged her mother's skirt.

"Rebecca! Get back under the wagon!" Sue never took her eyes off the man. "Either you mount, mister, or meet your Maker. Now!"

The girl didn't move, frozen to her mama's leg.

"Well, well. What we got here? Ain't you a sweet youngun? An' purty as yer ma."

A foot stepped forward, and in one swift move, he grabbed the end of her flintlock, pointing it skyward. Sue pulled the trigger. The night exploded. She released the spent weapon, and then drew her pistol. Blue Dog leapt across the distance in a flash, latching on to the man's arm.

Levi jumped onto the intruder and wrapped his arms around his neck. They both went to the ground. Sue held fast to her gun. "Get back, Levi! Get away!"

The little girl pierced the night with her high-pitched screaming.

Henry stepped to the edge of the camp, but stopped as Levi backed away like a crawfish in the dirt under the wagon. The boy retrieved his long gun.

Sue stood, her pistol aimed at the man's belly. "If you don't want to die, mister, get on your horse and light a shuck." She held the weapon higher, pointed right at his head. "You've got one chance before I blow your brains out. Now mount!"

Her nephew stepped out with the butt of his rifle on his shoulder, aimed at the man. "You best follow my aunt's orders."

The man stumbled. Weaving, he tried to get to his horse. "Whoa, whoa now. Don't get your dander up, ma'am. Didn't mean no harm." He held out an arm with his head lowered in submission. "Just riding through." He winked at her. "No offense, mis'ess." He picked up his hat and dusted it against his knee.

Saddle leather creaked as the unwelcome visitor struggled to mount. Until he disappeared, the intruder kept an eye on Blue Dog. Blue followed the varmint off into the darkness, and Henry stepped into the light.

Sue glared. "Thanks for all your help, Mister Buckmeyer."

"You did a right fine job all by yourself." He looked to Levi. "You, too, son."

Levi spit to the side. "I ain't your son."

SUE'S KNEES SEEMED LIKE PUDDING. She slid down the wagon wheel and sat on the ground with Becky still clinging to her.

Levi bowed up to Henry. "You shoddy coward! Jig's up! Running off, hidin' in—"

"Levi!" She silenced him.

Henry looked at her nephew, shook his head, then walked over and kneeled beside her. "You all right?"

She nodded. "No thanks to you."

"See if you and Rebecca can sleep." He looked toward the east. "Couple of hours yet before first light."

"I couldn't; I'm wide awake." She stood. "Might as well get the day going. I'll make some biscuits and heat the beans."

By midmorning, she drove the lead wagon into Cuthand, surprised by the number of folks at the trading post and livery. Henry walked beside her. She scanned the area, shaded by tall pines, then looked down at her hired man. "We'll stop the wagons at the livery."

He nodded as though it was his idea and then headed toward the trading post. The aroma of tobacco tainted the air. Two ladies in full-length dresses tucked hair under their bonnets, glanced at her, then looked away. She sat a bit taller, then laughed at herself for letting their judgments bother her.

Under a big red oak, a little past the barn's side corral, a rough-looking man smiled and nodded her way. Dressed in homespun clothes and a fur cap, he exchanged a long-stemmed pipe with a group of Indians. Caddo, she figured; one of the more friendly tribes, so she'd heard. She held her chin high and pulled up the team, then climbed out of the wagon and made her way to the forge where a big, burly man worked. Becky followed.

"Good morning, sir. Have any feed and mule shoes you can spare?"

The smithy set his hammer down and wiped his brow on his sleeve then his hands on his stained leather apron. "Some. How much you be needing?"

"A set of iron would suffice, and a bushel maybe. More if the price is right."

"That bunch of cotton grangers tapped me hard, but I

could let you have a couple of bushels, say four bits a hundred. I'll throw in the shoes for a dime more."

Sue started to protest. No doubt the man was taking advantage, but he was the only show in town; there didn't appear to be any other options. "Done. Those farmers you mentioned, when was their train through?"

"Came the first time late last Thursday, I suspect. Then went and got one of their wagons stuck in the bottoms. Rolled in again Saturday morning wanting me to go fix the axle they broke getting unstuck." He turned his head and spit a brown stream into the dust. "Pulled out again after Sunday services."

"Which way were they going?"

"Headed southwest, said they's taking the ferry this time." He laughed.

"So two days, you say?"

"Yes, ma'am. Some of them wanted to leave out first light, but the ladies insisted on hearing the circuit rider's sermon." He took the coins she extended, stuck them one at a time between his teeth, and then pocketed them. "I got a good team of oxen if you're in the market. Bought them and that broke wagon, but I ain't had time to fix her yet."

"Thank you, but I have no need of an ox."

"Suit yourself."

She turned around and found her nephew watering the mules. "Levi, would you please help the smithy load the two bushels of grain and set of shoes I just bought?"

He looked over and smiled. "Sure thing, Aunt Sue."

"Thank you, dear." She hurried to the trading post, holding her daughter's hand.

Henry kneeled in the dirt, studying some intersecting lines a distinguished looking older man scratched with his long knife.

A pure white long beard covered the man's cheeks and chin, but from his ears up, his hair remained black as midnight. His mustache—she'd never seen anything like it—was two-toned, black under his nose, white over his lip.

"Did you hear, Mr. Buckmeyer? We're only two days behind the train. If we hurry—"

He held up his hand, but didn't lift his eyes from the dirt map. "Yes, ma'am, I heard. You hear why?" He gestured toward the man drawing in the dirt. "He says 'cause the bottoms are still muddy. We'll go on to Ringo's Landing like the rest of them and cross the Sulphur on the ferry."

She rubbed her brow. Would this man ever understand that she was the boss? "But we can get ahead of them on the trace going through the bottoms. Becky would have her best friend Sassy to play with, and I would enjoy a woman's company, too. We'll never catch up if we trek west all the way to the ferry then have to double back."

He said something to the old-timer, then stood. "Getting stuck, we could lose a heap more time, but it's your call."

She hated his consistent insubordination, then false acquiescence. "The only reason they came back to Cuthand was because one wagon broke an axle."

"That's right, but it broke because its wheel sunk in the mud. It took them a whole day to off-load the cotton, then another to get back here."

She looked him square in the eye. "It's Tuesday. There's been almost a week of hot and dry since they tried to cross the bottoms. We can make it."

"You have a point."

"Yes, I do."

"The smithy have grain and iron?"

"Levi's seeing to getting it loaded now."

"He say what he wants for that yoke of oxen?"

"No, and I'm not interested."

"They'd make things easier."

She shook her head. "Listen to me well. I will not have any oxen pulling any wagon of mine. Not now, not ever."

HENRY STUDIED HER A MOMENT and decided to hold his peace; the oxen would be nice, but four more mules would be much better. The bit of panic he saw in her eyes belied the hardness of her words. He decided to ponder all that later. Right now, he'd best see to getting everything he might need. A right hilly trail and two waterways separated his little caravan from Titus Trading Post, the next planned stop at Pleasant Mound, thirty miles away.

Pulling out, he rode the lead wagon. Levi walked, and Sue drove the second team. Rebecca had asked to ride with Henry, and her mother agreed, so the nine-year-old sat beside him singing a ditty with Blue Dog curled at her side.

"You have a lovely voice, Miss Rebecca."

She looked up and smiled that miniature smile of her mama's. "Why thank you, Mister Henry. I love to sing. I wish all the people in all the world would sing everything they ever said. Don't you think that would be great if everyone sang instead of talking?"

"I'm not a good singer."

"Well, I've never heard you sing. Why don't you sing a song with me now, and let me be the judge of that?"

"I don't sing."

She huffed out her exasperation. "Oh, bosh! Everyone sings. All you have to do is make your words float out on a tune. It's easy as pie."

He laughed. "I'm not a baker either."

"Well, maybe you just don't know many songs. What songs do you know? Pick a song, and I'll sing it with you. My friend Sophia Belle says I know all the words to all the songs, even the ones I haven't heard." She giggled.

"I don't know any songs." Was she going to talk nonstop the whole way? Next time he wouldn't so readily agree to this arrangement. He bumped her with his arm against hers. "You are certainly a little chatterbox, aren't you?"

"Well, I don't know about that, but I bet you do know how to sing. I know! 'Mary Had a Little Lamb'! You certainly know that one, don't you? Everybody knows that song."

Not only did she smile like her mother but she'd inherited that ill-fitted stubbornness, too. He leaned in close and half whispered, half sang "Mary had a little lamb, little lamb—"

Rebecca burst into a fit of laughter, hugging his arm with her inside hand and patting his chest with her other. "Stop, stop!" she squealed, then tried to talk between giggles. "I never heard anyone sing that bad! I think you're right, Mister Henry. You're much better off talking." Her laughter died down, but she did not release his arm. Instead, she used both hands to hug it and laid her head against it.

"Mister Henry?"

"Yes?"

"I've been praying." She didn't look up or move, just rested against him with her little hands wrapped tight around his arm.

"It's good to talk to your Maker."

"Well, I was wondering 'cause I've been praying for a daddy. You got a wife back home?"

Her innocence kept no bridle on that powerful curiosity. "No, ma'am, not married."

"So then you haven't got any children, right?"

He didn't know if he liked where this was heading. "Nope, no kids."

She looked up and smiled. Her little face shone like an angel's dappled by the sunlight shining through the tree-covered trail, but no way was he ready to be anyone's daddy or the answer to the child's prayer.

She bumped his arm. "Ever been to Memphis?"

"No, ma'am, never have."

"Do you think you might want to go sometime?" She looked up at him and batted her eyelashes. "I hear it's a very nice place."

He laughed, then flicked the reins and swallowed hard. Even the little girl knew about her mother's vow. But then why wouldn't she? Most everyone in the Red River Valley knew the beautiful Widow Baylor had vowed not to marry again without her father's blessing. She'd for sure have already been snapped up if the man didn't live so far away in Tennessee. Too bad for the others; worked to his advantage though.

Of course, he'd considered her, asked around, ever since seeing her that day at the trading post with that storm blowing in, her leaning into the wind. What had it been? Four years? And he'd never heard an unfavorable word about her. With prospective wives few and far between in the territory and far more available men, he should've got over there sooner, let her know of his interest, but he wanted to impress her, be ready for the journey east. Then his mother . . .

"Get up, Brown Mule." He hadn't thought of being a father to this miniature Sue. He'd only considered the widow, the possibility of making her a part of his life. But, now that Rebecca had brought it up, he pondered what all that having Sue entailed. The widow definitely came with some baggage, including the boy.

The girl bumped his arm again. "Mister Henry?"

"Yes?"

"Please promise not to tell Mama. About me prayin', I mean. I figure it should be our secret for now."

He grinned. Smart like her mother, too. "Yes, ma'am, little miss. Our secret; I promise."

Glancing up through the dancing leaves, he breathed a heavy sigh. The morning sun sparkled on them, through them, as though diamonds were the trees' fruit. They'd soon turn colors and another fall would arrive with its cooler weather. He loved autumn best of all. He looked back down at the top of the child's head. So, she'd been praying for a daddy. Poor little gal.

The wheels rolled against the hard-packed trail, spitting out occasional rocks. Wooden boards creaked under their load, and the mules' hooves kept a rhythm with the wagon's groans. Amazing how a man's life could take such a turn in two short days. Before the widow rode into it that morning, he'd never thought once about being anyone's father.

The trail had been on a descent all morning. A little after noon, he smelled the river and, soon enough, heard it. The little girl's chatter had finally stopped. He guessed she'd fallen asleep against him. He chuckled to himself. Again, so much like her mama.

He steered the team to the left, looking for the crossing the old man had told him about. Couldn't have missed it, though; the banks on both sides had been worn smooth. He stopped the team short, locked the brake, eased Rebecca awake, and then jumped down. Directly, Sue appeared at his side. He looked past her. "Levi, keep them back. We best water the mules before we cross."

Sue grabbed his arm. "Why do that? They just had a drink not two hours ago."

He leaned back against the wheel and threw his right leg across his left knee. "We don't want them stopping for any reason when we cross. Better safe than sorry." He tugged off his right boot and sock.

She nodded. "And why are you taking off your boots?"

He looked at her a minute. Why, why, why. She was as bad as her little girl. "I'm going to walk the crossing before we take these wagons into the water."

"Oh. Well. That's a good idea." Her eyes twinkled with what looked to him like playful admiration.

"Well, thank you, ma'am. Glad to hear you think so."

She smiled and even let a chuckle out. "You're so welcome."

He pulled his other boot and sock off, then handed the pair to the little girl. "Keep them dry for me up there on the seat." He turned back to Sue. "Could you please hold the team?"

"Certainly, glad to." She walked up to the mules and rubbed Daisy's muzzle. "Whoa, girl."

He walked in right where one wagon wheel would travel. The water was a bit cool, but not too bad. The river flowed a little above his knees at its deepest. He reached the far side, then came back where the other wheel would travel. It was narrow like the old man had said, but appeared more than wide enough to accommodate the wagons.

Levi busied himself hauling buckets of water to let the mules quench their thirst while Henry checked the riverbed. Sue met him at the bank on his return, still smiling. She was even prettier when she smiled.

"Looks like it'll be fine. Best we all get to waxing the wagons. Levi, you can help me with the underside." With that chore accomplished, Henry handed Sue his paraffin. "Tell the boy to hang back while I cross. Once I clear the far side, he can come hold that team, and I'll get on back over here."

"Now, Mister Buckmeyer, I'm perfectly capable of driving my wagon across after you."

"No doubt, ma'am, but it wouldn't do to get that cotton wet." He didn't mention keeping his tobacco or pelts dry. "How about you let me get this first one to the other bank? I'll have a better feel. Then we'll see."

"Fine, fine." She held her hands up to her daughter. "Come on down, Becky. You wait here with Mama."

"But I want to ride across with Mister Henry." The little girl frowned and stuck out her bottom lip.

"Rebecca, I agree with your mother. It's safer to let me go it alone, so why don't you jump on down like your mother said?"

She turned her frown on him, then smiled and jumped off the sideboard. He climbed back into the first wagon. "Ho, now. Let's go." He shook the reins, and the team heaved the load forward.

Keeping a close eye on the far bank, he urged them into the water. "Slow, now. Steady." He spoke in calm tones.

On the far bank, the mules pulled the load out, and water, rushing off the wagon and wheels, ran back into the river. He took a deep breath, thankful the crossing had gone without mishap. He drove the team well up on the south side, then jumped down, hoping the lady wouldn't insist on driving the other wagon across. "Levi, come on over and hold this team."

The boy shook his head and glared. Henry hated it that the youngster acted so mad all the time, but he figured his bad attitude stemmed from not having a father to teach him to be a man. No way could a woman do that, no matter how hard she tried.

"No need. He can ride over with us," Sue lifted Rebecca

up and then followed her daughter into the wagon. Levi climbed in on the opposite side. "Ho, Mil! Come on, Mabel."

Why did she feel the need to prove herself all the time? He was already duly impressed by her capabilities. "Keep 'em coming. Don't let 'em stop."

Safely on the far bank, she pulled the rig up next to the first and climbed down with an ear-to-ear grin and her chin held a little high. "I did it, Mister Buckmeyer, didn't I?"

He smiled more at her elation than the successful crossing. "You sure did, ma'am." Without a single hitch, both wagons crossed the Sulphur River and nary a drop landed on the lint or any of his goods. "Maybe some dinner while we're stopped?"

She nodded. "We've got biscuits."

"That'll work, especially with a bit of my honey." He turned to Levi. "Grab the buckets, and we'll fill the barrels." He faced her again. "You do like honey, don't you?"

"Yes, indeed, and we can certainly take time for a noonday meal." She appeared to be altogether happy with life. "Especially since we crossed the Sulphur so easily. I mean without incident, basically no trouble of any kind. Can you believe it?" She cleared her throat and laid one palm against her cheek. "Of course now"—her eyes twinkled—"I'd never be one to say I told anyone so."

He nodded. "Good." Before he put his boots back on, he waded out midstream, waited for the water to clear, then dipped the bucket full, handed it to the boy, and took the empty one. He had to figure a way to adjust that boy's attitude. And the woman? She had no idea how many things could've gone wrong.

CHAPTER

SEVEN

Toward the end of the first hour back on the trail, Levi came trotting up beside Henry. "Aunt Sue says for me to relieve you."

"She's the boss."

The boy jumped aboard, then settled in to the seat next to him, but didn't offer to take the reins. "I never took you for a coward."

Henry glanced over at him. "I didn't take you for a fool either, but you're sure talking like one."

"Oh, you think so? It was you ran off in the middle of the night when that stinking drunk came into camp."

"That what you believe?"

The boy sniggered. "It's what I know, mister; saw it with my own eyes."

Henry shook his head. He hated explaining himself, but the boy needed a lesson. "What if there'd been more of them?"

"There wasn't."

"And you knew that right off?"

"Well, no, but the way I see it, a man meets whatever he has to head-on, not sulking around in the dark."

"I prefer to know what's afoot, how many I have to fight. It's best to have all the advantages you can get going into any scrap."

Levi studied Daisy's rump like he was trying to figure things out. After a bit, he turned back and stared at Henry a few minutes before saying anything. "What would you have done if there had of been more of them?"

"Whatever it took."

The boy gave a quick nod and then reached over and grabbed the reins. "Aunt Sue said she'd like a word with you."

Henry jumped down and slow-walked until Sue's wagon pulled alongside. Blue Dog trailed him. "You wanted a word?"

Rebecca leaned out across her mother. "Why is it you're walking when it's always my turn after Levi?"

"Guess we both can walk."

"Sure you can." Her mother shook her head at Henry. "Why don't you jump on down, Becky? You've gotten plenty good at it. Play with Blue and spend some of that energy of yours."

"All right, Mama, thank you! I'll keep you in sight. I won't forget!"

He adjusted his hat, gesturing to Sue before setting it a little further back on his brow. "That word?"

"Oh, I was just so excited that we got across the Sulphur with no problems and didn't have to go so far out of the way over to the ferry, I hadn't told you how much I'd appreciate it if you could stop underestimating me." She smiled down. "I mean I realize men think women are helpless without them, and I don't mean to be rude, but I have taken care of myself and my business without a man's help for a long time now. And I drove my wagon across that river with no trouble."

He could hardly believe his ears. "Don't believe I have underestimated you, ma'am, but I apologize for giving you that impression. I've actually been quite astonished with your achievements. These sixteen bales of cotton on their way to market are a mighty testament to your abilities, Sue."

"Oh. Well." She cleared her throat. "Thank you, I guess."

"And I was right proud of you for chasing off that horrible man this morning, too."

"But you didn't think I could drive my own wagon across the river."

"Wasn't that at all, ma'am."

She looked off as though considering. "Then what was it?"

He shrugged. "Nothing to do with your capabilities, just wanted to be sure the load didn't get wet."

"Well." Her foot tapped the boards, then stopped. "All right. Since that's out of the way, I've thanked the good Lord for our safe crossing, and I wanted to thank you, too. For making sure it all went well and everything."

"You're welcome, ma'am." Seemed to him that the Lord always got a lot of credit for things a man did, but she could believe what she wanted.

"Also want to ask you, if you get a chance, would you talk to Levi? He's—"

He waved her off. "We talked. We're good."

"Excellent. He is a precious boy."

He looked off to Rebecca romping with Blue and laughing. "You've done a fine job with the both of the children, Sue; another of your impressive achievements."

"Why thank you." She didn't say anything for a while and fidgeted with runaway strands of her hair, working them back under her hat. "Well, I guess that's all. I'm glad to know you think a little more highly of my efforts and wishes; especially since I—well—hired you to come along to assist us."

Man, she just couldn't let it go. "Yes, ma'am. Sorry you got the wrong idea that I didn't."

Rebecca ran up beaming. "I sure love your dog, Mister Henry."

He gave the little girl a wink, then looked back up at Sue. "Mother always said, 'Takes more than brawn to survive Texas.' "

A hint of blush flushed Sue's cheeks. A smile tried to form, but she stopped it. "Well, thank you, Henry." She wouldn't meet his eye, but it was the first time she'd used his given name since she came to his place. He liked the sound of it on her lips. "That's so kind of you to say."

"Believe in giving credit where it's due."

She faced him, but this time she smiled.

He loved that show of gladness on her face and wished he could make it happen all day long, but he still had to address the next topic. "We've got the worse of it ahead of us, though, to get out of these bottoms. If you're in agreement, I'd like to camp this side of White Oak Creek."

Her smile disappeared. "Why not push on? We just crossed a river. A creek shouldn't be any problem. For the life of me, I cannot understand why you're always so intent on slowing our progress."

"Not at all, ma'am, but I hear tell the double branch of the White Oak is more treacherous then the river. Unless you say otherwise, I'd like to take them on with fresh mules and a full belly."

"How much farther can we go?"

"Hour, two at most."

She glanced toward the sun, then looked back and shrugged, obviously perturbed again. "I would like to keep going."

He nodded, tipped his hat, and then increased his pace. Every time he thought he'd gotten through to her, she went right back to her old way of thinking. He hated that she was so stubborn.

Past his turn to ride, he kept walking. If he'd told the widow thanks but no thanks, he could have had that last batch of seed ready and be on his way to St. Louis, but no. He'd hired on to be a nursemaid. Rebecca climbed into the wagon with Levi. Shortly, the girl's laughter, then her singing, interrupted his sour mood. How could anyone stay grumpy around her?

He continued to walk until the creek came into view, then turned around. Levi stopped his wagon a few feet before the bank sloped into the water. Sue pulled her wagon next to the boy's. He glanced at the sun and then stared at her. "Still want to cross this afternoon?"

She glared for a bit, then looked skyward and shook her head. "It would appear to me that the best idea would be to cross in the morning. The mules will be fresher then, not so spent; and so will we. We'll cross after breakfast." She climbed down from the wagon.

He nodded. "Probably for the best." The urge to smile almost overwhelmed him, but he kept a straight face. "I'll see about catching some fish for supper."

With camp set, Levi seeing to cleaning and frying up three nice-size catfish, and corn bread baking in the Dutch oven, Henry offered his hand to Sue, who kneeled by the fire.

"Care to do some scouting?"

"Scouting? Why? What do you need to scout?"

He shook his head. "Never mind."

He stormed off toward the creek tired of all the woman's whys. She couldn't seem to accept that he had a good reason for everything he did. No, she insisted on questioning every move he made. Why, why, why.

He stopped short, sat on a fallen tree, and yanked off his right boot and sock. She walked around the trunk and sat down. He glanced over.

She sighed. "Didn't mean to upset you, but I can't for the life of me understand what's wrong with me asking you—"

"There's a reason for everything I do, and you're always second-guessing me."

She sat there silent for longer than he liked. "I don't know what to say, Henry."

"Care to get wet?"

She looked at him, eyes questioning, but didn't ask why.

"Figured we should check out the creek bottom."

She smiled. "Sure, why not? Doesn't look too deep." She leaned over and started unlacing her high-top shoes.

He got his other boot and sock off, then waded in. "It's not so deep, but the bottom is said to be tricky."

She eased her first shoe off, then tugged at the thick, masculine sock. Laying it over her shoe, she looked up. "Andy's. I prefer wearing them when I'm working." She started on her second foot, wrestling with keeping the trouser leg up out of her way. Seemed a bit of a chore, but she finally sat the shoes together, laying her late husband's socks carefully over them. She rolled up both legs all neat like, then pushed herself up and walked toward him. "Same with his britches; just seem so much more practical for chores than petticoats and skirts."

He ignored the comment and nodded toward his right. "You want to check that side?"

"Happy to." She stepped into the water, then hiked her pants legs up even more. "Oh, it's cold." She grinned, then made an ugly face. "And the mud is so squishy. It's nasty!"

He chuckled but continued walking to the other side of the shallows. On coming back, he checked a little more downstream. He crossed several times, noticing she followed his lead. "What do you think?"

"The mud's a little deep, but the water's shallow. It seems a little rockier over here. I think it's a decent place to cross, don't you?"

He nodded and resisted the urge to splash her with creek water. How could she do that to him? One minute, she made him so mad, then the next, made him feel like a schoolboy. "We shouldn't have any trouble with this one."

Heading toward the bank, he climbed out, then waited on her. He extended his hand. She slipped hers into it, and he pulled. He loved the feel of her skin, even if it was her calluses against his. Sue's hands were so much smaller than his mother's.

She climbed onto the bank, stared at him for a moment, and then slowly withdrew her hand. "I best go check on Levi. He might burn the fish if I don't help."

He nodded and stepped gingerly back to the felled tree. His tender feet found the knee-high grasses scattered with unseen stones and summer's stickery seeds barely navigable. He quickly replaced his boots as Sue did—sitting so close, and yet so far away—then went on back, leaving her to finish without having to work so hard at keeping her bare ankles from his view.

He appreciated a modest woman—even one in britches.

He smiled, thinking of what his mother would say about that. The way Sue had looked at him when she stepped out of the creek encouraged him. He hoped what he'd seen in her eyes was at least a bit of what grew in his heart.

CHIRPING BIRDS WOKE SUE. Her eyes opened to the gray light of false dawn. She lay there relishing the benefits of a decent night's sleep. She looked over at her little girl snuggled up in her quilt on the furs and thanked God again for the child who gave her a reason to live. So much like her father. As hard as Sue tried to remember, she'd forgotten exactly what he looked like, but Becky kept a part of him alive in her heart.

She smelled her favorite early morning aroma and rolled over.

"Morning." Henry squatted next to the fire. He held up his tin cup. "Coffee?"

"Yes, sir, thank you." She crawled from beneath the wagon, stood, and stretched her hands toward the sky. "I feel so much better this morning than yesterday. Rested and more refreshed."

He handed her a steaming cup. "We all needed a good, long, quiet night."

"Don't you figure we're at least a day or two ahead of the train now? Bless the Lord."

"Well, for sure we're bound to be ahead of them. We've had a good start." He drained his cup and tossed the dregs toward the fire. "I've got biscuits in the Dutch oven. If you've a mind to tend them and maybe fry some salt pork, I'll rouse the boy, and we can get the mules seen to."

She nodded. "How long have they been cooking?"

He glanced at the eastern sky. "Five minutes or so."

She busied herself with breakfast and picking up and stowing the pallets, except for Becky's. The little sleepyhead would've slept all the way to eating time had it not been for Blue Dog. He nosed his head under her hand and, when he got no response, put one paw on her chest. It tickled Sue that he wanted her awake. The dog finally licked Becky's face, and she opened her eyes.

Right as the sun burst over the eastern horizon, Henry doused the cook fire with creek water and faced Sue. "If it's fine with you, I'll take the first wagon."

She realized it was more of an order than a suggestion, but she did prefer how he framed it. "Yes, you go ahead. That will be fine." She made one more visual sweep of the camp. Everything was stowed, and other than the wet remnants of charred firewood, they weren't leaving anything. "I'll wait until you're across and top the far bank."

He nodded, then faced Levi. "Ride with me."

The boy shrugged. He'd seemed a little easier to get along with, but still acted as if he resented the man being there. They both climbed aboard the lead wagon, and Sue said a little prayer. It seemed to take some extra urging to get the first team going. But they soon were in the water just below their knees.

"Ho, Brown Mule. Pull. Get up, Daisy."

Slow but steady, the mules made progress crossing the first branch, probably twice as wide as the Sulphur if you counted the swampy conditions on both sides of the actual creek. The team moved along doing so well. Sue hurried back to the second wagon and climbed onto the seat for a better view. She wanted to see exactly where and how Henry went. It just wouldn't do for him to make it and her to fail.

She glanced away quickly to check on her daughter. Blue Dog ran alongside her. "Becky, come, get in!"

Watching Henry again, Sue realized she didn't remember seeing her little girl running or sitting or laying in the grass looking up at the clouds without Blue Dog right there beside her. She appreciated the hound taking such an interest, and had to admit that she liked the animal—more than she would ever have thought possible.

Following Henry's progress, she held one hand on her chest. Once the wagon's wheels pulled out onto the far bank, she remembered to breathe. She faced her daughter, who climbed up beside her in the nick of time to celebrate Henry's crossing. "Yes!" Sue patted her chest repeatedly and sighed. "That seemed easy enough."

Becky stood on the seat and clapped her hands above her head. "Yay! You did it! Hooray for Mister Henry! Hooray for Levi!"

Sue looked up at her daughter and joined the celebration. "Whoopee!"

Becky's smile spread over her face like bluebonnets on the Texas prairie in April. She beamed. "Mister Henry can do anything."

"Oh, you think so?"

"Yes, ma'am, he surely can." Becky sat down and straightened her skirt. "But I remembered not to hurt Levi's feelings and hollered for him, too, at the last."

"That was certainly nice of you. I'm proud you remembered."

"Yes, ma'am, but I'm sure Mister Henry didn't need any help from him. Most likely, he did it all by himself. He can"—Becky looked up and nodded like the little priss she was—"do anything!"

Sue wanted to argue with her daughter, and tried to think of something he couldn't do, but she couldn't come up with a single thing. Maybe he could do whatever he set his mind to. The first wagon stopped on the ridge of the far bank. She clucked the mules to life. "Hey, now." She snapped the reins, and the wagon lurched forward. She would have preferred a bit more speed, but the wooden wheels knifed into the water and kept on rolling.

She prayed all the way across and encouraged the team until she pulled onto the opposite bank, climbed it, then stopped a bit past the first wagon.

Henry smiled on her way by. "Well done."

"Thank you, sir." She looked to the sky. "And thank You, Lord."

After a hundred yards or so, she topped the next ridge, and her heart skipped a beat. The wagon with the broken axle sat on the bank of the second branch of White Oak Creek, a ghoulish reminder of her friends and neighbors' failed crossing. It taunted her jubilance and screamed of doom. Her mouth went dry, and all smiles vanished. She stopped the mules and locked the brake.

Henry pulled up next to her. "The old-timer said this was the bad one, deeper water and not a lot of bottom. This is why the train turned back and took the ferry."

Sue tore her eyes away from the water and looked at him. "Did the old man mention how we might get across?"

"Claims there's a rock path." He jumped down and extended his hand. "Want to help me find it?"

She took his hand, steadied herself, then stepped down. For a second, he didn't let go. A tingling danced up her arm, but she pulled away, extinguishing the sensation before it reached her heart. She had no time for entanglements now, and especially not with Henry Buckmeyer—or did she? "Guess we need to get wet again."

Unlike the first branch of the creek, these beds had holes filled with deep mud. Henry crossed back and forth, as did Sue, time and again. In one spot, she stepped onto a thin layer of rocks. "Over here. Check this out," she called.

He walked back and forth over the area she'd found, sloshing through the water several times, then across from one bank to the other as many times. "It's the best we've found."

She hated the thought of trying to cross it, but gave herself no choice. She definitely did not want to go back to Cuthand then all the way to Ringo's Landing. But if she didn't get her cotton to market, all her hard work and cash spent would be for nothing. Without the cotton money, it'd be doubtful she could even survive another year, certainly not with hers and Levi's land intact.

She faced Henry, who wore a grim expression. "What do you think?"

He shrugged and sighed. "It can be done, but there's not much room for error."

She bowed her head, then nodded. "Let's get to it."

He waded to the middle of the rocks and studied the tree line. "Seems to me we need to line up on that pine." He held his hand up and gestured a straight line toward a tall single pine that stood in front of a wall of hardwoods.

She joined him and imagined the line. "Looks good to me."

He faced her. "Want me to drive both wagons?"

Her first notion was to agree, but the stronger impression, the one born in the stubbornness of her heart, wouldn't have it. From that first horrible year, she'd succeeded on her own, alone. She did not need this man or any other to do what she could handle.

"No. We'll do this one as we did the last. You go first, and I'll cross once you're on the other side."

He waded back onto the bank, retrieved his boots, then headed for the wagon he'd been driving. She could tell that he didn't like her answer. Why? Did he think he was invincible or something? If he could do it, so could she. Picking up her footwear, she glanced back at the creek, then to the broken-down wagon. Her confidence drained away. As she followed him to the wagons, a knot formed in her throat.

Why did she always have to be so willful? She already regretted her headstrong proclamation. But she'd said it. And now she had no choice but to do it. And do it she would! If he could, then so could she. But then the possibility that even he wouldn't make it swept over her. What could that mean but turning back? At least it wouldn't be her fault.

"Lord, don't let the load get wet."

Then again, Becky said the man could do anything. Sue wished she'd immediately agreed to let him drive both wagons. It would've been so easy then, but no. Who thought they were invincible? While she chided herself, without a word, he climbed aboard the first wagon, released the brake, and headed toward the entry point they'd decided on.

He aligned the team exactly with the pine and then urged them forward. As though he'd been doing it every day of his life and twice on Sundays, Henry drove across the second and worse branch of White Oak Creek like it was a picnic. He stopped at the far ridge and jumped down hollering something.

She couldn't hear him, but her insides had settled a lot, having seen that it wasn't as hard as it appeared after all. Her confidence returned. If he was hollering to try to get her to let him drive the second wagon now, he might as well save his breath.

"Hang on, Becky. Here we go."

The front wheels cut into the water. He ran toward her, waving his arms. Why was he doing that? Levi joined him, waving his arms, too. What were they saying? She couldn't stop now. She'd get stuck for sure. He should know that. She slapped the reins on the mules' backs. Just as the load passed into the water, she finally heard what they were hollering.

"Watch out for the snake."

"Snake? Where?"

Henry pointed upstream.

She looked, and her heart sank to the pit of her stomach. A huge water moccasin swam straight toward them. She'd never seen one so big before. "Oh, God, have mercy." She kept the team moving. "Easy now. Good." She clicked her tongue. "Get up, Dex. Good boy. Keep us moving." She couldn't stop, she couldn't.

Her mule must have spotted the reptile first. He whinnied and shied. Mabel followed his lead. Sue fought to keep them on the rocks and heading straight, but felt the wagon roll backward. The back wheel sunk into a hole, and the wagon tilted precariously and jerked to a stop, throwing Becky sideways. Sue screamed and grabbed her one-handed just as her daughter fell off the wagon.

She went to her stomach on the bench and grabbed her little girl with both hands, then pulled with all her might until the child was safe in her arms. "Becky, oh, Becky. I got you!" She had to be all right. "Did it bite you? Did you get bit?"

Becky leaned back, crying, and shook her head. "No! I don't think so, Mama."

Both mules brayed and reared. They pawed the creek water wildly as the moccasin disappeared from her sight somewhere under or around her team. For a terrifying second, it seemed the whole wagon was going onto its side, but thankfully, it stayed upright. As quickly as it had come, the snake floated downstream without any apparent damage.

Sue slapped the reins, urging the team forward. The beasts strained. They snorted and pulled, but the wagon didn't budge. "Oh, blast!"

CHAPTER

EIGHT

HENRY RAN TO THE EDGE OF THE CREEK. Why hadn't she stopped? He watched for a moment while she urged the team, but they couldn't pull that much weight out of the hole. "Don't." He held his hands up. "Stop. I'll get the other team." He half turned, then looked back, confirming what he thought. The off mule's head drooped. Oh, no. He jerked his boots off—should never have put them back on—and waded into the creek.

"What's wrong?"

"Looks like this one got bit."

"Oh, dear, no! Will she die?"

He reached the animal and felt along her chest and neck. His fingers moved over a swollen spot on the mule's lower chest. "I don't know." He turned around. "Levi, fetch Mil." He started taking Mabel's harness off.

"What can I do to help?"

He looked up. Sue was unlacing her boots. "Sit tight. Shouldn't take us too long if it's going to work. You'll need to drive."

First, he replaced the snake-bit mule with Mil, giving Mabel to Levi. "Don't worry with hobbling her right now. Just fetch the other two out here one at a time." He worked on modifying the harness hookup with chains from the wagon to accommodate the two extra mules. Levi returned with Brown Mule first, and Henry set about hooking him in front of Mil. By the time he got his animal set, the boy had led Daisy out, then helped Henry get her ready.

"Thanks, Levi. Now I'll go to the back and lift on the corner that's in the hole from the deep side." The boy started around the wagon the other way. "No, no. You'll need to stay up there to urge the front team forward. Your aunt's reins won't reach them."

"Yes, sir."

Henry waded along the low side. "We're almost ready, Sue. When I give the word, take 'em out slow and steady if we get it out of the hole."

She nodded. "I will."

He moved on back and shouted at her, "Let's go."

"Hey now, Mil!" She whacked the reins against the closest mules. "Let's go, Dex." The animals strained and pulled.

Levi jerked on the front mules. "Ho now, mules. Get up!"

Even little Rebecca joined the ruckus. "Get up, now!" she screamed at the top of her lungs. "Come on, mules, pull!"

Henry sucked up a breath and lifted and pushed with all his might. He grunted and strained against the wagon with his shoulder. His thighs burned.

The teams' hooves sucked mud as they tried to dig in against the soft bottom again and again. The wagon moved ever so slightly. With no other option, Henry quit before he busted a gut. The wheel refused to climb out of the hole.

"Stop. Wait."

Sue eased up on the mules. "Whoa, now."

He walked to the front of the wagon. "Where did we stow the ax?"

"In the back of the other wagon."

He held his hands up toward her. "Come on. I'll carry you to the bank."

"What? Why? What are you thinking? We've only tried once. Let's try again. We've got to get this wagon unstuck."

He nodded. "I plan to, but that wheel is too deep. The load's too heavy. Four mules can't pull it out."

"Then what are you going to do?"

He looked down, gathering his peace, and let his hands fall to his sides. Would the woman ever trust him? He hated being expected to explain himself at every turn. Would nothing satisfy her until she knew his every thought? He flexed his jaw a couple of times, then looked up. "I'm going to find a male bois d'arc and cut him down. I'll use—"

"A male bois d'arc? How can a tree be male or female?"

Wonderful. Facing a crisis and she interrupts so she can know everything. "The males grow straighter. The female tree bears the horse apples, and the fruits' weight bends her limbs and even the trunk." He turned to Levi. "Get the chains and harnesses off the mules. We'll let them graze."

"Oh, no! Is it going to take that long?" She looked so disappointed that she might cry, but then she bit her lip, obviously trying to recover her self-control. She cleared her throat. "I never knew that about trees. Why won't any tree do?"

He shook his head. She was simply not going to let up. He studied her a moment and then decided he'd better give details, lay out every plan if he was ever going to get to work. "I need to make a fulcrum to raise the corner of the wagon. Hopefully, using it, we'll be able to lift the wheel out of that hole. I want a bois d'arc because its wood is extremely dense and strong."

Levi chimed in. "So less likely to snap."

Henry and Sue both looked at the boy. Henry hadn't realized he was even listening. "That's exactly right."

"Levi, I didn't realize you knew about trees. Where did—"

"Oh, I was only guessing from what Mister Henry said." He grinned and headed toward the bank with the first team.

"Anyway, it'll take a while. You and Becky need to get to shore." He held his arms out again. "Want to stay dry?"

"I'm already pretty damp." She sighed. "Can't we at least try one more time?"

"To what end?"

"Oh fine, Henry Buckmeyer." Her tone was not of resignation but frustration tinted with a bit of anger if he read her right. "By all means, carry me to shore. Guess I can put some beans on to soak since it looks like we'll be here awhile." She stood, turned slightly sideways with her back mostly toward him, then fell into his waiting arms.

Her weight took him by surprise. She felt light as a feather but remained fairly stiff. Her face was so close to his. Why couldn't she relax? Maybe lay her head on his shoulder? He enjoyed the feel of her.

"I'll be back for you, Miss Rebecca."

The little girl grinned and held out her dress. "I'm already wet, but I'll wait for you to carry me, too."

He headed for the far shore. "I'd like you and Rebecca to get a fire going. A big one. When it's going good, throw some damp leaves on it. Lots of 'em."

She held herself out from him and wrinkled her brow in puzzlement. "Why in the world do you want us to do that?"

He should have known. "To make smoke. We need smoke, lots of smoke."

She still looked stumped. "What for?"

"A signal. The Caddo have been known to help distressed travelers."

"What if we call Indians from the wrong tribe?"

"The Caddo populate this whole area. Any others would be traveling through and aren't likely to respond to our signal anyway." He sat her down on the bank without another word and waded out for the little girl.

Levi followed him. "I'll carry Bitty Beck, and you can start loosing the second team."

Henry didn't much like the boy telling him what to do, but decided to let it go. He stopped next to Mil and began unbuckling the leather straps.

"No! Get away!" Rebecca stomped her foot. "Mister Henry said he would get me."

The boy held out his arms. "Come on, now, Bitty Beck. Jump!"

"No, I won't!" She crossed her arms over her chest. "You always think you are the boss of me, but you are not! Now you go get those mules, and let him carry me like he said he would."

The boy's face reddened. "You are such a little spoiled brat, Rebecca Ruth!" He wore a hard expression but relieved Henry from the mule duty without saying more.

The little girl stuck out her tongue to his back, then clapped her hands. "Come on over here and catch me, Mister Henry!"

He held up his arms, and she propelled herself from the wagon. He didn't really need to catch her as she wrapped both arms around his neck.

She laid her head on his shoulder and whispered into his ear, "I wanted you so I could tell you something."

"Oh, yeah? What's that?"

"I think since I asked Him, God sent you to be my daddy, and I love you, Mister Daddy. Isn't that a good name to call you? But only when it's just me and you." She gave his neck a little squeeze then leaned out and looked him in the eye. "I need to get used to calling you Daddy." She bent over closer to his face. "Don't you agree?"

He smiled, not sure how he should answer the girl. How could such a small female know how to worm her way into his heart? Her daddy. The little gal needed some discipline sure enough. "You calling me Daddy, huh?"

She nodded. "Well, Mister Daddy, on account of I should show some respect."

He glanced at her mother, gathering kindling on the shore. She hauled it to the top of the rise. He'd have to win her to make it happen, but he couldn't deny the idea of being a daddy was growing on him. "Wouldn't we have to let your mother in on our secret? I mean—"

She giggled. "That's why I said when it's only us. I'll still call you Mister Henry in front of everyone else. Might be best if Mama doesn't know just yet. Besides, I like having a secret with you."

Walking ashore, he threw her into the sky amidst abundant giggles before sitting her down. She ran to her mother. "Did you see me? Did you see how high I went?"

Her mama smiled, though shaking her head. "Yes, I saw. I hope you didn't hurt your cousin's feelings."

"Well, Mister Henry"—she glanced over at him and winked—"he'd already said that he would carry me. Levi should mind his own business."

Henry chuckled and grabbed the ax that Sue had obviously gotten out and leaned against the wagon for him. "I'll be back."

The woods were cooler and the sounds of the little one and her mother faded. He hadn't realized how long it'd been since he'd been alone. He truly enjoyed the peace and quiet. Silently passing through, he kept an eye out for the distinctive bark of the bois d'arc. Wouldn't bother him a bit if it took a while to find one. Blue Dog came running up to his left, doing some scouting of his own.

He hadn't gone too far before he saw exactly what he hunted. A tall, straight bois d'arc, and it wasn't too old, perfect for his fulcrum. Blue disappeared; he must have gotten bored. Henry rested his musket on the trunk of a nearby tree, spit on the ax blade, and went to work.

SUE FANNED THE FIRE and glanced for the hundredth time at the wagon stuck in the creek. It was all that snake's fault! If it hadn't been for that moccasin, she could have made it just fine. Dumb snake! And with both the guys hollering at her at the same time, how was she supposed to make sense of what they were saying?

She stopped in her tracks and stared at the ground. She'd seen the first time Henry hollered and waved his arms perfectly well. He'd plainly meant for her to stop. But she was already in the water by then. Still, why did she have to be her stubborn, proud self? Just to prove to Henry that she could do whatever he could?

What was so bad about following his directions? Like she had an aversion just because the order came from him. Order. Maybe that was it. He always ordered everyone around! And they all obeyed. But not her! She couldn't let him think even for a minute that he was the boss. And look where her pride had gotten her.

Pride goeth before a fall. She glanced up at the sky. "Is that what it is, Lord? You're punishing me for my pride?"

It was never like that with Andy; she had no trouble submitting to him. From the start, he was her hero, her champion, and her head in every respect of the Word. He also loved her enough to listen. He would sit for hours and discuss her ideas and dreams. She smiled, remembering how he always told her how smart she was. He'd said every other girl he'd ever spent much time around had embarrassed him, but that she never had.

Maybe she should give in and let Henry take the lead for the time they were on the trace. So what if she paid him a salary? Truth was, she'd hired him to get them there, whatever it took, and if it took doing things his way . . .

One thing for certain, her cotton would be a lot closer to Pleasant Mound by now if she hadn't been so hardheaded. If only she'd let him drive both the wagons across like he'd offered.

It was all her fault.

Becky came running up barefoot in her wet cotton bloomers and slip. Sue saw no reason her daughter couldn't have a little fun playing in the water while she helped accomplish the chore Henry had put them to. The girl dumped an armload of leaves that she'd dampened at the creek onto the fire. They almost put the flames out.

"Becky, Becky, not so many at one time."

"Sorry, Mama."

She skipped off, going deeper each time into the woods to gather twigs and leaves for the grand fire. Sue watched until she disappeared behind the hardwoods and brush, then fanned the flames again, sending roils of smoke into the sky. So Indians would come. He wanted to call the Indians.

She sighed.

Never would she have sent smoke signals to call savages to her location. Never. As far as she was concerned, the safest bet was to assume that more violent tribes roamed the untamed territory than friendly ones. She steered as clear as she could from all of them.

Levi came back after retrieving the cooking pots from the stuck wagon and dropped them on the ground. "Want me to drag up some deadfall?"

"Sure, I suppose we're ready for some larger logs." The muscles across her shoulders ached from one side to the other. She tried to stretch her neck some, relieve the pressure. This day—getting stuck and it being her blunder—had almost gotten the best of her. "Guess I might as well get some dinner going."

She checked the swollen beans and got out her ingredients for corn bread, then got busy making a cook fire and getting the pintos to boiling. Next time she looked over, Levi had the signal fire blazing. "Maybe you should trench around it."

"Yes, ma'am." He headed toward the shovel she'd used for her cook fire, then got to work digging a ring.

She looked toward the creek, then along the woods. She stood and went to the other side of the wagon. "Levi, have you seen Becky? She's been gone—" Sue tried to remember exactly when she last saw her daughter. How long had it been? "Uh—a long time." Just then, as though she'd been reminded of Becky's absence by the Lord, a terrified shriek came from the woods.

Becky!

Sue dropped the Dutch oven, spilling the corn bread batter, and ran toward her daughter's screams. Before she reached the edge of the woods, Becky burst into the open. Close behind her, a black bear crashed through the trees.

"Oh, God! Help me!" Sue looked around frantically. Where was her gun? "Becky, run to me!" She ran toward her daughter. Waving her arms hysterically, she screeched at the wild beast. "No! Get out of here." She slowed only a bit and picked up a chunk of wood, then hurled it at the bear. "Go away!"

From nowhere, Blue Dog appeared and charged the beast. Sue kneeled, and her daughter ran into her arms. "Oh, Becky, Becky, Becky!" Tears streamed down her face as she hugged her little girl. Sobs racked her being. The whole day. Getting stuck. "Oh, Becky, Becky." What would she have done if that awful bear had gotten her baby? She couldn't stop crying.

The bear and dog circled each other. Blue Dog barked and barked and bared his fangs. The bear stood on its back legs and growled, showing fangs of its own.

Levi appeared with his long gun, aimed, and fired.

CHAPTER

NINE

HENRY DROPPED THE AX at Rebecca's first scream, grabbed his musket, and dashed back to the others. Blue's bark and the bear's growls spurred him into a dead run. His heart pounded. A shot rang out. Crashing through the woods, he leapt over deadfall and threw up his arms to block limbs. He pushed his legs faster; in his mind everything slowed as he prepared to battle the bear.

He exploded into the open. Sue had Rebecca. Blue Dog lay beside them. Henry scanned the area immediately, but the beast was gone. Levi stood holding his long gun, looking proud of himself. The mules huddled together but appeared to be fine, except the snake-bit one's head hung low.

Henry bent over and grabbed his knees. He blew hard until he found his breath. His insides quivered, but he willed them still and walked to the boy. "Was it a sow bear?"

"Don't know; everything happened too fast."

Henry glanced at the girl, who still hugged her mother, and walked toward them. "She all right?"

"She will be."

"And you?"

"Fine, but I'm still shaky." It sounded as though her voice nearly choked her. "I was so scared." She put a hand on either side of her face and shut her eyes. "I hate this day!"

"I hit the bear, Mister Henry. I know I did. Wasn't a kill shot, but I know I got a piece of him." Levi held the long gun.

"That's ace-high, son. You did great."

Sue rose, smiling at the boy, and threw her arms around him. "I'll say you did. I'm so proud of you, Levi." She left one arm on his waist, clinging to him.

Henry hoped the bear had run the other direction. "You re-load yet?"

"Uh, no, sir. I didn't think about it."

"Better see to that."

The little girl hugged the dog's neck but left him to join her mother. She hugged her almost-brother's leg. "Thank you, Levi. Thank you for shooting that bear and saving me and saving Blue Dog, too." Tears flowed down her cheeks, and her bottom lip quivered. "I'm sorry I was mean to you before. Forgive me?"

Levi kneeled and returned her hug. "That's all right, Bitty Beck, and of course I forgive you."

She wiped her face dry. "Good."

Henry motioned for Blue to stay, then walked out a ways. He soon found the blood trail. For a moment, he debated on whether he should follow it but decided it would be best not to leave the woman and girl alone. When he returned, the boy was still busy reloading the long gun.

Henry joined Sue and Rebecca near the cook fire. "That old bear scare my best girl?"

She looked up and nodded. "I was gathering leaves to get wet, and I didn't see him. Then he was there, and he growled at me real mean, so I ran."

"You did good raising a ruckus and getting yourself some help." He smoothed her hair. He wanted to scoop her up and hold her tight, but her mother might not understand. She didn't know that her little girl had called him daddy. And that's what he wanted to be. He could handle her being a spoiled brat, but all of a sudden, he couldn't imagine a life without the little one in it.

He swallowed hard and blinked the bit of moisture in his eyes away. "I was almost finished chopping that tree I need. You ladies want to come and help me drag it back?"

Becky jumped up and grabbed his hand. "I do. Come on, Mama."

"Well, if we're going to have any corn bread with our beans, I better stay." She looked up. "You don't really need my help, do you? If you want Levi to lend a hand, take him. He can help watch Becky, too, if she's set on going. I'll be fine here."

"You sure?"

She nodded and scratched the scruff of his hound's neck. "You're a good dog, Blue." She pulled his face next to hers. "You're a wonderful, powerful good dog." She sighed and looked up at Henry again. "You were absolutely right about this animal. There's no way I could pay enough for what he's done."

"Yes, ma'am." He turned to the boy. "We'll get going then. Leave the long gun for your aunt."

"He can take it. I'll get my flintlock and keep it close."

Becky ran to hold her cousin's hand, then looked to Henry. "Can Blue Dog come, too?"

He glanced at the dog, then held out his hand to her. "He better stay here with your mama."

SUE WATCHED THEM LEAVE. She regretted not going some, but she'd be fine. Alone, she bowed her head, and tears flowed down her cheeks. "Thank You, Lord, for putting it in Henry's heart to come with us. Oh, God, draw him to Yourself." Images of the black bear right behind her little girl flashed across her mind's eye. "Thank You for bringing that man and his dog into our lives."

She remembered her best sister-friend. "Thank You for Elaine, too, for her insisting that I ask him; and for softening my hardheadedness." She smiled.

A peace settled over her, and she wiped her wet cheeks. She had corn bread to fix. No matter what, they had to eat.

HENRY SEARCHED THROUGH THE TREES and brush for any sight of the bear. Then the rhythmic pound of the sharp ax against the tree took his mind off the too-close call. Chips flew through the air and fell all around the forest floor. Levi's long gun rang out.

Rebecca clapped her hands. "You got him! We'll have rabbit for supper now, I'll fetch it."

In no time, the bois d'arc fell. "Think you can handle the top end?"

"Yes, sir!"

After trimming the tree, Levi helped him lift the bottom of the trunk into the air, and Henry got it on his shoulder. Then Levi got under the opposite end.

"I'll carry the ax." Rebecca grabbed the handle.

"Let's go then." Henry headed back to camp. The girl ran up beside him.

"Mister Da— Uh." She giggled. "I mean Mister Henry. You going to use this log to get the wagon unstuck?"

"Hope to."

"How you gonna do it?"

For the rest of the way back to camp, he explained his plan.

The wagon came into view, and Becky ran ahead. "Mama, look at that big old bois d'arc tree. It's extremely heavy. Can you believe that they can carry it?" She held the ax up. "I helped, too."

Henry placed his musket against the wagon's wheel, then faced the boy. "Let's ease it on down here for now."

"Sure." Levi lowered his end of the trunk to his waist. When Henry rolled the big end off his shoulder, the boy let the smaller end on down to the ground. He held up the rabbit, grinning. Got you something to fry up, too."

Letting the tree fall the rest of the way, Henry pushed it out. "How 'bout you get to work on that oak over there?" He pointed to a medium-size tree a bit off the trail. "We're going to need a good-size chunk of it."

The boy nodded, apparently wise to his plan. Henry liked it that Levi didn't ask a heap of questions. Later, as he took a turn swinging the ax, it dawned on him that the opposite was true about Rebecca. He considered that for a while as he worked. He always enjoyed having something to ponder while he did a repetitive task; it made the time pass faster. In the end, he reckoned it was because he'd fallen hard for the miniature Sue.

He really had barely tolerated Levi. The kid's rudeness, his suspicion and resentment, his sarcasm didn't sit too well either. But then, the young fellow had never had a man in his life, at least not since he was old enough to remember. Henry stepped back and handed the ax to Levi again. "Want to take him on down?"

"I'd like that."

After fifteen more whacks, the oak fell exactly as planned. Henry walked to the log and pointed to a spot about two feet from the end. "Now we need to cut him off here."

The boy spit on his hands, rubbed them together, then hefted the ax. "Yes, sir."

Henry liked all the yes, sirs. Maybe he'd misjudged the boy. When the chips stopped flying quite as fast as before, he took the ax. "Get a blow and a dipper of water if you're of a mind to."

"You want one?"

Henry nodded, then went to work. Shame he'd not included a crosscut saw on his list, but he hadn't, so he continued swinging the ax. Soon enough, the boy returned with the dipper.

"Aunt Sue said dinner would be ready in a few minutes."

Henry drained the water, then nodded, wiping his mouth on his sleeve. "Want to finish this one before we eat?"

"Might as well. How many more chops you think he'll take?"

"Hopefully only one more, but the doing will tell."

After too many swings to count, Henry and the boy had the stump cut off. "What say we sit a spell and eat some beans and fried rabbit? You game?"

"Yes, sir."

There it was again. Maybe shooting the bear had changed Levi's attitude somehow. Henry would have to think on it some. Whatever the reason, he appreciated it. Like his mama always said, it never hurt to show some respect.

After too short a dinner break, it took Henry and the boy almost twice as long to get the next chunk of the oak cut and split. Henry wiped his brow, then studied the west sky. Not much daylight left. "I think we're ready, but best we wait until morning and get a fresh start on it. What do you think?"

Levi, who looked worse than Henry felt, stood a bit taller, then nodded. "I'm with you. Time we got the mules hitched and everything in place, it'd be nigh onto dark-thirty."

Henry swung the ax one-handed into the end of the log, then released it. "Or later." He smiled. "I'm plum tuckered."

That night while he waited for sleep to find him, Henry contemplated the boy's change in manner and the lack of protest from Sue when he'd informed her that they were knocking off early. The look in her eyes belied the words that came out of her mouth. He figured she'd swallowed a scalding protest. Apparently, though, he looked even worse than the boy.

He resolved to be nicer to Levi, treat him more like a man than a boy. That thought gave way to the first time he'd seen the kid—only knee high to a grasshopper—with his aunt at the trading post four years back. His favorite image of Sue came next: her standing on the porch watching a storm blow in. A powerful breeze caught her hair and sent it flowing out behind her, but she leaned a bit into the wind. How many times had he fallen asleep studying on that remembrance?

The weather didn't seem to faze her; there'd been no fear in those beautiful eyes.

That vision of her standing there had frozen in his mind. Nothing he'd heard or seen of her since had changed his first impression of what a beautiful, fine, strong-willed lady she was.

CHAPTER

TEN

After getting dinner ready, Sue had used her time to clean up a little, and had decided to change into her skirt. With all the pondering her being alone allowed, the thought that Henry had been divinely handpicked to accompany her tickled its way through her considerations. Well, she had most definitely been wrong about him being soft and lazy. He worked hard, and no one could say he wasn't polite. She couldn't have been more mistaken about the man if she'd tried.

That he'd agreed to come after she insulted him with her honest-work comment proved the provision to be divinely influenced. She had no doubt now that she needed his help, but it would certainly be easier if he could act like less of a king. And she wished there was some way she could lead him to accept the Lord. Surely, that was a part of God's plan.

As soon as Becky fell asleep, Sue pulled her own pallet out a bit from under the wagon to look at the stars. They always reminded her of what a big God she served. A million brilliant, twinkling lights studded the dark sky and took her breath away; they did every time.

They always took her back to the first night she and Andy

had slept out under the stars as man and wife, made her feel close to him. More love than sense had driven them into the adventure of starting their life together in the new territory.

If only her father had given his blessing when Andrew asked and not made her choose between them. Why couldn't he understand she didn't have time to wait? Maybe then her husband would still be alive, and Becky would have known what it was like to have a daddy. Sue deserved whatever God meted out for her rebellion, even losing her husband after only a year. But her innocent little girl had done nothing to warrant her loss. Sue regretted most that, because of her own poor choices, her daughter had suffered.

Sue missed her daddy. She often wondered what he was doing and whether or not she'd ever see him again. It was a desire of her heart, and the Good Book said God would give you the desires of your heart, so she hoped she would. First thing, she'd ask her father's forgiveness. Had he ever gotten her letters? She hoped no response didn't mean that he hated her or that he had died.

Sue sighed at the high price she'd paid for disobeying and not honoring her father. A long time ago, she'd promised God that, if He would forgive her, she'd never marry again without her daddy's blessing. In the nearly ten years since Andy's death, plenty of suitors had called, but when they talked marriage, her vow always dampened their affections.

Over and over, men tried to convince her that it was not so much the asking but the traveling all the way to Tennessee. Oh well, her vow had proved to be a right good measure of their true intentions and how deep their love ran. She might never be blessed with another love, but if it happened, the man's commitment would certainly be tested.

"Penny for your thoughts."

She scooted around and sat up, then smiled at Henry. "Oh, just reminiscing a little, I guess. The stars do that to me."

"Mind some company?"

"Not at all. Levi bedded down?"

He chuckled. "Yes, ma'am. I think that ax wore him plum out." Henry had a nice laugh. The first time, she'd heard it on the heels of her honest-day's-work insult. He'd taken it with such grace even if it had embarrassed her at the time.

She tried to think but couldn't remember another time since that he had laughed. "Yes, he looked pretty tuckered."

Wait. At the Aikins' place with William and again with that Lizbeth.

Henry took a seat against the wagon wheel a respectable space away, but not so far that she couldn't make out his features in the pale moonlight. "Bad break, that water moccasin."

She nodded. "Indeed. We would have been halfway to Pleasant Mound instead of stuck here."

"Yes, ma'am. And it sure looked to me like you were right on track to cross with no problems."

"Well, if we can get out pretty quick in the morning, won't be too much time lost."

"Yes, ma'am." He looked up and pointed. "A shooting star."

She followed his finger in time to catch the star's dying trail. "Wow. I haven't seen a shooting star since we came west." She studied the heavens and looked back ten years. "Me and Andy were so young and so in love and on such a grand adventure. Slept out under the stars all the way."

HENRY STUDIED THE WIDOW; maybe now was a good time. "I never had the pleasure to meet your husband or his brother, but

I've heard tell . . ." He let his words drift off; maybe she'd take the bait and talk about her lost love.

She closed her eyes. He hoped he hadn't lost his chance to hear about Andy. "We had such plans for our future, and the Baylor brothers were two of the hardest working men I'd ever known."

"That's what everyone said."

"They should have quit that day when it started to rain, but they had promised to deliver the load the next afternoon . . ." She shivered and hugged herself, like instead of just remembering, she had traveled back in time. She fell silent.

Could he keep her talking without being blatant? "Ma'am?"

"It was the most horrible day of my life; still haunts my dreams. I was expecting, of course, though I didn't know it at the time." She took in a deep breath. "We had to cross Langford's Creek. Levi and I made it no problem in that very wagon over there, but we had all four mules. You knew his mother died from complications shortly after his birth, didn't you?"

Henry nodded. "I'd heard that."

"Anyway, the drizzle was heavy, and it was getting dark fast. Andy walked by the yoke, urging the oxen to the top of the hill. Jacob brought up the rear, pushing. A bolt of lightning struck too close, blinded me a heartbeat, but in its afterglow, I saw their team rear. The oxen bellowed something awful."

She shuddered. "The off ox started slipping and fell. His struggling pulled him down the bank. The wagon teetered on two wheels a second, but the back axle broke under the timber's weight. Tie ropes snapped, and the logs rolled off. First ones knocked Jacob down. The rest kept hitting him and rolling over and over where he'd landed."

Henry started to stop her, but then figured it best to let her get the telling out.

"The wagon tumbled down the bank side over side until it finally settled at the bottom. One wheel was spinning in the air. Funny what stands out, the details you remember." She looked up at the stars again. "Andy disappeared in the melee. Logs lay strewn all over the place; horizontal, vertical, sticking into the air like ghoulish omens. I ran from log to log across the side of the incline. Then I spotted Jacob covered in mud head to boot, as lifeless as the logs."

Her pain cut his heart. He wanted to see to it that nothing so horrible ever happened to her again.

"I didn't want to look. I didn't want to see his face, but when I made myself, his open eyes stared into the rain. I knew he was gone. I screamed for Andy but couldn't find him. Then at last I heard him calling my name. I was so relieved. His voice was faint, but I heard it and found him. That black mud caked my shoes so heavy I could hardly walk, but I found him. He was trapped under the wagon, its sideboard across on his belly. He was so covered in blood, I thought he'd lost his eye.

"One of the oxen kept screaming—the most horrible sound I've ever heard to this day. Andrew wanted me to see to Jacob." She shook her head. "I told him he was gone. Then he sent me to get the gun and put the ox out of its misery. He had me reload quick as I could and shoot into the air, hoping someone might be close enough to hear and come help."

Henry wanted to hug her, make all her pain and bad memories go away, but that would be the wrong thing to do.

"I'd never killed anything. Never saw a dead man either. Mr. Foglesong heard the shots and came. Took us most the night to get Andy out and home. He passed three days later. He never even knew I was pregnant."

She looked skyward. Henry watched with her for a bit, then

turned his attention to the widow. She was about the most handsome lady he'd ever laid eyes on; no wonder nearly every eligible bachelor or widower in the Red River Valley had come calling. "Most women would have given up, Sue."

"Maybe, but I just couldn't quit, though there were plenty of times I thought about going home to Daddy. Andy and Jacob had tied up everything they owned in the land and their steam-powered sawmill. They were so proud of that. I couldn't simply walk away and give it all up. I'd be robbing the children of their inheritance. Besides, the hardships drove me closer to the Lord. I prayed a lot. He got me through."

Henry laughed. Why did women always want to give a heavenly father credit for what they had done? "My mother always said the Lord did this or God did that when it was her all along. She did it. She was alone, and she did it by herself—just like you, Sue—by her own strength of character and will."

"So." She paused as though choosing her words carefully. "You aren't a believer."

"Well, yes and no. I do believe there's a God up there somewhere, but no, I don't have much use for organized religion with all its thou-shalt-nots. I've never been one to turn the other cheek."

"Just believing there is a God isn't enough. The devil believes that, too. I know all the rules do make it seem hard sometimes, but thing is, no one keeps 'em all. No one can."

SHE LOVED IT THAT HENRY called her by her nickname all the time now; he must consider himself a friend. Had the Lord opened his heart? At least the man wasn't cutting her off or being rude. "The fourth commandment says to obey your parents, and I didn't. Still, He forgave me. That's one reason why I promised Him that I'd never marry again without my father's blessing."

Henry's eyebrows lifted a bit, and he smiled. "Yes, ma'am. Heard about that. Never knew the whys of the promise though. So Andy asked, your father said no, and you did anyway?"

"Yes, he did ask for Daddy's blessing, but my father the judge thought we were too young to know what love was. He said no, that we should give it a couple of years, but there wasn't time to wait. Andrew was leaving to go in partners with his brother." She didn't want to mention Andrew's poor financial position or that her daddy held it against him that he had no trade. The scenario fit Henry too well. "So, I just ran away, left home, and married in rebellion. Haven't seen or spoken with Daddy since. I'm not even sure if he knows he has a granddaughter."

"You never sent word?"

"I posted three letters with folks going east, but never got a response. Daddy may not have got them, but even if he did, he didn't write back; probably hates me and decided long ago I was dead to him whether I breathed or not. I always figured if he received them, he'd insist that I come straight back to Memphis. I never wanted to leave Texas."

Henry laughed. "So you're an independent, are you?"

She loved it that he laughed all the time now. Had she had a part in that? She hoped so. "Aren't you? Don't you want to see Texas a republic? Free of Mexican rule?"

For the next few minutes the man expounded on how the territory was part of Mexico and should stay that way. He finally stopped talking. Though she didn't care much for what he was saying, she could have listened to his voice all night.

He stood. "We best get some shut-eye. Tomorrow promises to be a tough one."

With her pallet back under the wagon, she considered how the question of the territory's future had turned the conversation from religion to politics, and his views were as opposite in one area as in the other. Disappointed that she'd let the opportunity to witness to him slip away so easily, she promised herself she'd bring the topic up again before the journey was over, maybe on the way home.

But one way or another, she fully intended to be God's vessel to bring this man—although clearly a morally good man—to salvation. If she knew anything, she knew that being good wouldn't get anyone to Heaven. And without a doubt, his mother wanted to see him again on those golden streets someday. Sue would gladly be the teapot the Lord used to pour out some truth on the man.

She smiled at herself and at the Lord. He had always amused her with His awesome sense of humor. She remembered laughing aloud at more than one inappropriate time because He'd gotten her tickled.

A cool breeze stirred the leaves and a nightingale sang its praise.

Pondering what she'd come to know about Patrick Henry Buckmeyer on the trace—had it only been three days?—she recalled how weary he looked after the day of chopping down the bois d'arc and the oak. And that following the extra work to hitch the four mules to the wagon she'd got stuck. Yet he hadn't complained once, or said I told you so either.

Her precious little girl was smitten with him, but probably only because she'd never had a father. Sue patted herself on the back for swallowing her pride and not insisting that he keep working when he'd called it an early day with so much daylight left. She'd let him burn it without saying a thing. And she didn't even get angry!

What a day it had been.

Conflicted at every turn, she teetered between laughing and crying. Even though she didn't understand why she'd had to get the wagon stuck, she had faith that everything would be all right. No doubt about that. God had proved Himself trustworthy to her time and again since she'd been living alone on the Sulphur Fork Prairie with two children.

Mama—God rest her soul—had taught her never to give up. She'd be proud. Her sweet prayers for others—even on her deathbed—had always awed Sue. How could she not love God after living with a mother like Patricia Abbott for twelve years? Sue still missed her.

"Father, You have blessed me so," Sue whispered toward the sky. "Your faithfulness, Your mercy, Your everlasting, never-ending, loving-kindness. They are all so amazing."

Even if she'd made a bad choice, she had repented.

Still, what if God had intended all along that she miss the Jefferson buyers? What would she do then? And she'd blown her chance to get Henry saved. She missed Andy and she missed her daddy and her wagon was stuck in the creek. A tear rolled down Sue's cheek as a mountain of self-pity smothered her.

How could she be so happy and full of faith and so overwhelmed and sad at the same time? Thinking back to the last time Eve's curse had visited, she chalked up the mood swings to it coming again soon. Great. That was all she needed out here on the trace. She gave in to the depression and cried softly.

CHAPTER

ELEVEN

HENRY HEARD THE LADY CRYING in the night but decided not to go to her. He had no idea why she would be sad but figured she might be praying. Some women seemed to cry every time they prayed; his mother often had. He didn't understand that at all. How would their earthly fathers feel if they cried every time they talked to them?

Too soon the next morning, he woke. Every muscle ached and begged to stay horizontal longer, but a hard day lay ahead and wouldn't wait. He eased up, stretched a bit, and then silently went to work on a fire and getting the coffee on. With those chores seen to, he decided to handle the necessaries.

On his return, he carried a clutch of duck eggs he'd spotted in the pale moonlight right as he finished his business. He hoped Sue would be pleasantly surprised. More and more, it seemed about all he could think of was pleasing her. He wanted to see more of that smile of hers, a lot more.

"Good morning."

He turned his head, and there it was. He didn't know what had made her so happy so early, but he was thankful. "Morning to you. Ready for some coffee? It's almost done."

"Yes, sir." She stood and stretched.

He should look away but couldn't help enjoying her fine figure in the flickering firelight. He cleared his throat. "Got a surprise for you."

She pulled her shawl around her shoulders, hugged herself against the cool morning, and came toward him smiling. "Oh, you do?" Amusement filled her voice. "I can't imagine what that might be out here in this swamp."

"Found a clutch of duck eggs." He pointed to his hat. "Levi and the little miss like eggs?"

She smiled again.

How could he live without seeing that every day?

"Yes, they sure do; we all do! What a wonderful gift from the Lord." She went over and peered into the hat. "How many is in there?"

"Nine. Want to splurge or save some?"

"Depends. How much do you like cake?"

"Ummm. I love cake." He grinned. "You got everything you need?"

"Well, now, there is one contingency."

He loved that she had a good vocabulary. Having grown up with a lady of letters, he'd been put off over the years by pretty girls with a limited selection of words. "And that would be?"

"How much honey you're willing to part with. I have everything else."

He laughed. If only she knew the real reason he'd brought the honey jars. "I'm willing to provide a healthy sopping's worth if the cake's a good one."

Her lips spread a bit, but she made them straighten. She did a thing with her eyes that he liked, moved them up and down quickly. He got the impression she flirted a bit. "Don't cotton to braggin' on myself, but I guarantee you that you haven't eaten cake, Mister Buckmeyer, until you've tasted mine."

He nodded. What he wanted to do was scoop her up and hug her until the sunrise came together with the sunset and all the time in between, but that wouldn't do. He had to play the game according to the rules, be polite and a gentleman at all times. "Want me to fix the biscuits?"

"No, sir, I'll make 'em. I like mine better than yours, if you don't mind me saying."

"Why would I? I like yours better than mine, too. So, won't bother me a bit. As a matter of fact, if I never had to fix another meal for the rest of my life, that'd be fine with me."

"Truly? I would have guessed otherwise."

"No. Between Mother and the army, I got real spoiled to having my meals prepared."

"I see." She studied the fire's embers. "So were you really with Jackson at New Orleans? I've heard stories—"

"Yes, ma'am, sure was."

She went to the wagon and retrieved the Dutch oven, frying pan, mixing bowl, and her fixings, talking as she went. "But I never believed them totally. How could it be true? Battle of New Orleans was in 1814, right? So, that's what? Eighteen years ago? You're not that old."

He squatted next to the fire, enjoying its warmth. "I was always big for my age, and lying came real easy back then. By the time the Colonel found out I was only sixteen, I'd proved my worth. We were always outnumbered, and since there really wasn't anywhere to send me, he made me his personal orderly. But I saw about as much action as anyone else."

She looked up. "So you're . . . thirty-four?"

"Yes, ma'am, and too much a gentleman to ask your age." He stood. "Looks like we need a bit more firewood."

"Still in my twenties, but barely." She smiled—again! "If you could watch the fire a minute more, I'd like to take a little walk. Be back directly for that cup of coffee."

"Yes, ma'am, of course. I can gather more wood later." He watched her bending over and tying her shoes. Her feet seemed so small and dainty. Then he gazed after her as she walked away into the darkness, taking pleasure from her every step. He loved her smooth pace and the soft swing of her skirt. He liked that way better than those britches she'd been wearing.

No, sir, he wouldn't mind making Susannah Baylor his own one bit, and gaining his little miss in the deal would be ace-high. All he had to do was convince Sue to forget that vow of hers.

SUE TIPTOED OFF, making sure she was well out of sight without going any farther into the woods than absolutely necessary. Gathering her skirt up, she searched the shadows for that bear and kept her ears keen for any sound of footfalls on the forest floor. Several pieces of good-size deadfall that she could handle lay near and, once finished with her morning routine, she picked them up.

She'd surprise Henry.

False dawn's first light grayed the night sky as she made her way back to the camp. Becky would be so surprised, eggs and a cake! This day had to be better than yesterday, and Sue gleefully anticipated getting the wagon freed and back on the trace.

Even with the whole of yesterday lost, she and Henry were still at least two days ahead of the train. It shouldn't be any problem beating them to Pleasant Mound. The moon still shone bright, and by the time she reached the fire, she was humming a tune. The words came to her, so she sang softly as she prepared biscuits and then got the cake batter ready for the Dutch oven once the biscuits finished baking.

"I know that my redeemer lives. What comfort this sweet sentence gives. He lives, He lives, who once was dead. He lives, my ever-living Head." Those were all the words she could remember, so she went back to humming.

Henry came back into camp. "Ready for that coffee now?" He grabbed a second cup. "You have a beautiful singing voice."

She laughed and shook her head. "No, not me. Now my husband? He could belt out an amazing tenor. Thank goodness Becky took after him. And yes, I would love a cup. Got so busy mixing and making, I didn't pour myself one. Thank you."

Henry chuckled. "Yes, your daughter and I discussed music and singing. She gave me no peace until I sang so that she could be the judge of my abilities—or inabilities, as is the case." He laughed a little harder and handed the filled cup to her.

She accepted it and took a cautious sip. His story tickled her even more because she knew her daughter so well. "My little angel can be powerful persistent."

He gave her a look as though he knew that. "Like I said, she made me sing, but then begged me to stop."

"She didn't!"

"Oh, yes."

Sue could not keep her composure a minute longer and burst out laughing. She held her coffee out to keep from spilling it and bent at the waist, holding her side with her other hand. She let it go, couldn't help herself. "Oh, no!" She gasped for air. "Please tell me you're making this up."

He joined in laughing with her. "No, ma'am. Not one word of it. She was beating me on the chest begging me to stop." His body heaved, and his shoulders shook. "Said I should stick to talking." He spoke between spasms and looked like he'd almost bust a gut.

"What's so funny?" Becky sat up on her pallet under the wagon.

Sue glanced at Henry, who was looking at her daughter, obviously trying to recover his breath. She spoke to give him more time. "Oh, I'm just so happy and excited about this day. It's sure to be a good one."

The little girl crawled out, ran to her, then hugged her neck. "I love it when you laugh, Mama." She looked at Henry. "She doesn't hardly ever laugh, you know. I mean she never thinks anything is funny."

"Rebecca Ruth! That is not the truth."

The little one made an incredulous face. "Is so." She glanced at Henry, nodding her head as fast as she could. "It's true, I swear. What'd you do to make her laugh so hard?"

He chuckled. "Oh, I suppose I hit her funny bone, and she hit mine back."

"Well." Becky put her hand on her hip. "I think this really is going to be a great day, like Mama said."

"Um-hmm." Sue picked up the makeshift hat-basket. "And see what we're having for breakfast? Mister Henry found them."

Her baby girl peeked inside, then ran and hugged his waist. "Oh, I love eggs. I've missed them since we've been on the trail." She grinned up at him. "Where'd you get 'em?"

He stroked her hair. "Saw them in the moonlight. They were laying there shining almost as bright as a lamp, so they're my surprise for today. And I didn't even know how much you like 'em."

"Yes, sir." The need must have hit her. "Well, I've got to go. Beck'll be back in a bit." She ran off toward the woods giggling at her alliteration.

Sue watched her, then turned to Henry and held up the coffeepot. "That was a close one."

He tossed his coffee's cooled remains and extended his empty tin cup. "Sure wouldn't want her to think I'd betrayed our private talk. She's a mighty fine young lady."

"Yes, sir, I agree. I'm so proud of her." Sue filled his cup, then poured herself another one, too. About that time, Levi roused. "Morning, sleepyhead, want some coffee?"

"No, ma'am. Not unless Mister Henry's willing to let go of some of his honey. I don't know how y'all drink it black and bitter. I can stand it without milk, but not without something sweet."

"Why, you Baylors would have both my honey jars empty by the time we get to Jefferson if I didn't keep a tight hold on 'em." Levi's expression was priceless, but then Henry busted out laughing again. "Of course, you can have some, son. From what the ladies both say, it is going to be a great day."

Levi grinned. "You had me going there for a minute." He nodded.

Breakfast was a hit. The fellows and Becky had two eggs each, but Sue had only one to save two for her cake. Henry even suggested a spoon of honey for the biscuits since it was already out. Levi seemed as giddy as Becky over the announcement of cake for dessert after supper.

"I could sit here all day if we were having a picnic, but there's work waiting, and we're burning daylight." Smiling at her, he stood.

Levi immediately rose as well. "What are we doing first?"

"Well, you men go on with whatever you need to do. As for me, I have a cake to bake." Sue caught Henry's eye. "Unless there's something I can help with."

"Baking that cake will do fine." He tipped his hat and headed off with Levi at his side.

Sue's heart was light and her spirits higher than they'd been since she left for the trading post in Sulphur Fork Monday morning. All was well in her world. Getting along in such a fine manner with Henry brightened her mood—much better than being at odds—and she'd thoroughly enjoyed the belly laugh they had shared. He was a good man and about to get her cotton back on the trace.

She could hardly wait.

IN NO TIME, Henry had everything in place; the stump sat right behind the stuck wheel, and he wedged the bois d'arc pole in under the wagon's frame and on top of the oak. It stuck out a good ten feet. The boy held an assortment of wedges at the ready.

Henry jumped and threw all his weight onto it, then tried to bounce the pole down.

"That raised it maybe an inch, but not enough."

Henry stepped back. Sue and Rebecca watched from the shore. "I need your help, ladies."

"What can we do?"

"Wade out here. I need more weight."

"Of course, but Levi weighs more than both of us together. How about I take his place, he helps you, and Becky stays here?"

Henry would rather not have Sue anywhere near the wheel or even in the water, but getting unstuck was vital. "We can try that." He pointed at Blue Dog. "You stay with Rebecca."

After he'd tried every combination, Sue insisted he hitch the four healthy mules and attempt getting the wagon out using his bois d'arc pole to push rather than as a fulcrum. Nothing worked.

Finally, with more than enough of failure and tired of being soaked to the bone, he headed toward the shore. "Let's think about this."

Sue waded after him. "But what's there to think about? We have got to get this wagon out of the creek. Not take breaks. I didn't say anything at all yesterday when you wanted to quit early, but now . . ." She looked at the sun. "Why, it's past noon already!"

He spun around. No woman had ever so pushed his patience. Harsh words danced on his tongue, but the pain in her eyes caused a pause. He swallowed and deliberately softened his tone. "I'm open to any ideas you may have."

"Well, Mister Buckmeyer, I don't know. Your fulcrum sure didn't work." She stepped out onto the bank and shivered. "We've already lost a full day yesterday. I guess for nothing since your bois d'arc plan went bust."

For the longest time, no one said a word; even the normally chatty Rebecca fell silent. His heart hurt for the lady, but what else could he do except tell her it would get done when it got done? "Sue, we will get the wagon out, but it's going to take more time than I thought." He headed back into the water. "Come on, Levi."

Once the beasts were hobbled and grazing again, he found Sue busy tossing leaves on the signal fire. "There is another option."

She looked up. "What's that?"

"I can light out for Cuthand; buy that yoke of oxen. I'd be back late tomorrow."

She shook her head. "I hate the beasts."

Of course she did, blamed them for her husband's accident. She turned away and looked skyward, then directly turned back around and leaned in close. "And besides, I'd rather lose the cotton than spend twenty-four hours here without you."

All right, maybe things were looking up after all. He liked hearing that his presence meant so much to her way better than her sounding as if she wanted to cut his throat.

"I mean—after the bear and the smoke signal to the Indians—I, uh—"

"I didn't like the idea much myself."

CHAPTER

TWELVE

THE UNANIMOUS DECISION to get serious about calling for help gave Sue new purpose. She assigned everyone something to do. Henry and Levi went into the forest time and again dragging out deadwood. Becky gathered twigs and kindling, having to go farther and farther away for it, but Sue didn't worry. The incident with the bear had made a serious impression on her daughter, and she pretty much stayed in sight.

Besides, the dog watched over her. Oh, how very thankful she was that Henry had insisted on bringing him. Most definitely, she understood why Blue was the best dog he'd ever had and agreed with his high opinion of the canine.

On one of the trips out of the woods with deadfall, Henry dragged it to the fire and swung it on, then sidled up to her. "Got one more option. Thought about it this morning first thing, but didn't want to bring it up."

"What?" Her voice sounded short, though she didn't want it to. She longed to be patient, but another day was swiftly passing, and her cotton remained stuck in the creek. She made herself smile. "What did you think of first thing?"

"I say we give this signal fire until morning. If no one

shows, we'll hook up the mules and start dumping the bales."

"Into the creek?" She couldn't believe her ears! "Are you crazy?"

"See why I didn't want to mention it? But it may come to that if no help shows."

Sue flounced her skirt and stormed off. This topped it all. Throw her cotton into the creek? What a plan! She might as well have sold the harvest for the two cents Littlejohn had offered. What could Henry possibly be thinking? She spun around and pointed her finger at him. "Absolutely not. We'll all go back to Cuthand if that's what it takes."

"How are we going to do that?"

"We'll take the other wagon back."

"The one in the water is blocking the only safe crossing."

She huffed and puffed and steamed inside. "Then we'll ride the mules. Becky can ride double with me."

"And you'd leave your cotton, and your wagon, and all my goods? Do you honestly think it would be here when we got back?" He shook his head. "Are your mules broke to ride? What about saddles?"

She held her chin, tapping two fingers across her lips. Mister Croaker had a negative answer for every idea she offered. Where were all his ideas? Oh, yes, throw her cotton into the creek! "There's just got to be another way! We all worked too hard, planting and chopping and pickin'. This harvest is the best I've ever had, and you want me to dump it?"

Levi came out into the clearing. He hefted the log he carried onto its end. "Want this on the fire now?"

"By all means, throw it on!" She waved her arm, pointing to the log, which stood almost twice as tall as the boy. "Might as well call every savage in the territory!"

Her nephew stood there with his mouth gaping, then looked at Henry.

"What are you looking at him for? Throw it on! Call the Indians and anyone else who might see it before my employee dumps my cotton into the creek!"

Looking to Henry again, Levi shrugged as though apologizing for her. She wanted to slap him. How dare the little ingrate? He end-over-ended the log onto the fire.

It sent embers flying, and she turned away. "What about loading enough cotton onto a raft to keep it dry and lighten the load?"

Henry glanced at her nephew, then to her. "We can try. Liable to take a week."

"A week? Why in the world do you think it will take a week?"

"Chopping down enough trees, lashing them together."

"You and Levi can chop, Becky and I can lash. That wouldn't take too long."

"Building the raft and unloading those five-hundred-pound bales will take three or four days. Then it'd take that again to get the wagon reloaded."

Becky strolled up carrying a pile of leaves. "What will?" She threw her load on the fire.

Levi faced his cousin. "The wagon will."

"Will what?"

"Come out easy if it's empty."

"Oh well, how are we going to get the cotton off?"

"Never mind!" Levi looked to Sue. "What's with all her questions?"

She glanced skyward, blew out a heavy sigh, then faced him. "Please don't. I'm in no mood for bickering."

"But she's driving me crazy questioning everything!" He looked to Henry. "What do you think, sir?"

Sir? Sir! Oh, what a little manipulator. Conspiring with the hired help right there in front of her. She could hardly believe it.

"Oh, no you don't. You're not dragging me in."

Well, what did she know? He'd actually stayed out of her business for once. Good. She glanced at the boy. Never did she intend to hurt him. His expression held something more, like Henry had sent him a hidden message and Levi had seen the light. She hated Henry Buckmeyer going and making secret deals with her children.

"Well, then, we've got a raft to build. Since it is well past dinnertime, I say we take a break, eat, then have some cake."

He sighed. "Then we'll get to cutting down this forest."

Becky jumped up and down, clapping her hands. "Take a break and eat some cake! Take a break and eat some cake!"

Levi shook his head and swiped at his little sister-cousin. "Come on, Bitty Beck, let's go wash up."

DINNER CAME AND WENT, but Henry would remember that piece of cake forever. She was right. Somehow here in the Sulphur River bottoms, he'd eaten the best cake ever. Shame she was so stubborn. Susannah Baylor was the hardest-headed lady he'd ever known.

In an odd way, though, he kind of liked that about her. He never could stand a wishy-washy woman. If Andrew Jackson was a female, he'd be Susannah Baylor. Smiling, Henry thought about it and decided it might be prudent not to mention that comparison to her. Could get his face slapped. Though to him it was a high compliment, she probably wouldn't relish being compared to Old Hickory.

"I'm thinking cedar is the lightest and likely has the best buoyancy. Plus it's a bit easier to cut and abundant." He looked over at the boy. "If you concur, and if I remember right, there's a nice stand pretty far in. What say we get to work?"

"Cedar's fine by me, and I'm ready when you are. I'll get the ax." He went off to the wagon.

Henry appreciated the boy's willingness to tackle the job. "Grab my canteen."

"And is there anything you'd like Becky and me to do while you're gone besides see to supper?"

"No, ma'am. Except keep the fire going."

She put her hands on her hips as though he'd insulted her. "Anything else?"

"No, that's all."

He headed off into the woods with the boy in tow. A comfortable silence settled between him and Levi, broken only by the call of a hawk that pierced the air. The woods, though not too overgrown, provided enough shade that it seemed even cool. As Henry had figured, the first tree came down fast and easy. The second one took a little longer. By the fourth cedar, neither he nor the boy made the chips fly powerful fast or far.

"Here." He tossed the canteen to Levi. "Let me take a turn."

Levi passed the ax, then guzzled water. He caught his breath, then took another long drink. "You really think this raft idea is going to work?"

"Maybe, but after your aunt pitched such a fit, I wasn't about to press the issue." He spit on the ax blade. "Don't know how many women you've been around, but Susannah Baylor is about the most hardheaded woman I've ever run across."

Levi laughed. "Bitty Beck may be worse."

Henry's hands didn't want to swing the ax anymore, but he swung it again. For sure, his back and arms and shoulders had had enough, but he willed them to swing that ax, again and again. Halfway through the tree, the boy stepped up and traded the canteen back for the ax.

On his first swing, he bent into it, and the ax blade totally missed the tree. The handle hit it instead. Its crack reverberated. The head went flying.

"Stupid ax!" He went after it and picked it up.

"Broke?"

"Yes, sir. I'm sorry." He hung his head.

"You do it on purpose?"

"No, sir."

"Then don't worry about it."

The boy stood a bit taller. "Yes, sir."

SUE AND BECKY HAD STAYED BUSY dampening loads of leaves and putting them on the fire all afternoon. If anyone was anywhere in the vicinity, she couldn't imagine them not seeing the billowing smoke. She loved working with her daughter better than about anything. Becky always had a thousand questions, so the talking never really died between them.

But the girl took after her daddy in that she could go to sleep in a breath. Late afternoon, she'd gone under the wagon and lain down on the furs. A minute later, she was sound asleep. Sue thought seriously about joining her, but no way did she want Henry to come back and find her napping. Sometimes

Andy'd slept for only fifteen minutes, but he always said a nap refreshed him to finish whatever the day held.

If she dozed off, though, she'd probably sleep until someone woke her.

Besides, Blue Dog lay right beside Becky with his head resting on her hip. Sue sure had come to love that hound. She wondered how old he was, and if Henry might ever think of selling him. She'd have to wait for the right time and ask. The thought of parting her daughter from him at the end of the journey hurt Sue's heart.

It wouldn't matter what he asked, whatever the price, she'd pay it. Henry might not be willing to sell him, though. Best dog he ever had, he'd said. She sighed. She'd just have to talk him into it. After all, he seemed to really care for Becky. Except he never called her that; he called her Rebecca or little miss. Sue had loved the name when she gave birth, Rebecca after Andy's mother and Ruth after her own. Her daughter carried both her grandmothers' middle names.

Maybe it was a good sign.

Just then, Blue Dog lifted his head off Becky and stared past the wagon. Sue followed his gaze. A mean-looking Indian warrior stood not fifty yards away. The sides of his head were shaved, leaving a streak of black hair from his forehead back. His bare chest glistened in the sun, which also glinted off large silver earrings.

He wore only a breechcloth and moccasins, and his nakedness embarrassed her, but she couldn't look away. Her heart beat double time, and her pulse throbbed against her temples.

Blue Dog growled low in his throat, then stood and positioned himself between the savage and his little girl.

Oh, great. Where was Henry?

CHAPTER

THIRTEEN

HENRY SPOTTED THE CADDO standing on the north side of the clearing, staring at Sue and Rebecca, who sat near the fire. Blue Dog had claimed a point between the visitor and the girl. That dog would die before he let the stranger get to her. His hound had taken to Rebecca almost as much as he had, maybe even more if that was possible.

Shame the boy hadn't broke the ax four trees ago.

Henry raised his hand palm forward and walked toward the man. The Indian mimicked the sign and came toward him, closing the distance and leaving the lady to the side of the path. Levi followed a little behind and to his left, carrying his long gun. Henry gestured eating by bringing his fingers pinched together to his mouth. "Hungry?" He pointed at the guest and repeated. "You hungry?"

The man shook his head and extended his clay pipe. "Tobacco?"

Henry nodded and headed toward the wagon, proud he had traded for the tobacco and had it available now. He retrieved a small leather pouch from his kit, then turned, but Sue blocked his way.

"It's all right. He's Caddo. Friendly."

Her voice was shaking. "I'm so glad you got back when you did. I know we called him with the fire and all, but I hated him coming with you gone."

"You stay with Rebecca. I'll deal with him."

She hurried back to her daughter, and he strolled toward the Indian, handing the pouch to him as soon as he got there.

The Caddo untied the leather laces and held it to his nose. The sweet aroma of Virginia mild wafted on the air. The visitor smiled and nodded. "Good tobacco." He pinched enough to fill his bowl, and then picked up a little stick off the ground and made his way to the fire. Blue Dog followed him. Sue moved backward, scooting and clutching Becky to her.

"Is he a savage, Mama? He doesn't act so mean." She turned to the Indian. "Are you? Are you a savage?"

"Becky! He probably doesn't even understand what you're saying, but still, that was rude! You shouldn't ask a question like that."

The Caddo smiled and nodded at her daughter. He bent, held an end of his stick in the fire until it caught, then lit his pipe and headed back over to Henry.

"He didn't mind, Mama. Even if he did understand, he knows I'm just a little girl."

Walking back, he grinned like a kid with a new pup. He sat cross-legged on the ground, so Henry squatted in like fashion in front of him. The guest offered his lit pipe. Henry took it and pulled hard on the stem, puffing the tobacco. The bowl glowed. He inhaled, then let the smoke curl from his lips and nose. He wanted to cough, needed to, but, by his will, kept his peace and smiled at the man.

"Tobacco good."

SUE'S RACING HEART had resumed a more regular rhythm. From startled to curious to amazed, she studied the not-so-savage visitor. It amused her that Henry played his game so well. He shared the pipe, then offered food. She heaped two plates of supper for them at his request. The men ate and laughed and talked and signed until their plates were empty. Then Henry insisted that their visitor have a piece of her cake.

He hollered and instructed her to put a heaping spoon of honey on both pieces as well. Sometimes he could be so exasperating. His being over there having such a good time with his new friend and totally ignoring her and the children just irritated her to no end. Then he had the gall to boss her around as though she worked for him! She fed her children and fixed her own plate, wishing she cared less about his disregard.

She'd stop this nonsense if her wagon wasn't stuck. That savage could help. Or could he? Was he only here to smoke up Henry's tobacco and eat all her cake? When would he ever make the deal to get her wagon unstuck? He stood and walked toward her.

She held up her hand. "If he wants more cake, he can forget it!"

Henry grinned, which only served to upset her more because she knew he was laughing at her. "No, we just got around to how much he'd charge to help us."

"Oh, really? Finally?" She gazed past him to the Indian enjoying the last crumbs of his cake. Or should she say her cake? "Please do tell. What does he want?"

"The long gun that Levi's been holding on him."

Well, that was never going to happen. There was no way she could ever replace that gun.

"A bag of powder and some shot for it." He looked at her straight-on. "A pound of my tobacco."

Well, that wasn't so bad; she had no use for the smelly smoke.

"And three of your mules, but not the snake-bit one."

"Well! Is that all? What a generous soul. Looks like your signal fire worked about as good as your fulcrum!" She crossed her arms over her chest. "That crazy Caddo! What did you say?"

"Nothing yet, wanted to speak with you first." He moved closer, almost touching her, like he didn't want the Indian to hear or something. "It's your wagon, and you'll be the one paying him."

At least he had that right. "What do you consider fair? What are you thinking of telling him? We certainly cannot give him three mules. If we did, we might as well dump the cotton."

"How about we offer the snake-bit mule?"

She turned and looked at the grazing animals. Mabel still appeared to be feeling under the weather. Sue loved her mules. They weren't just working stock to her. "But I've had her over ten years. She's like a family member; they all are."

"Well then, how much of my tobacco would you like me to offer him?"

She hated that she was going to have to give up any of her profit, but they'd tried everything else. "What's tobacco going for these days?"

"Two years ago, the price was only five dollars a hogshead. But it's been steadily rising. I was hoping to get between eight and ten."

"A hogshead? What kind of measurement is that? How much in pounds?"

"Well, it's a wooden barrel that holds about a thousand pounds."

"Do you think he'd help for twenty pounds?"

"I can ask. Anything else you want to offer?"

She sighed. "I don't know. Can't think of anything." He turned to go, but she grabbed his arm and stopped him. He met her eyes. "Make the best deal you can for me."

She had to trust him, but it surprised her how easy it seemed, especially after knowing him such a short time. What had it been? Only five days! It seemed that she'd been on the way to Jefferson for a month or more. Anyway, she'd known of him for years, but had carried that bad, terribly wrong opinion from listening to those gossips.

And even though he wasn't a Christian, trusting him was comfortable. He was a moral and honorable man.

He returned to his negotiations with the red man. Sue sighed and glanced toward the darkening sky. A little of Your favor for Henry would be appreciated. She watched the Indian as the sun sunk behind the tree line.

The private confab seemed to go on forever. Was he planning on spending the whole night in camp? At last, Henry came back to her. "He says the only way he'll help is for one mule, one rifle, and ten pounds of tobacco. Plus the powder and shot."

"That's out-and-out thievery!" She crossed her arms again and tapped her foot. "But. The only. Option. I see. At this point." She shook her head and huffed out a heavy sigh. "Will he guarantee to get it unstuck?"

"We won't pay him anything until he does. He'll be traveling back to his village to fetch relatives and friends to help him, so getting it out should be a done deal."

She hated to even ask since it was her wagon and all, but she couldn't imagine parting with one of her mules. "How will I ever decide which one?" Her eyes watered full, and she swiped at an escaped tear.

"He can have my mule."

"Oh, could he?" She looked into his eyes. "I'd pay you top dollar for him, of course. You wouldn't mind? I'd be so grateful. I just can't think of giving up one of ours."

He nodded. "No problem. What about the weapon?"

"Well, I can't ask Levi to give his up. That was his daddy's long gun. And mine was Andy's, but . . ." She looked at him. "I guess I could let it go."

"Sue, everything I've got is for sale. I don't mind letting him have mine."

That statement thrilled her in more ways than one. "Excellent! Thank you! So what are Brown Mule and your musket and ten pounds of your tobacco going to cost me?"

"I did turn down seventy dollars for the animal, but I'll sell him to you for sixty. And how about I loan you the rifle, and you can buy me a new one when we get to Jefferson?"

He looked at the sky, so she did, too, following his gaze. The first star shone bright. The depth of the man's integrity impressed her. In a position to easily gouge her, he instead had made her an even better deal than he'd already turned down.

"I'll tell you what. You can just replace the mule, too, and let's forget the tobacco. I'll throw that in."

"Why, thank you, sir. You're a true gentleman."

He smiled a you're-welcome, tipped his hat, then returned to his new friend.

A dreadful heaviness she hadn't even realized was weighing

her down suddenly lifted. She could breathe easy again. It really was going to happen. They would be on the trace tomorrow morning. She wished she had thought to ask Henry to get a commitment on how quick the Caddo would return with his friends, but he was already deep in conversation with the man, making her the best deal he could.

In almost no time, Henry stood and walked back long faced. "He wants one more thing."

"Oh, my word!" She'd already agreed to pay so much. Why couldn't God make him accept what he said he would take? If she agreed to whatever this latest demand was, would he ask again for more? "What else could he possibly want?"

"The rest of your cake."

She laughed with relief at the request.

"He wants to carry it home to his wife and children. He has three little ones."

"Fine, fine then. Did he happen to say how soon he could get back here?"

"In the morning."

"Early?"

Henry shook his head. "He has a way to go, so probably more like midmorning."

"And he's certain he can get us unstuck?"

"He's sure. Evidently, he's done it plenty before."

That night while lying next to her daughter on Henry's plush furs, she considered that at four cents a pound, or twenty dollars a bale, she'd just spent almost four bales! She wholeheartedly regretted not having thought things through sooner. She should have just let Henry dump the cotton, or even thought of it herself the first day. She would have at least saved the two days and most likely been with the train by now, visiting with Shannan and Mrs. Foglesong, and Becky could be playing with Sassy.

Poor Henry, giving up his musket and mule and tobacco, too. He was such a good man, so unselfish. She liked that; most would have told her she needed to pick a mule no matter what. She so appreciated him for considering her sentimentalities. If she only got four cents in Jefferson, after paying him back she'd barely have enough to buy Blue Dog for Becky. That was her one ray of hope.

He did say out of his own mouth that everything he had was for sale, so that meant she could buy the dog. But what if it meant selling some land? Was Blue worth that?

CHAPTER

FOURTEEN

THE INDIAN AND HIS ENTOURAGE showed up later than Sue expected, more midmorning than early, just like Henry had said, whooping and hollering. But her heart still rejoiced that her wagon would soon be freed from its hole. By the end of the day, she'd be on the trace again and on her way to Pleasant Mound. There was still a chance she could catch up with the train and be so much more at ease the rest of the way to Jefferson.

Six Caddo rode in on three horses that all wore collars. The man who'd showed yesterday and one other came afoot. Henry and Levi got the four mules hitched to the wagon. Brown Mule, Henry's rifle, and the tobacco were set off to the side ready for payment once they successfully pulled her wagon out of the creek.

The Indians quickly fastened a rope to each side of the three horses' collars, for a total of six ropes. One Caddo stayed on each of the ponies. Henry and the five other Indians waded to the back of the wagon—she supposed to lift and push—and Levi drove the team. Sue and Becky watched the show from shore. Everything was packed and ready to go.

It was quite obvious the Caddo had done this before; they worked with amazing precision and teamwork until all sat at the ready. One of the riders gave what sounded like a victory whoop, and everyone went into motion.

Levi slapped the mules. "Go! Go! Pull, Dex; come on, Mil!" Leather popped and wood creaked. The men heaved and groaned. The animals snorted and strained against the weight of the load.

For half a breath, nothing happened. Only a lot of effort exerted with no results.

"Lord, help, please."

Then suddenly, the wheel came free, and the load rolled across the creek all the way up onto the dry shore. She and Becky held hands and jumped up and down together cheering. The Indians hollered and held their arms in the air celebrating with her. Levi's smile stretched wide. Then tears blurred Sue's vision, and she couldn't see more than the men's forms.

"Thank You, Lord, thank You."

To her amazement, Henry sloshed out of the water and to the wagon, where he retrieved two handfuls of his jerky. He passed it out to the savages as though the high price she had already paid wasn't enough. They all kept on eating and talking and celebrating way too long, definitely past the time that he ought to have been seeing to getting her back on the trace.

"Levi!" She called her nephew from the group of men, where he was laughing and obviously enjoying himself.

He ran over. "Yes, ma'am?"

"Looks to me like Henry might just party the whole day away, and I do not intend to spend one more night here. I want you to start hitching Dex and Daisy back to the other wagon. Maybe he'll take the hint."

"But, Aunt Sue—"

"We've lost two full days and most of this one sitting on the bank of this forsaken creek. The wagon's unstuck now, and I'm ready to go! I can't believe Henry isn't."

Levi turned and got busy doing what she said. She knew he loved her all right but also that she tried his patience. As soon as he was old enough to build himself a cabin and be his own boss, she figured she'd lose him for sure.

BACK ON THE TRACE, Henry drove the second team and pondered the Caddo. He really liked the lot of them; they were his kind of people. Drove a hard bargain, laughed a lot, and worked hard at keeping their word. If he'd been willing to call their bluff, he might've struck a better deal, maybe all the tobacco to keep his long gun. He did hate to part with it since Old Hickory himself had given it to him. But no way would he have asked Levi to give up his daddy's or Sue to let go of her late husband's.

What he should have done was to buy her load of cotton and dump it into the creek that first morning. If he'd known for sure there would be a buyer for his seed, he would have, but if there was none, it would have taken a big chunk out of his honey money to pay her off. Getting into the cattle business would take a right smart stack of coin.

He smiled. He did like the fact that she owed him now. A mule and a brand-new gun. Not that the musket President Jackson had given him wasn't a fine piece, but he'd been hearing about a new one, a Hall breech-loading rifle, a fifty-four-caliber with a round barrel almost thirty-three inches long. Might even be one for sale in Jefferson.

Would he really do that to her, though? His gun was old after all.

The late afternoon sun warmed him whenever it peeked

through the wall of trees, but it didn't hold the midsummer burn he hated so much. Past ready for the heat to break, he looked forward to the fall colors showing up as he always did this time of year. Autumn was by far his favorite season.

The boy sat next to him. Henry figured that he and Levi were about as tuckered as the animals were well rested. Even the snake-bit one appeared fine. Since it would be a short day anyway, he figured everyone should ride. Pretty soon, the grade dropped down, and the tall hardwoods and pines disappeared. Other than a smattering of cedars, nothing but bois d'arc lined the trace on both sides. Their fat, ripe, green horse apples dotted the ground everywhere.

But he had no time and no storage and no place to wash them.

About as quickly as the thorned trees started, they ended, and the trace began a gradual incline. After a mile or so, he handed the reins to the boy. Levi looked up at him. "How come you had to give up your mule and your musket and your tobacco, but she didn't give up anything?"

"Oh, I'm not married to any of it. We needed help."

"What if she can't sell the cotton in Jefferson? What are you going to do then?"

Henry chuckled. "I don't borrow trouble. Today has enough problems of its own. We'll let tomorrow—and the day after—take care of their selves."

"Well, tell me this. You said yesterday that you could've sold Brown Mule for seventy dollars. Why didn't you? That's more than he was worth, wasn't it?"

"Value's often hard to measure. He was going to be worth more than that to me; it wasn't like I could go and replace him. Every mule and ox in the area was already pressed into service pulling cotton on the trace."

"Couldn't you have sold him and then bought him back when everyone got home again? Or at least another animal just as good, and made a profit?"

"For a fact, I could have. But then I had no intention of hanging around until they came back. My intent was to get myself to St. Louis."

"Why St. Louis? Ain't that up north?"

"To sell my seed. And yes, it's up on the Missouri."

"I saw you stowed some sacks away. What kind of seed you got?"

"Bois d'arc."

The boy sat back. "You're kidding me! Who in their right mind would pay good money for horse apple seeds? Especially when a bois d'arc ain't nothing more that a thorny trash tree. Those Northerners must be crazy."

"Up in the high plains, there isn't much wood to build fences. Bois d'arc makes great hedgerows. Keep 'em trimmed down, and, after two years most animals won't go through." He held up his hand, forming a circle with his thumb and forefinger. "After three, they can't."

"So after you gather the horse apples, what do you have to do?"

For the next mile or two, as the trace rose higher, Henry explained the laborious task of harvesting the bois d'arc seeds. Each step of smashing the lime green apples, picking out the seeds, washing them, then washing them again and drying them. He gave Levi the whole story, even included a few tricks he'd come up with.

The boy didn't ask, and Henry didn't volunteer that he figured his sacks of seeds to be worth more than all of his aunt's cotton. Nowhere was it written a body had to tell everything he knows.

CHAPTER

FIFTEEN

THE WIND SHIFTED, and then freshened to fifteen or twenty miles an hour. The temperature dropped as many degrees or more. Henry stood and glanced over his right shoulder. A wall of boiling black clouds filled the sky, moving rapidly from the northwest toward them. The wind swirled and gusted hard right at him, like a Union Jack eight-pounder, but he didn't see any way to dodge this one.

He looked to Levi. "Hold on." Henry slapped the reins hard. "Let's be to it, mules. Storm's coming." He needed to find a big tree on level ground before that rain came.

He pulled next to the other wagon. Sue gave him a puzzled look. He nodded to the right. "Best we find somewhere flat."

She looked for herself, then sat back down and draped an arm around Rebecca. Leather slapped across the team's backs. "Oh, my! Slow down, wind, give us time!"

For a good two hundred yards, the wagons raced side by side. He didn't spot anything that would offer protection. Finally, at the top of the knoll, he found it. He hollered toward Sue and pointed. "On the right. Let's put the wagons together under that big oak."

She nodded and reined in the mules, turning and pressing hard on the brake. He matched her, and the wagons stopped side by side, right under the tree, exactly like he planned. He intended to tell her what a good job she'd done, but first, he needed to get everything set up before the rain reached them.

For the next few minutes, he concentrated on untying and then retying the canvas covers to where the wagons were double-tarped with a couple of feet of open space between them. He then went to help Levi, who worked at unhooking and hobbling the animals. Once they were seen to, he and the boy joined the ladies.

Sue stepped to the edge of the canvas and studied the dark wall. "Sure is moving fast. Suppose it might just be a lot of blowing?"

A flash of lightning danced across the sky, followed almost immediately by a double clap of booming thunder. Henry walked up next to her. "Could be, but I wouldn't bet on it."

"At least we had time to get here." She smiled at him. "I did tell the wind to slow down and give us time."

Another bolt of lightning streaked its way to the ground and blinded him for a moment. Seconds later, the rain blew in. It poured down in sheets. The dark sky looked like night, though the day was barely half over. He stepped farther in beneath the tarps. "Guess I'd win that bet."

After watching the downpour for a minute, she pulled her shawl tighter around herself and moved back as well. Big drops of rain dappled her skirt. She was one handsome woman. "Are you a gambling man, Mister Buckmeyer? Seems you talk a heap about betting."

He gazed away, studying the storm, and thought about it. "Was once, but I prefer not to now. I hate to lose."

A close lightning strike with its instantaneous boom of thunder pulled her further away from the opening. Rebecca ran to her mother and hugged her legs. "Mama, I'm scared."

Kneeling, Sue stroked the child's head. "Remember, Becky? We never have to be afraid because God is always with us." She sat on the dry ground, and the nine-year-old cuddled in her lap. She looked up to Henry and smiled.

"Your mama's right, you know. Scriptures say not to fear three hundred sixty-five times."

Becky's eyes widened. "That's once for every day of the year!"

Sue looked him square in the eyes. "If you don't mind me asking, how is it you know the Bible so well?"

"Mother pointed out that fact." He loved the woman's directness. "But she also taught me to read with the Good Book. Read through it cover to cover, more than once."

She fell silent. He saw the question dance across her eyes but didn't think now was the time to discuss religion. Besides, he had a question of his own that he wanted answered before he bared that much of his heart.

Rebecca raised her head off her mother's chest and rubbed Blue Dog's head and ears. "Hey, Levi and I read the Bible, too. Mama makes us; well, she makes him." She nodded toward her cousin leaning against one of the wheels, whittling on a piece of wood he'd been working. "I like reading, so she never has to make me." She raised her eyebrows and nodded slowly, as though giving great affirmation to the truth. "I can read anything."

He bent toward her and smiled. What an arrogant little angel. This miniature Sue was every bit as strong and sure of herself as her beautiful mother. How could he ever go back to his life without them in it? He couldn't; even though he'd spent less than a week around the woman and her child, his heart belonged to them.

He reached and tousled Rebecca's hair. "I'm sure you can."

The young mother might not be willing to admit it, but she and her little girl needed him as much. The package deal suited him fine. He wanted both of them, and the way the boy was coming around, he'd gladly take him, too.

He faced Sue. "Ever read anything other than the Good Book?"

"Some, when I can take the time, which isn't as often as I'd like. There's always so much work to be done. How about you?"

"My mother insisted I read the Federalist Papers—and Poor Richard, of course. She even pounded enough Latin into me so that I could read Caesar's commentaries."

"Latin? You read Latin?"

He nodded. Maybe he shouldn't have brought Caesar into the conversation. He'd never intended to make himself out to be more than he was. "Some, but I'd walk over a dozen leather-bound Latin volumes for one good newspaper."

She waved him off. "I wouldn't have one of those vicious rags in my house with all the muckraking and backbiting."

He glanced up at the canvas. It shed the torrents without any apparent leaks. "Well, this upcoming election doesn't seem to be as bad as 'twenty-eight, but from what I've read so far, it isn't far behind." He looked toward the girl. "Can the little miss really read anything?"

Sue smiled and nodded. "If she doesn't know the word, she'll sound it out then pester me until I tell her what it means—that's if she can't get the gist herself from the context."

Henry laughed. He wouldn't want a newspaper anywhere

around Rebecca either. "No newspapers it is then." Another flash of lightning lit the sky bright as the near noon it actually was, but the thunder didn't follow right after like before. He started counting; the boom came thirty-four seconds later. "Good, seems to be moving off."

"Guess it passed as quickly as it blew in. No doubt it will outrun us. Maybe we can get back on the trail."

"I don't think so, if you don't mind me saying."

THE YES-I-DO-DEFINITELY-MIND didn't make it through her lips. Sue might be hardheaded, but not stupid. After that stuck wagon incident, prudence insisted that she not only hear what he had to say but pay good attention. They'd be with the train already if she'd listened to him.

"And so, tell me. Why do you think we should sit here and not move on?"

"If the old man was right, we've got four or five more miles before we get completely out of these bottoms."

"So? That seems more an argument for my way of thinking, which is to get after it. We can make five miles if we get started and be up and out of this swamp by the end of the day." She looked out. The rain had lessened to a soft drizzle, and the sky was already brightening. "One thing is for certain. Sitting here, we'll be burning daylight in no time."

"We could get hitched back up and, by then, maybe have three hours or so before dark." Henry glanced away, obviously frustrated.

Why were men that way? Why couldn't he just explain his obstinate self? It seemed as though he felt like she should trust him without question, do everything he said with no input at all. Why, it was as if he really were the king or something.

"So you say three hours? I'd think more like four, but even if, at a mile and a half an hour, we're out of these nasty bottoms in no time."

He nodded. "Probably right, if it wasn't wet. Looks to me we got better than two inches. You know how this black dirt gets. Slick and sticky. We're already a mule down, and—"

Levi laughed.

Henry faced him. "You know something funny?"

The boy chuckled again, grinning at him. "I wasn't going to mention this, but that young Indian, the one riding the paint?"

Sue poked his shoulder; she hated it when they ignored her like she wasn't the boss, the one paying all the bills and with everything to lose. "What's that savage got to do with anything?"

He shrugged. "Claims we overpaid. Said they would have pulled us out for the gun and a few pounds of tobacco. Could've kept Brown Mule all along."

"Really?" She faced her employee. "So it seems I overpaid." She loved it, the great Patrick Henry Buckmeyer had blundered, and she had a witness.

Becky placed a hand on Sue's cheek. "Mama, just because that Caddo boy said it, doesn't make it true. Surely, you have heard that Indians are known for lying like dogs and making sport of white folks." She gave her cousin a sideways glance with pursed lips. "Levi should know that, too."

He stood and came toward her. "He was telling the truth, you little scallywag! You think you're so smart and know everything, don't you?"

Sue drew her daughter into an embrace. "Now, Levi, calm down. You know she meant no harm."

Becky stuck out her tongue and gave him her pinched ha-ha-ha face.

Sue didn't want to hear that she'd been bilked out of the price of a mule. Neither did she want to stay there wasting time discussing whether or not she'd overpaid for the assistance. She had something on Henry no matter what Becky said, and everyone knew you could hear a lot in a long day. Where did her baby girl hear such a thing anyway?

"All that is not an issue right now because the fact of the matter is, it's over and done." She let Becky sit straight but kept holding her hand. "What is important is getting out of these bottoms and on to Pleasant Mound. There may still be a chance to catch up with the train there."

Levi shrugged. "Well, I'm with Mister Henry. I don't think we should try getting out of here today. It's too wet. Those wheels will get caked with mud, and no way could we make more than a quarter of a mile an hour, especially since we are a mule down."

Becky climbed out of her lap and stepped to the man's side, like she needed to physically support him. "Me, too. I'm with Mister Henry."

Sue threw up her hands. "Oh, sure, jump on the bandwagon! How can I fight you all?" Besides, she'd never hear the end of it if something bad did happen. "So fine! I'll not chance being blamed by the lot of you for anything that goes awry. So, against my wishes, we'll spend the night right here."

Henry nodded. She saw the faintest grin that he obviously worked at keeping hidden, like he'd won or something. She wanted to slap—or kiss—that silly grin off his face. No! What? Why would she even think such a thing? She put that thought right out of her mind. He was her employee, a heathen to boot, and nothing more. She was paying for his advice as well as his strength, so why shouldn't she get her money's worth and take advantage of both?

"It's still dripping some, so let's give it a bit to stop completely before we see if we can spark a fire."

There he went again. Giving orders. And she was downright tired of it. Who did he think he was? Was he totally incapable of not being the one in charge? She turned away with her heart pounding and her face burning. Mad at him, but just as upset with her own self. Why was she being this way? He was only doing what he thought best.

He'd been the one who thought of wax to coat the wagons and keep her cotton dry, and his wonderful dog had saved her most precious daughter from the bear, and Henry had insisted on that signal fire. Without it, the wagon might have still been stuck in that creek when the rain came. She shuddered to think.

Why did she always have to be so cross and stubborn? But in the same way, why couldn't he understand that she had to get her cotton to Jefferson? That she had to sell it for enough money to get her little family through another year. She knew why. Because he had no idea what it took. He had no one but himself to be responsible for; only knew fighting and hunting and trapping and fishing and living his good ol' bachelor's life of ease.

She wanted to scream. Instead, she made herself go to the larder and get everything ready to start on supper. They had to eat, and seeing to that was her responsibility.

Without any prompting, after Henry got a cook fire going, he and Levi retied the wagons' canvases and gave them a good oiling. Why hadn't she thought of that? Well, probably only because she wasn't as used to traveling, and apparently he'd been on more journeys than he could count.

No doubt he'd learned a heap about what to do when he was in the army. President Jackson must have pounded all that into his thick skull. She pondered on his fault of having to be the one in charge and wondered if Old Hickory taught him anything at all about submitting to authority. Surely he had; and, most likely, the young Henry had no trouble following the man's orders.

She put all of that out of her head until the last of the day's chores were completed. All evening, she'd forced herself not to think about the lost time or overpaying the Caddo or how insubordinate her employee continually acted. She'd concentrated instead on finishing the day, in order that another one could start.

Tomorrow, maybe she could catch up with the train and get her cotton to market without any further delays.

Once the opportunity to finally lay her head down presented itself, she pulled the already sleeping Becky to herself. At that moment, it all came crashing in on her. A powerful sense of dread and doom covered her like an early morning fog hovering on the creek bottoms back home. Home. Would she ever see her home again? Oh, Lord.

"You awake?"

She looked to the other wagon, which sat too close. Henry stretched out, resting his head on one hand. He smiled.

She rose up and put her forearm under her head. "Yes, sir, I am."

"When we were racing the wagons ahead of the storm, you drove that rig like you'd been mule skinning your whole life."

She nodded. What a left-handed compliment. But at least it was a compliment. "Thank you."

"And you were right about your cake, too."

"I was? How's that?"

"It was by far the best I've ever eaten, exactly like you said."

She smiled, but only a small, quick one. "Proud you liked it."

"No, ma'am. I loved it. I'll remember that cake forever; far better than good."

"Well, now you're exaggerating, but still, thank you, Henry. That's kind of you to say."

"You're welcome." He lay down, then raised right back up again. "I also want to thank you for being sensible. I mean, not insisting that we leave this afternoon."

Another left-handed compliment, but again, an accolade. He'd called her sensible. Sensible! Why all the flattery? Maybe he'd picked up on her depression, how she felt unappreciated, alone, rejected, and unloved. "Well, you're welcome, but the three of you forced my hand."

He nodded. "I admit it, you're right. We sort of did, but you are the boss, and if you'd said go, we would have gone, mud or no mud."

"Is that so?" The many times she'd told him that she paid his wages so she was boss came to mind, and here he was, admitting to that very fact. But she'd gone against him at the creek and got the wagon stuck. "And how much grief would I have caught if something bad had happened?"

"None from me. I learned a long time ago not to second-guess authority." He smiled, then lay back down.

Would this man ever stop amazing her? Out of his own mouth, he'd confessed she was the boss. He'd testified that he'd do whatever she decided. She liked that. Maybe things were looking up, at least enough to put an end to her morose mood for another day.

Oh, how she wished that she could trust God more and let Him lead her. She identified with Paul in the respect that she did what she didn't want to do and didn't do what she knew she should. Chief of sinners, the apostle called himself. But he hadn't known her.

CHAPTER

SIXTEEN

WETNESS ON HIS FINGERS. Henry awoke instantly; Blue Dog licking his hand was not a good sign. Something his dog didn't like was afoot. He lay there and listened, hearing nothing. The hound whined ever so softly and then looked east. Henry grabbed his pistol, stuck it in his belt, and shook the boy awake.

Levi threw an arm, and Henry dodged. "What?"

He put his finger to his mouth, pointed to Levi's rifle, then quietly crawled to the other wagon. Blue silently padded along beside him. He laid three fingers on Sue's arm and patted softly until her eyes opened. Then he immediately removed his hand.

"Henry? What are you doing?"

If she had been a man, he would have covered her loud mouth with his hand, but instead he crossed his lips with a finger. He nodded toward the dog, then half mouthed half whispered, "Blue says someone or something is out there."

She looked from him to the dog. Then realization appeared in her eyes. "What should I do?" She'd lowered her voice to match his volume.

"Your gun at the ready?"

"Yes." She sat up. "Where do you want us?"

He leaned in close to her near ear. "You and Rebecca stay behind me."

She nodded, and he joined Blue, who faced east, searching the dark and darker shadows. Levi eased up next to him, pointed to where the dog stared, and then scrunched his shoulders. Henry shook his head. Then, as if the intruders wanted him to know, a long howl sounded soulfully. Two shorter, mournful howls cut through the night and landed square in Henry's gut.

Wolves. He hated wolves. And they were close.

He nudged the boy, no longer keeping his voice quiet. "Get the fire going, if you can." He turned around. Sue, with the still sleeping Rebecca clutched to her bosom, sat between the two wagons right behind him. Her pistol lay at her side within easy reach. He shook his head. "There's at least three of them. Hopefully, it isn't a full pack."

"You think they're after the mules?"

"Could be. If it's a full pack. But I don't think three could cut one of them out and take it down."

"Even hobbled?"

As though on cue, the mules snorted, and one brayed. The howls had obviously set them on edge.

"They can still kick."

"So you think they're after us then?" She gasped and pulled Rebecca closer.

He nodded. "They'd definitely see us as the easier prey."

Blue's growl pulled him around. The dog's hackles rose, and he stood at the wagon's end with his teeth bared. Henry joined him. Right where the dog stared, he could make out an extra-dark shadow, maybe one of the wolves, but he didn't like shooting at shadows.

Levi held on to his long gun with one hand and, with the other, pulled out the last of the deadfall they'd gathered that afternoon and stored under their wagon. He tossed it on the low-glowing embers from their last meal's cook fire, then faced Henry. "Should I get more?"

"No, they're right out there."

"Where do you want me?"

"Get on the back side of your aunt. Stay low so you can see under both wagons."

"Yes, sir." The boy did as he was told.

SUE'S HEART BEAT WILDLY against her breast. She hated wolves; the vicious creatures didn't have the fear of man that most wild animals did. She had only encountered them once before, on the trip west with her new husband. They'd come in the night then, too, just after she and Andy went to sleep. Except she and Andy hadn't had a good watchdog like Blue. By the time she woke, four pairs of glowing eyes stared from the darkness. They vanished once her husband stoked the fire and shot at them, using up half their powder. Nothing in her life to that point had frightened her as much.

Her nephew, at her back side, comforted her more than the man-child would ever know. She could even breathe some. She swallowed and squinted against the night, searching the shadows. Just then, she spotted the first pair of eyes reflecting the fire's brightness.

Blue Dog had saved them all again. She rocked Becky and waited. After an internal debate whether or not to wake her, she decided against it. Her daughter would be up soon enough if the pack attacked, but if a standoff ensued instead, it might last until daylight, and her baby could get a fearless, full night's sleep.

Sue eased her daughter down so her hands would be free. She leaned over as close to the ground as she could get. Easing the sleeping girl to lay on her skirts on the left, she settled her without waking the child. She picked up her pistol and cocked it. Henry carried her flintlock since trading his musket. He moved back toward where she sat, stopping short and not turning around. "I think there's only three. I'm figuring a mother and two near-grown pups."

"That's good, right?"

"Depends on how hungry they are."

Just then, right in front of the wagons, a scraggly looking gray with bared fangs leapt straight at Henry. Blue flew through the air at the form and knocked it to the ground. Before the attacker could regain balance, Blue landed on top of him, eating fur. A second wolf came in from the side. A shot rang out from behind Sue. She spun.

Levi shook his head. He immediately worked on reloading his rifle. "I don't think I hit him."

Becky sat up, looked around, then screamed and kept on screaming.

Henry ran toward the second wolf but couldn't bring the flintlock around quick enough to shoot. The beast hit him full force, and they both went down. The animal relentlessly assaulted him. His pistol, flying from his hand, lay almost under the wagon. In seconds, Blue left the one he fought with and jumped onto the one trying to get to Henry's throat.

Sue rose to her knees and made herself focus on the first wolf, the one Blue had just abandoned. She pointed her pistol, but before she could fire, from behind her, a shot split the night, followed by a high-pitched yelp. The aggressor fell, staining the ground with its blood.

Sue immediately turned back to the wolf that had been on Henry. Blue warred in a fang-to-fang battle with the larger animal. Bleeding, Henry retrieved his pistol and the flintlock and turned in circles, searching the camp's full perimeter. He obviously watched for the third animal. She had to help Blue, but what if she missed? She pointed her pistol toward the two fighting canines.

"Shoot it, Auntie!"

Becky jumped up and ran toward the dog. "Don't shoot Blue, Mama!"

Sue's heart stopped. "Becky!"

The wolf had gotten Blue Dog down and was on top. Becky closed the distance to the snarling battle. Sue scrambled to her feet. She had to do something. The intruder opened his mouth wide. Evil fangs glistened in the firelight.

For only a moment, the wolf turned its head toward her daughter.

Sue aimed and fired.

Becky screamed as the wolf fell on top of Blue. Her baby grabbed the wild animal by two handfuls of hair and dragged the carcass off her dog. Blood covered poor Blue. Becky fell across him crying. Another shot rang out. Sue whirled in time to see the third wolf fall from midair right behind her. A faint whisper of smoke wafted from Henry's pistol.

She stared at the animals, looking from the one she'd shot back to the dog. The pistol fell from her fingers. She gasped for air, filling her lungs. She couldn't remember when she'd breathed last. Reality hit her all at once.

She crumpled back to the ground, her head in her hands. "Oh, dear God, no! I've killed Blue."

Becky ran to her. "Blue's all right, Mama. You didn't shoot him. You saved him."

Henry was also instantly beside her. He kneeled and laid his cheek on her head, hugging her with one arm. "Susannah, it's over. We're all fine. It's all right, Sue. Everything's all right."

She gritted her teeth, then slapped her skirts. "Every. Night. It's something! Drunks! Bears! Storms! Wolves! What else? I can't stand anything else!"

Sobs racked her being. Tears streamed down her cheeks. "Over!" she screamed. "I want it to be over!" Becky backed away, and Sue turned, flinging her arms around Henry, holding on for her sanity, his strength. He held her, and she cried on his broad chest. A sense of being safe there washed over her. How long had it been? She hugged him tighter. "I want it to be over."

He didn't loosen his hold on her either. "It's all right; it's over. Shhhh."

Soon enough, her sobs turned to whimpers. Finally, she swallowed and could breathe again. Still, she didn't withdraw. She rested in Henry's strong embrace.

"Oh, Blue, don't die. Don't leave me. I love you too much."

Sue pushed back and looked at her daughter and Blue. The dog lay perfectly still right where she had last seen him. Was he dead after all? Oh, no! Jesus, Blue Dog can't be dead. She stepped to him and kneeled beside her daughter. He looked up with sad eyes and whimpered. Several deep cuts covered his face and shoulders with blood.

Becky turned and took hold of her arm. "Help him, Mama! We've got to save him! What can we do?"

"Let's get these wounds cleaned to start with. Fetch the coal oil and a rag. Do you know where it is?"

"Yes, ma'am." Becky stood, took a few steps toward the wagon, then stopped. "But it will sting him so bad."

"Maybe not; dogs are different from people. Even if it does, though, it will help him. We need to get his wounds clean as we can." She couldn't let Blue Dog die. Not now. Not this night.

Henry kneeled beside the dog and examined the wounds. "I don't think it's as bad as it looks."

Sue hoped above hope that would be the case.

Becky returned with the coal oil and wrapped her arms around the man's neck. "We've got to save him, Mister Henry. I can't stand it if Blue Dog dies."

He hugged her back. "I don't think he's going to die, Rebecca. I know it looks bad, but there are only a couple of deep cuts. I can sew those up, and your mother can help me clean all the blood; then he'll look better. Might take a few days until he's back to his old self, though."

The little girl pushed off his chest. "I can sew. I'm an excellent sewer. Should I do it?" She wiped her tears.

Henry looked to Sue.

"She is an excellent seamstress, but do you think—?"

"Mama! I know I can do it. Let me help Blue Dog!"

"All right, all right, Becky. Of course, you can do it if that's what you want. If it's all right with Mister Henry." She rose. "I'll fetch the sewing box."

When Sue returned, all Becky's tears were gone, obviously replaced by a strong resolve to do what she had to do. She gently cleaned the wounds, wiping the blood from the hound's dappled coat. It made Sue so proud of her little girl. She wasn't sure she could do as well. She handed the box down to her. "Here you are, Doctor."

Becky opened it and peeked inside. "Which thread should I use?"

Henry peered in and moved some of the spools aside. "I suppose the black or white would do, or would you like pink better?"

She giggled. "Oh, Mister Henry, you're so funny. I'll use the white then. It may show up best." Becky bit off a long piece, turned toward the firelight, and threaded her needle. She looked up to Henry. "Now do I sew just like I was sewing a tear in a skirt?"

"Yes, ma'am, exactly like that. Here, let me hold him for you."

"Now, Blue. This is probably going to hurt me more than it hurts you, and I don't really want to do it either, but it's because I love you so much."

Sue watched her most precious daughter lovingly poke the needle into her friend's skin and then watched it come out again on the other side of the wound. A wave of queasiness washed over her. She turned away and looked up at the sky. One more time, a horrible danger had been overcome, and all was well.

Never in a million years would she have imagined so much trouble on the Jefferson Trace. Elaine had been so right when she said Sue could not go alone. She sighed, so grateful—again—that Henry had come along. "Thank You, Lord."

Levi busied himself dragging the three carcasses into the woods.

The sky, no longer black, still twinkled with stars, but the false dawn would soon brighten the new day. She would see to breakfast, totally appreciative of another day with everyone safe and Blue still alive to heal. What day was it anyway? Could it be Monday morning? Had it been only seven days ago that she and the children had headed to Sulphur Fork's trading post with the cotton?

"My, my, my, only a week on the trail, and we've experienced enough adventure to last a lifetime." She shook her head and got her mixing bowl and biscuit fixins from the larder. "Bless the Lord."

CHAPTER

SEVENTEEN

THE DAY DAWNED TOO SOON FOR HENRY. The lack of sleep was wearing on him. He sure was proud everyone, including Blue Dog, survived the wolf attack. Rebecca had done some mighty impressive stitching. Only thing happened to him seemed to be a couple of rips in one of his favorite shirts. He'd have to get Rebecca to fix it for him. And that pair of his trousers that had a seam coming loose while she was at it.

He flung out the cold dregs in his cup and walked to the fire. "Got more coffee?"

Sue looked up and smiled. Her beauty caught his breath. "I certainly do." She wrapped a rag around her hand and lifted the pot from the fire. He held his tin cup out, and she filled it. "Breakfast is about ready." She smiled again.

It made him laugh inside.

Quick as he finished his last biscuit, he stood. "Let's get the mules hitched. The trace is waiting."

The boy threw back his last bite of biscuit and rose. "Yes, sir, I'm past ready."

Before the sun barely cleared the horizon, he pulled the second wagon back onto the trail, following Sue. She had seemed to be glowing all morning. The woman certainly brightened his life, as did the little girl sitting beside him. She insisted on riding by Blue, to keep him comfortable, she'd said.

A sense of well-being settled over Henry's heart; he'd get Sue to Titus Trading Post maybe this afternoon, tomorrow morning for sure. Even if their neighbors were ahead of them, they'd be on the main trace after Pleasant Mound. More than likely, they could find someone to team up with.

The boy had volunteered to take the first walking duty, which today would also include frequently scraping the wagon wheels and picking the mules' hooves. Henry wouldn't let him go too long, but sitting here next to Rebecca sure was nice.

"Mister Daddy?"

"Yes, darling daughter Rebecca?"

She giggled. "I like that! You're so funny. You make me and Mama laugh all the time." She wrapped her inside arm around his and squeezed. "I just love you so much."

Oh, wow. Her declaration rendered him speechless. What should he say? He couldn't imagine her loving him like that after such a short time. The little gal obviously needed a father, and if he married Sue, he'd be it. He wiped his face before a tear rolled down and she spotted it. How could he ever go back to his solitary life without them?

He couldn't; even though he'd spent less than a week around the woman and her child, his heart belonged to them. They needed him. Rebecca kept a tight hold on his arm. "Anyway, I was just wondering."

He waited and waited awhile longer to find out what she wondered about, but she never said another word. He leaned out and glanced down to discover that she lay sound asleep against his arm. What an angel. And so quiet when asleep. He grinned. Didn't mind that much at all, except . . .

He'd hardly been able to get Sue's embrace off his mind. Sipping coffee, eating breakfast, harnessing the mules, and getting back on the trace, he couldn't shake it. Not that he wanted to. It was and would always be the best hug he'd ever gotten in his life. No matter what happened in the future, he would never forget it. He loved the way she held him close, the way she surrendered the entirety of herself into him, almost melting through his skin and becoming one with him.

It was for certain. He would ask her to marry him when the time was right. He knew she was the one. The one he'd waited so long for. Years ago, when he'd noticed her at the trading post, he'd first thought of making her his own. She'd taken off her hat and shaken her long hair loose, running her fingers through it, letting the brisk wind blow it away from her face. He'd asked around about her several times since, finding out what he could without being too obvious.

It hadn't been too long ago that he thought he'd missed any chance he might have had. Heard tell that a widower with two children over near Jonesboro had proposed. He didn't ever hear exactly what happened, but a marriage never took place. Figured her vow had something to do with it. But no matter, he would not miss this chance. Before he got off this trace, he would ask her to be his forever.

He only hoped her religion wouldn't interfere.

SUE HARDLY REMEMBERED cooking or eating breakfast. She'd spent the time chiding herself for falling into Henry's arms like a foolish, scared schoolgirl. That angry self battled inside her head now with other intense emotions that tried to make her believe she was sixteen again and in love for the very first time.

Except she couldn't be.

She was a middle-aged widow for Heaven's sake!

She loved Henry insisting on an early start that morning; certainly he'd done it to please her, and he had. Most everything about the man pleased her. Or made her so angry that she couldn't see straight. How did he do that? Play so with her heart. One thing she knew, she absolutely could not let herself be carried away by emotions.

She might as well get him out of her mind because she could never disobey God by yoking herself unequally with a heathen—no matter how good and kind and handsome he was. Sue Baylor! She had to quit thinking such thoughts. That devil! The father of lies and master of deceit. He was the one who had played his hand too boldly. She saw her infatuation for exactly what it was—an evil device to bring her and her little family to ruin.

But what of her daughter? She already saw Henry Buckmeyer as her hero who could do anything. Perhaps Sue shouldn't let her ride with him, should keep her close and protect her daughter's heart. It couldn't be a good thing to let her get any closer to the man or think any more highly of him than she ought.

Sue recalled the feel of her cheek on his chest, his hands on her back. Butterflies in her belly had her feeling like she might take flight herself. No! She must not think on that. She would concentrate on whatsoever was lovely and pure and worthy of a good report. How shameful would it be for anyone back home to find she was out here on the trail hugging a single man, then daydreaming about the embrace?

Though when he had held her last night, right after he saved her from that wolf, she didn't want anything more than to be in his arms. The safety of his embrace overwhelmed her. But he wasn't even a Christian. She just couldn't let herself get all weak in the knees. Besides, it was ludicrous to expect that he might even consider spending the rest of his life taking care of and supporting a used-up widow and her two children.

Henry lived a life full of adventure. He had no one to answer to, and she knew full well he liked it that way. After all, there had to be a reason he was thirty-four years old and never married. He obviously loved living his life loose and free, going where he wanted when he wanted. He didn't even want to obey God, knowing full well the great love story if he'd read the Bible through like he said.

No, being tied down to the responsibility of a ready-made family would be the last thing in the world he'd ever consider, much less choose.

Besides, she didn't want to be, wouldn't be, the one who brought him down. He was fine just the way he was—all free and strong and adventurous and kind and handsome and gentle and sweet. She shook her head. There she went again. He wasn't fine at all. He was lost, and she needed to help him find the Lord.

She looked to the heavens. "Father, help me and give me strength to stand in obedience to You. Help me keep my distance until the journey is done."

The day went by uneventfully. Henry insisted that only he and Levi take turns walking as the scraping and hoof cleaning turned out to be a dreadfully strenuous chore. Very slow and mostly steady, the teams moved the four tons of cotton over the muddy terrain. The two men worked so hard on so little sleep they both looked tuckered by early afternoon.

Sue didn't object at all when Henry suggested they set camp well before sunset. As a matter of fact, she couldn't wait to get supper behind her and go lay down. Battling with herself all day, talking herself out of love, had worn her out. Why object? She was too tired to have any fight left. Her internal warring quenched any unction to quarrel with the man.

The sun dipped with unprecedented glory into the western horizon. The brilliant purple and pink and golden hues painted by God's own hand took Sue's breath away. Night fell on the trace with a starless sky. The clouds almost obliterated the moon as well, but it did shine through now and then, though it was darker than usual.

After supper, she and Becky got the dishes washed and put away, then curled up together by the fire both for its light and its warmth. Sue pulled her shawl tighter around herself and her little girl and yawned.

Henry and Levi busied themselves with their normal chores, seeing to the mules, greasing the wagon wheels, and all the other things they took care of without her ever having to ask. She appreciated that. Her nephew came over and sat Indian style next to Becky.

Her little tomboy balled a fist and hit his arm. "Hey, Levi, where's Mister Henry?"

He held up a fist himself. "We trading punches, little girl?"

She squealed, then laughed. "No, no, no! I won't do it again, don't hit me!"

"All right then, keep your word, or you'll be in big trouble, you hear me?"

She nodded, but still made a face at him. "So where is he?"

"You keep making those ugly faces, and one of these days, one of 'em'll freeze up just like that. Then you'll be sorry the rest of your life." He looked over and grinned. "Mister Henry went to get some more firewood, said he'll be back directly."

Sue pulled Becky into a head lock and squeezed gently. "You best listen to your cousin." She laughed, then stood. "I think we should turn in. I'm so tired."

Levi locked his fingers behind his head and stretched. "Me, too. So, tomorrow we'll be in Pleasant Mound, right? Sure is taking a long time, and we sure have had more than our share of trouble."

"Yes, indeed." She pulled Becky up. "Come on, little girl. To bed with you."

"But I want to stay up and wait for Mister Henry."

Exactly what Sue wanted to avoid; she wanted no discussions regarding that hug. Better to go to bed and try to catch up on missed sleep. "Rebecca Ruth."

Becky pouted. "Oh, all right. But I'm not tired, I had a nap today." She heaved a heavy sigh and stared at Blue. "Come on, boy." She bent over, kissed the hound, then turned to Sue. "He's feeling much better, but I don't want him away from me, especially while he's still recovering."

The dog raised his head and stared into the darkness. Silence filled the campsite. Blue Dog stood and took one step toward the woods. A low rumble started deep in his throat.

Sue's heart beat faster. "Levi, go grab your long gun and fetch my flintlock, and my pistol, too. Becky, you stay right by me no matter what. You hear?"

"Yes, Mama."

The rumbling in the dog's throat increased in volume, and he showed his fangs. It wasn't long before Sue heard the footfalls that Blue had noticed before. She took a deep breath that lifted her shoulders. What now? Where was Henry?

Her nephew returned and handed her the flintlock, then the pistol. He slipped off into the darkness, leaving only her and Becky by the dwindling fire. She wondered where he went, why he would leave, but she didn't think long on it because a man called from the darkness.

"Hello to the camp."

Blue Dog growled louder but stepped closer to the visitor. For some reason, the man sounded familiar, but that didn't squelch her uneasiness. "Show yourself, sir. I'm not accustomed to speaking with a man I can't see."

"Wanted to say something since I saw your boy got your gun and all."

"Fine, so you've announced yourself. Now come into the light."

"Yes, ma'am, I am. Don't shoot, Mis'ess Baylor. And I'd appreciate it if you'd call off your dog, too."

Becky leaned forward and clapped her hands softly. "Blue! Come here, boy." The hound obediently returned to her side but never took his gaze off the dark woods. She put her hands around his neck and kissed his face. Blue returned the affection with a quick lick to her cheek.

Who could it be that knew Sue's name? Her mind raced, trying to place the voice. She tucked her pistol into her skirt's waistband and stood with the flintlock pointed in the direction of the voice. "Come in." She waited with bated breath.

"Mister Littlejohn! What in the world! Why are you here?" Indignation trumped astonishment. Her hackles rose. Her daddy always told her that if a man would lie to you, he would steal from you. "State your business, sir."

He smiled his big old phony smile, the one he'd used when he told her he'd pay three to four cents a pound for her cotton depending on its quality. "Well, now. You've almost made it to Pleasant Mound, haven't you? All alone and almost halfway to Jefferson. I must say, I'm impressed. You are some kind of woman, Susannah Baylor."

"You have not answered my question. What is your business here?"

"Well, you see, I've had time to reconsider, and, frankly, I've come to the conclusion that I really do want your cotton, ma'am, so I've come to get it."

"I told you before my cotton is not for sale to the likes of you!"

"No, no. Don't you worry, I've come to pay your price. I believe you last offered it at three and a half cents, did you not?"

"You may have changed your mind, but I most certainly have not changed mine! I thought I'd made myself clear. I'd burn it before I'd sell it to you. You wasted your time coming here. Now be on your way."

"Why, ma'am, you do surprise me. How could you be so inhospitable? And quite un-Christ-like as well, I'd think. But then, I also thought you might say that."

She stepped in front of Becky. "I owe you no hospitality. You are unwelcome here, and I've told you to go. If you do not, I will blow your kneecap off. If you still don't leave, I give you my word, sir, that I'll put a bullet right between your eyes."

At that instant, a second man leapt from the rear of the wagon and grabbed her from behind. He knocked the flintlock from her hand and pulled her pistol out, waving it at Littlejohn. "Got it, boss."

Becky screamed, and Blue jumped on the man's backside, tearing into him.

"Run, Becky! Run into the woods!"

The girl got up and took off. Littlejohn caught her by the arm.

"Get your filthy hands off her!" Sue glared at him.

Becky struggled and slipped out of his grasp.

"Run, Becky! And don't stop!" Sue fought against the man who held her hands behind her back. To her relief, Blue took off after her daughter.

A third henchman strolled in smiling. He had Levi by the collar. "Just like you said, boss. A piece of cake."

Littlejohn lost his fake smile. "Good job, Skunk."

The name certainly fit. The man reeked of body odor and only God knew what else. His grin showed rotten and missing teeth.

Littlejohn walked over to her. "Sorry it had to be this way, Mis'ess Baylor."

She spit on him. "You're despicable!"

Then, like a flash of lightning, Blue Dog reappeared and leapt onto Skunk's back, lashing at his neck. The man let go of Levi and ran screaming louder than Becky had into the darkness with Blue leaping and tearing at him every step of the way.

In the melee, Sue writhed and wiggled to free herself, but Littlejohn grabbed her from the front and whirled her around. He pulled her tight against him. A shot rang out. The man who had been holding her went down. A red stain grew on his shoulder. Littlejohn pulled a knife and put it against her throat.

"Drop your long gun, son, or I'll be forced to slit your aunt's throat from ear to ear."

Becky came running back into the firelight. "Mama!

Mama!" She ran over and kicked Littlejohn. "You let her go! Let her go now!"

Kicking out to the side, he sent her little girl flying through the air. Sue would kill him with her bare hands if he didn't kill her first.

Levi raised his long gun with a bead on Littlejohn's head. "I am not your son. Now let her go."

"Why, you're just a kid. You've never killed a man, have you? You know you'll go to Hell for sure if you shoot me, boy. Best drop that gun. I'll not tell you again."

Henry walked into the light and right toward the thief with his pistol held out. "You are a dead man if you so much as spill one drop of this woman's blood. I promise you. This is over." He took another step toward him. "I've killed seven men. Shot six and beat one to death with my bare hands. You'll be number eight if you hurt her." With the blade of the knife pressing against her throat, Sue's heart beat against her chest with such force she thought she'd surely faint. Her eyes begged Henry. She wasn't ready to die!

"Collect your friend there and hightail it out of these parts as fast as you can travel." Henry's eyes were like steel. "Do it now."

What Sue could see of the man's arm and pudgy hand glistened with sweat in the firelight. He fidgeted, holding the knife a little way out from her skin. "But, but, the minute I let her go, you'll shoot me dead."

"No, not in front of this little girl and her mother. But be it known, you best travel far and fast. I ever see your face again, wherever it might be, you're a dead man after what you tried here tonight."

The one Levi had shot writhed on the ground. "Do it! Let

her go and get me to a doctor, you fool. Only a woman and a boy you said! Chowderhead!"

Levi kicked him. "Shut your mouth, you no-good worm. I hope you die, and that I'm the one who gets to send you straight to Hell. Say another word! Go ahead." He poked him with the barrel of his long rifle.

Henry held his cocked pistol pointed at her captor's head. "I won't tell you again. Let her go. Now."

The man dropped the knife and released her. She ran to Henry and held him with all her might. He kept aim on the thief. Littlejohn helped his friend up and half dragged, half supported him, getting into the darkness and disappearing as fast as he could move.

Becky ran to her and hugged Sue's leg with one arm.

She looked down at her daughter, her vision blurred by the tears in her eyes. Her little one's other arm wrapped Henry's leg. "Are you all right, sweetheart?"

Becky nodded, her face glistening with tears as well. "Yes, Mama. It hurt my leg the worst when he kicked me, but I'll be fine."

Sue realized Henry's arms were around her, again. Oh, his embrace felt so wonderful and safe. She could stay there forever, but she pushed away and looked into his eyes. "Thank you." She gasped for more breath and to stop from releasing the sobs rising from deep inside. "So much." She lifted a hand to his cheek. "One more time, you've saved my life."

CHAPTER

EIGHTEEN

THAT NIGHT AS HENRY WAITED FOR SLEEP, he stared at the sky, watching shades of gray move past, and replayed the evening's events. Oh, how he wanted to kill that no-count Littlejohn, wanted it bad, but more than anything, he wanted to keep Sue and Rebecca safe. Plus, he'd never want to disappoint either of them by killing a man in cold blood. How things had changed.

It did concern him that she had pushed away so soon. He would have preferred to hold her longer. He did save her life after all. She might have at least given him a longer hug, and maybe even a kiss—on his cheek would have been nice. Some might have expected it. Why had she pushed away? Was it her God keeping her from giving her love, or even showing her gratitude?

Sleep found him before any conclusions regarding Sue's change in attitude. For a while, he dreamed of Littlejohn, but instead of his henchmen, the no-count was teamed with the wolves, and, instead of only three, he traveled with a full pack. Henry shot, and Sue reloaded, but he couldn't kill them fast enough. The beasts kept leaping at him, on him. Finally, when one had Blue by the throat, the wolves and Littlejohn vanished.

Then Henry found himself back in that Kentucky tavern.

He relaxed, exactly like he had that November night so long ago. Sipping on a beer, he sat against the wall minding his own business. The barmaid didn't flinch when he added the beer to his stew order. She did want to see his coin though. Halfway through his second drink, the front door flew open. At first, he didn't pay any attention to the two lumberjacks who filled the tavern with their boisterous voices.

It was his birthday, and all he wanted was the present he'd promised himself.

The taller of the two men looked around, spotted Henry, and slapped his fellow's arm. "Ain't that the schoolmarm's boy sitting there against the wall sipping beer?"

The other one looked. "You've got an eye, mate. It is him." He wiped his mouth. "Hey, boy, tell your mama I need some schooling."

Henry shrugged and took the bait. "Sure, what's your name?"

"What? You don't know your own daddy's name?" The man laughed. "That's what I am, your pap, and that's the gods' truth, son."

Henry stood, staring at the man. He wanted to tell him that he knew full well who his father was, a respected man of letters, but he didn't say anything. Figured he'd best get on home. He shook his head, spit on the sawdust floor, and walked toward the door.

Footfalls pulled him around. The man ran toward him but stopped short. "Where you going, boy? Just now, I told you a thing. Ain't you going to say otherwise? Or is it you don't know for sure that I ain't your pappy?" The guy leaned forward, exposing his chin, like he was begging Henry to take a swing. "Maybe it's 'cause you know your mama's honor ain't worth defending. Is that it?"

For a heartbeat, he stared at the man. He clenched his fists but kept them at his sides. No matter how good it would feel, smacking the brute wasn't worth it. He turned away and grabbed the door's latch. An open hand slapped the back of his head. He spun around.

"Where you going, son? I thought we'd share a beer, talk a bit about that handsome mama of yours."

"Don't hit me again."

The man stung Henry's cheek. "What about slapping?" He laughed even louder. "Does that count?"

Henry's fists balled. He swung and kept on swinging. The drunk went down. Henry jumped on top of him, pounding on his face. The man's friend joined the fight, pummeling his head and back, but Henry kept on swinging anyway. Inside, he screamed at himself to stop, but he didn't. He couldn't. He jammed his fist into the disrespectful, loathsome man's face time after time.

Until a hand grabbed his arm.

The tavern disappeared. He looked up.

Sue kneeled beside the wagon he and the boy slept under. She stared at him. Her hand still held on to his arm, gently shaking it. "You awake now?"

He shook sleep and the bad dream away and peered into her eyes. "I am. What's afoot?"

"You were shouting in your sleep to stop."

"Was I now?"

She nodded. "Want to talk about it?"

"No." What he wanted was to pull her to himself and smother her with kisses. Instead, he played the gentleman's game and only smiled. "I'm sorry I woke you. Let's get some rest. Maybe aim for another early start tomorrow."

She scratched her ear, nodded, then crawled back under her wagon and the soft piles of his furs.

SUE LAY THERE AWAKE with her mind going as fast as that storm had blown in. The frogs sang to each other, and if she listened, really listened to their song, she could imagine they were croaking their praise to the Creator. A breeze rustled the drying leaves, and they, too, sent their song to the heavens. The owl joined in with his whoo and made her think he might be asking who was more glorious than God. Could there be any more beautiful a symphony?

She didn't want to think about Henry at all, but that's exactly where her thoughts kept returning. His eyes haunted her; in a good way, but still, she wanted her musings to go somewhere else. That look, though; had there been something there? Like he wanted to hug her and kiss her. But she couldn't let that happen, no matter how she felt.

Besides, she wasn't sure she'd even seen it. Could be that was only what she wanted, all wrapped up in her sinful nature. She'd probably only invented what she hoped to see there in his eyes—or what the devil wanted her to see.

He didn't have to be such a handsome man. Not in a pretty-boy way, but a rugged, manly kind of way. Why he hadn't been around more sure posed a mystery. Especially since every other single man on the Sulphur Fork Prairie had eventually come calling to court her. Young and old alike, from nineteen to seventy-two years old. She smiled remembering. What an old geezer he was! Probably showed up on a dare.

It was all confusing. None of them had ever made butterflies swarm her belly like Henry though. But him not being a believer . . . She sighed. Maybe he had no interest in marriage and being tied down anyway. What she knew was that she was absolutely not interested in that kind of relationship with any man unless it led to marriage, and that debate—so far as Henry Buckmeyer was concerned—had been settled in her mind after the first hug.

She would never marry Patrick Henry Buckmeyer. She'd never tie him down. And she'd never marry an unbeliever. Besides, he'd admitted out of his own mouth that he was a killer—had killed seven men.

Arriving in Pleasant Mound; that's what she'd think about. Seeing the Foglesongs again and Becky playing with Sassy. And the Howletts; Sue enjoyed Shannan so much, and it would be good to have the long trip to visit with her and Berta and Benny. The women always shared their fresh revelations. Why didn't more men spend as much time in the Word as women?

Henry not being a believer was dreadfully worrisome. How could he have read the Bible through so many times and not have seen the Truth? And her Levi, too, he'd never asked Christ into his heart. Maybe because he'd been forced to grow up way too quick, and even though she'd done her best and truly loved the boy, he just always seemed unsettled.

Oh, she needed to quit thinking and get some sleep! Counting her blessings might work. Maybe that would help her keep her mind off Henry. But it didn't. She kept counting him! Henry, Henry, Henry! Why had he been yelling "Stop" in his dreams? When had he killed those men? And why? Were they the ones who haunted his dreams?

She yawned and finally dozed off with the heathen on her mind.

HENRY SLAPPED THE MULES' BACKS. "Hey, now." The beasts lumbered forward amidst the rattle of the trace chains and the wagon's wood creaking and straining. As the day before, Rebecca rode with him to see to Blue Dog's comfort, even though her mother had put up a little fuss. He couldn't see what it mattered all of a sudden.

As far as the dog was concerned, though, he'd seen how the old boy sprang into action when he was needed last night. But he sure enough played the invalid again that morning. How could anyone claim dogs were only dumb animals? Not his Blue.

His little miss tugged on his sleeve. "Mister Daddy?"

He loved hearing that; it warmed his heart. He didn't want to ever stop hearing her call him that. "What, Rebecca?"

She sniffed and looked up. Tears filled her eyes. "I don't want you going to the bad place." Concern etched her face.

"Don't intend to, sugar. Why would you think such a thing?"

"But last night, you told that bad man that you killed seven men."

He nodded. "I did, that's true." How much should he tell her about his life? "I've got a past I'm not so proud of."

"One of the Ten Commandments says don't kill."

"But every time, it was in self-defense; I didn't have a choice. I'm sure the man upstairs understands."

Her concern eased. "I hope so, because I wondered if I still wanted to go to Heaven if you weren't going to be there."

His breath caught in his throat. She loved him that much? How could he ever love any little girl more? Not sure she wanted to go to Heaven if he wasn't going to be there. He wanted to hug her tight and never let her go, but he just tousled her hair instead. "Seems Blue was a bit more spry this morning."

She shook her head. "No, he's still real sore and needs plenty of rest. I don't want him doing anything for a couple of more days."

He smiled and nodded. "Whatever you think, Doctor Rebecca. Noticed your stitches held tight, even after last night."

"Yes, sir. I did, too. I truly am an excellent seamstress. Mama taught me."

Sue, who had insisted on taking the first walking turn, stayed close to the front wagon, spending her time talking to the boy, best Henry could see. He still hadn't resolved what exactly her pushing him away so abruptly meant. Didn't like it much that she was the one who woke him from his nightmare either. Seemed if he mentioned or even thought about his past, he relived it in his dreams.

Had there not been plenty of witnesses to what had happened, he might have landed in the calaboose. But everyone agreed it was self-defense, though maybe a bit too vigorous, so no legal ramifications followed. The fact he'd been only fifteen, and the logger a grown man known for being a troublemaker, silenced even the other lumberjacks. Furthermore, Henry had cuts and bruises aplenty.

For a while, he'd let his life play out, but thinking on the progression of years, he came to concede that the tavern fight had been the first peg to fall that brought him all the way to Texas. He couldn't imagine being a woman widowed at only nineteen and pregnant in the wild territory. He shook his head.

Sue slowed her pace and came abreast of his wagon. "Ready to switch?"

"Past ready." He handed the reins to Rebecca and jumped down.

In a more graceful motion than he'd seen her make a week and a day before, she climbed into the wagon with it still moving. He smiled at her. She smiled back, but at best, he'd rate it a weak grin. Not the dazzling one he loved so much. What was wrong with her? What had he done to get her so upset with him?

He walked beside the wagon for a bit, then looked up. "If I've got it right, we should reach Titus's Trading Post mid-morning."

She nodded. "Good. Maybe things will at last be easier from there on."

"I was thinking, even if we've missed our neighbors, there should be others coming from the west heading for Jefferson. If you're a mind to, we could team up with some of them."

"Sure, that's a good idea, but I hope we haven't. Becky and I have good friends traveling with the train, and I'm really looking forward to spending time with them."

So she wanted to spend her time with anybody but him? He had no idea what had upset her or why she acted all of a sudden like he had the plague. Could it be because he'd admitted to killing those men? If it bothered her, why wouldn't she talk to him about it? Women. They were such enigmas. Did he really want to tie up for life with any of them?

He dipped his hat once, then increased his pace until he walked beside the lead wagon.

SUE HANDED THE REINS TO BECKY. "Hold these a minute, please." She yawned and stretched.

"Tired, Mama?"

"Yes, I am. Didn't sleep so good last night." Between Henry's nightmare and her taking so forever to go to sleep, it had been too short. She took the driving back. "How about you? Were you able to get some rest?"

"Yes, ma'am. I'm not tired at all."

Sue watched Henry walking beside the front wagon talking with her nephew and wondered what the conversation might be about. Had finding out Henry was a murderer changed Levi's opinion of the man as it had hers? She was actually glad to know the truth. It shored up her decision to steer clear of him. And how had it affected her daughter? She looked down at her. "What are you thinking about, Becky? You sure are being quiet."

Her little girl rubbed Blue Dog's side. "Oh, I was thinking about Mister Henry."

You, too, huh? Sue put her hand to her mouth. Praise God she'd only thought that! She should have known. That man! How did he weasel his way into everyone's thoughts like he did?

"I really like him, Mama. Don't you?"

She knew she'd better weigh every answer. "I like him all right. He's helped us a lot."

Becky twisted away from the hound and faced her. "Yes, he certainly has, and don't you think he's powerful nice, too?

Why, he saved us from the bear and those wolves and that awful Littlejohn man. And he thought of calling the Indians, too, and—"

"To tell it true, it was Blue there that saved you from that bear. Mister Henry arrived a little late on that one."

"That's right, but Blue is his dog after all."

"I'll concede that it is a good thing he's been with us on our trip, Rebecca."

"Good, because I think we really owe him a heap."

"Well, when we sell our cotton, we'll pay him for helping us, so that's his job. It's why I hired him, to help us."

She hoped her daughter understood that it wasn't all out of the goodness of Henry's heart that he was along. While she did agree a hundred percent that he had been a blessing, she preferred not to encourage the girl's obvious infatuation with the man. No way would she put her in a position to be hurt by the likes of Henry. She needed to have a talk with him and tell him to back off.

This was not going the way Becky had hoped that it would, Sue was certain. She knew her daughter well enough to know she was trying to get her to think differently about Henry. She probably hoped that he would be her new father, and thought that Sue was muddying the water being so negative. She'd heard her daughter pray for a daddy, and her being without one broke Sue's heart.

But Henry was not that man, even if Becky thought he was, wanted him to be. She hoped her little girl didn't already love him. No doubt she'd blame her mother for messing everything up when it didn't turn out as she would like.

"Mama? How much do you think I'm worth?"

"Why, you are priceless, my dear." She hugged her, one

armed. "You're my gift from God and worth more than all the money in the whole world."

"All right, fine. I thought you might say that." Becky giggled. "So what I want to know is if you want me to be happy for my whole life."

"That's a silly question! Of course I do. I'll always want the very best for you."

"Good, proud that's settled." The girl returned her attention to her patient. A diligent doctor indeed.

Sue shook her head and smiled. Her little one never failed to astonish her with bizarre conversations. Sue only wished she could be sure that Henry didn't reside at the bottom of her daughter's deep thoughts, but she feared he was exactly the motivation for Becky's strange musings.

CHAPTER

NINETEEN

Like Henry figured, he pulled the first wagon's team to a stop in front of Titus's Trading Post a bit before high noon. On both sides of the well-worn road, a smattering of buildings stood in various stages of completion. He liked progress, and Pleasant Mound looked progressive. Might even make a town before too long.

The other wagon pulled in behind him. He looked back at Sue. "What do you think, boss? Want us to unhitch 'em?"

"Let's hear the news, and then we can decide."

He chuckled on the inside. Exactly what he'd supposed she'd say. "Sounds good." He locked the brake and tied the reins off, patted Blue, then jumped down. He held his arms out. Rebecca fell into them like she'd been doing it her whole life. He put his mouth close to her near ear and whispered, "See if you can find something you want, my treat."

"Anything?"

He laughed. "Maybe not anything, but if you really want it, I'll see if I can't dicker for it." He set her on the wooden porch leading into the trading post.

Sue hurried past, giving him a disapproving look on her way into the building.

What had he done to deserve that?

Women, would he ever understand them?

ONCE INSIDE, when her eyes had adjusted enough to find the proprietor, she held her hand out across his countertop. "Sue Baylor, sir, from Sulphur Fork. Has the cotton train from up my way made it through yet?"

"Yes, ma'am. They pulled out yesterday morning before the sun showed." The man held out his hand. She grabbed it and shook halfway between the light touch of the gentlewoman she'd been raised and the firmness of the granger she'd become. "Andrew Titus, ma'am. This is my trading post. So you folks from up by the Red?"

She looked down as though studying his wares, but her true purpose was to hide her disappointment. Only a day behind. If she just had listened to Henry, they could have beaten them here by what? Two days. She chided herself and felt bad about it all over again, then met the man's eyes.

"Very nice to make your acquaintance, and yes, sir." She smiled. "I have a little over nine hundred acres about twenty-five miles south of the river."

Becky strolled past, carefully scrutinizing all the merchandise the man had on display. She looked up at Mister Titus. "Yes, sir. We've got a right good block of black dirt four miles south out of Sulphur Fork." Becky grinned at Sue.

She chuckled. "My precocious daughter, Rebecca."

Levi hurried by as though above window-shopping. "Any paraffin, sir, and oil for the canvases?"

Sue nodded in his direction. "And Levi Baylor, my nephew."

"Pleased to meet you, sir." Titus pointed. "You'll find both in the back left corner." He looked past Sue to the outside. "That your husband watering your mules?"

Her heart skipped a beat, startled her. "Hired man."

Titus nodded. "You heard the news?"

"What news?"

"The cotton buyers are leaving out early, not staying much longer in Jefferson. Sent word down the trace. That's why your neighbors lit out 'fore sunrise."

"When? Do you know?" She looked toward Henry. A rock grew in her belly. "Any idea of how much time I might have?"

The man counted on his fingers, then pulled a stubby pencil from behind his ear and scribbled on a pad. "If I'm counting right, you've got three days at most."

"Counting today?"

"No, ma'am. Four counting today."

Sue did the math. It meant better than thirteen miles a day, if they could make another eight today. "Why are the buyers leaving so soon?"

"Seems the election is doing funny things to the price of everything, especially lint."

"That doesn't make sense."

Titus shrugged. "That's what I thought." He smiled. "Anything else beside the wax and oil I can help you with, Mis'ess Baylor?"

She shook her head. "Thank you, no, sir." She had to get the wagons back on the trace. She turned and headed toward the door. Should she give up, turn around, and go home? How could she after all they'd been through? But was it a waste of time to go on and try to make it?

HENRY PASSED SUE as she headed out, her head hanging. He'd heard it all. If they needed to be in Jefferson in three days, then that's where he'd have them. He marched up to Titus. "That your team out back?"

"Yes, sir. Traded a man on his way home out of them a few days ago. Got the mules and his wagon. You in the market?"

"Harness, too?"

"Yes, sir. I'll make you a deal on the lot."

"Don't need the wagon, but I might be a buyer on the mules and harness, if it's trail worthy and the animals are sound."

The man's thumbs pulled on the bib of his slightly stained apron, then he smoothed it all out, like he needed to think a bit. "Oh, yes, sir. Those four fine mules are fit as a fiddle. Hadn't had a better set here in a spell. Leather could use some oil, but what harness couldn't?"

Henry started to say his, but figured why antagonize the man? No need to, especially when he was trying to trade him out of his team. "You drive 'em?"

"No, sir, but I saw the fellow work 'em. Not a stubborn one in the lot."

"They catch easy?"

"Hadn't tried."

"They got hobbles?"

"Yes, sir. I'll throw them in."

"You got plenty of grain?"

"Oats, corn, a right smart load of wheat, all good enough to grind, but fine feed for sure. Plenty of miles in my grain, man or beast."

Henry nodded. The shopkeeper was selling him, but he'd heard it all before. "What you want for the lot?"

Titus wiped his mouth, tugged on his apron again, then smiled. "Three hundred gold or silver coin." He closed one eye, then bobbed his head side to side like he was counting. "That includes two hundred pounds of grain, your choice."

Before Henry could counter, Rebecca sidled up next to him and took his hand into hers. He looked at her and smiled. She smiled back. "I found what I want."

"Really, what is it?"

She pointed to a shelf behind the man's shoulder. "That ring right there, the shiny green one."

Titus turned, grabbed the ring, then held it out. "This what you want? That's an emerald, and it's real gold, missy."

She took it and slipped it over her ring finger. The band was at least three sizes too big. She held her hand out in front of herself admiring it, then handed it back. "Yes, sir, that's the one." She tugged on Henry's hand until he bent down to her level. She spoke softly into his ear. "Thank you for the ring, Daddy." Then she kissed his cheek.

He straightened up and faced the man. "How much?"

Titus rubbed his tongue over his teeth, then smiled his trading-post smile. "Seven dollars; it being gold and all."

Henry nodded like he was going to pay full price for what he wanted. He searched the store, then spotted the boy in the far corner fingering a shirt. "Levi, find anything yet?"

"Yes, sir." The boy laid the shirt down and headed toward him. "There's a pair of boots."

"Anything else?"

"Maybe some powder and shot?"

Henry nodded, then pointed to a jar that rested next to

where the man had pulled the ring from. "What you got there?"

"Hard candy. Best I've ever had."

Henry laughed at himself. Was he really contemplating spending a month's worth of gathering and cleaning seeds on these children? His answer came in the affirmative; that's exactly what he was going to do. Warmth spread through his heart. Could this be what splurging on your own kids was like? He smiled. Must be what love did to a person.

NAUSEA WAVED OVER SUE. If the last half of the trace went one iota as bad as the first half, she was sure to miss the buyers. She held on to the edge of the wagon and tried to steady her insides. She looked toward the trading post. What in the world could Henry and those two children be doing?

Eight more miles today, then thirteen a day for the next three. How could they ever cover that much ground? So far, she hadn't done thirteen even one day, much less three in a row. She looked to the sky, almost mad at God for the cruel turn. She definitely was in no mood to rejoice or give thanks or say anything kind to anyone at that point.

She had trusted Him, and here He was, letting her down. So what if it was the best crop she'd ever made? What difference did it make if she missed the buyers? It seemed all for nothing.

She had no fight left, no hope. She looked again at the three of them still chatting away with Titus like they had all day to waste and nowhere to go. She wanted them to come on. But then again, what did it matter how long they stayed? She'd never make it in time anyway. Might as well resign herself to it and start thinking what she was going to do next.

Maybe she'd just give up and go home to her daddy. She climbed into the wagon and sat there crying on the inside.

Becky came running out with her fingers clutched tight. Keeping what she had in her hands hidden, she carefully climbed the spokes, then sat beside Sue. "Mama! I have a surprise for you. Mister Da—umm, Mister Henry got it for me and you! Pick a hand." She held out both fists in front of her.

Sue shook her head. She did not feel like playing any games. She did not want to be happy. Her life was ruined, and all she wanted was to be left alone.

"Go ahead! Pick one, Mama."

Should she make her daughter share the weight of the world? No. But how could she act like any surprise pleased her? Becky was obviously so excited about it, but Sue couldn't think of one thing good at that awful minute. She sighed, trying to relieve some of the pressure on her heart, and looked into her little girl's smiling, glowing face. She tried to smile and tapped Becky's left hand—since nothing was right, after all.

Becky opened her fist, revealing a golden piece of hard candy. "It's butterscotch! You get the butterscotch!" She opened her other hand showing a red piece. "Mine's cherry!" She popped it in her mouth and closed her eyes. You could tell she enjoyed it. "Ummm, oh, Mama! Roll it around so it'll touch every part of your mouth. It's like Heaven." She opened her eyes. "Why aren't you sucking yours?"

Sue shook her head. "Watching you, I guess. So do you like it better than my cake? Is it your new favorite?" She fully expected the child to choose it over her vanilla pound cake.

Becky took the hard candy out of her mouth and turned it in her fingers, staring at it. "Oh, my goodness, no! This is a one-time chunk of cherry. Delicious, but your cake will always be my favorite in the whole world for my whole life." She stood and hugged Sue's neck. "Don't be sad, Mama. Eat your candy. Suck it slow, so it'll last a long time, and it'll make you feel better." She popped her cherry piece back in her mouth, then put her sticky little hand on Sue's cheek. "Everything will be all right. You'll see."

"I love you, Becky."

"I love you, too. It just isn't the end yet. You have to wait for the end to know how everything turns out."

"You're one wise little cookie, daughter of mine."

Becky kissed her cheek. "Well, I got to go now because I need to see how Mister Henry is doing. I'll tell him you're in the wagon ready to leave, and then we'll probably be back quicker."

What a bright ray of sunshine Becky was, spreading her innocence and joy everywhere she went. Such a wonderful wee optimist. Sue usually considered herself an optimist, but she knew enough to know when everything had gone south and when it was time to give up, too. She studied the candy a little longer, then closed her eyes and popped it in, sending it with her tongue to every part of her mouth. And she remembered to suck it slow.

Ummm, it was like Heaven.

HENRY LOOKED TO THE PILE he and the children had accumulated, and he patted the goods. "This and the four mules, harness, hobbles and two hundred and fifty pounds of grain, my choice, and I'll give you a hundred in gold coin, U.S., ten furs, your choice, and five pounds of tobacco, Virginia mild, the best, smoothest smoke around." He stared at the storekeeper, willing him to take the deal, but not really expecting him to.

The man shook his head. "Two hundred gold, weighted out and proved, all your furs and twenty pounds of tobacco if it is as good as you say."

"No, sir, can't part with more than ten furs. Let's say one fifty gold, proved any way you want, and all the tobacco."

Titus stuck out his hand. "One seventy-five, the tobacco, and I get my pick of the skins."

"One fifty-five, the smoke, and you pick five, I'll pick five."

The storekeeper kept his hand out. "One sixty, the tobacco, and I pick six, you four."

"Done." Henry grasped the man's hand and shook. He faced Levi, who had been standing next to him the whole time. "Would you fetch my smallest honey jar?"

"Yes, sir."

Henry didn't think he'd ever get tired of the boy calling him sir. He grabbed a cloth from the pile, spread it out, then emptied the hard candy jar by turning it upside down and tapping on the bottom. "This should work."

Rebecca tugged on his pants leg. "What are you doing with that candy? And why did you send Levi after the honey? That wasn't part of the deal."

He smiled and winked at her. "You'll see quicker than I can tell you."

The boy returned carrying the brown jar. "Aunt Sue said she'd like to leave, if it isn't too much trouble."

Henry took it from him. "You tell her what we did?"

"No, sir. Figured you'd want to surprise her."

"Good man." He popped the heavy wire that kept the honey's lid tight, then started pouring the thick liquid into the emptied candy jar. Once it began flowing, he tipped the jar he poured from closer to level and leaned over where he could watch its bottom. When almost all of the honey had run out, he spread another napkin and reached in and pulled a handful of coins out onto the cloth.

Rebecca clapped her hands. "I see now! You've been hiding your money in the little honey jar. I love it! It's honey money!" She started jumping up and down and turning around. "Is the big one full of gold coins, too?"

Levi scowled at his cousin. "Bitty Beck! You do not ask a man about his money."

Henry fished out another handful and counted them. "Don't trouble her, son. The other one doesn't hold any coin." Henry hoped she wouldn't press it. He wouldn't lie to her, but he sure didn't want her quizzing him about the larger jar.

Real quick, the coins were cleaned, weighted, and put in the man's pocket. "Let's see to the furs and tobacco, then I'll help you hitch 'em up," Titus said. "You good folks can be on your way."

SUE WATCHED as Henry and Mister Titus paraded out to the other wagon, where Henry's wares had been stowed. He pulled out his furs and spread them, and the storekeeper began examining them immediately. Well, she supposed they'd be sleeping on the hard ground the rest of the way. She certainly didn't look forward to that.

Levi came out carrying an armload of goods. He stopped next to her and started pointing out all the wonderful things Henry had bought for him. "Look here, new boots! And he said to get two of these shirts. I got extra shot and powder, too, and oh, yes, a new hunting knife in a tooled leather sheath. It's, it's"—he shrugged—"better than grand! And wait till you see what he got Bitty Beck." He carried his haul on back to the second wagon.

Why was he acting like a five-year-old at a Sunday all-day dinner and singing on the grounds?

When Becky finally came out of the trading post, Sue could see only her hands and legs. The pile she carried covered everything else. Oh, my goodness, what had the man gone and done? This was ridiculous! Enough was enough, and too much was—Well, now she saw a dreadful, undesirable trait in Henry.

"Mama!" Even muffled, the excitement in her daughter's voice came through. "Wait till you see! Just you wait!"

Sue huffed. All this time she'd been sitting here ready to go. She'd decided to try and get to Jefferson before the buyers sailed. Turning back seemed illogical and senseless. From that point, she'd been past ready to leave. How dare he buy all that without consulting her? She couldn't believe he had the nerve to spoil her children in such an extravagant manner, as though she couldn't provide.

And he had burned daylight doing it!

When the cotton sold, she intended to get them each a pair of shoes and fabric to make some new clothes, but with all these expensive, ready-made purchases of Henry's, anything she planned seemed paltry. No one would be excited after this! Who did he think he was? And where did he think she was supposed to put it all?

"Mama, you're going to have to help me. I can't climb up there with all of this."

"Rebecca Ruth! Did you ask Mister Henry to buy all of that? You cannot go around begging for things. That's terrible!"

Sue stood. "Step back so I won't knock you over, and I'll climb down."

Becky retreated a few steps. "He told me to find something I wanted. I didn't beg or even ask for all this. I just told him I liked the ruffled apron, and he said, 'Get it!' And I was only admiring the doll, holding her and looking at her face when he hollered, 'Bring that here!' I promise, I did not ask right out for anything you see."

"He bought you a doll?" Sue could hardly believe her ears. "Dear Lord, what am I to do?"

Her daughter did her best to shift the load and look around from one side to see her. "Well! If I were you, I'd tell Mister Henry, 'Thank you, thank you, thank you so so so very very very much. You have blessed my family.'"

"Rebecca Ruth! You're such a scallywag sometimes." Sue took a new pair of shoes from one of her hands and peeled off a blue dress and the ruffled apron from her pile.

"And I got a new blue bonnet that matches my dress, too." Becky giggled. "You just wait till you see what all he got. Mister Henry sure must love me."

Love her? She thought Henry loved her? She'd be so crushed when they parted ways. Sue had to talk to Henry and tell him not to be so nice to her daughter! Well now! That sounded stupid, even to her, but she couldn't let him hurt Becky's heart. "Oh? So you think he loves you, do you?" Sue unfolded the napkin full of the heavenly candy and shook her head in disbelief.

"I'm sure of it, Mama, aren't you?" Her answer more than stunned Sue. Becky handed over a sack of cornmeal and a big package wrapped in brown paper. "It's salt pork." Her pile was now down to manageable. She wrinkled her nose and lifted her shoulders. "He got you something, too. Wait till you see." She literally sang the words, but softly; obviously so that Henry wouldn't hear her share his surprise.

"Well, he shouldn't have!" He got her something, too? Sue wondered what in the world it might be, and the butterflies came back. Suppressing any show of anticipation, she took the rest of the booty from her daughter's arms. "Now where are we going to put all this?"

Becky ran ahead to the back of the second wagon, holding her new doll by both her hands, making her dance in the air. Sue followed at first, then stopped abruptly. "Levi Baylor! What are you doing?"

He looked up. "Oh, uh, sorry, Aunt Sue. Uh, Mister Henry. He told me to uh, unhitch these mules."

"What! Unhitch the mules? Well, that's it! He's gone too far!" She stormed back to where Titus had heaped Henry's furs over his arm. "Henry Buckmeyer! Why did you tell my nephew to unhitch my mules from my wagon? You knew full well that I have been ready to go this whole time. Trying. To. Wait. Patiently on you, and, and your—your incredulous liberality!"

She dumped the load of Becky's stuff in his arms and marched back to the first wagon, where Levi worked on harnessing Dex and Daisy in front of Mil and Mabel.

Like a sledge to her left temple, it hit her. That man had gone and bartered her wagon and half her cotton for all the stupid stuff. Well! She never! It wasn't his to trade; every bit of it was hers! Well, not the furs, but good Lord have mercy! How dare he!

The man was worse than Littlejohn! She walked back to where he stood still holding Becky's things. She forced herself to be calm, as much as possible. "Henry."

He turned around holding what appeared to be all his tobacco and smiled that infuriating, smirky smile of his. "Yes, boss?"

She closed her eyes and nodded toward the side of the trading post. "I need. A word. If. You don't mind." She walked ahead of him into the shadows.

Not soon enough, he joined her, still smirking. "Something I can help you with?"

"Did you barter half of my cotton and my wagon to Mister Titus for all that merchandise you just bought and gave to my children?"

"No, ma'am."

His answer shocked her. She'd been so certain. "But. Then. Why is Levi—" At that exact moment, the boy hurried past her toward the back of the building. "Where is he going?"

"Around back."

"I can see that." Icicles dripped from her words even though the temperature had to be over ninety. "What is he doing back there?"

"Titus needed some help."

She closed her eyes, sure that smoke wafted from her ears and nose. She willed herself to be civil. She was about to slap him. If he didn't tell her what was going on, she might just lose all composure and do exactly that. He deserved worse for that smirky grin of his. A close snort pulled her eyes open.

Levi and Titus led a team of four harnessed mules right toward them.

Totally confused, she managed only . . . "What—"

"I traded for 'em." Henry moved to her side. "If we've only got three more days to get to Jefferson, I figured we'd need some extra mules."

She was speechless. Oh, Lord, why could she never hold her tongue? Why? Why? Why did she always have to jump to conclusions? Shoot her mouth off? Her face burned; it had to be three shades of red. She sighed and wished she was invisible, then spoke softly. "Henry, I can't pay for those mules."

"Don't have to. I already did."

"But—"

He waved her off. "When we're done with 'em, I should be able to get my money back. I mean to get you to Jefferson in time to sell your cotton, Sue."

She lowered her head and cleared her throat. "Thank you, Henry."

"You're welcome."

CHAPTER

TWENTY

SUE WAS PLEASED to be on the trace again and could hardly believe how easily her four mules pulled the load now. It pained her so bad that she'd been such a shrew with Henry for taking so long and buying so much. Good Lord, she chided herself, he was only trying to be wonderful. The poor man had only wanted to do everything he could to get her cotton to Jefferson in time.

Forgive me, Lord.

What a shame Henry Buckmeyer was such a confirmed bachelor, because he would make some woman a near-perfect husband. Well, except for his being unsaved. Any God-fearing woman would know better than to yoke herself up to a nonbeliever. Sue had never known a man like him, though, not even her Andy.

Henry's selflessness amazed her, especially seeing as how he'd been alone all these years. His thoughtfulness, too. He acted so much like—so much like—Christ. What a paradox.

Never ever would she have considered buying more mules to help get to market in time, but he did and wanted to please her. Had she done anything on the journey, since she'd first ridden into his yard that day, specifically to please him? She couldn't remember a thing and was shamed by that.

Oh, wait, she'd picked up a couple of pieces of deadfall. Mostly, though, she'd given him nothing but grief. She'd been stubborn, and short, and bossy. Elaine's words about trying not to be so bossy came back to her. She should have listened to her friend. But why would Henry want to be so nice to her after all that?

Probably just another one of his admirable traits—doing whatever it took to get the job done. Maybe that was it, and he hadn't done it for her sake at all, rather just to do what he'd been hired to do. No, that wasn't it. She'd seen the joy in his face when he told her he bought those mules. He'd definitely done it to please her, help her.

She remembered what Becky had said, that he'd gotten her a surprise, too, and wondered if her daughter meant the new team. They weren't really hers. They were his mules; he'd paid for them and even mentioned selling them later to get his money back. She loved the way he thought.

He wasn't just handsome and selfless and thoughtful and generous, the man was extremely intelligent, too! She sighed. No matter how good he was, he needed the Lord. So what did she do? Live a horrible example of a Christian right in front of him. Why, a stranger would think he was the saved one and she was lost!

She sighed again, disgusted with herself.

Well, remaining single must be his life choice, because no doubt every unmarried woman he'd ever met did everything in her power to hook him, whether he was saved or not. Sue thought back to Lizbeth Aikin and had a whole new appreciation for the girl's crush. Back then, Sue hadn't known him that well yet. Henry had handled the young woman so gently and sweetly.

A perfect example of what she was talking about. How in the world had the busybodies back at Sulphur Fork gotten it so wrong, saying that he was a no-good layabout? She needed to set those ladies straight.

A small incline to the horizon made Sue realize again the ease with which the four mules pulled the load compared with only two on each wagon. She might actually be able to make Jefferson in three more days. She could hardly wait until her turn came to walk. She wanted to ask Henry how many miles per hour he thought they were making now.

She searched to her right and to her left, looking for her nephew, but he was nowhere to be seen. Probably back behind, walking next to Henry, enjoying talking to the man. Both the children seemed to prefer him over her, but that wasn't hard to understand. So did she. The admission made her smile to herself.

Levi needed to be around a strong man. The difference in the boy— Well, she would hate to see him lose Henry's fellowship. Being around the man had caused such an incredible growth in him, almost like going from a child to a grown-up. She knew how to teach a girl to grow up to be a proper woman, but how could she know how to turn a boy into a man? She had no clue.

Maybe Henry would allow Levi to visit and even stay with him some after the trip was over and everyone went back home. But then, she needed Levi's help, too. Could she keep the place up and running without him? Even the thought of having gotten the cotton harvested without his help was daunting.

Where was that boy? She didn't want to wait anymore. It

seemed like it'd probably been almost two hours, and it was her turn to walk. Besides, she didn't take pleasure in not having anyone to talk to. She stood to look for him. "Leee-vi!" She turned her head the other direction. "Le-viiiiii!"

In no time, he came trotting up beside her wagon. "Yes, Aunt Sue?"

"I'm ready to walk awhile. Come on up, would you?"

"Sure." He climbed aboard.

She handed him the reins. "How are the new mules doing?"

"Oh, they're great. Good, well-mannered animals. Mister Henry seems real pleased with them."

"Well, that's excellent." She rose to jump down. Looking toward the moving ground gave her pause every time, but she'd learned how, even if she would never enjoy it. "Sure was a grand idea." She grabbed her skirt and took the leap, landing on her feet.

"Yes, ma'am," Levi hollered. "That man is chock-full of great ideas."

Sue walked slowly; the second rig rolled toward her. She couldn't wait to talk to her children's new favorite person. Though she found it a bit difficult not to be a little jealous, especially with Rebecca, she reveled in the children's relationship with such a wonderful role model, and she decided she wouldn't change a thing.

She and her daughter had always been best friends. At the same time, Sue couldn't fathom being a little girl with no daddy at all—or a daddy like Henry either. She only hoped the man's leaving at the end of the journey didn't break her little girl's heart. Maybe she could hire him to help around the place sometimes.

The mules got even with her. They truly were fine-looking

specimens. When they passed, she looked back. Her daughter slept soundly, leaning into Henry. He finally came alongside.

"So, Levi says the new team is doing great. They're beautiful animals."

Henry nodded. "Yes, ma'am. As advertised; I'm happy with 'em. Titus bought the lot off a man going west on his way home."

She had thought about what exactly to say and how to say it, even practiced while riding alone, but now that the opportunity to speak with him lay before her, she forgot everything she had rehearsed. "Henry, I, uh. Well, I wanted to tell you that I'm sorry."

"For what?"

"I guess for being me. I know I can be difficult at times—and that's putting it mildly."

He smiled. "Nothing to worry over."

"But I just cannot seem to stop my tongue from wagging or being so sharp. It seems I'm always on the edge. I don't intend to be mean, I truly don't." He looked down at her. She gave him a half smile, then faced the ground. She was proud she could have this talk without actually being face-to-face; it was easier not to have to look him in the eyes. "Holding my tongue has never been an easy thing for me. Lord knows I've prayed enough about it."

He looked down and smiled. "I've taken no offense, Sue."

"I'm so proud for that, but I'm afraid it's one of my bad traits. I do seek God's will daily."

He smiled, but this one held no hint of smirk. "Hope that helps."

Taken aback a bit, she speculated on exactly what he meant by that but decided not to pursue it. "So, to change the topic—and I thank you for letting me off the hook so easily—I've been wondering how many miles you think we're making an hour now? I can hardly believe how much easier it seems for the mules."

"Hard to say. I think we can make a fork Titus mentioned in a couple of hours. I'll know better once we're there. Should be a good place to camp."

Two hours? He was thinking of stopping so early?

"But, Henry, shouldn't we push on? How far is it anyway? And what makes it a good camping place?"

He sighed. "High ground."

She looked toward the sun. "We've got better than four hours daylight." With that, she made herself bless the Lord and, with great force of will, hush.

"If you want, we can go until dark or dark-thirty."

Why did he have to speak in that tone and look at her as though he couldn't believe what she'd just said? She hadn't been sharp in the least; she was sure of it. Didn't he appreciate that? Realize the effort it took?

"I'd like that better."

"I'd like plenty of light to see to the new team. See how they do with your mules."

"Aren't they doing great? Levi said you said they were good animals. Why would you think there might be problems? Why is it necessary to lose a whole hour or two of daylight by stopping so early? Especially when we're making such great time."

He sighed. "It's your call, boss."

She sensed irritation. "All right. Well, I'll think on it then."

"If we reach that fork before we stop, Titus advised we keep to the west. It's a bit farther on to Daingerfield's Springs, but the folks living the other way reported it being soggy after the storm. Think on that, too, and let me know. I should be in front by then."

"I will. Thank you." Well, at least he had given in on going on longer—if that's what she wanted to do. It clearly was not his preference. She let the wagon pull ahead, then slipped into the woods to take care of some pressing business. She wished she'd seen to it when in Pleasant Mound, but after the bad news about the moneymen leaving early, she hadn't been thinking too straight.

She looked toward the sky. "Oh, Lord, please don't let the buyers be gone."

Ready to drive again by the time her hour of walking had ended, she caught back up with Henry. "Want me to relieve Levi and send him back here?"

He thought about it only a minute. "I think you can handle this team fine. They're good actors. I'll hop down and walk awhile if you want to come on up."

She didn't remember until she sat next to her daughter in the second wagon that the man hadn't answered her question about how far that place was where he wanted to turn. And he had disappeared. "Becky, did you hear Mister Henry say anything about a fork?"

"No, ma'am, but Mister Titus did when we were leaving." She hugged her doll. "Is my walking turn next? I think Blue Dog needs some exercise."

Sue rolled her eyes. That dog surely was taking full advantage of his injuries. He'd been healing nicely, though, and she was thankful for that. "We'll see if there's enough light for you to have a turn this evening. Do you remember if Mister Titus mentioned how far the fork was?"

Becky nodded. "Yes, ma'am, he did. Said it was about eight miles."

Eight miles, huh? That meant Henry thought they could be doing better than two and a half miles per hour if he believed they might reach the fork with daylight left. That was wonderful. She started calculating when they should arrive in Jefferson. Taking the longer west fork meant two full ten-hour days to get there on the third day. That sure would be cutting it close if the buyers left on Friday instead of Saturday.

Gratitude for the extra four mules washed over her again. Getting there in time with just her four would've been completely impossible. So, she had to decide. She had no doubt Henry would want to stop early and go the long, drier way. Maybe she should simply agree and do what he wanted. That would be the prudent way to go.

She really would rather have the comfort of pulling into Jefferson late Thursday night, but even going the shorter route, that would mean twelve-hour days. She sighed and looked down at Becky. A ten-hour day on those hard wooden seats wasn't easy for her, and certainly not for a nine-year-old.

Sue had to trust that God knew exactly when she needed to be there. She pondered it awhile longer, then made her decision. She settled on doing what would please Henry. A peace washed over her, and she knew with certainty she'd made the right choice. That led her to a confidence that the buyers would still be there until Saturday waiting on her.

She really hated being the last one to arrive though. The others would probably all get a better price.

"So, Becky."

"Yes, ma'am?"

"When you said Mister Henry had gotten a surprise for me, too, were you talking about the four mules?"

"Well, sure."

Sue's heart fell, but she was glad in some way that he hadn't gotten her anything. It wasn't like she'd even thought about buying him something. "Well, I love them, and I'm so proud he did. They are certainly a big blessing. We're able to go much faster now, and we'll be there by Saturday morning for sure. Will you be glad the trip's over?"

"Sort of yes, and sort of no. It all depends." Becky made her doll dance in her lap, then held it to Blue's face as though the doll was giving him a kiss. "But that's not all."

"What's not all? What are you talking about?"

She looked up at her with an exasperated expression. "The mules, silly!" Then her eyes sparkled, and she grinned, nodding her head. "Mister Henry got you something else, too."

CHAPTER

TWENTY-ONE

Her agreeing to stop earlier pleased Henry. He'd have been more than disappointed if she'd chosen to push on. After all, it certainly looked as though he'd made it possible to get her cotton to Jefferson before the brokers sailed back to New Orleans. As he unhitched his mules, he tried to put that city away from his mind's eye, but that awful memory of fighting for Old Hickory wouldn't be denied. Made him relive those horrible days when he'd seen things no human being should ever see. For too long, he fought the battle again, then a hand touched his shoulder.

"You all right, Mister Henry?"

He focused. The boy stared at him. "Hey, Levi, you see to the other team?"

"Yes, sir. Want me to help you?"

"That'd be great."

For the next bit, he and the youngster unhitched and then hobbled the new team without a word or any trouble. He loved it that the boy didn't have to be told twice about a thing. "Thanks for the help."

"Any time." Levi smiled. "You sure surprised Aunt Sue."

Henry laughed, then nodded. "You hurrying past us when you went to help Titus was perfect timing, then you and him coming back with the team so quick. I loved it, even if it was just a little cruel."

"Maybe so." Levi laughed with him. "But the look on her face was something I don't think I'll ever forget."

Henry gathered his new harness; it needed oil more than he'd thought. "I know I won't." He looked off, thinking of her. "She's one fine woman, that aunt of yours."

"Yes, sir. She's been right good to me." The boy leaned back against the wagon. "Sir, can I ask you a question?"

"Sure, what's on your mind?"

"You told Littlejohn that you'd killed seven men. I know for a fact you're not a liar, but I can't imagine you— Was it true?"

"Afraid so."

"And you beat one to death with your bare hands?"

Henry nodded. "On my fifteenth birthday." He hated telling the story, hated reliving it in his dreams even worse, but if anyone other than Sue needed to know about him, it'd be Levi. "Like the fool I acted back then, I decided to give myself a couple of beers to celebrate my birth."

Sue's nephew stepped closer, appeared to want to quiz him, probably about the beer, but held his peace. Henry launched into the tale, stating the facts without any relish or embellishment. He sidestepped exactly what the lumberjack had taunted him about; surely the boy could figure it out himself.

"So I kept on hitting him. A part of me wanted to stop. I knew that I should." He took a deep breath, then let it out. "But I didn't."

"What about the other six?"

Henry glanced over to see where the ladies were and saw

only his little miss playing with Blue, lying stretched out near the cook fire. "Five in the war." He pulled his shirt up, exposing his side. "See that scar?"

Levi leaned in and stared. "What's it from?"

"An Arkansas toothpick."

"Wow, a cut like that, and you still were able to get the other guy?" The boy shook his head.

"Two men jumped my mother and me right after we left Kentucky on our way to New Orleans." He retucked his shirt. "I took the knife away from the guy who gutted me and killed his partner with it."

Levi seemed all wrapped up in his story. "What happened to the one who cut you?"

"Mother shot him." Henry looked at the ground.

"Oh." The boy stared off at the horizon. "I told that Skunk guy that I hoped he died and that I was the one that sent him to Hell."

"I heard you."

He faced Henry again with his eyes watery. "I didn't mean it. I was glad I didn't kill him. It was bad enough that I had to shoot the man."

Henry dropped the leather and pulled the boy to his chest, embracing him. "Son, you did what you had to, the right thing." He held him tight and spoke directly into his ear. "I have bad dreams sometimes about the men I killed, especially that first one, but I've not lost a bit of sleep over those two evil ruffians that tried to rob us. No telling what else they had in mind for Mother and me."

For the longest time, the boy let himself be hugged, then pushed away. "Would you have really shot Littlejohn while he had ahold of Aunt Sue?"

"Yes, I would have gotten closer and aimed away from her as much as possible."

Levi nodded. "I was not happy when she showed back up at the Dawsons' with you. Thought I could handle the hundred miles to Jefferson no problem; that we didn't need the likes of you."

Henry smiled. "Figured as much. You weren't hiding your feelings."

Levi glanced at the last of the day's light fading on the western sky, then looked back. "I was wrong, so wrong. We'd all be dead—or worse—wasn't for you." He stuck out his hand. Henry took it. "I want to thank you proper and all, and tell you that I'll be pleased as a fat tick on a hound to have you for an uncle." He grinned.

WITH THE CORN BREAD ON, Sue had innocently stepped to her larder for the potatoes and heard the men talking. She really wasn't listening until she heard the name Littlejohn coupled with seven dead men. Then she quietly turned and leaned against the far side of the wagon in the shadows. Curiosity got the better of her; she just couldn't help herself. Besides, as far as she remembered, no Scripture condemned listening in on a private conversation.

And at least she'd found out the stories on those men he killed without having to ask. She'd been wondering and pondering on how she might bring the topic up. Soon as their discussion ended, and her nephew started apologizing for his early-on bad attitude, she hurried silently to get back to the fire and cut up the potatoes.

By now, Sue counted any vegetable other than beans a treat, and fried taters always excited Becky. She scooted the Dutch oven full of corn bread to the edge of the fire and then dumped a big blob of lard into the skillet that held the browning salt pork. She looked over at her daughter. "Don't you think that dog is milking his injuries a bit too much?"

Becky faced her with a frown. "No, Mama! What in the world would make you ask such a thing? This dog saved all our lives; mine twice in the last week." She went back to rubbing him, shoulder to hip. "He's a courageous dog, the bravest dog I've ever known. I love him."

Sue smiled. "I knew that, and it's pretty obvious that he loves you just as much. Want to help slice the potatoes?"

"You're frying taters? Yes, ma'am, I'll help!" Her little girl patted the animal. "You rest, Blue. I won't be gone long." His tail whacked the ground twice, but he didn't raise his head.

Henry moseyed over with his new harness on his shoulder and an oily rag in his hand. Sue looked up, and he smiled.

She smiled back. "Hey, how'd your mules take to being hobbled?"

"Good." He dropped the leather next to a big pine and sat down, leaning against the tree. "Stood still like they'd done it before."

"Excellent. Shouldn't be too long before supper's ready." She looked past the man to where the boy stood playing mumbley-peg with his new knife in the last of the daylight. "I could use a bit more deadfall if you've a mind, Levi."

He glanced at her and nodded. "I put some under the other wagon. That all gone?"

"I don't know. Maybe you could check."

He wiped his knife on his breeches, put it away, and then walked toward the other wagon.

Henry looked up at her and grinned. "Reason I wanted to stop here, besides having enough light in case there was a problem with the new team, is that I figure we can make Jefferson in two more days."

Rebecca dropped her jaw and held her mouth open too long. "Two days, only two and we'll be in Jefferson?" She ran off. "Hey, Levi."

Sue dumped her last potato in the hot grease and shook her head in disbelief. "You really think we can make better than twenty miles a day?"

"Yes, ma'am. Once when we had to, Jackson force-marched us over a hundred miles in four days. Like to of killed the mules. Matter of fact, we had a couple that didn't make it, but we replaced them before they dropped. Old Hickory was hard, but never stupid."

"Two days?" She could hardly believe it. She'd never dreamed. "That's wonderful! So we'll have a whole extra day." She wanted to hug him, but restrained herself. She shouldn't tempt herself—or him.

"If we roll out in the morning way before the sun, and blow the mules pretty regular, grain 'em extra, and stop with the last of the light, it can happen. On your word, we'll do it."

She nodded. "Of course! I'm so excited! We'll get there in time, Henry! Why didn't you tell me this before?"

He shook his leather and poured a bit more oil onto the harness. "The off lead mule stumbled a half mile or so out of Pleasant Mound."

She grimaced. Why had he said that? So the off lead mule stumbled, so what? "I'm sorry. I don't understand what that has to do with getting to Jefferson."

"I didn't see anything for him to stumble over. If he wasn't sound, we couldn't do twenty mile a day. I watched him, but decided not to stop. He didn't do it again."

"So, you think he's fine?"

"Yes. No heat or swelling. Might be a trick he picked up. Act lame to get a break. Mules are twice as smart as horses. He may have been testing me." He chuckled, then looked toward the young doctor and her patient. "Kind of like Blue's testing your girl there."

Sue smiled. "That dog is truly something. How long you think he's going to let her keep nursing him?"

Henry shrugged and returned her smile, but this one had more little boy than she'd ever seen before. She'd never thought he was so cute as that very minute. Made her want to see if he could come out and play. Good thing she didn't have a bucket of water near, or she might have had to pour it on him.

Her musings got the butterflies to fluttering in her tummy again. Oh, if only it might ever be possible. How could she be thinking such thoughts? Could she really be falling in love? But he wasn't a Christian.

She swallowed hard and compelled herself to behave. She had to stop revisiting those notions, not allow herself even to ponder on his kindness, his patience, his intelligence, his generosity . . . how handsome he was, how he took care of everything. An uncomfortable silence ensued. What had she been talking about? Blue!

She cleared her throat. "Well, in my personal opinion, that hound has earned all the nursing he wants."

"I suppose." Henry sniffed. "What's frying?"

She glanced toward the smaller skillet. "Threw some potatoes in with the fatback. Might want to find a stopping point with your oiling there; supper's about ready."

HENRY WATCHED HER hurry back to the other wagon. He loved the way she moved. A lady's lady, but hard as a bois d'arc stump. It showed in her walk, too. He'd never known a woman so genteel and hard at the same time. He noted where he'd gotten to on the harness, then stood. The aroma of sizzling grease pulled him to the cook fire. He loved all things fried.

Levi smiled as he stepped into the firelight. "Corn bread, fatback, and some of those taters you traded for fried up all crispy. Man, I'm past ready for supper."

Sue strolled back loaded with empty plates and a jug of water. "Thank you again for all the trade goods you bought us."

"You're welcome."

She took to filling and passing out plates. She always made Henry's first. Handing him his, she added, smiling, "Even though you may have been a bit extravagant."

He ignored the comment. Other than the ring that remained his and Rebecca's secret, Titus pretty much had thrown in everything else. Well, not the bolt of cloth his soon-to-be daughter claimed would be enough for her mother's wedding dress. He didn't think he'd been extravagant in the least.

Bless her heart; Sue had been fighting money so long trying to make a living by herself, she didn't recognize any deprivation, even her own. Whatever these two youngsters wanted or needed, he'd do his best to get it for them, show them how much he appreciated—and loved—them. But Susannah would always come first.

He took the heaping plate of food from her. "Thank you, ma'am."

"You're welcome, sir."

He watched her serve the children while he ate. Once she got her own plate and sat down, he pointed his knife at her. "How'd you do it, Sue?"

"Do what?"

"Make a go of it all these years?"

She nibbled a bit of fried tater, then cocked her head. "Well, at first, we lived off the timber Andrew and Jacob—that's Levi's dad—had already cut before the accident. Then the Lord sent one nice chunk of money in from a load of saw boards they had shipped to San Antonio." She took another bite, then shook her head. "I'd forgotten all about it. A teamster we used brought it. That money was like manna from Heaven. God never let me down." She popped the rest of the fry into her mouth.

"By that time, it had become quite apparent I couldn't cut the timber or operate the steam-powered saw, so I sold the whole kit and caboodle to Phillips over DeKalb way. He's still sawing lumber last I heard." She took another dainty bite. "Then I figured, if I couldn't log our land, I'd farm it. The brothers had already cleared so much of it."

"How many acres you got?"

"Total, a little over nine hundred. Half of that belongs to Levi, though; his inheritance."

Henry smiled at her, then her nephew, giving him a little nod. She made it sound so simple, but he knew firsthand how hard it was to grub a living off the land. Her doing it alone while raising two kids, as far as he was concerned, was beyond remarkable. "How much did you farm this year?"

"Thirty-two acres of cotton, three acres of sweet corn, and another two in our garden."

"Thirty-seven with just you and Levi? That's mighty impressive."

Rebecca waved. Her faced screwed into a pinched pout. "I helped, too! Mama said she couldn't have done it without me."

Henry laughed. "I should have known that. Sorry I left you out, little miss."

"Oh, I forgive you, although it is very hard for me to even think you'd ever forget me."

"I just didn't—"

"Rebecca Ruth, quit making Mister Henry feel bad."

The girl jumped up and ran and hugged his neck. "I didn't mean to make you feel bad!" Up close, she whispered in his ear, "I'm sorry, Mister Daddy."

He hugged her back. "No, no. Don't you worry about it. You didn't hurt my feelings."

She looked at her mother, but held her tongue and went back to her plate. "I love fried taters, Mister Henry. Sometimes, I think better than candy. Oh, um, speaking of candy . . ."

"Re-bec-ca." Sue shook her head no at her daughter.

"Oh, Mama, I was just saying—"

"I heard what you were saying, young lady."

Henry laughed. "Well, even if she hadn't mentioned it, I was going to suggest we all have a piece after supper. If it was all right with you."

Levi chimed in. "Sounds good to me." He glared at the girl. "If Bitty Beck didn't ruin it already."

She stuck her tongue out at him.

Sue stood with her empty plate "Oh, I suppose we'd all enjoy that very much. It'll be all right since Mister Henry said he was already going to offer." Levi handed his plate to her. "After all the dishes are dried and put away," she added, taking her daughter's plate.

Rebecca jumped up and down, clapping. Blue was at her side wagging his tail like he was going to have a piece himself. Knowing Rebecca, she probably would be sharing.

CHAPTER

TWENTY-TWO

HENRY'S EYES POPPED OPEN. He listened for a bit. Frogs croaked to each other, locusts played their hectic, overlapping songs, and a distant owl bragged over his wisdom asking Whoo was as wise? Henry scooted over and peered at the moon. It rode the western night sky, casting enough light to catch the mules by.

Levi lay on his stomach, dead to the world. Henry decided to let him sleep awhile.

After the necessaries, he stirred the cook fire, added kindling and then a few medium-size branches. It first loosed an ascending trail of smoke, then came to life.

"Morning." Sue rested her chin on her propped-up hand, staring at him from under the other wagon. "Anything you'd especially like for breakfast?"

He laughed. "I'd love some bacon, three eggs over easy, four of your ace-high biscuits—two smothered in thick, creamy gravy, and another two dripping with honey." He held a finger up. "And ice-cold milk, half a gallon at least."

She grinned. "You don't want much, do you?"

He dipped the coffeepot full from the water barrel,

dropped in a handful of coffee grounds, and then set it on the fire. "Hey, you asked."

"When we get back home, I promise to make you a breakfast like that." She scooted out, then pulled herself up with the wagon wheel. "I was thinking more along the lines of frying up some potatoes and fatback again, if you wanted, or I could save the grease for gravy. It'd have to be made with water and not milk though, and biscuits, of course." She scrunched her shoulders and reached for her shawl. "With or without some of your honey. I sure am enjoying these cooler mornings."

"Yes, ma'am. I'll take my biscuits with, and might be a good idea to make a second batch, maybe grease up four potatoes and let them bake for later. You might not want to cook tonight. It'll be a hard day."

"I can do that."

He looked toward the still sleeping Levi. "When the coffee makes, best get my right-hand man up and at 'em."

"Of course."

He nodded, then walked out hunting mules. He found his four grazing together fifty yards from the wagon. Starting with the off back mule and finishing with the one that had stumbled, he caught, grained, watered, and then harnessed each. Before he chained them to the wagon, he ran a hand over each leg, checking for hot spots or swelling, talking to them as he went. Each in turn proved sound.

All sixteen hooves were examined and picked clean, with attention to smelling their frogs. After he secured the last chain, Henry stood straight and tousled the near ear of the off lead mule. He asked himself as much as them, "You boys ready? Got a long day ahead."

They didn't answer, but he figured they were, and so was

he. Not that he looked forward to it. He'd done it before, except that time he didn't have a boy and little girl to see to or a boss he was in love with. Well, he sort of loved Old Hickory, leastwise really respected the man. That march of his had put everyone to the test. All had done what he said, but there wasn't a one happy about it.

Sue strolled toward him holding two steaming cups. "Saw you were finished hitching your mules, and thought you might be ready for some coffee."

He took the cup she offered. "Yes, ma'am, thank you."

"Sure. Breakfast is getting close."

"Good." He looked to the eastern sky, not even false dawn yet. "I'd like to pull out first bit of light we get."

She nodded. "Levi's almost got my mules hitched and ready."

"Did you notice if he grained them extra?"

"Yes, I noticed; and he did. Said you told him to."

Henry smiled. "That's one good boy you've got."

"Thank you."

"If you're of the same mind, I think we shouldn't have anyone walking, and that I need to be in front the whole time."

IF YOU'RE OF THE SAME MIND, Sue repeated with a cynical tone in her head, like it made one iota of difference whether her mind matched his. No matter what, he wanted it his way and no other. Patrick Henry Buckmeyer thought he always knew best.

She made the disgusted ooooogh sound in her head but refrained from giving it voice, still feeling a little indebted to Henry's generosity, but she had stopped early yesterday like he wanted. So . . .

Instead of acting ugly, she willed her volume soft and her tone sweet and was proud of herself for it. "Oh. I thought we needed to save the mules. That isn't important anymore?"

He sat his coffee down and rummaged in the wagon, bringing his honey jar out, then picked the cup back up and headed toward the fire. She followed. His usual eating position was sitting by a tree, leaning his back against it, so it didn't surprise her when he went straight for the biggest tree close to the fire.

With one leg stretched full out, he bent the other. She tended to breakfast and wondered if he might ever be planning to answer her question. Was he really trying to irritate her?

He took another sip. "With four mules to a wagon now, I figure we should save the people instead." He grinned. "The smidgen of weight saved isn't worth wearing any of us out."

That sounded logical. He always sounded so logical. But being afoot for a piece didn't wear her out. "I enjoy my turn walking." She took the biscuits off the fire and turned the fatback. She could feel him watching her. Why was he doing that? "Don't you?"

"If you choose to walk, that's your prerogative, of course."

Why, thank you, Mister Buckmeyer, for noticing. In her head her words dripped sarcasm. Her prerogative, indeed. She glanced over at him. "Would it offend you if I asked why you want to be in front all the time now?" She didn't care to eat his dust the whole day. That time, her spoken words carried a tone, but she really didn't mind so much.

He tossed his dregs and made his way to the coffeepot. "Not at all."

She lifted it and poured his cup full again.

"Thank you, ma'am." His words were gentle and kind and

free from irritation. "You have any idea how to pace a team to make two mile an hour?"

"Hmm, no." She hadn't thought of that. Now he was making her sound stupid. "Speed 'em up a little, make them go faster, I suppose."

He grinned his crooked, little-boy grin and raised both eyebrows. "I see. So, that's how. Now do you want to drive lead then, boss?"

"No, I suppose not." What a—a wise arse! Oh my goodness! Susannah Baylor! What are you thinking? It relieved her that response stayed in her head and didn't travel to her lips. "I was just wondering. I mean I've driven the lead wagon most the way here."

"And done a right fine job of it, too."

She glanced at him, then started filling the first plate.

Levi moseyed up. "Looks like I timed that pretty good."

"Would you get Becky up, honey?"

"Yes, ma'am." He went to the closer wagon, kneeled beside it, and used his singsongy voice. "Bitty Beck, Bitty Beck. Always last in bed. Time to get on up now, you little sleepyhead."

She sat up and grinned, then threw her arms around his neck. "Give me a ride to breakfast, Levi!" He stood with his giggling cousin hanging on and lumbered back to the fire.

Sue handed Henry his plate heaped with food. "So how far is it to Captain Daingerfield's Springs?"

" 'Bout twelve miles."

"Six hours, huh? Maybe a little less. So we'll get there around midday?"

He had filled his mouth with a chunk of biscuit covered in gravy, so he only nodded. She handed Levi his plate, then got her daughter's.

Once Henry had swallowed, he put up a finger. "You make a fine water gravy, and yes, around noon's what I figured."

"Twelve miles by midday. Why so quick? You planning on going more than twenty if we can?"

"No, thinking to cover the majority in the cool of the day, less later." He passed the honey to the boy.

Sue finally settled with her plate in her lap. "Well, that's a good idea. Plus, it'll give us some time to fill the water barrels at the springs."

He smiled and nodded.

She was glad he didn't say that's what he'd planned, although she figured he had intended to. He seemed to stay ahead of her all the time.

During the rest of breakfast, talking dropped to a minimum. As soon as Becky finished her plate, she hurried out of camp. "Come on, Blue, let's take a little walk 'fore we go. I'll find me a bush, and maybe you can find you a squirrel!" The dog followed her with his tail awaggin'.

Levi stood, too, and handed Sue his empty plate. "Thanks, Aunt Sue. Sure was good." He turned. "Anything else you need me to do, Mister Henry?"

"Checked your mules' hooves?"

"Yes, sir. They're all ready to pull out. Yours need anything?"

"No, sir. They're ready, too, but thank you." Henry pointed to his honey jar. "Suppose you could stash that for me?"

"Glad to." The boy picked up the jar. "You had any yet, Aunt Sue?"

"Thank you, Levi, I'm fine."

He turned and headed toward the far wagon.

Sue smiled after him, then faced Henry, letting him share the boy's smile. "Thank you for being so good to him. He needs more time with a man, and you're a great influence. You wouldn't believe the difference I see in him." She finished her last bite of biscuit. "Maybe once we're back home, you could come get him from time to time, take him fishing or hunting with you some. I'm sure he'd enjoy that."

"You've done a fine job raising him up, Sue. He's going the right direction." Standing, Henry reached toward the sky and stretched. "Guess I'm ready to go when you are. Let me know." He yawned and turned.

Sue stood, wondering why he didn't readily agree about having Levi over. But never mind that, she had more pressing issues. She grabbed his arm. "Wait, Henry. There's something I need to talk with you about."

"Sure. What's on your mind?"

She could still offer up another subject, maybe him not answering about having Levi. No, she knew it was the Lord. He'd been convicting her until she fell asleep last night and then started again that morning about the eavesdropping. She had to get the guilt off her chest if she was going to have any peace.

She drew in a big breath. "I need to ask you to forgive me."

A shocked look came across his face. "What for?"

"I didn't mean to, except I guess I did. I could have left." Tears welled in her eyes. Shame gnawed at her, but she did not want to cry like a little girl in front of him. She turned and opened her eyes wide so the tears wouldn't fall and give her away.

"What are you talking about?"

She faced him again, then examined the ground in front of her, rubbing her forehead. This was harder than she'd expected, but she had to spit it out and get it over with. "Oh, I was at the wagon getting potatoes for supper last night. I heard Littlejohn's name mentioned, and I—I—well, I didn't leave. I turned around like a sneak in the shadows and listened to yours and Levi's private conversation." She looked up at him. "I'm glad to know the circumstances, though. Glad to know that none of those killings were your fault, Henry."

His eyes, like daggers, bore into hers, cutting into the depth of her soul.

She'd never seen him angry before. "I'm sorry. Will you forgive me?"

He took a turn looking at the ground. When he finally raised his head again, he took a breath and blew it out. "What else can I do? Of course, I forgive you."

He stood there, not moving, as though he would like to say something else.

She wanted to step in closer and let him wrap his arms around her and hold her and comfort her, but she held still.

WITHOUT SAYING what was on his mind, Henry walked to his wagon and began checking the harness. "Levi!"

The boy ran to his side. "Yes, sir."

"How about you ride with me?"

"Sure, be proud to."

"Take care of that fire 'fore you board, would you?"

"Yes, sir. Sure will."

Henry pulled out in the lead before false dawn and chided himself for not asking her about Andrew when he'd had the chance. Though he didn't like being spied on, it actually relieved him that she knew, especially about the time when he was fifteen. No way should she have been listening in on a private conversation, but confessing sure took a heap of guts; all the more a witness to her courage and strength, her asking him for forgiveness.

He grinned. More than he'd done that night he eavesdropped on the Dawsons' porch.

Besides, he'd intended to tell her anyway.

Less than two hours out, a few cabins dotted either side of the trace, marking the place Titus had told him to turn back east toward the springs. He'd met Major Pitts, who first settled the area a couple of years back; if he'd had more time, he'd try and locate him, but he'd have to get back to Pittsburg some other day. He wanted to make Captain Daingerfield's Springs by noon.

Henry shook his head. "Territory sure is growing."

"Yes, sir." Levi nodded. "I been hearing Jonesboro and Pecan Point was busting at the seams, over a hundred families in either one now. Even Sulphur Fork, number of folks on the prairie's about doubled in the last year. You hear about that convention they had back in the spring?"

Henry turned the team and headed southeast. "Indeed, I did. Friend of mine attended and stood with the rest demanding that Mexico legalize whites' immigration."

"I don't understand why they don't want folks coming to settle Tejas."

"Well, the way I heard it, a couple of years ago, Mexico's President Bustamante outlawed all immigration from the United States—that's what the convention was all about. And he ordered all the slaves released. Cotton grangers didn't much care for that. Religion's an issue, too. Mexicans are mostly Catholic."

Levi sat up straight and stretched. "Used to be a few of those *presidios* around our parts. Wasn't any fighting, but they up and left anyway. Would you fight over the land?"

"All depends." Not fond of talking about war, Henry brought the topic of conversation to a close. "Don't suspect there's anything the Mexicans can really do about all the easterners flocking in."

Right about then, a dog from one of the homes ran out to the road barking and checked the wagons' smells. Old Blue Dog's neck hairs had to be bristled, but no fight ensued. Henry's dog never did like another mutt around. He could just picture Rebecca making the hound stay down on his sick pallet.

Midmorning, the off lead mule stumbled again. Henry watched him hard, then decided to ignore it. The old boy must be ready for a blow. "Remind me to check my off lead mule when we stop. He stumbled again."

"Yes, sir. Sure like this pace we're on. Like visitin' with you, too, sir, about important things. I'll tell you true, I love Aunt Sue, and Bitty Beck, but women, well, sometimes, they about chatter my ears right off."

Henry laughed. "Know what you mean, son."

"I don't know why the women can't just stick to riding together and leave us men to discuss politics, the war, and what's happening in the territory. Or ride quiet, you know? Women seem like they have to be talking all the time. You'd think they enjoy each other's conversation same way we do."

They rode in silence until the houses ended again and the land stretched out before them. "Ever seen pines tall as these, Levi?"

"No, sir, never did."

By the time the sun neared straight overhead, the next smattering of cabins came into view. Most were rough-hewn log and cedar-shingled hovels, but one good-size, downright impressive clapboard home anchored the settlement.

"Wow, Aunt Sue didn't think Daingerfield had a store or nothing."

"Didn't last time I was through."

"Why's there so many people then? I counted more than thirty."

The wagon rounded a curve. "There's your answer."

"What's that?"

Henry pointed up ahead. "That's why. See that fellow talking to the others?"

"Yes, sir."

"Well, he's pitching those folks to sell 'em some miracle potion that he claims will cure consumption or whooping cough or take warts off your nose. Maybe all three." Henry shook his head. "Don't ever believe a guy like that. All his little bottle will do is get you soaked, maybe worse. He's trying to bilk 'em out of their coin."

As the wagon pulled closer to the springs, even more people clustered together in little groups. Women tended fires and children scampered wild, obviously thrilled to have playmates to romp with. Wagons dotted the area for a good ways out. "Now what do you suppose this is all about? Think they all came for the springwater?"

Henry pointed to the right. "Somebody's set that tent up over yonder. May be having a camp meeting."

"Aw, no! Aunt Sue's going to want to stay and hear the preaching, I guarantee it."

Henry laughed. "Best not guarantee what a woman is liable to do." He winked at the boy. "I suspect she'll not want to be here a moment longer than necessary."

Levi nodded. "You're likely right; I'd say Aunt Sue wants to get to Jefferson more than anything. Seen it before, her getting a powerful bug about a thing. Just like that cotton. I's ready to give up on it more than once, but she wouldn't have it. Never got so sick of anything as chopping them cotton rows."

"That's hard work, all right."

Levi grinned. "While she prayed for rain, I asked for hot and dry so the weeds and grasses wouldn't grow. Should've known the Lord wouldn't have listened to me over her. Rains came, weeds growed, and I hoed." He held out his hands palms up. Calluses on calluses. He stared at 'em a minute then wiped 'em on his britches.

"Those show you're a hard worker. I'm sure your aunt appreciates all your help."

"Yes, sir, I suppose."

A couple of buckboards sat off to the side of the tent, and a string of horses stood tied to a picket line. Some of the men threw horseshoes, and a group of boys played mumbley-peg. A mess of tables sat end to end, and several ladies scurried around loading them with covered dishes and loaves of bread wrapped in towels and jars of various colored liquids.

"I sure wouldn't mind staying for dinner unless they're eating after the preachin'." Levi laughed. "Them church ladies can lay down a spread!"

Henry stopped at the springs behind a buckboard. A man and boy worked at filling their water barrel. He nodded toward a big post oak up the hill and to the south a ways off. "Good spot to let the animals blow a bit; want to take them over once we're done?"

"Yes, sir. Should I unchain them?"

"No, they'll be fine staying in the traces."

"I'll go let Aunt Sue know what we're doing and see if she wants to stay and eat."

CHAPTER

TWENTY-THREE

SUE REINED IN THE MULES in line behind Henry. Before noon, just like he'd said. And the team hardly acted tired at all. The people everywhere excited her, and Becky obviously couldn't wait to get down. Since the outskirts of the settlement, Sue had searched the crowd for her neighbors, but hadn't seen any.

Levi walked up next to the side opposite her. "Hey, Auntie." He pointed up a hill. "After our turn, Mister Henry's planning on blowing the mules up there by the big post oak."

Becky stood on the wagon seat. "I want to go play."

Sue knew her daughter so well. "I suppose that'll be all right. Don't go far; stay in sight."

"Whoopee! Catch me, Levi!" She sailed through the air and into his arms, and then squirmed to be down. He held on, though. "Let go, put me down! I'm going to play."

He held her even tighter, but she squirmed and looked almost too strong for him. "See that big oak over there?" He pointed, then tickled her with his pointing finger.

She wiggled and giggled. "I see it; I see it. Now put me down!"

"That's where our wagons will be when we get done here. Understand?"

"Yes! All right, let me go now! Bye, Mama! Come on, Blue!"

Levi stood there a minute. Becky ran toward the children with her tail-wagging shadow on her heels. "I'll pull your wagon up if you want to get on down, too."

"Well, thank you, son. I'll take you up on that." She took his hand and climbed down.

Henry pulled up close when the buckboard in front moved off, and Levi urged the second team forward, then locked the brake and hopped down. Sue straightened her shawl and watched him get to work helping Henry without a word. The man grained using his hat while Levi hauled water to the barrel and filled the bucket to give the mules a drink.

She stretched her back and then lifted her hat and fanned herself a bit before heading down toward the tables. A woman stepped forward and offered Sue her hand. "Hello, saw you folks pull in." She smiled and looked toward a group of children. "That's my daughter, Nancy, over there who your little girl's playing with. My name is Louise, Louise Koiner. I have a fresh pot of coffee if you'd like to sit a spell."

"I'd be proud to, thank you. I'm Sue Baylor."

The lady took her arm. "I have a son, too, Michael. How old is your boy?"

"Fourteen, he's my nephew, but I've raised him, so he is mine."

The woman led Sue to their campsite and spread a quilt. "Richard dear, would you please hand me that cup right there?" He did, and she poured it full. The coffee smelled wonderful.

HENRY FINISHED WITH THE SECOND WAGON, then drove it up next to the first one. He made sure all the mules rested in the shade, then jumped down, checking the sun's position. Another half hour might be in order. He strolled to where he'd seen Sue visiting and, on the way, spotted Rebecca with Blue right beside her.

He then found Levi with boys about his size. He grimaced when Levi took what looked to be a coin from one of the others. Henry shook his head, certain the boy's aunt wouldn't approve; she'd asked if he was a gambler. Maybe the boy needed him even more than he thought.

A man greeted him with an extended hand. "Good to meet you, Mister Baylor; your wife tells me you're on the way to Jefferson."

Covering her mouth, Sue made a little choking noise. Henry took the man's hand and shook vigorously. "Name's Buckmeyer, sir. Patrick Henry Buckmeyer. Go by Henry."

Sue cleared her throat. "I employed Mister Buckmeyer to help me get my lint to market."

The man touched the brim of his hat. "Sorry for the misunderstanding; pleased to meet you, Henry."

He nodded and let himself be introduced all around, then listened politely to the conversation for a bit before excusing himself. "Good to meet you folks." He turned toward Sue. "With your leave, boss, I'll be about finding someone who's traveled the trace from here to Jefferson. Care to join me? Or do you prefer to visit a little longer?"

She rose. "No, no. That's a good idea. I'd enjoy accompanying you, Henry." Turning, she leaned in and hugged the lady. "Thank you, Louise, for your hospitality." She faced the men and took their leave, as did Henry. He held out his arm, and she hooked hers through it.

He headed toward the springs. "Could I ask a question?"

"Of course." She smiled as if he'd walked right into a trap. "If I can ask one of my own."

"Deal." He took two steps. "You still in love with your husband?"

She showed no change of expression but patted his arm. "Andy and I met my last year in school; he only courted me a few months, but I suppose I loved him. Lord knows I missed him something terrible after he passed, but I did my grieving. With so much suddenly on my plate, wasn't much time for sadness. I believe God's healed my heart."

He liked her answer, but it led to another question.

Before he could frame it, she pulled him to a stop and stepped out in front. "Why'd you have such a reputation as a layabout?"

He smiled and looked to the ground, shaking his head. "Best I can figure, it started four years ago. One night, I ran into a couple of men I knew from the war. They told me about Jackson finally getting voted in." He shrugged. "They also were hauling a big load of rotgut. We got to toasting our new president.

"Next thing I knew, the three of us were under their wagon drunk as skunks, and it was the middle of the next morning. Of course, it happened right by the Jonesboro ferry, so every gossip who didn't see me heard about it soon enough. Mother got twenty-something reports."

"Are you accustomed to drinking a lot?"

He smiled at her. That was two questions. "No, ma'am. Never liked beer; haven't had a drop of hard liquor since. I was sick for a week." He held a hand up. "Back to the layabout thing. Wasn't too long after, maybe January or February of 'twenty-nine, anyway three of Mother's lady friends came to visit.

"I'd been out hunting most of the night. You should have seen the disapproving looks when I came out of my room mid-afternoon rubbing sleep from my eyes. Mother wasn't the type to make excuses; she hated gossips anyway. I figured between that and the time at Jonesboro—throw in not going to church with Mother—must have kept tongues wagging to this very day."

Sue nodded. "You're probably right. I heard how sorry you were more than once. Can I ask why you didn't attend services with your mother?"

"What's this, a three-for-one deal?" He laughed. "I'd like to delve in and find out exactly what you heard sometime, but right now, I've got another question of my own to get us back to even." Besides, he deemed his a more important topic. "Our third night out, you cried yourself to sleep. What was that about?"

"Oh, a combination of things. Recounting Andy's accident earlier—that's a recurring nightmare—made me miss Andy and my daddy." She shook her head. "The wagon getting stuck, not trusting God. Doubtin' I'd get to Jefferson." She glanced toward where the church family sat, then turned back. "Plus, I thought I'd missed a chance and let the Lord down. Just one of those nights, I guess. You'd be safe in saying I was feeling all sorry for myself, doing a little wallowing in self-pity."

Something pulled his attention away from Sue; she followed his gaze. Levi squared off with one of the boys, and a man hurried toward them.

Henry nodded. "Come on, looks like Levi might need some help."

Her nephew held out his open hand, palm up, obviously arguing, but she couldn't hear exactly what was being said. The other boy glanced at the man hurrying over. "Pa! This son of Satan's bilking me."

Henry broke into a lope. For a few strides, Sue matched him, then pulled ahead.

The father stopped next to his son. "Wait just one minute here." He stared sternly at Levi.

For a few beats of her pounding heart, Levi stared back, then looked away just as Henry reached the fast-growing circle of onlookers. He turned back. "I'm no cheater; beat him fair and square. Your boy owes me two bits copper."

The man looked at his son. "That true? Were you gambling?"

"He made me, Pa. Said I couldn't play with them if I didn't."

The real bilker's pa turned back. "That right?"

Levi shrugged. "Yes, sir. All of us were matching for money when he first came up, but we didn't make him play. He watched awhile then wanted in the game."

The man drew his boy behind him and stepped toward Levi. "Are you a child of God, boy; saved and properly baptized?"

"Well, no, sir. I—"

"Then you are a son of Satan, like my boy said. You need to repent and be baptized, or you're going straight to Hell, condemned for eternity! Sure as me and mine will go to Heaven."

Sue stepped into the circle. "You, sir, need to shut. Your. Mouth."

"I'll tell you one thing." Levi joined her. "I may be Hell bound, but your son's a cheatin' liar. Last I heard, God doesn't cotton to either. A bet's a bet, sir, and I expect him to pay up. You want to go to your pocket, that's fine with me."

"Why, you little devil." The man lunged toward Levi. Sue moved to step in from of him, but a blur suddenly appeared from her left.

Henry stood between her and the man. "Levi is not a devil. Your boy played, he needs to pay."

The man looked around the circle of young men, who chimed right in.

"Levi's the one telling the truth."

"Yeah, your son made the bet."

"And he lost, too."

"Yeah, fair and square!"

Others gathered on its perimeter, the circle now two, even three deep in places. The man leaned back a bit, then stuck out his jaw. "Our money is for the Lord's work."

Levi stepped up next to his protector. Sue loved having Henry on her side. The boy touched Henry's arm. "It's fine, sir. If he allows his boy to be a cheater, so be it. It's only two bits."

Henry looked from the man to Sue, then exhaled. "All right then, it's your call, son. You ready? Best we be leaving."

"Yes, sir. I am."

The man's voice boomed from behind him. "You still need to repent, boy! Hell's fire awaits you. Tomorrow is never promised."

Henry spun around. "If you don't shut your loud mouth, I will shut it for you."

"You cannot silence God's message or his messenger."

Henry balled his fist and moved closer. Levi grabbed his arm. "Leave him be, Mister Henry, please. Ain't worth it."

Sue pulled on his other arm. "Henry, don't let that chowderhead get your goat. Let's leave." For a heartbeat, she thought he wasn't going to come and tugged harder. He glared at the rude preacher but finally came with her. Levi followed. She slipped her hand into Henry's.

Levi cupped his fingers beside his mouth. "Hey, Bitty Beck! Time to go. Come on."

Her daughter put her hands on her hips. "But I'm having so much fun! Can't we just stay a little longer? I have a new friend." She turned and went back to her game.

Sue could hardly believe it. "Rebecca Ruth! Now! I know you hear me." She turned toward the children. "You do as Levi told you, young lady, and get over here! We're leaving."

Becky stomped her foot but obeyed. She marched up the hill staring at the ground the whole way. On arriving, she pinched up her face at her cousin. "I don't know why we have to go so soon."

The troublemaker called again. "Repent, stop your sinning, and be baptized, boy, before it's too late."

Sue spun. "Oooo!" She faced her nephew. "Get her into the wagon, Levi."

He grabbed his cousin's hand and kept walking.

Becky wiggled. "Stop! You're hurting me." She stuck her tongue out.

"Come on, and then I won't!" He stuck his out right back. "You're so spoiled, you stink!"

"Levi! How old are you?" Sue turned from her nephew to the girl. "Rebecca Ruth, behave!" She stormed down the hill. "Now, you listen to me, Mister Preacher Man. You'd best not say another word to my boy. Do you understand me?" She shook her finger in his face. "Love is patient and kind, and you're being nothing but ugly and rude, sir. We are to lift up the name of Christ, and then He—not you or any other man—will draw men to Himself. Or haven't you read the Good Book? 'There is therefore now no condemnation'!"

"To those who are in Christ, sister. Your son admitted by his own word that he isn't walking after God, but the devil. Why, he led my son straight into sin, and then tried to bilk him."

That scripture had backfired on her. Flustered, she tried to think of another about not condemning. "I have no doubt in my heart that Levi will one day come into God's Kingdom, sir, but not from being ridden with guilt and shame by the likes of you! He'll accept Christ because of love, not the hate you peddle or your so-called Christian son's bad example."

The man waved her off. Pieces of scripture raced past her mind's eye, but she couldn't grab ahold of any. Oh, she wanted something to hurl at this self-righteous oaf. "You low-down—"

"Sue, come on, let it go." Henry gently took both her elbows from behind and spoke close to her ear. "There's another thing about love to remember; it hardly even notices a wrong done. Let's get on back on the trace."

She let him turn her around. "Jesus told that woman caught in adultery that He didn't condemn her, didn't He?"

"He did."

She glanced over her shoulder at the offensive croaker, then back to Henry again. "I wish I knew the scriptures better! And could quote them when I needed to."

He didn't answer.

She did know the Bible, but it all got mixed up sometimes. Be angry and sin not. How could she do that? Henry did. How could he remain so calm and composed in light of such injustice? Like, like—just like Christ. She shook her head and stared at the ground. Her actions certainly hadn't glorified the Lord. Yet she was the one claimed to belong to Him.

Walking beside Henry, she became aware he held her hand again and remembered taking his earlier. It felt so good and seemed so natural. His being right about leaving earned her appreciation for getting her out of there, and also for standing up for Levi. Having a wonderful man on her side, especially a strong, wise, and gentle man like Henry Buckmeyer, made such a difference.

She looked at him; he headed straight toward the wagon. She loved that face. The realization shocked her. When had her heart let him in and come to love him so deeply? Indeed, she loved him. She squeezed his hand, and he glanced over and smiled. She loved Patrick Henry Buckmeyer. Unsure exactly how, she determined to spend the rest of her life with him.

Just then, at the height of her sweet revelation, the promise she'd made to God reared its head. The vow had served her well, weeded out those who professed love, but would it hurt her now? Every suitor had quit coming around once she told him. What if Henry did likewise? Or if her father refused again to give his blessing?

Could she marry him without it? Or without him being a believer?

And if she did, would he die, just as Andy had?

She shook her head. Faithfulness to God trumped everything else. No way would she go back on her promise. No compromise either. Henry had to agree to go and get her stubborn daddy's blessing. Then her father had to give Henry her hand; he simply must, and she refused to think on any other outcome.

Sue looked toward the sky and silently prayed, "And God, it is Your business to get him saved before we get to Daddy's. You know he'll never give his blessing if Henry isn't a believer."

CHAPTER

TWENTY-FOUR

HENRY HELD SUE'S HAND until he reached what had become her wagon, then still didn't let go. He bent and braced his knee, lifting her hand, and she used him to climb aboard. She finally pulled away and seated herself. Levi heaved his cousin up on the other side, and Blue jumped up at the girl's feet.

"Mama, Levi said I had to ride with you! It's not fair!" Becky sat forward on the bench with her arms crossed over her chest. "He got to ride all the way here with Mister Henry, so it should be my turn. Tell him! Tell him that it's my turn, and he has to ride with you!"

"Well, my, my, my. What a sad thing to have to spend a little time with your mother, Rebecca Ruth. How would it make you feel if I didn't want to ride with you?"

Becky dropped her hands to her lap and hung her head. "I'm sorry, it's just that—"

Levi spit, then threw his hands in the air. "You can ride with him tomorrow, stinky." He glanced up at his aunt, shaking his head. "You've spoiled her so bad!"

Sue looked to each of the children and then at Henry. "So, I guess everyone would rather ride with you." She smiled.

"But what can I say? I certainly understand. I'd rather ride with you, too."

He shook his head and smiled back. "We best get going."

Once aboard, Henry unlocked the brake and waved the reins over the team. "Hey, now." The animals tossed their heads and threw themselves into moving the load. They were a good team; he should be able to make a profit on them. Circling back around toward the trace, he recognized a granger waiting in line at the springs on the Jefferson side.

He handed the reins to the boy. "Keep 'em at a good clip, I need to talk to that man. I'll catch up." He jumped off the wagon and waited for Sue to come beside him, then nodded toward the springs. "I'm going to see if there's any news. I'll be back directly."

She nodded and slapped her team's backs with the reins. "Come on now."

After a quick handshake and hello, Henry quizzed the man. While the granger talked of the trace and cotton prices, Henry kept an eye on the wagons. Once the man went to talking about the weather, Henry excused himself and ran off after Sue's wagon. Didn't take him long to catch up.

She glanced down when he came alongside. "What'd you find out?"

"Good news is, the buyers are still there and paying six cents a pound for high-quality lint like yours."

"Oh, Henry! Six cents?" Her face shone. "That's a wonderful report!"

"Bad news is that their steamer is getting full fast, and he said there was a long line when he left."

The glow faded. "Oh, no! Do you think we'll make it in time?"

"We're going to give it our best. He said there's two steep pulls between here and Jefferson, and that the trace is in fair to good shape. Bad ruts in a few places, but with four mules to a wagon, shouldn't be much of a problem. Only those two hills might slow us down some."

"How far is the first one? Will we get to it today?"

"Not sure, he didn't say."

Becky stretched out and grinned a big ol' grin. "Me and Trudy, that's what I named my doll. Anyway, we get to ride with you tomorrow because it's my turn. How close will we be from Jefferson then?"

"We should get there tomorrow evening."

"Oh, good, so I'll get to ride with you for the whole day." She opened her eyes wide. " 'Cause I have some things I want to talk with you about, and we'll probably need the whole day." She nodded that fast little nod of hers where she kept on nodding.

Sue looked at him and shook her head. "What have you done to my children? What did you ever do to win such admiration from the little darlings? Tell me, please." She laughed.

He shrugged. "I don't know. Like a new toy, I guess. Best get on back to Levi. We need to pick the pace up a bit."

He ran ahead and climbed into the wagon. The boy handed him the reins. Henry urged the team into a faster walk and, though he hated repeating himself, told the boy everything he'd just told his aunt. For a while, the ride was quiet, but the peace didn't last long.

"So, Mister Henry, how fast do you think I had 'em going, and how fast would you say they're going now?"

"You were at a mile or a little over; I'd say we're closer to a mile and a half or two now, maybe even a bit faster."

"How can you tell? Do you pick a tree up ahead and count or something?"

"No. You get a feel for it. Comes from experience. You'll have to go through the mill, but you'll get it by and by."

The boy sat silent awhile and then nudged him in the rib with his elbow. "So when are you going to ask her?"

Henry started to play dumb, but he knew exactly what Levi was talking about. He didn't have the answer though. "I don't know. Think I ought to wait."

"For what?"

"Maybe until we get to Jefferson and get her cotton sold."

"But why wait? Even I can tell that you're perfect for her. You're exactly what Aunt Sue needs."

He pondered on it before saying more, and then sighed. "Well, then there is the vow."

The boy sat back and grinned. "Oh, so you've heard about that, have you?"

Henry looked over at him. "Who hasn't?"

SUE RODE AWAY THINKING on what Henry had told her. She tried to figure out what she'd do if the buyers had all the cotton they wanted. She'd not considered that scenario at all, never even thought to. If there were no buyers, she didn't know what she'd do except hope and pray that Henry would have a plan.

One thing she did know. She'd learned long ago that worrying about tomorrow never changed a thing, so she dismissed that elusive day and its troubles and focused on a completely different subject. That wasn't a hard thing for her.

Henry.

She'd been thinking a heap on him of late. Never would she have imagined how much she missed the simple act of strolling along on a man's arm; the sense of belonging, of having someone. Admitting she loved him, even to herself, had not come easy, but now she knew how powerful much she wanted to spend the rest of her life beside him.

But what if he didn't feel the same way? She certainly hadn't been acting as though she had any interest in him past getting her cotton sold then safely back home. Maybe he couldn't wait until he made it back to Sulphur Fork and was rid of her bossy, angry self. But then, his eyes . . .

Oh, Lord, let it be. Let him overlook my bad qualities, and let it be Your will. Surely it was; after all, God had arranged the whole journey. She had to trust Him to bring Henry to salvation, but trusting Him came easy. He'd proved Himself so many times, she couldn't even count.

She glanced over at Becky. No doubt her daughter would be thrilled to call Henry daddy. Her little one sang a lively tune that she was obviously making up as she went along. Her doll danced in time on her lap.

"So, happy girl, what do you need to talk to Mister Henry about?"

"Oh, Mama, don't you know that we talk almost the whole time when we're riding together? We talk about Blue Dog. How much better he's getting." She looked at the sky as though thinking. "Um, we talk about singing some." She turned, dipped her chin toward her chest, and looked up from under her eyebrows. "But you knew that, didn't you?" She giggled. "He really sings more terribler than anyone I've ever heard, Mama. Wait till you hear him!"

"There is no such word as *terribler,* young lady. Seems to me that you're avoiding my question. Did you think I'd forget it if you stalled long enough?"

The little girl held her mouth wide open like she was aghast. "I was answering the very question you asked, Mother."

"Um-hmm."

"And!" She paused. "I saw you holding Mister Henry's hand at the springs."

"Oh, you did?"

"Yes, ma'am, and I'm so proud to see that you've finally come to your senses, Mama. He loves you, you know."

Sue couldn't believe what had just come out of her baby's mouth. How could a nine-year-old know such a thing before she even knew it herself? "You really think so, do you? What in the world would make you assume that?" Those silly butterflies swarmed her tummy again.

Becky rolled her eyes and shook her head. "Mama, I do not assume it, I know it."

"How? Did he tell you?"

"Well, not in so many words, but—"

"There, you see?"

Becky looked all around and puckered her lips over to the side as though trying to decide a hard problem. "Well, what I was going to say is, he may not have told me right out that he loves you, but remember, I know all what he bought with his honey money." She glanced over and winked. "And he got you those mules. They were dreadful expensive, by the way."

"But those mules are really his. He said he planned to sell them and get his money back."

"And he got you something else, too."

Sue leaned over against her daughter and tickled her ribs.

"What else did he buy, Rebecca Ruth Baylor?" She tickled her more, enjoying Becky's throes of giggles. She loved that her child lived so carefree. Sue had worked hard at that, keeping all the burdens at bay. "Come on, you silly willy! You know you want to tell me."

"No, I don't! I do not!" She bent at the waist and gasped for air. "Stop, stop. You're killing me."

Sue quit tickling her. "Now tell me true, Rebecca Ruth, what did Mister Henry buy for me with his honey money?"

Becky reached up with one hand and placed it on the center of her chest. "Do you really want to know? It's supposed to be a secret."

"Yes, I do, or I wouldn't have asked."

"I can't tell you!" She bent over laughing.

"Rebecca Ruth, that is not nice to tease me."

"I'm sorry, Mama." She grinned. "All right then, I'll tell you one thing, but I can't tell you what kind or what it's for."

Sue reached over and squeezed Becky's cheeks together so that she made a fishy-kiss face. "Stop talking in riddles. What is it?"

Her daughter looked to both sides, then behind her. "Fabric, Mama, but you can't get me to say what kind or what it's for. And that's not all either."

If Henry had bought her material, Becky had probably told him that she'd like it, and that's why he'd bought it. He certainly had been more than generous.

Was it only yesterday? Time on the trace always seemed so much longer than it actually was. They had been on it barely over a week now, and it seemed like a month or more. Sue was so tired of travel and troubles and trying to figure Henry Buckmeyer out. Her daughter obviously knew him better than she did.

But he was so good for Becky. What a great father he'd make. He was good for all of them. Levi had matured so much just being around him. For that matter, Henry Buckmeyer was probably good for everyone he was around at any given point in time. She wished she could be more like that. But he wasn't even saved.

What a wonderful Christian he would be! Why wouldn't he give in? He had to be under conviction.

Could what Becky thought be true?

Sue wondered what else he'd bought—besides those mules and the material—which her little hard nut to crack refused to tell her about. And what could the fabric be for? Maybe he'd only chosen a bolt or two for the Aikins, and her daughter had misunderstood. "Now, listen to me, Rebecca Ruth."

"Oh, this is going to be important."

"Listen, I don't want you to tell any secrets or break any promises; your word is powerful important. I always taught you that. But seriously, if you could let me know, I sure would like to find out what Henry got. I'd rather not be surprised."

"I suppose I could give you a hint. Want one?"

Sue thought about it a minute. She couldn't imagine what it might be, and she really wanted to know. She nodded. "Why, yes! Give me a good clue; then if I were to guess, it wouldn't be like you telling me."

"You. Are. Going to. Love it!"

"That's my hint?" Sue shook her head and sighed, totally drowned out by her daughter's cackling. This was going nowhere. "What kind of clue is that, anyway?"

Becky threw her head back, laughing and laughing harder. "The best kind you're ever going to get out of me!"

Sue sighed. "Well, I guess I'll just wait to find out then. It doesn't matter to me anyway. He shouldn't have spent all that money, much less bought anything for me."

"Oh, Mama, don't be like that. He's powerful nice."

Sue smiled at her daughter. What would she and Becky do if Henry didn't want a ready-made family? "He is nice." Thinking on the man and all his awesome qualities, she was rudely interrupted.

Her precious one stood up and faced her, hands on her hips. "And, Mother, please, please, puh-leeese, do not ever tell him about that vow of yours!"

HENRY HANDED THE REINS TO LEVI. "Want a biscuit?"

"With some of your honey? And a big chunk of jerky?"

"Thought your aunt Sue didn't want you eating my horse."

"I don't think she ever mentioned it. Anyway, I ate some when you passed it out to all the Caddo; that young buck who told me we overpaid gave me some."

Henry jumped down. "Want your tater now?"

"No, thanks. I'll save mine for supper."

Henry waited until the second wagon drew abreast, then climbed up next to Rebecca. "Hey, little miss, you and Blue Dog about ready to walk a bit?"

She looked from him to her mother, then back to him. "No, sir. I like it just fine right here. Besides, Mama said you said we didn't have to take walking turns today."

Sue smiled at him. "You hold her, Henry, and I'll see if I can count her ribs."

Rebecca jumped to her feet. "Don't you do it, Mister D—uh—Henry, sir. She's been tickling me all afternoon, trying to get me to tell."

"Rebecca Ruth, I have not."

Henry raised his eyebrows. "Tell what?"

Rebecca climbed over Henry, then rode the wheel down. "Come on, Blue, I think they want us to skedaddle." She looked up as the wagon went on past her. "Ain't that right?"

Sue looked beyond him and started to say something, but Henry put his hand on her arm. "She give away any of my surprises?"

"I didn't know she was such an avid little secret keeper. She did tell me that I'll like what you got me."

"Did she now?"

She smiled. "So, what did you get me?"

"Well, that all depends."

Her expression held confusion. "On what? Haven't you already got it?" An understanding came. "Oh, you were thinking about giving me those mules if I wanted them and not selling 'em after all. That's it, isn't it?"

He smiled. "No, wrong."

"Then what could it depend on? I'm confused."

He grinned playfully. "Well, that's not like you."

"What?"

"Being confused. You usually have a strong, solid opinion on about every topic. Hadn't seen much confusion in you, Susannah Baylor."

She sighed. He must think she was just horrible, a stubborn, headstrong, controlling witch. "I've been such a shrew." She looked into his eyes. "Will you forgive me, Henry? Could you ever?"

"Mis'ess Baylor, I can't say that you haven't been trying at times, but you're a product of the life you've lived. I don't hold that against you, nothing to forgive."

Product of the life she'd lived? What could he mean by that except past her prime years? Did he consider her an old-maid widow?

"Becky!" Levi's holler pulled her attention toward the lead wagon.

The sight of her little girl falling off the side horrified Sue. Becky landed on the ground with a thud. She didn't move. Not a leg or arm. Nothing! And she wasn't crying or making any noise either.

God, no!

Could she be dead?

Henry leapt down. Sue reined in the mules, set the brake, and followed him.

CHAPTER

TWENTY-FIVE

A KNOT IN SUE'S THROAT threatened to choke her completely. She could barely breathe. Her legs wouldn't cooperate and get her to her daughter fast enough. Rebecca lay perfectly still on the hard ground. Oh, Lord. How had she fallen? What had she been doing on the side of the wagon anyway? She'd surely broken some bones.

The lead wagon stopped, and Levi ran toward her, too, but Blue got there first. Henry beat Levi by a few steps and checked Becky over; head, chest, arms, and legs. "Where does it hurt, Rebecca?"

The dog licked her face like he could fix every problem with his slobber. The little girl finally gasped. Thank God! Sue could swallow again and caught her own breath.

"Nowhere, I don't think." Becky pushed the hound away and then rose up. "Get back, Blue. I'm fine." She smiled at Henry. " 'Sides being hard to catch my breath, maybe I'm fine, and I'm not going to die."

Sue raced to her side, proud to hear she wasn't hurting anywhere. "What were you doing, young lady?"

Rebecca grabbed Henry's hand and let him pull her up. "Levi wanted me to get us something."

Sue dusted her dress. "You about scared us to death!" She looked to Henry, who tilted his head and mouthed no. "Well, at the least, you gave me heart palpitations. Why in the world were you climbing around on that wagon when it was moving? What were you after?" She glared at Levi. "She could have been killed!"

Henry touched Sue's arm. "I guess it's partly my fault. I told Levi we'd eat on the go and that he could have some honey with his dinner. She was probably trying to get everything ready for when I came back."

Sue shook her finger at her nephew. "I can't believe you'd do such a thing!" She grabbed Becky's hand and turned the child to face her. "Are you sure you're not hurt? That you're all right?"

"Yes, Mama, I don't think my bones are broke or nothing."

"Or anything, Rebecca."

"Yes, ma'am."

"Well, if you're sure, come on then. You're riding with me. We've wasted enough daylight, and now the mules are going to have to work extra getting us rolling again."

THE LITTLE GIRL LET HER MOTHER PULL HER ALONG, but she turned sideways and winked at Henry, then mouthed a thank-you, too.

He smiled after her, relieved more than he was ready to admit that his little miss hadn't hurt herself bad. She sure picked a fine time to fall, right when his conversation with her mother was getting serious. He wanted to hear more of what Sue had to say. And tell her what his gift for her depended on; at the same time, though, he enjoyed keeping her guessing.

He faced Levi. "Get them going; I'll be right there." He grabbed the smaller honey jar and hurried to Sue's wagon. "Here, keep this with you." He took a napkin full of cold biscuits from her, and then hurried back to the lead wagon, grabbing his big jar, then joining the boy.

After he and Levi got good and sticky, Henry decided he needed to talk to the boy. "You've already mentioned about me being perfect for your aunt, but you've been the man of the house. I want to know what you think about me being Rebecca's daddy and your uncle."

"You kidding me? Sir, if I got to handpick from all the men in the world, you'd be my first choice. You serious, then? About asking her?"

"Been thinking on it. Think she'll say yes?"

Levi laughed. "I'm sure of it. Wow. That's top drawer. But wait; what about her vow? You don't plan on going to get her daddy's blessing, do you?"

"Of course. What's the problem?"

"How? He lives in Tennessee."

Henry went to licking the honey off his fingers. "Guess we'd all have to go."

"What about our mules? And the wagons? Auntie prizes them highly. We can't drive them all the way to Memphis. It'd take forever." Levi sat back. "I want to get home, sir. Ground needs breaking, time to get some wheat and oats in. A dozen other things need doing. We've been gone so long already, and we never even planned to go at all."

The boy had a point, but none of it mattered. Henry would go to war again if that's what it took to make Sue his wife, and he hated war. "We'll figure it all out."

"Why don't you just forget that old man? He's probably dead now anyway."

"I don't think she could do that, so, neither can I."

SUE WANTED TO FIND A PEACH SWITCH and threaten Becky good, but her daughter had seen through that ruse years before, not that she needed much discipline. Both she and Levi had been wonderful, obedient children—most of the time. Sue couldn't have been blessed any better and had no complaints. "What exactly were you trying to get?"

"I can't tell."

"Why not?"

"Levi made me promise."

"That doesn't count. If he's telling you to do something that dangerous, then making you promise not to tell when you get hurt—no! That's not going to work. Now what was it?"

"He didn't tell me to, I went all on my own, but I promised not to tell." She looked up and pouted. "I don't want you to be mad at us or Mister Henry."

"Mister Henry? What's he got to do with it?"

Becky raised her eyebrows.

"Fine, I promise not to be mad at anyone. This is much too wonderful a day to be upset about anything, so tell me now, and tell me true. What were you after when you fell off?"

"Levi gave me a bite of the jerky he'd been sneaking from Mister Henry's tucker. It's so good, Mama, and I was hungry.

I wanted some more, but he said you didn't want us eating horse, and it'd get Mister Henry in trouble if you found out." Her eyes filled with tears. "So, why's it a wonderful day any-way?"

"Oh, nothing, sweetheart." Sue hugged Becky.

"He asked you to marry him, didn't he?"

"Why would Mister Henry do such a thing? He lives a quiet life; free to go where he wants when he wants. He wouldn't want to settle down with a ready-made family."

"But he loves me, I know he does. And I'm sure he loves you, too."

"How could anyone not love you? You are wonderful and so lovable. But I don't want your heart to be hurt if he doesn't stay with us, Becky." Even more so now since she hoped herself the man might want to take her for his wife, stay forever. Becky's wouldn't be the only heart broken. And Sue wasn't free to say yes even if he asked.

Like her baby could read her thoughts, she laid her head against Sue's arm. "But if he did, what about your daddy? And your stupid vow?"

"Rebecca Ruth! You should not call my promise to the Lord stupid. That's rude. After your daddy passed, you weren't born yet, and I was so alone. Drawing close to God . . . Well, He got me through those hardest times." It choked her to think she might never be alone again.

Sue sighed and straightened her back, swallowing to regain her composure. "I don't know what he'd say about the vow. If he really loved us—" She burst into sobs.

"Mama! Why are you crying? I'm sorry I called your promise stupid. I really am."

Sue wiped her eyes and face. "Oh, sweetest heart, I just

don't want you to be hurt. I love you more than life. Promise me you won't. I don't see how he could love me."

"Oh, Mama, you're easy to love, too, just like me. And I love you better than life, too." Becky took the reins. "I'll hold these if you want to cry all those tears out. And I do promise you I won't be hurt. I'm so happy! But not like crying happy, more like singing happy!"

So her beautiful and wise daughter sang at the top of her lungs. "I am happy, oh so happy! The Lord has made me happy! I am happy, yes, I'm happy! I'm happy deep in my soul!" Sue didn't know if Henry could hear her, but she hoped he could. While Becky made melody in her heart and thanked God for a daddy, Sue buried her hands in her face and cried.

What was she going to do? She could not, would not go against God; she feared the consequences too much. Fear of the Lord is the beginning of wisdom. She sobbed. But what could she say to Henry if he did ask? How would she ever make him understand? There was nothing, no thing she could do—except pray, of course.

And she did.

After she could see straight again, she took the reins back. Becky didn't say anything for a while, but curiosity must have finally gotten the better of her. "So then, if we've got to go to Tennessee, how are we going to get there? Won't that take a whole year? Think we have to ride these wagons all the way? Couldn't we just go home together and you and Mister Henry can get married at Sulphur Fork? That's where all our friends are."

"No, silly. Tennessee isn't that far. And I'm sorry, but as much as I might want to do just that, I promised I would not marry again without my father's blessing."

Sue cleared her throat. "When I was young, I ran off with your daddy against my daddy's wishes, then before you were even born, he was dead. It's all my fault you grew up without a daddy, and I killed Levi's, too. I'll not be disobedient to God again. You know honoring and obeying your parents is one of the Ten Commandments, but I ignored it. I made a bad choice and paid the consequences of my actions, but so did you and Levi.

"Remember that, Becky; you can learn from your mother's mistakes."

"But, it was an accident. You didn't make it rain; you didn't make that stupid ox slip. You didn't kill my daddy, or Levi's either. You would never do such a thing. God knows that."

"Yes, the rain came and the ox slipped, but it all happened because I disobeyed my father. I know it sure as we're sitting here."

"But you were grown, Mama."

"Scripture doesn't stipulate any age. John and Patricia Abbott will always be my parents, and I will always be their little girl, no matter how old I get or how far I run away. Just like you'll always be mine even after you're married and have children of your own. Nothing can change that. I'll always love my little girl."

HENRY TOPPED A LITTLE KNOLL. The trace curved a bit, then he saw it. A steep hill that was more than a pretty good pull. He checked the western sky. Another hour or better of light, but not enough to tackle it this late. He reined to the side, then turned around and signaled for Sue to stop next to him. "Let's camp here tonight."

She pulled her wagon parallel to his and stopped with about ten feet between them. "We've got better than an hour of light. We can make another mile or two, can't we?"

He jumped down, went around, and pointed at the incline. "That's a hard pull, Sue. We may not make it without doubling the teams. We won't know until I try, but we'll have a better chance with fresh animals."

She looked to the west and then faced him. "You're right; first light will be best."

He couldn't have been more pleased or proud of her. Not even a debate. He held out his hand, and she took it and stepped down.

Rebecca stood on the edge and held out her arms. "Catch me."

He did and then leaned in close to her ear. "After supper, before you go to sleep, give me the ring, all right?"

She nodded with tight lips so as not to give any secret away, then slid down.

By the time Henry and Levi had seen to the mules, Sue and Rebecca had a cook fire going with fatback sizzling in a thick layer of sliced potatoes. Henry stopped at the back of his wagon. Someone grabbed his pants leg, and he jumped. Rebecca stood behind him holding the ring out.

He bent and took it. "Ah, thank you, darling daughter."

She giggled and hugged his waist. "You're welcome." Then she stopped abruptly and pointed.

The hairs on the back of Blue Dog's neck bristled.

"What is it, boy?"

CHAPTER

TWENTY-SIX

SUE TOOK BECKY'S HAND, then joined Henry and Blue Dog at the top of the knoll they'd stopped on. She could make out the shape of a wagon. Its canvas top's lighter gray contrasted against the darker shades of the far tree line. The sound of tinkling brass drifted on the evening breeze. "Are those bells I hear?"

"Afraid so." Henry kneeled beside Blue, whispered something in his ear, and then pointed toward the woods off to the right. The dog trotted off.

Levi stepped to the side of the man he'd come to admire so much with the powder horn draped over his chest and his long gun in hand. "Where you want me?"

"Ease out with Blue, but stay where you can see them. Warn me if anyone slips out of the back or the bottom of their wagon."

Sue moved closer and spoke under her breath. "Do you know who they are?"

"Only ones I know who bell their teams are gypsies."

She'd heard stories about the traveling vagabonds but had never been around any. "I thought they were fortune-tellers and jugglers and the like, happy heathen who entertained." As the wagon neared, the bells' tinkling increased, and she could make out a man and woman in the driver's seat.

"True enough. They'll do all that while they're stealing you blind."

"Really?" She hadn't heard anything about that.

He looked at her and nodded. "Yes, ma'am. They sure will." The visitors pulled up to the top of the knoll where he and Sue waited. Henry waved and smiled. "Hello."

The man reined in a scraggy pair of mules. "Smelled your smoke, neighbor. Mind if we camp here with you? For the fellowship and safety. We've got plenty of food to share."

Becky stepped out. "Are you gypsies?"

The older woman in the seat burst out laughing. "Oh, my, no, child. My husband's a gunsmith by trade." She turned to Sue. "You have a beautiful daughter. I've got two girls of my own in back."

The news of girls to play with obviously thrilled her daughter. Becky jumped up and down. "Can they stay, Mister Daddy?" She quickly covered her mouth, "Oops. Can they, please?"

"What did you just call him?"

"Sorry, Mama, didn't mean to."

Henry looked to Sue. She smiled and held her hand out toward their fire. "We were about to have supper. Certainly, you're welcome to camp with us."

The gunsmith nodded and waved his reins over the mules. "Thank you, ma'am. Mighty grateful for the hospitality and company." He drove his team near the other two wagons and set the brake.

"Come on, girls. Come meet everyone." Two comely young

ladies climbed out from the back of the wagon. The younger appeared to be about Levi's age, the older in her early twenties maybe.

"They're old!" Becky pouted. "I wanted to play house with our dolls."

The older of the two kneeled beside her. "Oh, but a girl is never too old for that. Let me see your baby. I still love playing house. Don't all young women?"

While Becky showed off her Trudy, Levi came trotting into camp with Blue and his eyes seemingly glued on the younger daughter. He was smiling ear to ear. The girl acted somewhat shy but kept looking back over toward him. He walked up to her and extended his hand, pulled it right back and rubbed it on his breeches, then held it toward her again. "My name's Levi Baylor. What's yours?"

She offered the tips of her fingers. "Grace. Pleased to make your acquaintance, Levi."

After introductions and pleasantries were exchanged all around, Henry went to help the man hobble his mules, and his wife brought a slab of ham and sweet potatoes from her larder to add with what Sue already had cooking. Sue made room for her pan on the fire. "It's been a while since we've had ham."

"We bought it already butchered for our trip north and after we get settled. We've been eating high on the hog I guess you could say." She laughed.

"So how long have you been on the trace now?"

"We're two days out of Jefferson. Them mules he bought off those gypsies don't seem very healthy. Had a heap of trouble getting over two pretty good-size hills. One's just there behind us."

"Yes, we wanted our teams to be fresh to go over, so figured we'd wait till the morning." Sue checked on the Dutch oven. "Biscuits are almost done, and there'll be plenty."

HENRY HANDED THE RIFLE BACK. "Nice piece, a bit heavy though."

"It's that, but shoots true for better than a hundred paces." The man set the long gun back in his wagon. "Anything else you interested in?"

"No, sir, but thank you. Any news you care to share?"

For the next few minutes, while the ladies finished supper, He listened to the man run down President Jackson and praise Henry Clay, his opponent. Henry had not expected the news to be a lecture on the evils of Andrew Jackson. Finally, he held a hand up, palm toward the visitor. "May all be true; but I don't think so. We don't need a bunch of banknotes floating around getting people cheated out of their hard-earned money. To my thinking, Jackson's the better man."

The smith looked like he wanted to fight, might have started something if he'd been a few years younger. "You can't say that. You have no idea what he's doing to the country."

Henry did know, leastwise best he could from month-old newspapers that he got semiregularly. The man's older daughter joined her father, so Henry decided not to say more. Ladies usually didn't care for political discussions. He nodded as she slipped her arm into her father's.

She smiled. "Did I hear right? Your name is Buckmeyer, and the lady is a Baylor?"

"That's correct." He turned back to her father. "When you get to Titus's Trading Post in Pleasant Mound, ask the man for some tobacco for your mules. Looks like they may be wormy."

"Hadn't thought of that, but I sure will. Thank you kindly."

The girl smiled every time he glanced her way and batted her lashes a bit too much. "Oh, I almost forgot. Mama sent me to fetch you men. Supper's ready."

Through the whole meal, Henry could feel the young woman's eyes on him. He avoided even looking her direction. Were all girls that age man crazy? Or was it really baby crazy, and they just needed a partner? He was proud Sue had never acted like that, at least not with him, but he figured Andrew Baylor may have gotten a good dose of it.

He noticed her watching the girl watching him a time or two. He loved what a lady she was. He faced the girl's mother. "Ma'am, might I impose on you and yours to keep an eye on our little miss? I'd like to take Mis'ess Baylor here on a little walk."

The woman nodded, glancing at her older daughter, then looked back. "Well, certainly, we'll be glad to."

Rebecca jumped to her feet with a grin wider than Levi's. "And I won't be hard to watch either. It's about time for me to get to sleep anyway."

Henry smiled at her and stood. "Yes, ma'am, you're right. We'll need to be gone first light." He extended his hand toward Sue. "Ma'am? A walk?"

She let him pull her to her feet but didn't release his hand. "Of course."

He led her to the top of the knoll, then started down the other side. "You're such a lady, Sue, and I sure do appreciate you."

"Oh, I don't know. You might not say that if you knew what I was thinking. In my mind, I sent Blue after that young woman three times. He just didn't get the message. You've got to teach me how to do that thing you do with him."

"You might sic him on me then." Henry laughed.

"Never! And he probably wouldn't mind me anyway." She straightened her shawl, pulling it tighter around her. "Now with Becky, he might just take her side over yours."

"I best not ever cross her then. Don't know if I could whip Blue in a fair fight."

"I don't think there's anyone you couldn't whip, fair fight or not."

He laughed again. "Now don't go to thinking that. I wouldn't want you matching me against one of the prizefighters. Those monsters are vicious."

She stepped in closer and put both of her hands on his chest, then peered into his eyes. "Wouldn't matter how big or vicious they were, you'd win."

He loved hearing her tell it, but he wasn't so sure. He had taken a few beatings in his day. But he needed to get to it; he hadn't brought her out there alone for small talk. "Want to keep walking or sit a spell? Thought we might star-gaze some."

She leaned back, looking a bit surprised, then smiled. "Sitting would be fine. I do love enjoying the beauty of the Lord's night sky. I love the stars."

He helped her to the ground, then sat close beside her with his back to a pine. He had practiced this but seemed all out of kilter. How to start?

"Aren't they beautiful? Like diamonds in the heavens. Did you know God has every star named?"

"One of the later Psalms, near the end, David said God has them numbered and calls them all by their names."

She leaned out from the tree. "Henry Buckmeyer, you never cease to amaze me. How is it that you've read the Word enough to know such things yet escaped God's wonderful plan of redemption?"

"Isn't God or His Word that I have trouble with. It's men and their religious rules, judgments, and self-righteousness. No one could look at such a sight"—he waved his hand across the expanse of the starry sky—"and not believe in a higher power."

He rose and turned toward her on one knee, looked her square in the eye. "Sue, I've come to admire you more than you can know. These days on the trace—they've been the happiest days of my life. I can't imagine going back and leaving you. I love you, Susannah Baylor, and I'd be the proudest man in Texas if you'd agree to be my wife. Will you marry me?"

She sat back, stunned. "Marry you! Marry you?"

"That's right, Susannah. I'm asking if you'll spend the rest of your life with me, because I sure want to spend mine with you."

Total fulfillment and elation soured to heartbreak in the time it took for her to digest his proposal. The yes died on her lips. She never looked away from his eyes. "Oh, Henry! There's nothing I'd ever want more! But I can't say yes, even though my heart is aching inside to have to tell you that I can't." She shook her head. "It was my fault Andrew died. I made a vow to the Lord that I cannot break no matter how much I want to."

"Let me rephrase my question, then." He grinned. "Susannah Baylor, if your father gives us his blessing, will you marry me?"

Her heart leapt and skipped a beat, and a tear flowed from her blurry eyes to her chin. She couldn't believe it. She didn't deserve it. Oh, God, how could he love her? "Oh, Henry, how did you know about my father?"

He slipped his hand over hers. "Men and boys don't sit

around and gossip all day, but we do talk about the important things, like the most beautiful widow in the Red River Valley."

She laughed, tears streaming over her cheeks. "Oh? And what do they say?"

He took her face in both hands and gently wiped her tears back with his thumbs. "Consensus is she'll be a good-looking widow the rest of her life."

"Well, why do they say that?"

"Seems most of them figured going all the way to Tennessee on a maybe wasn't ever going to happen."

"And you? What about you?"

He squeezed her hand. "First time I saw you, standing in front of the Sulphur Fork Trading Post with your hair blowing in the breeze staring down that storm; so beautiful and strong. I should have paid a visit back then, told you. I have no excuse. I'd never seen a more desirable woman before and still haven't to this day."

Her cheeks warmed. She sat back, hoping the darkness concealed her blush, and smiled. "What a kind thing to say. I'm glad you liked the wind was blowing my hair."

He chuckled. "Yes, ma'am. You looked that day exactly like I've come to find you are. Beautiful but resolved, passionate but with a kind streak I could drive both wagons through. You're so much like my mother, but even more. You've succeeded where she failed." He smiled. "Susannah Baylor, I love you more than life, and if your father is half as smart as you are, he'll see it."

She searched his eyes and adored what she saw. He loved her! He wanted to marry her! And was willing to get her father's blessing! She was getting married! She threw her arms around his neck. "Yes, yes! I will marry you. I'll be the happiest woman on the face of the earth."

He stood, pulling her to her feet and hugging her so tight, she became a part of him. She floated back into camp, his arm around her. When he said good night, she thought he might kiss her, but was glad—well, sort of glad—when he didn't for the sake of being right before God.

Sue lay on her pallet of his furs. She could hardly believe everything that had happened. The difference one day made simply astounded her. She never wanted this day to end, and yet, the stars twinkled in the night sky, marking its demise. The last day that so changed her life had been for the worse.

Back then, she'd never dreamed living would be sweet again, but along came Patrick Henry Buckmeyer. Oh, how awful she had been to him in the beginning. She couldn't imagine why he would still want to love her, but, oh, how she loved him now. This day, the change had been a joyful one. She couldn't wait to tell Elaine and all her friends back home.

Then a question sauntered through her mind. It wasn't one she asked herself but came from outside her own thinking.

What have you done? You cannot marry an unbeliever.

Indeed.

What had she done?

CHAPTER

TWENTY-SEVEN

SLEEP ELUDED HER. Sue's mind kept spinning, thinking on every detail. She should be overjoyed; they'd be in Jefferson tomorrow. She'd sell her cotton, probably for six cents a pound. More money than she'd ever dreamed. Then Henry would take her and the children to Tennessee. She'd see her father again, and he'd meet his granddaughter that he never even knew he had.

But would Daddy give his blessing? He might not even speak to her. Maybe he had received her letters but written her off as dead to him. Surely he'd want to get to know Becky, though, even if he couldn't forgive Sue. And now, she'd gone and fallen in love with another poor man with no trade. Would it be the situation with Andy all over again? And even worse; Henry wasn't a Christian.

What would she do if it turned out that way? Could she live her life without Henry now?

She rolled over, wide awake, and stared at Becky.

It all swirled across her mind's eye. There should have been a background of white, puffy clouds floating in sunny, blue skies with birds singing. But instead, a dark storm loomed and overshadowed all her happy thoughts.

What had she done?

Did she just forget what God's Word said? What was she thinking? Wait a minute. That was the problem, she hadn't been thinking at all.

She must talk with him first thing in the morning. It wouldn't be fair to let him keep assuming the only hurdle was her father's blessing. More than anything she ever wanted, she wished it would be as simple as leading him to salvation, but no doubt his mother had tried a hundred times.

Sue had to dig deeper, not let him off the hook so easy with his "I have no trouble with God or His Word." She could not let him get away with that; she must find out exactly why he rejected God's sacrifice of love. She had to overcome whatever his objections were. He couldn't have any decent reasons.

It shouldn't be hard. If he loved her, he'd share his heart.

She turned toward his wagon and wondered if he was asleep. Tomorrow, Jefferson. Surely, she'd be in time. Henry had seen to it. The buyers just had to still be there so that they could purchase her cotton.

It would be a long trip to Tennessee, probably as far as from home to Jefferson, or even farther. Then certainly farther from there back home again. Such a long journey. Should she even drag the children all that way if he refused straight up to be saved?

What if her father had passed or moved back east? What if he hated her and slammed his door in her face? He'd never answered any of her letters. But then, had he actually received them? Ten years was a long time. If he wasn't there, the journey would be for nothing. She'd wanted to go visit, but the years had slipped by.

Maybe she should talk to Henry about all that. Would he

still be willing to risk going? There'd be no need if he wouldn't repent and accept Christ. Oh, she wished she could just go to sleep. She closed her eyes and tried not to think anymore.

She could send a letter now. From Jefferson! It'd be more likely to get there, but how long might that take? If she wrote and told her daddy about her life in Texas and how much she loved Henry, she could ask him to forgive her and please bless this marriage.

But what if she never got an answer back? She didn't want to wait forever to marry Henry. But the vow could not be broken as long as her father lived to give his blessing. But also, it didn't hinge only on the blessing. She'd made the vow, and she'd keep it, but blessing or not, she couldn't marry an unbeliever. She would never take such a chance with Henry's life.

She rolled onto her back and stared at the bottom of the wagon.

Why borrow trouble? She would speak with Henry and see what he said. She didn't want to mull all the negative what-ifs. She only wanted to think of the man she loved and how wonderful he was and how he loved her, too—enough to ask her to be his wife. He chose to forgive her ill behavior and stubborn streak and see through all that ugliness to her heart.

Isn't that what the Lord did?

He always knew her heart—the only salve to her wounded spirit when she failed to hold her temper. Only God could manage Henry seeing through all her faults, and she thanked Him profusely as she finally drifted off.

The next morning, she woke with a smile and the aroma of brewing coffee. Today was the day! As had become her custom, she rolled from under the wagon and pulled herself up using the wheel. Henry's team stood waiting, already harnessed, and it looked like he was helping Levi get her mules ready. The gunsmith's wife had her own Dutch oven already sitting out of the coals and ham in her frying pan.

"Good morning." Sue pushed a stray curl back into her braid, retrieved her cup, and then made her way to the fire. "The coffee smells wonderful."

"Rough night?" The woman she'd thought a gypsy looked up from the cook fire.

"Yes, ma'am. Had trouble getting to sleep. Too much on my mind."

Henry walked up finishing a biscuit, then nodded toward her wagon. "Best we take your team up the hill first."

"Good morning." She placed her hand on his face and smiled, looking into those deep eyes she loved so much. "You in a big hurry today?"

He laughed. "Sue Baylor, you've been in a hurry ever since we left the Red River Valley. I mean to get you to Jefferson today." He faced Levi. "You keep the other one down here, get 'em all set to go. Once we get your aunt Sue to the top, ease them on out."

That suited her fine. She liked being in the lead anyway.

Levi grabbed another biscuit with ham. "Yes, sir." He turned to the cook. "Thank you, ma'am. That porker's delicious."

She smiled and nodded. "My pleasure."

Becky crawled out from under the wagon, came straight over to Henry, and tugged on his shirt. "Don't forget it's my turn to ride with you." She rubbed her eyes, then grinned. "I want to hear all about it."

"How could I forget my best little miss?" He tousled her hair. "You should get something to eat. We're leaving pretty quick. I'm going with your mama right now, but I'll be back. You stay with Levi."

"Yes, sir."

The visiting lady grinned. "Your children certainly are polite. Here, darlin'." The woman handed Becky a biscuit with a slice of ham in it.

"Thank you very much, ma'am."

Sue accepted a biscuit with ham, too, smiling at the gunsmith's wife. "You are such a blessing. I pray our paths will cross again one day, and I can repay your kindness." In love with life, she hugged the woman, then climbed aboard. "Ready when you are."

Henry jumped up beside her. "Then let's see if we can pull this grade."

"Hey, now!" She waved the reins against the animals' backs and clucked. They pawed the ground and threw themselves into moving the load. Wood creaked; leather stretched; and metal rings and chains clanged. Sue waved good-bye to the family staying behind and left the last camp before Jefferson.

She prayed for God's favor and blessings, with Henry's salvation heavy on her heart.

As they neared the base of the hill, he jumped off. "Don't stop; let them take it at their own pace." The wagon passed him.

As soon as the team hit the incline, the mules slowed, but they never quit moving along, higher and higher. The closer to the top, the more all four strained, but they kept pulling. "Come on, Dex; come on, Mil. Y'all can do it. Get up, Daisy! Good mules, almost there." The wagon slowed to a crawl nearing the top. It barely moved at all, but the wheels kept turning.

She couldn't believe how easy it was going, with four mules to the wagon, thanks to Henry. She was so, so blessed!

Then they were there. At the top. With a long, easy descent in front of her, she reined the mules in, set the brake, and jumped down. "We did it!"

Henry joined her, breathing hard. "Yes, we did."

"Henry!" She put her hand on his chest. "Were you pushing the whole way?"

"No, just the last bit, when it looked like they might stop." He turned and took a step down the hill back toward camp.

She grabbed his hand. They were alone. She should say something, tell him she couldn't marry an unbeliever. "Wait, catch your breath."

"I'm fine." He looked north. Levi waved. The other wagon pulled out of camp. "Best beat him to the bottom."

She watched from the hill's crest, hoping the second wagon would make it as easily as hers. And just the same, the team pulled it straight to the top without any problems. "Yay! We made it! God is good!"

The second hill before reaching Jefferson wasn't as bad as the first and didn't pose one bit of trouble. Before noon, she drove the team up under a shade tree and set the brake. She kept wanting to tell someone Henry had proposed; she'd been tempted to say something to Levi all day, but decided that she should tell Henry about her reservations first, get him saved, and then break the good news to the children together.

She couldn't stop smiling though.

While the men grained and watered the animals, she and Becky prepared dinner, bringing out Henry's honey for the biscuits. After all, a celebration was in order, even though a small stretch of trace remained to navigate. It was the last stretch and all downhill now.

Then she was there!

Coming into Jefferson was like entering another world. People milled everywhere. She asked directions and made her way to the wharf, with Henry following behind. She immediately spotted the Howletts in line next to a big wooden dock. She set the brake, jumped down, and ran to them.

"Are they still buying?"

"Sue!" Shannan opened her arms wide. "What are you doing here? I thought you sold your lint to Littlejohn."

Sue hugged her good friend tight. "He turned out to be a weasel and a thief, but that's a long story. What's going on? I heard they were paying six cents a pound!"

"Nothing is happening. We've been waiting all morning, but haven't had our turn yet. They're supposedly counting now. The steamboat captain will only let them carry sixteen hundred bales, and they think they might already be at their limit."

"Oh, no. What will y'all do?" Sue shook her head and looked up and down the wharf at all those still waiting. "Y'all? Oh, dear, I meant what will we all do!"

"Trust the Lord, I say."

Sue smiled. That's the way her friend was and one of the reasons she loved her so. Sue faced her and took both her hands. "I'm in such a tither, Shannan. I've got good and bad news. I need you to pray in agreement."

"What is it, Sue?"

"I've fallen in love again, and he loves me. Henry Buckmeyer has asked me to marry him, and I was so excited that I said yes. Please pray with me that God will draw him to salvation."

Shannan moved Sue's hands together and drew them to her chest, looking her in the eyes. "Susannah, are you sure? I loved his mother, but—"

"I know, I know. Everything you've heard about him isn't true, though, except that he isn't saved. I've prayed, and I know he's going to accept the Lord. I just know he is. God is the one Who brought us together—I hired him to help me get my cotton here. Henry's no layabout, I can tell you that without reservation. Those old biddies back home are nothing but gossipmongers, and their scuttlebutt, nothing but lies."

"But, dear one, you must not marry so long as he's a heathen. You do know that, right? Not to unequally yoke yourself? Assure me that you are not thinking of going through with any marriage until he is saved."

Sue dropped her chin to her chest and stared at the dock's boards. Yes, she knew; of course, she knew. Raising her gaze to meet her friend's eyes, she smiled. "Yes and no. I won't wed until Henry's a born-again, bona fide, baptized follower of Christ." Tears welled and blurred her vision. "But I love him so, Shannan, and he loves me—and Becky, too. She wants him to be the daddy she's prayed for. I wasn't looking for a husband. Will you pray?"

Her friend pulled her into a big tight hug and whispered in her ear, "I will, and I'm so glad for you. God can do all things. Praise the Lord; but, Sue, what about—"

"As soon as we sell the cotton, he's planning on going to Tennessee so he can ask my father, but I don't know if we even should if he isn't saved. I've got to tell him, but the time hasn't been right. He thinks Daddy's blessing is the only thing standing in the way."

Her friend hugged her again. "Well it's true, you do; I'll pray for the perfect time and for his heart to be receptive. I'm so happy for you, and don't worry. If God is in this, it will all work out. If He isn't, you don't want it to anyway."

Sue could always count on her friend for wise counsel. She confirmed that Sue should proceed only by the book, the Good Book. She and Shannan chatted, exchanging stories until a man with a foghorn appeared.

He spoke from the steamboat's high deck. "Folks, thank you for waiting. I regret to inform you all that the boat is indeed full, and we cannot take on even one more bale of your fine cotton. If you care to wait, we'll return in nine days, Lord willing."

NINE DAYS? Henry didn't want to wait nine hours, much less nine days. He locked the brake and then jumped down. "Stay with the wagon, Blue Dog." He glanced at the hound, winked at Rebecca, then trotted to the other wagon. Sue stood beside it with her chin on her chest and tears rolling down her cheeks. Levi looked lost.

Henry lightly touched her hand. "Don't cry, sweetheart."

She looked at him. "And why not? Didn't you hear what the man said? Nine days! We can't stay here for nine days! That would cost a small fortune!"

"And we won't. Listen, we passed a livery a ways back, and I noticed on a side street after that, there's a nice looking boardinghouse." He stuck his hand in his pocket and pulled out several coins. "You and Levi take the teams and stable them, then get us two rooms. This should cover it."

She held her hands out, palms facing him. "I can't. You've already spent too much."

He reached and took her hand, then placed the money in it and wrapped her fingers shut. "Take it. See to the teams, pay extra to put the wagons inside, and get us two rooms."

She nodded. "What are you going to be doing?"

"If I can, I'm going to fix this, but I'm not sure I can. Please, do as I ask. And leave Blue with the wagons. I'll be back directly."

SUE WATCHED AS HE SPOKE with both the men from Sulphur Fork who hadn't sold their cotton, then hurried down the street. She lost him when he turned a corner.

"Come on, son; you heard him. Let's see to the mules." Levi hopped down and went to the second wagon.

Sue remembered passing the livery and traced her way straight back to it. While Becky played with a Shetland pony penned at the end of the hall, Sue negotiated stalls for the eight mules and a roof for the wagons, but insisted she and Levi would see to graining them. After all, she had her own oats Johnny on the spot. She did buy hay for them and had Levi toss it in each stall after getting the mules grained and watered.

Becky gave Blue Dog a big hug. "You're staying here, but we'll be back, so don't worry. Just guard the honey, Blue!" He settled down with his chin on his paw. "Aw, look, Mama. He thinks he's done something wrong." She hugged the hound again and kissed his face. "You're a good dog, and I love you! We'll be back, I promise."

He barked twice.

Sue left with a bag that carried a change of clothes for her and Becky, then turned back and got Levi a clean shirt. From directions the livery boy gave, she made her way to the boardinghouse, a lovely brand-new two-story with a large porch all the way across the front and even down the side. When Sue walked inside, the plush furnishings and richness brought memories of her childhood home flooding back, except everything was so new and fresh.

"Mama, it's so beautiful."

Arriving at the front desk, Sue almost fainted at hearing what two rooms would cost. She paid from the coin Henry had given her but was not happy about it. She didn't fuss though; it seemed all her spunk had leaked right out after she heard the buyers would be leaving without her cotton. She opened the first room.

Levi walked through the door and took the place in. "Now, Aunt Sue, I'll be staying in here with Mister Henry. I'm getting too old to bunk with the womenfolk." He stretched himself out to his full height, now well above hers. "I figured on heading on back to the livery to keep an eye on things there. Matter of fact, I may even spend the night with the wagons. Wouldn't want our cotton to disappear—or Mister Henry's honey either."

"Well, I suppose you're old enough to do that if you want." She wrapped her arms around him. Not only was he taller than she was, but thicker than she remembered—becoming a man. "And here, I brought your shirt thinking you might want to bathe while you had the chance. Promise to stay out of trouble."

"Won't have any problems, Auntie."

His calling her auntie like he did when he was a little boy always made her go soft inside. She couldn't love the boy more if she'd birthed him. Where had all the years gone? He'd soon be a man and already stood a head taller than her. She and Becky went to the second room, and first rattle out of the box, her energetic daughter went to bouncing on the bed.

"Rebecca Ruth! We do not treat other people's furniture that way!" She surveyed the accommodations. She could certainly put the washbowl to good use. "Now come here, and let me get some of that grime off you."

The child obediently hurried to her. "I'm sorry. I thought this was our room now."

Sue poured water from the ceramic pitcher provided into its bowl. "Only for tonight. Mister Henry was kind enough to pay the owner of the room so that we could all have a bed to sleep in. Isn't he wonderful?"

"Yes, he sure is. So, Mama, you got anything to tell me about?"

What a little fisher she was. But Sue wanted to speak with Henry before saying anything. "No, nothing except I've never seen you so dirty!" She stripped Becky to her slip and bloomers, then went to work with a washcloth and a perfumed bar of soap the boardinghouse had provided.

The girl wrinkled up her nose and sniffed. "Mmmm. It smells so good. Could you wash my hair with the soap, too, Mama?"

"That sounds like an excellent idea." Sue smiled and had her daughter hang her head over the bowl. Pouring more water to wet her hair, she lathered it, and the whole room smelled sweet, like lavender and honeysuckle. After a good rinsing, she wrapped a towel around her daughter's head, rubbed it good all over until Becky giggled with glee, then started combing out the tangles.

"I can't wait for Mister Daddy to see me all clean and smelling so nice."

"Maybe I'll clean up as well." After she braided her daughter's hair, she went to refreshing herself. Oh, it felt so wonderful to wash her face and arms, be clean again.

Becky fell fast asleep on the bed, so Sue used the time

to wash all over. That invigorated her so that she decided to wash her hair, too. She redid her braid, then twisted and pinned it into a bun at the nape of her neck. She put on her change of clothes, pinched her cheeks, then sat by the window and waited for Henry to come and for her daughter to wake up. So many folks scurried here and there along the dusty streets of the river town, but she never caught a glimpse of her betrothed.

Once Becky woke up, she and Sue ate a bite in the dining room, then went to sit on the front porch in side-by-side rocking chairs and passed the time watching for Henry. Like her daughter, Sue couldn't wait for him to see her all clean and smelling so sweet. But wait she did. She waited and waited the afternoon away.

What could be keeping him? She wanted Henry back with her. Had he run into trouble? Or someone he knew? Maybe an old flame? Or perhaps he'd met a new one. He'd said he'd be back directly. She huffed and rocked faster, tapping her foot on the floor and getting more upset by the minute.

The daylight sunk into the horizon, leaving a pink, purple, and golden sunset that would usually take her breath away, but she was too irritated to give it proper attention. Not much after night's cloak fell, the streets darkened, mottled with dim lights cast from coal oil lanterns that sat inside nearby windows.

Sue could not imagine where Henry had gone off to, and what he planned to do to fix anything. He could have given her a little more information before leaving her alone. The more she thought about it, the angrier she got. It really perturbed her that he didn't discuss things with her.

Another thought struck her. Would he still expect her to pay him for coming along? She didn't think so. Besides, that way, he wouldn't have to feel bad about bossing the boss around. She smiled, but only momentarily. Her foot went to tapping faster and harder.

What was he doing, for Heaven's sake?

Becky had climbed up into her lap and fallen asleep again. And why shouldn't she? It was well past her bedtime. The girl's head rested on Sue's arm and had made her hand go to sleep. It tingled something fierce before Henry finally came sauntering down the street like he had not a care in the world. Was he whistling? Sue resisted the urge to holler at him to hurry.

He walked up onto the porch with saddlebags she hadn't seen before hanging over his shoulder and smiled his victory smile. As infuriating as he could be, she did love it that he was so even-tempered all the time. She needed even-tempered. But he acted like he couldn't even tell that she was upset or would ever imagine she might be.

He held out his arms. "Here, let me take her." He hefted poor Becky over his shoulder like a sack of potatoes, then pulled Sue out of the rocking chair. "My, you ladies are smelling very nice." He opened the front door for her. "Where's your room?"

How could she stay angry with him? It might not be easy, but she was determined. He carried her baby upstairs, and she opened the room's door. She pulled the spread and top sheet down, and he laid the sleeping child on the big bed. Becky looked so small. Sue covered her, then turned to him.

She whispered, "Henry Buckmeyer, where have you been? And what in the world have you been up to?"

He smiled, then nodded toward the door. She showed

him his room and gave him the key. He walked in and set the saddlebags on the bed. She stopped at the door.

He turned around. "Would you be more comfortable talking on the porch?"

"This is fine. I wouldn't want to get that far away from Becky."

"Want a chair?"

"No, I've been sitting all day." She interlocked her fingers just beneath her bosom. "Are you going to tell me or not? I've been here all afternoon—and evening—waiting and wondering." She looked into his eyes. "If we get married, then I—"

"If? It isn't settled?" He took off his hat and slung it back onto the bed, grinning at her.

"Well, I've been wanting to talk to you. There's my father's blessing, but—"

"That is not going to be a problem." He ran his fingers through his hair and shook his head.

"You don't know my daddy." She put her hands on her hips. "Quit getting me off the topic. I was saying, when we're married, I—"

"I like that much better."

She glared at him. "Sir! Will you please let me get a full sentence out?"

"Sure. Go ahead. I promise not to interrupt."

"As I was saying." She stood there silent a minute, looking at him, and then dropped her shoulders and gazed at the ceiling. "What was I saying?" She shook her head. "Now see what you made me do?"

"You were saying, 'When we get married.' "

"Oh yes, now I remember. When we do, I want you to talk

to me and tell me your plans and perhaps even let me in on making a few together with you. Then I was going to ask, where have you been? And what have you been doing? But there's a whole other topic I've been needing to discuss."

"You sure are a sassy little thing, aren't you?" He smiled his crooked, little-boy playful smile. "And always full of questions. First off, I found a drummer heading to St. Louis and sold him my seed." He gestured toward the only chair in the room.

"Thank you, no. I'm plenty comfortable standing."

He stepped in closer. "So, next I found a crew that will take our cotton to New Orleans. If you're agreeable, we can leave midmorning tomorrow."

What? Had she heard what she thought she'd heard? Maybe she had misjudged the man after all. Then again, she couldn't believe he would propose just to get his hands on her cotton. "Did you just call it our cotton?"

"Well, I did say *our,* but I was referring to your cotton that we brought up the trace, and the eight bales I bought this evening."

"Henry Buckmeyer! If you wanted some lint, why didn't you get mine? Lord knows, I probably owe most of it to you anyway. Who did you buy from?"

"Our neighbors. I offered to let them go with us to New Orleans on the flatboat, or sell me their lint. They wanted the money and to get back home." He smiled.

"Oh." The tightness in her neck released. When was she going to stop jumping to conclusions, especially when they regarded him? "Flatboat? We're going on some little flatboat all the way to New Orleans?"

"It isn't too little. It'll carry both of your wagons, the sixteen bales of cotton, and your mules. Would have fit my team, too, if

I still owned them. The crew's loading twenty beeves of their own, and there's still room."

Would this man ever stop amazing her? Praise God she hadn't said more. "Well, I can certainly see that you had a busy day. What'd you pay for the cotton?"

He smiled. "I gave them a nickel a pound, half of what I heard it's bringing in New Orleans."

"Half? They're paying ten cents now?"

He nodded. "Yes, ma'am. Heard it more than once. Big run on lint; seems the mills back east and in England can't get enough."

"Ten cents!" What wonderful news. She should never think for one minute that God would let her down. He always came through! She started the calculations in her head, but Henry interrupted her mental math.

"Now if you're a mind, I've got a buyer for any or all of your wagons and mules."

Her head spun. He was going too fast. "I can't sell my mules. I've had them too long, I named them; they're like family."

"I know, that's what Levi said. But think about it. We're going to have to go to Tennessee from the port. I suppose we could stall them here and pick 'em up on the way back, but it'd be a far piece out of the way. How about the wagons?"

She shook her head. "Well, one of them is rightfully Levi's. His daddy owned one and Andy the other. What do you think? Are we going to need it?"

After a brief discussion and her promising to think on it, Henry grabbed the door's knob, then stepped closer. "We best get some rest. Tomorrow's shaping up to be a busy day."

She nodded, but didn't want to leave. She'd spent most of the day and all evening away from him, and now he was sending her to her room. "It does at that." She backed into the hall. She still needed to bring up his salvation, too, but it never seemed like the right time. And she had practiced what to say, how to broach the subject all afternoon, too. She had to be careful, especially remembering what he'd said that first day she'd gone and asked him to come with her.

She couldn't find the words. What had she decided to start with? "Did you check on Blue? Or see Levi?" Well, that sure wasn't it.

"Levi said he was going to stay at the livery. Blue Dog's with him."

"Do you think that's all right? I guess he's old enough."

"He is, and I do." He eased the door half closed. "He's a good kid. Best get some rest."

He needed to know—and better sooner than later—that his lack of faith would keep her from marrying him even though she loved him with her whole heart. She had learned her lesson the hard way. She sighed and wished she knew when and how would be the best way to tell him. "Henry?"

"Yes?"

"There's that thing I need to discuss with you. Remember when I said *if* we get married?"

"Of course, you just said it, Sue. What's the matter? Is there something wrong?"

She sighed and looked up into his endlessly blue eyes. "You probably know how scripture says not to unequally yoke yourself."

"Seems like I read that. In one of Paul's letters to the churches, wasn't it?"

"I'm not sure where, but that's not important. It's in there." She took his hand and studied the scars and calluses a minute.

"Henry, I have to tell you that I said yes to your proposal too quick." She looked up again. "Please know there's nothing I want more in the whole world, but I can't go against my Heavenly Father any more than I can go against my earthly one. I cannot marry a nonbeliever."

"But I told you. I don't have a problem with God. I do believe."

"But you're not a Christian. You haven't asked Jesus to be your Lord or been baptized into the faith."

He glanced off and shook his head. "I'm fine with the man upstairs. We're on plenty good terms. Trust me, it isn't a problem." He lifted her chin. "Better go and get some rest; got a long day ahead of us tomorrow."

"You're right." She tried to smile, peering into his eyes. "Henry, I love you, and I do trust you. But, dear man, you must understand that I cannot unequally yoke myself. I refuse to put your life in any jeopardy." She placed her hand on his chest. "You know what I've been through with Andy. If it isn't a problem for you, why don't you make it official for me? Confess Him before men. Get baptized in a church, for my sake. Will you think about it?"

He closed his eyes and nodded slightly.

"Thank you." She turned toward her room, leaving him standing in his doorway.

HENRY WATCHED until she reached her room, then eased his door shut and exhaled. What a woman; what a day. He hated it that the condition of his soul concerned her so. He set the bags under the bed, kicked his boots off, flopped down, and tried to find sleep.

The evening's events churned in his mind. He didn't know exactly what bothered him, but at least he knew now what had been troubling Sue, what she always seemed to have on the tip of her tongue that she couldn't spit out. He shook that off and thought again how everything had fallen into place that afternoon. He loved trading.

He'd found the drummer and made that deal, then overheard the flatboat captain and made that deal. His neighbors were still at the wharf, though why they were hanging around was a mystery, but he was grateful that they'd wanted the money now. He tried to count how many of his coins he had spent and how much profit lay ahead. The numbers ran together in his head, then melted into Sue's beautiful face.

The deal making had been exciting, but it paled when compared to making her his own, her saying yes. Had that been only yesterday? He didn't understand why his getting baptized was so important to her when he'd told her he believed. Maybe she was still worrying about her father's blessing. While he tried to count the days until he could have them in Tennessee, he drifted off.

His eyes popped open. He jumped up and walked to the window. Nothing stirred that he could make out in the bit of moonlight that cast an eerie glow on the street below. He retrieved his saddlebags and then hurried out. A ways off, a rooster crowed. A closer one answered. The kid in him wanted to join the competition, but he resisted the urge and hurried to the livery.

A growl greeted him as he slid the barn door open enough to slip in. "Blue."

The dog hushed, then padded softly to him and nudged his hand with his nose. "What is it, boy?"

CHAPTER

TWENTY-EIGHT

HENRY FOLLOWED HIS DOG toward the wagons. Blue whimpered a couple of times. It wasn't like him to whine. He trotted up to the sleeping Levi and licked him, looked at Henry, and whined again.

"What is it?" Henry kneeled beside Levi and saw the bottle still in his hand. A pint of whiskey with not much more than a swallow left. He slipped it from the boy's grasp and poured it out. "Get up, you rowdy." Henry grinned. "Jig's up."

Levi moaned and rolled away from him.

Henry stood and pushed the boy's hip with his boot. "Come on."

"Leave me alone. Sick. Head hurts something awful."

"I don't doubt that. Let's find some coffee and get you cleaned up before your aunt sees you." Henry rocked him harder with his boot. "Get up. I'm not leaving."

The stench of alcohol preceded Levi as he crawled out from under the wagon with his head hanging. "I tell you I'm sick."

"No, you're hungover."

Henry helped the boy stand, then leaned him against the

wagon. He grabbed Levi's new shirt lying near, then pulled out a big chunk of jerky and tossed it to the dog. Blue caught it midair. "Stay."

He draped an arm around Levi and helped him out of the barn. False dawn draped Jefferson in hues of gray. He eased the boy down the street a block, then cut over on a side street where he'd noticed a barbershop last evening. "Good, they're open."

Half an hour and half a pot of coffee later, he and the boy emerged. Henry looked to Levi. "You better?"

"Yes, sir. I could have stood a lot longer in that hot bath. It was great. But I'm ready for whatever."

"Let's get the wagons and pick up the ladies." Henry headed toward the livery. "We've got a busy morning ahead."

Levi caught up. "You going to tell her?"

Henry rubbed his smooth chin. He never should have told the boy about him having those beers when he was fifteen. At least the boy hadn't got into a fight and killed someone, just sowed some wild oats and, Henry hoped, learned a lesson.

"No, not this time."

THE SOUNDS OF TRACE CHAINS clanging and leather popping opened Sue's eyes. Were they leaving without her? She lay there a minute adjusting to the unfamiliar surroundings. It suddenly dawned on her where she was, and she sat straight up in bed. Sunshine peeked through the lace curtains, casting tiny rays to the far wall, which it studded with points of light.

Oh, dear. She had thought she slept late yesterday. She couldn't remember the last time the sun had beat her up. She ran to the window. Both teams stood harnessed and hitched to the wagons below. Levi smiled up at her and waved. A knock on her door pulled her from the window.

"Sue, you up?"

"I am now." She frantically shook Becky. "Wake up! Wake up, little girl, we've got to hurry!" She scurried around the room in her chemise and pantalets, rounding up her and Becky's clothes. "Give me a minute, we'll be right down."

"Sure. I've got coffee."

Lord, bless that man! Sue dressed her daughter and then herself in record time. Thank goodness she'd braided Becky's hair last night. She picked at hers, unpinned it, letting the braid fall down her back, and grabbed her hat. She threw their dirty clothes into her bag, searched the room for anything she might be leaving, then tied the girl's bonnet under her chin. "All right! Let's go!"

Henry waited in the lead wagon. Becky waved at him. "Good morning! I'll ride back here with Levi so you and Mama can talk." She scampered out of sight. He smiled and leaned over, offering his hand.

Sue grasped it, climbed aboard, and accepted a cup of steaming coffee. "Thank you, my dear." Sitting back admiring him, she rubbed his smooth cheek. "My, don't you look nice."

"Thank you. You look better than nice." He patted her hand.

"So what's our first order of business this morning?"

"We're heading to the wharf to show our neighbors where to off-load my lint." He snapped the reins, and the team came to life. "What have you decided about your wagon and mules?"

"I can't part with them. I know it's silly. How much would it cost to stable them?"

"I thought you might say that. I asked Doug Howlett if he

would mind driving them back for you. He said he'd be pleased to if he could have the use of them. Wants to haul extra goods home and work them in the fields once he gets there. Shannan can drive one, and her son, Samuel, the other."

"Sounds great, everyone wins."

The parade passed the turnaround basin on the Big Cypress Bayou before the sun topped the lacy cypress trees. Four wagons in all. The flatboat and its crew were waiting. Cattle in a wooden pen nearby bellowed like they thought it was time to eat. Henry set the brake, jumped down, and then turned to help Sue. He caught her at her waist, and she floated to the ground.

He was so strong, and she could hardly believe she might soon be his wife. He only had to profess faith in Christ. Was that really so hard? And then her daddy better give his blessing. He had to this time.

Pulling her aside as Levi drove the first of her wagons onto the flatboat, Henry stepped away and hollered orders at one of the men working on the boat.

What compelled him to boss everyone he came around? And was it some kind of air about him that made people duty bound to obey him? Lord knew she'd have saved a heap of time and grief letting him run things from the start. But she never got past those blue eyes of his to detect any airs. She smiled.

The oldest and best dressed of the boatmen joined them. "Once we get your other wagon unloaded and those beeves onboard, you want to shove off or try to find more cargo?"

"I want to leave as soon as possible."

"Yes, sir." The man saluted, then went back to supervising the cotton's loading.

Sue couldn't believe what she'd just seen and heard.

"Henry, why did he do that? Who exactly are you that men let you boss them around the way you do?"

He laughed. "That guy there? He's the captain of this flatboat. Seeing as I'm the owner and his new boss, and him wanting to keep his job, he's doing the smart thing."

"Your boat? You bought this boat?"

He nodded and turned her around. "See that man over there leaning on the corral post?"

She looked until she spotted the guy. "Yes, I see him. Who is he?"

"I traded him my mules and harness for the craft. He wanted to sell the boat so he could buy himself a good team." Henry shrugged. "Guess you could say I was in the right place at the right time."

"I certainly would say that! Do you realize how blessed you are? That this is all God's doing?"

"Maybe, I don't know. You might be right, but I—"

"Trust me, Henry. You. Are. Blessed." She took his hand and squeezed. "And so am I!"

"Well, I am going to marry the most beautiful woman in the Red River Valley, so who am I to disagree?"

She laid her head against his shoulder and watched as the last of the cotton and then the bellowing cattle were loaded onto the flatboat and silently prayed. Oh, dear Lord, please bring him to salvation. Whatever it takes. Henry had the men tarp all the cotton and then stowed all of their other belongings inside the structure that sat in the middle of the craft. She paid extra attention to the boat's waterline, but even with everything loaded, it hadn't gone down much at all.

Henry had amazed her, buying the four mules from Titus back in Pleasant Mound, and then, when she missed the Jefferson buyers, trading them for the boat she needed to get her cotton to New Orleans. Plus he'd blessed the neighbors and bought their eight bales to sell. She wondered just how much money the man had, because he seemed to be going through it like water.

In no time, the men had her mules split and harnessed to her wagons and Henry's team delivered to their new owner. With a final request for Doug and Shannan to drop the hobbles and other borrowed items off at the Dawsons' and to let the Aikins know she hadn't forgot their fabric, Sue hurried across the gangplank and joined Henry. Becky and Blue stood by his side. Henry nodded to the captain. "We're ready, let's shove off."

Sue waved to the Howletts. "Stay safe! Be blessed!"

They waved back. "Y'all too! Love you!"

Sue looked around. "Wait! Where's Levi? I haven't seen him for a while."

Becky looked around Henry. "He's sleeping."

"During the day? Is he sick? Where is he?"

Henry nodded toward the boat's quarters. "In the cabin. He's fine."

Before Sue could ask more, the captain and his four crewmen pushed the boat away from its mooring with long poles. Once out a ways, two of the men raised their poles and ran to the other side. The captain went to the back and lowered another long pole with a fat end that ran through an iron ring. How the men navigated through the water and the speed with which they poled the craft along amazed her. She watched awhile, then faced Henry. "How long will it take us to get there?"

"About five days."

Henry slipped his hand into Sue's. "Care to inspect the accommodations?"

"Sure. Becky?" She held her hand out. "You coming?"

"No, Blue and I want to watch for a while. 'Sides, I've already seen the whole boat."

Henry's gut twisted a bit as he strolled toward the cabin, but as much as he didn't want to, he had to tell her. Once inside, he pointed out the different rooms and where she and Rebecca would be sleeping. He showed her his and Levi's berth, where, like Becky said, the boy sawed logs. He took her to the mess area and offered a chair. She sat, and he joined her.

"Want anything?" He nodded toward the cookstove. "We could fry up some fatback and potatoes if you'd like. Or chicken. Did I tell you I bought a few chickens? Are you hungry?"

"What's wrong, Henry? Is there something on your mind?"

He nodded. Could she read him so well so soon? "Yes, actually two things. It's been on my mind since you said it, and there hasn't been a good time to bring it up."

"Believe me, I know what you're talking about."

"You do?"

She laughed. "Not what you're going to say, but about finding the right time."

"Do you remember when you said Andy's death was all your fault? What did you mean by that?"

Her gaze dropped, and she went to fussing with her fingernails. Finally, she looked up. "He passed because I didn't honor my father like the Good Book says. His death was my punishment. It's why I refuse to go against God where you're concerned. I won't chance it."

"But what about grace? What about God's mercy and forgiveness? Mama always told me the only unforgivable sin was blaspheming the Holy Spirit. Have you repented of not honoring your father?"

"Of course! What a silly question."

"Then how is it you still blame yourself and carry so much guilt?"

"I—I don't know."

"Doesn't His grace and mercy and forgiveness apply to you?"

"Of course it does, and I hear what you're saying. You are an amazing man, Henry Buckmeyer."

"Glad you think so. Give it some thought, will you?"

"I promise."

"And the other thing, well, I don't like talking about it, but you need to know. You may not think I'm so amazing after all."

She looked into his eyes and smiled. "Don't you worry. Whatever it is, there's absolutely nothing in your past to make me stop loving you or thinking you're the greatest man who ever walked the face of this earth. And besides, we still have some more talking to do about getting you saved."

He wasn't so sure about that and couldn't see how him getting baptized was any of her business. It might not even matter once she knew. She probably could hear it all right, but would she still want him? "Sue, my mother and father never married. That man I killed when I was fifteen, that's what he was taunting me about."

She reached out and took his hands into hers. "Is that all? Why, it doesn't matter one iota to me what mistakes your parents made. My goodness, Henry, you were innocent."

He nodded. He'd heard it all before, but a part of him still believed it flawed him somehow. "It pleases me to no end that you think it doesn't matter. But what about your father? What's he likely to say?"

"Nowhere is it written that a person is required to tell everything he knows."

He smiled. The knot in his gut disappeared. "I love you, Susannah. I can hardly wait until you're my Mis'ess Buckmeyer."

She returned his smile. "I love—" But before she could say another word, a scream followed by a splash pulled him to his feet and out the door.

CHAPTER

TWENTY-NINE

SUE RACED ONTO THE DECK.

Becky stood at the boat's edge looking as if she was fixin' to jump. "Blue, you get back here right this minute! Blue!"

The dog swam toward the shore, where a brute of a mutt paced, barking and growling at him. Sue grabbed her daughter's hand. "Blue! Get back here!"

"Blue Dog," Henry bellowed from behind her. "Come here." Like he was on a rope, the dog turned, making a wide arc. The shepherd mix on the bank leapt into the water, heading straight for him.

Sue looked back at Henry. One of his boots lay on the deck, and he worked on getting the other one off. "What are you doing?"

He nodded toward the unfolding scene. The mongrel was closing in. "Getting my dog."

After one long stride, he stepped onto the rail, then dove. The brute lessened the distance to his unsuspecting prey. Henry pulled hard toward them, but the larger dog swam fast.

"No!" Becky stepped closer to the edge. "Blue! Blue!"

"Rebecca!" Sue tightened her grip. "Hurry, Henry!"

Before he could reach his dog, the cur made contact. He climbed onto Blue's back and pushed him under the water. Frantic seconds clicked by.

"No! Stop it!" Her daughter squeezed Sue's hand. "Blue!"

The dog finally emerged, turned, and attacked.

Becky wrapped her fingers around the side of her mouth. "Hurry, Daddy! Hurry!"

Fangs flashed. Blood stained both animals' heads and necks. Henry neared, then, with one hard pull, propelled himself into the melee.

"Henry! Be careful!"

He managed to separate the dogs. "Blue, go back!"

Obedient hound that he was, he turned away and swam toward the boat. The shore mutt latched on to Henry. Becky pulled her hand from Sue's and kneeled on the edge. "Come on, Blue. Come back here."

The dog reached the flatboat, and one of the crew helped drag him aboard. Blood oozed from gashes all over his head and shoulders. Becky hugged him. "Oh, Blue, why did you do that? You scared me half to death."

The current carried them past the fight. Sue turned to the pole men. "Stop this boat! Do you hear me? Stop it now!"

The man and the dog disappeared beneath the surface. The pole men changed direction, pushing hard. The craft lunged, then lurched, but they only managed to slow it a bit.

"Henry!" She couldn't bear this.

The boat floated further down the river. Sue moved to the back of the deck. The fight raged. Henry struggled to keep the dog's head below the water. People on the bank screamed. The brute kept popping back up, fangs bared and slashing every time. Man and dog went back under together.

Time slowed. The bloody spot fell further behind. Sue held her breath.

Come up, come up, she willed.

But the water's surface stilled. It remained still much too long. Too long! Much too long! Numbness worked its way up from her depths. Her jaw quivered. This couldn't be happening! Not again.

"Henry! No! God! God, save him!"

Becky stood. "Daaadeeee!" Terror filled her voice! "Daddy!"

Time stood still. "Henry!"

Nothing happened. Silence boomed in Sue's ears, through her head. Her knees threatened to give way.

The murky red water spread and calmed. Sue's heart stopped beating. Oh, God, she couldn't stand it. She couldn't live without him. A rage rose from her belly. "Henry! You can't die on me!"

Her knees buckled. She melted to the deck, buried her face in her skirts, and sobbed.

Becky stood and screamed at the top of her lungs. "Daddy! Daddy! Come up now!"

Seconds seemed like minutes. No dog. No man emerged.

Then Henry burst up, gasping for air. He spun around as though getting his bearings, then swam toward the boat.

"Daddy!" Becky clapped her hands. "Daddy! Mama! He's all right! He's coming!"

Had she heard right? Sue lifted her head.

He swam toward the boat. Both his arms were bleeding, washed each time they cut through the water. Sue joined Becky, Blue, and two of the boatmen at the rail's edge. Tears streamed down her face as if they would never stop. Thank You, thank You, God! Thank You, thank You, thank You!

She could hardly wait to hold Henry and would never let him go again. God had spared his life; he was alive! She belonged with him, to him. And he belonged to her.

Oh, Father, thank You! Lord, save his soul now, please. Draw him to Yourself. You know I cannot live without him.

Though it seemed to take forever, Henry reached the boat at last, and the men pulled him aboard. He gasped again and again, like he'd never get enough air. Sue fell to the floor beside him and held his face between her hands. "Henry, Henry, I was so scared."

She bent down and pressed her cheek against his, whispering in his ear, "I thought you were going to die. I couldn't bear losing you. I don't want to live without you."

He rubbed the back of her head. "I'll never leave you, Sue. Never, I promise."

She collapsed on him and bawled.

Becky fell across her shoulders. Her little arms wrapped around Sue. "It's all right, Mama. It's all right now. Daddy's safe. He didn't die. See?" She patted and rubbed her mother's back. "Don't cry, Mama."

Blue whimpered. Sue looked up. Bleeding himself, the dog licked his master's arm. She rose off Henry. Bright red blood covered his arms and oozed from a gash in his scalp, too. "Henry, you're hurt!" She sat up and turned to the captain, who had joined them. "Do we have any clean rags? Fetch me something!"

Levi came stumbling out of the center room. He rubbed his eyes as though he couldn't see well. He blinked, then stared at Henry bleeding on the deck. He walked next to Bitty Beck and kneeled. "What happened?"

"A bad dog was after Blue, so Daddy jumped in to help him. It was a huge mongrel, twice Blue's size, and it was fighting Blue; then it tried to kill Daddy." Becky's eyes filled again with tears. "He went under the water, Levi, and he didn't come out. Not for a long time."

"He's safe now, though; he'll be fine, sweetheart." Sue appreciated Levi comforting Becky and continued trying to clean Henry's wounds.

The man looked at them both. "I'm fine."

"Well, you don't look even fair to middling, much less fine."

"I'm so sorry I was asleep. I could have helped." He turned and retreated into the cabin's darkness. It wasn't long until he reemerged. "Auntie?"

"Yes, Levi?"

"Soon as you can, could I speak with you a minute? In private?"

What in the world? Why was he acting so strange? "Of course, dear—at least as private as we can get on this glorified raft." She smiled.

"I—uh—I have to tell you something." He ducked back into the shadows.

Henry sat up, holding a clean rag to his head wound. "I'm fine, Sue. You go ahead."

She stood and followed the boy inside the cabin. "Well, what is it?"

Levi hung his head. "The reason I was sleeping and didn't help Mister Henry." He looked into her eyes without lifting his chin. "I'd been up most all night."

"Why, honey? Was there trouble at the livery? Something happen I don't know about?"

"No, ma'am, I mean, yes, ma'am. Well, there wasn't any trouble. Nothing like that. See, I, uh, bought a pint of whiskey, and I got soaked. That's all."

She pushed him back. "That's all? That's all! What in the world were you doing drinking hard liquor, Levi Bartholomew Baylor?" Her eyes bore into his until he looked away.

"I only wanted to see what it tasted like. Bought me a bottle with some of my winnings from playing mumbley-peg at Cap Daingerfield's Springs. I'm sorry, Auntie. I am so sorry. I didn't mean to drink it all. It burned at first, but then it got to tasting kind of good. Made me feel like I was grown-up or something, I guess. It was gone before I knew it. Can you forgive me, Aunt Sue?"

Her heart melted. She extended both arms, and he walked into her embrace. She spoke into his ear, "Of course I can. We all make mistakes that we're sorry for later." She held him out at arm's length. "But promise me you'll never do that again."

"I promise. I never felt so bad in my whole life. I don't know what I'd have done if Mister Henry hadn't bought me a bath and poured coffee down me."

So Henry knew and hadn't told her? How dare he keep such a thing from her? Levi was not his nephew—not yet—and she certainly had a right to know what was going on with her children! She gave Levi another hug and a little peck on his cheek, then went to gathering all the clean cloth she could find.

She insisted Henry let her see to his wounds properly but didn't mention the incident with Levi. She wanted to think on it before spouting off. She smiled. Maybe she had learned something at least. She led the man to the mess table and went to work on him.

Becky marched in holding out the sewing kit. "Are you going to need this, Mama?"

"I don't know." Sue looked at Henry. "What do you think?"

"Wrapping should do."

She liked that answer. She would hate hurting him even if

it was to help him, but perhaps that was exactly what she needed to do. She needed to bring up the subject again and try to share her testimony or something. Tell him she couldn't marry him unless . . .

Might as well get it over with. Hurt him to help him. Tell him that even with her father's blessing, she could not marry him; not until he accepted the Lord's sacrifice and free gift of salvation. She wet a strip of cloth, then wrung it out and went to cleaning the first gash near his shoulder.

But should she mention his sinner's state at all? Would it only serve to make him mad? Especially when he actually acted more like a Christian than she did. He'd proved that over and over again. Daubing the cleaned wound with coal oil, she remembered all the times on the trace when he'd acted like Christ and she was the one who didn't.

But she'd have to let him know that the issue wasn't resolved just because he'd said he and the man upstairs were fine. It would rip his heart in two—and hers as well—if she just refused to marry him.

But could she really do that? Moving on to the next deep cut, she dipped the cloth and began again. How could she live the rest of her life without him if he absolutely refused salvation? Then again, what if today had been a warning of what might happen if she did go ahead and marry him no matter the consequences?

Would God really punish her if she conceded to unequally yoke herself to this most wonderful man? And what about His grace and mercy and forgiveness—all that Henry had said? She couldn't think about it; she couldn't bear to, not now. She must put it all out of her mind, far away from her innermost heart, and force herself to focus on the task at hand.

Once she finished, he extended his left arm, the one with

the most and worst wounds, and examined her doctoring. "I think that will do fine." He smiled. "Thank you."

"You are welcome, sir." She faced her daughter. "Please put the kit back where it goes; unless we need it to see after Blue. Have you checked him out good?"

"Yes, ma'am." The girl took the small box and stood. "He's fine; I made him a pallet next to my side of the bed."

Sue nodded, waited until Becky had left the room, then took a deep breath and held it. She exhaled slowly. "Henry, there's something we need to finish talking about."

He laughed. "I've already promised not to ever do anything stupid like that again."

"That's good, and I do appreciate it, but it's Father—"

"Sweet Susannah." He patted her hand. "Don't worry about him. I'm sure he'll be reasonable. We'll convince him; there's not anything we can't accomplish together."

"Henry. Listen to me, please. You saying that everything's fine with you and the man upstairs does not make it fine so far as I'm concerned. I've tried to tell you again and again, but you don't listen."

'I want you to quit worrying about me, Susannah."

"But—"

He held up his hand. "No buts. Everything will be fine. I promise. Don't you trust me?"

With her whole heart, she wanted to believe him, wanted to trust him, but he didn't know her daddy, and he didn't know the whole story of why he'd refused his blessing when she married Andy. How could she insult Henry by saying he didn't have enough money? Or that he had no trade? And without him being truly born again, there was no chance.

Oh, God, dear God, save Henry's soul!

CHAPTER

THIRTY

Like always, Henry healed fast. The third day out from Jefferson, he and Levi took to helping push the boat. Working the long poles stretched out his wounds and caused him to catch thunder from Sue each time she changed his bandages, but it gave him and the boy something to do. Contrary to what the old ladies back home thought, he hated lying about doing nothing.

That third evening, a bit before sunset, he walked toward the front of the boat for another push. His relief man caught up with him and took the long pole. "Miss Sue says your supper's ready."

"Good, I'm hungry." Henry strolled toward the mess galley that Sue had made her own. When he got there, he was amazed with the feast. He would love her even if she didn't know how to cook, but what a bonus. While he enjoyed a cup of coffee after his meal, the captain hurried in and grabbed a plate. After a few quick bites, he set his fork down.

"Mister Buckmeyer, sir."

"Call me Henry."

"Yes, sir." The captain grabbed another bite and bolted it

down. "Sir, the men and I have been talking, and, well, if you're agreeable, we'd like to buy the boat from you when we arrive in New Orleans."

"Why not? I was planning on selling her once we got the cotton sold."

"I thought I heard you say something like that. We have a problem though."

Henry smiled. "Not enough coin?"

"Yes, sir, that's it on the nail head. We're hoping to make some good profit on the beeves and a few other trade goods we've got, but I don't think it will be enough." He looked at his hands for a second, then faced Henry again. "Sir, would you consider taking a note from us for the remainder?"

Henry leaned back and glanced again at Sue. She lifted one shoulder a bit, then pulled one corner of her mouth into a lopsided smile. He liked this man, and his crew seemed top-notch. The risk would be high, but nothing compared to what the Lord had blessed him with. "No notes."

The man's face fell.

"But I will consider partnering with you."

"Partners? How would that work?"

"I was thinking to ask three hundred gold for the boat. Can you and the men cover half that?"

The captain nodded. "Yes, sir. That shouldn't be any problem. I'm thinking we should be able to come up with even a little more."

"No. Keep any extra for trading and supplies."

"Yes, sir."

"Can I trust you to do that?"

"Absolutely, sir."

"When you get back to Jefferson—and don't take my half of

this boat anywhere else—find a banker and give him my half of any profits."

The captain looked as though he was replaying Henry's conditions in his mind, then started nodding with a smile. "Why, yes, sir. I understand."

Henry stared into the man's eyes. He neither flinched nor seemed to be making himself stare back. Henry stuck out his hand, then remembered the unequally yoking that so bothered his beloved. "If you're a God-fearing man, then it's a deal."

The captain grasped Henry's hand in his and shook heartily. "Yes, sir, I am. So, it is a deal indeed."

SUE TRIED TO ENJOY THE CAREFREE DAYS on the flatboat, floating down the Red River, but the unrelenting realization that she must speak with Henry stole her peace. Each time she convinced herself of exactly what to say and when and how to say it, her heart ached at the possibility of losing him.

And the resolve tied her tongue into knots. When she'd try to start, she couldn't form the words or push them over her lips. One thought kept surfacing, though. The question he'd asked the captain. Replaying the incident, her mind's eye watched Henry say, "If you're a God-fearing man, then it's a deal."

Why had he said that? What would it matter to him if the captain was God fearing or not? Hmmm . . .

Finally, the fifth morning dawned. The captain said they should reach port before noon. After a good scrubbing, Becky got her hair braided, and then she put on her new blue dress, matching bonnet, and white ruffled apron. Sue also got her own bath. Having a river full of water at her disposal was nice after nine long, dirty days on that hot, dusty trace. If only the water could wash away the ache that grew in her heart.

About a mile out, the captain ordered the pole men to reverse. Sue found Henry on the bow. “What are they doing?”

“We’ve got to slow down; he’s going to steer us to that stretch of bank where the cattle are. Livestock has to go into holding pens, so we’ll off-load the beeves there, then get in line behind the other flatboats to deliver the cotton.”

“Oh, I thought we could—” She stopped herself, since naïveté might expose stupidity. She wished getting the boat unloaded could go faster, but no doubt it would take all day anyhow. Oh, well, by the end of it, she’d surely have her cotton sold.

But then what? Procrastination was not working well for her.

Henry laughed. “I thought I knew how busy the wharf was, but I never imagined anything like this.”

The day wore on as they inched their way up the line. Steamboats and skiffs sailed past to further docks, but more flatboats and barges lined up behind them. Slaves worked everywhere; the men’s dark, bare backs glistened under the sun and their burdens, and the women, in ankle-length, full skirts and modest blouses with long, puffy sleeves hurried about, carrying water or a bite of food. Some balanced loads on their heads. Always moving, dodging, and swaying as if performing some bizarre dance on the wharf. Some sang as they worked, adding to the buzz that filled the air.

One gang of slaves pulled on ropes attached to a block and tackle at the end of a heavy wooden boom and off-loaded the cotton on the fourth boat ahead of them. Their speed amazed her. In just minutes, each bale swung from the boat over to a waiting wagon where a slave eased it into place, making neat, interlocking stacks. Before the hoist hovered back over the boat again, another bale waited, ready for loading.

Henry pointed to a group of well-dressed gents wearing top hats who stood on the wharf huddled by the third boat in front of them. "Those are the buyers. See those wagons waiting? They'll take the lint to wherever the big guns say."

"Oh, I see, I see."

"The captain said the butcher who bought his steers heard that the man from Liverpool was paying the most—if he liked the quality."

Becky pulled on her dress. Sue looked down, having been unaware that her daughter had joined them. "Where is Liverpool?"

Sue slipped her hand into Henry's and squeezed, hoping he'd get the message to answer her daughter's question.

He looked at the ever-inquisitive child. "England."

"But I thought we hated the bloody British."

He laughed. "We did, but not anymore. We kissed and made up."

"Oh, I see." She looked up at him, then Sue, and giggled.

The dance continued until Sue's turn to meet with the buyers finally arrived. Just as the sky's fiery orb melted into the delta, splashing the sparkling water with its reflected pinks and purples and golden hues, a buyer with a thick accent handed her a piece of paper. Another handed Henry one. He stepped back onto the flatboat, then held his hand out to assist her. In no time, all the cotton was off-loaded, and the pole men pushed them away from the wharf.

It happened that quickly. Her cotton was sold.

The captain with his first mate waved from the dock. "We'll find you."

Henry nodded, waved back, and then turned to her. "What'd you get?"

She took a deep breath, glanced at the buyers, who were already looking to the next flatboat, then back to her piece of paper. Would this be the end? "Ten and a quarter cents! Oh, Henry, I never dreamed—" She tapped a finger over her lips. Her chest tightened, and tears welled in her eyes. She wanted to jump up and down like a little girl, but now that she'd finally sold her lint, would there be anything to hold him to her after she told him she couldn't marry him? She swallowed and focused on the moment. "How about you? What did you get?"

He smiled. "Nine and three quarters, but I didn't have to work as hard for mine."

She wished he'd gotten the same price she did, but her neighbors apparently hadn't taken the care she and Levi had in picking and cleaning the lint.

"That's wonderful! You almost doubled your investment in five days. What have I said? More than once? You are amazing. When and where do we go to get our money?"

"First thing in the morning, we'll walk over to the Wilkins and Linton Counting House." He nodded toward her slip of paper. "That's a bearer note, so don't lose it. Anyone can cash it."

She thought about it only a second, then held it out to him. He should know that she trusted him completely even if she couldn't marry him. "Would you hold it for me, please?"

He took it, folded it neatly, then put it with his into an inside vest pocket. "Of course."

For one more year, she and the children would survive,

even have a bit of money extra. But would that mean anything without Henry at her side? She didn't want to go back to the way life used to be—not ever! But what choice did she have? She made herself smile and looked hard into his eyes, the windows of his soul.

How could he refuse the Lord's love and lose her?

Surely, he would come around.

She sighed, determined to trust the Lord to get through to him where she could not. Worry only hindered every promise of God, so she couldn't think on it and fret so much. They were already twenty feet or so from the wharf. "And where are we going now?"

"To the loading docks on the other side of where the steamboats are."

He and the captain had everything all worked out. A part of her wanted to tell everyone what to do and how to do it, but the bigger part sought just to relax and let Henry take care of it all. She smiled; especially since he enjoyed that so much. The thought of her sole job being to take care of him and the children was heavenly, but she couldn't, wouldn't let that happen. Her hardheadedness had already cost her Andrew and Levi his father; she'd not let Henry lose his life over it, too.

As she pushed the ache down, deeper into her heart, a realization came to her. "Weren't you going to sell your furs here?"

"No, ma'am."

"Why not? Is there a better place?"

"No, I've decided to keep them."

"Keep them? Why in the world have you decided to keep them?"

He smiled that little-boy grin that she loved so much and

would maybe miss the most. "I don't want anyone else having the furs you slept on."

"Really? Henry Buckmeyer! How sweet." She slowly shook her head. "That's a heap of money."

He shrugged. "I know a tanner who lives a bit out of Jonesboro. Thought I'd get him to cure them on out. Maybe you and Rebecca can make us something."

Would this man ever stop amazing her? Just because she had slept on them, he wanted to keep the furs. How could she not marry him?

Fix it, Father, fix it as only You can.

The flatboat reached the loading dock just as the night got good and dark, but numerous coal oil lanterns hung from poles attached to the wharf's edge. They lit up the area with a golden hue that cast eerie shadows but made it easy enough to see.

On into the night, men—slave and white—worked, loading the flatboats this time, Henry's included. Getting the captain and his crew ready for a return trip to Jefferson, the parade of stevedores and slaves carried wooden boxes and small bales aboard. It was almost too much. Some rolled barrels on their edges as fast as they could walk. The speed at which they worked flabbergasted her.

The captain came up waving and walked the gangplank onto the flatboat. He extended his hand and shook Henry's. His broad smile indicated his efforts had proved successful. "Got everything we needed and some ace-high trading goods to boot! My mate will be here directly."

Henry nodded. "Excellent."

The wharf's hustle-bustle seemed never-ending to Sue. "Will they keep at it like this all night long?"

The captain leaned out and looked across Henry. "No,

ma'am, not unless a storm's coming. It should slow down here in a few more hours."

One of the boatmen walked the gangplank, balancing a big rectangular box on his shoulder. Two black men followed him with identical but smaller boxes. Their new brass latches reflected the lantern light and sparkled.

Henry pointed to the cabin. "The big one goes in my room and the other two into the ladies' quarters."

"Yes, sir."

Sue watched the men for a moment, then faced Henry. "What are those?"

"Trunks. They call them steamer trunks. We need to pack them tonight."

She watched as the men returned empty-handed. "Why tonight?"

"We sail at nine sharp tomorrow morning."

"Wow, and you accused me of not letting any grass grow under my feet!"

He laughed.

She loved it when he laughed; it would be so hard not to hear that wonderful sound. Time to make her mind up whether to travel on to Tennessee and see her father was running out. On the map, it looked about the same distance from New Orleans to Memphis as it was to go home. Smiling at him, she shook her head. "When did all this happen?"

"This afternoon."

"But how? You never left the boat!"

He grinned. "I have my ways."

The captain nodded. "I believe if Mister Henry said frog, these boys of mine would outdo each other seeing how high they could jump."

He did have that effect on people; shame she'd had such a misconception of him in the beginning. Maybe she would have picked up on his natural leadership abilities and let him run her show sooner. "But I have to go by the countinghouse before we sail. I can't pay for steamer tickets until I do."

Henry held up a hand. "Everything is taken care of. We'll pick up our cotton money in the morning, and then stroll on down to the wharf, board, and steam our way to Memphis. Be there in less than a week."

At the mention of Memphis, her heart skipped a beat. He wouldn't need to go at all since her father's blessing was no longer the main issue, but his salvation. Should she, though? Becky had never met her grandfather. Yes, she would. Maybe there could still be a miracle. In her heart, she knew what she had to do, but would she be able? She looked skyward. Give me strength, Lord.

CHAPTER

THIRTY-ONE

A STEAMBOAT'S WHISTLE SOUNDED, and Henry sat up in bed. He blinked away the night, then realized he held his pistol. Hmmm, was he getting jumpy? He liked it that he never slept too deep. He patted the bed for Blue, then chided himself for being such a creature of habit. Rebecca had stolen the dog's heart same as his.

Well, the mutt did still mind him; at least that was the same. He pulled on his boots, then eased outside. The moon, three-quarters full, lay heavy on the western sky, but the stars still rode the heavens. He figured two, maybe two and a half hours until false dawn.

He slipped into the galley. Sue already worked on making coffee. He loved the way she looked in the early morning. She turned and faced him. "You'd think that steamboat captain would be a bit more considerate."

Henry shrugged. "He's up; why not everyone else?"

She didn't answer his question but asked one of her own. "You want breakfast now or later?"

"Whenever. You cook it, I'll eat it. But if you're of a mind to, we can wait until we're onboard."

"Now's good, I guess." She went to working on biscuits. "Becky and I have everything packed. When will we leave for the countinghouse?"

"The man said they open at seven on the dot."

"Did he say how far it is?"

"Only a couple of streets down and one over. I know the place."

She handed him a cup, then filled it with steaming brew. "How are we getting the trunks from here to the steamboat?"

He smiled. "The captain said he'd see to it."

"Are you and Levi packed?"

"Yes, ma'am."

She put the lid on the Dutch oven and set it on top of the stove, then faced him. "Take that shirt off, and I'll change your bandages."

"They're fine." He held his hands up. "See? Everything is going to be fine. We'll get our money and then sail on to Memphis. I'm looking forward to meeting your father."

She nodded, but tears filled her eyes. She blinked them away, then stared at him like she wanted to say more, but instead returned to tending the sizzling fatback.

He wished she wouldn't worry. She seemed so teary of late. "Sue? Aren't you anxious to see him again?"

She nodded, but didn't look up. "Yes, I suppose. It's been so long a time, and I guess I'm a little afraid of what he's going to say."

BY THE TIME SUE had the gravy close to perfect, Levi had joined Henry at the table. "Mmm-mmm, Auntie, you sure got things smelling great in here!"

She smiled at him, then listened to the males' banter as she heaped their plates full. Henry was going to have to separate his belongings out of their shared trunk; she had to give him time for that. The boy burst out laughing, drawing her attention. She smiled. Being around the man had made such a difference in her nephew. Another thing she'd miss by not having Henry in her life, Levi and Becky would suffer his loss as well.

Sue couldn't imagine what her daughter would do when she found out. Becky would probably hate her for not marrying him anyway, but she'd just have to understand that God must always come first. Henry was such a good man, but good wasn't enough; he had to be a believer. And she had to bring it up again. She would not risk his life, no matter what.

He set his cup down. "Levi, your aunt Sue and I need to go to the countinghouse this morning. How about you go to the steamboat with the trunks?"

"I can do that; want me to hire a wagon or something?"

"No, the captain said he would see to it, but I'd like you to be along."

The boy sat taller. "Yes, sir, I'll keep an eye on things."

Henry pulled out a wad of printed tickets from his inside vest pocket and handed one to Levi. "Put everything in our room."

"Yes, sir."

Oh, Lord, he'd already bought the tickets. Should she tell him before they even went to the countinghouse? Let him know not to load his things onto the steamboat?

At first light, she looked around. She hoped she hadn't forgotten anything. She'd cleaned and packed her skillets and Dutch oven after breakfast. Henry and Levi waited by the gangplank. Her nephew stood guard over the trunks and the bundle of furs that lay on top. Sue took her daughter's hand. "I think we're ready then."

She should say something. The longer she waited, the worse it would be.

A cloud settled over her heart. Would this be her last morning with him? The last hours and minutes she and Henry Buckmeyer would spend together? She hoped he'd be able to redeem his steamboat ticket. After she paid his wages and replaced his mule and musket, would she have enough money for the trip to Memphis and home again?

And what about Blue? She couldn't separate Becky from that dog, especially after taking Henry from her. Would he even consider selling Blue to her after she broke his heart?

Henry led the way off the flatboat while all her chaotic questions cluttered her brain. He waited on the dock for her, then offered his arm. She knew one thing for certain. She had way more questions than answers.

Like it was just another day with nothing special on her mind, she strolled with him to the Wilkins and Linton Counting House. As she walked, putting one foot in front of the other as though everything was perfectly normal, she guessed that it would just all have to come out after the money, because, well, there the place stood. The brick, two-story building looked rather ordinary except for the heavy oak door laden with brass hinges and a double lock.

Henry knocked. Shortly, a little window in the middle of the oversize door opened, and a man's face peered out. "Good morning, may I help you folks?"

"We have bearer notes we'd like to cash." Henry held up the papers.

The little window closed, and the big door opened. As soon

as she and Henry walked in with Becky and the dog following, the man shut the door and locked it tight. He eyed Blue and the girl but didn't say anything and gestured toward a table with chairs. "May I see your notes, sir?"

Henry handed them over identifying which was whose. Within minutes, the banker returned, carrying a tray laden with gold and silver coins. He stacked forty twenty-dollar gold pieces in eight neat columns in front of Sue, then placed twenty silver dollars behind them as though they were the poor relatives or distant cousins.

She'd never seen so much money at one time, much less owned it. All these weeks and months, this was the moment she'd been working toward. All the plowing, planting, hoeing, and picking—all that work. Finally. Paid off. She'd sown, and as scripture promised, she now reaped. God had indeed blessed the work of her hands. Tears filled her eyes.

Father. Thank You.

Then her elation fell to the pit. Staring at the fortune before her, Sue realized none of it was going to be worth anything without Henry.

Becky leaned over and stared at the stacks. "Mama, I think we're rich." She reached out and took a coin, examining it more closely.

"Well, I don't know about that; does look like we won't starve this year, thanks be to the Lord." Sue made herself smile at her little girl. But it was not a smile from her heart. There were no smiles in her heart. She couldn't go to Memphis. Oh, she'd told herself she and Becky would go to see her father, play it out and see what happened, but doing so would only send Henry the message that she would marry him with her father's blessing, and she could not do that.

She had to tell him—again. Maybe he'd listen this time.

The banker placed nineteen gold coins and another ten silver ones in front of Henry. He pushed a piece of paper each in front of her and Henry. "Please sign or make your mark." Reaching across the table, he tapped the line at the bottom of each of the papers.

Henry signed first, a quick scribble that she couldn't have read if she didn't know his name. Only a few letters in the scrawl were legible. She wrote her signature in the neat penmanship that she'd been taught so long ago.

Sue picked up a gold coin and closed her eyes, trying to remember the last time she'd held twenty dollars at one time. She set it back, then faced Henry. A lot of it was his anyway. "Would you please keep this safe for me?"

He nodded once and smiled. "My pleasure." He put all the coins in his saddlebag, draped it over his shoulder, then stood. He extended his hand, and she let him pull her to her feet. Becky followed beside Blue Dog. Her little optimistic world was about to be blown asunder.

Dear God, please prepare her, protect her heart.

Once outside, Sue let him lead her toward the wharf. With each step, the heaviness in her chest increased, until she could hardly breathe. Every time her heart pounded against it, she thought the organ might burst. He turned the corner. A steamboat slightly bobbed by the dock in all its pristine grandeur.

She stopped and pulled away. The tears flowed freely down her cheeks. "I can't. I'm sorry. We can't."

He faced her. "Sue, what's wrong? You can't board the steamer? Why?"

She ducked her head, then shook it slowly back and forth. Her shoulders heaved and her gut knotted. She made herself look him in the eyes. "I love you, Henry, I do, with all of my heart and every part of my being, but even if Daddy gives his blessing, I cannot marry you if you are not born again."

HE HEARD HER WORDS. He saw the tears. But nothing made sense. She loved him, but even if her father— "But, sweetheart? You're not making any sense. I told you—"

"Mama! What are you saying?" Rebecca grabbed her mother's hand. "It's all set! We're going to be a family! Daddy loves you. You love him. What's wrong with you?"

Sue looked from Rebecca back to him. "It's—it's—I do love you, but, Henry, you're not a believer. It would be a disaster if we married. You might die." She kneeled and hugged her daughter. "I'm sorry, Becky. I know you love him, too. But it would be just like me running off with your father. I couldn't stand it if anything happened to Henry because of my disobedience. I cannot marry him."

Tears wet her face and her dress, and she buried her face in her daughter's apron and sobbed.

Henry filled his lungs. He should have told her before, bless her heart. All this time, he'd thought she wasn't herself over meeting with her father, facing him again after so long.

The little girl took off her mother's hat and hugged her head to her chest. "No, Mama, you have to. Tell her, Daddy. Tell her." She laid her head on Sue's hair and wept right along with her.

It cut his heart to see her hurting so, to see both of them in such pain. He kneeled beside them. "Sue, look at me."

She shook her head. "I can't. Please, just go."

"Rebecca, will you look at me?"

The girl caught her breath, sniffed twice, then nodded and looked up.

"Good, thank you. Now will you please tell your mother that the Good Lord has saved my soul, and that I'm on my way to Heaven?"

Sue looked up. She stared at him as though she hadn't heard him right. "What? When? I thought you—"

He took a deep breath, then blew it out. "I'm so sorry. I should have told you. It happened in the water with that dog. For a bit there, I thought I wasn't going to make it, that I had gone and got myself killed."

She swiped at her cheek. "I thought so, too, and that it was a warning from God what would happen if—"

"But I cried out to the Lord, Sue, and He saved me."

She held up both hands and glared at him. "Why! Why didn't you tell me? You knew I was upset! How many times have I brought it up? I can't believe that you've let me—"

"I thought you were only worried about seeing your father again. Why didn't you say something?"

"Me! Why didn't I say something? Patrick Henry Buckmeyer! I did! More than once! And you just kept telling me you were fine with the man upstairs. Why couldn't you tell me when you got saved? I'd think you'd shout it from the rooftops! Why are you acting like it was nothing important?"

"Well." He searched her eyes. "I wanted to tell you, but I figured it best to wait."

"Wait? Why in the world wait? Why not just tell me what's going on with you? Why don't you ever tell me what's going on with you?" She stood and stomped her foot. "Would that have been such a hard thing?" She stared at him like she wanted to hit him.

He shook his head. "That dog had pulled me so far under, Sue, and I couldn't hold my breath another second. In my head, I hollered, screamed for dear life, 'Jesus! Save me!' Then, someway or another, I don't know exactly how, I was able to get a breath. He saved me. I knew it was Him. I was drowning, then suddenly, I could breathe."

"You've been saved?"

"Yes, Mama, didn't you hear?" Becky jumped up and down clapping.

Sue's lips thinned, and her eyes bore into him. She seethed inside. "So what? For five days now, you've been a Christian, and you didn't think I'd want to know that?"

He gave her his little-boy crooked grin, but she wasn't having any part of letting him off the hook! "I can't believe you, Henry!"

"I did want to make sure it was real, that He hadn't just saved my life but actually saved my soul." He added a shrug. "Guess I was waiting to get baptized, too, do it up right."

SUE'S LIPS SPREAD into a slight smile, and a weight that had been keeping her heart so far down she wasn't sure it would ever see the light of joy again lifted completely. The sky got bluer, and, all of a sudden, she heard the birds singing. She wanted to kiss him, but, at the same time, thought about slapping him. She couldn't believe he'd kept such an important thing from her.

"So is it? Real? Are you sure that you're really saved now?"

He nodded. "Yes, my love, it is. I'm sure. I gave my life to Him. I'm a bona fide, born-again believer in Jesus Christ and in what He gave so that I could be saved."

"And you're not just saying that?"

"No." He laughed. "It's real. For the first time in my life, I know my heart is clean. I want you to be my wife, and I promise you that I will get your father's blessing, no matter what it takes." He stood there holding out his hand to her.

Fear washed over her. "But what if—"

"Sue, have I ever let you down? Have I ever not kept my word to you?"

She took his hand and let him pull her close, then threw her arms around his neck. But suddenly, she pushed back and looked to the right and to the left. People all around had stopped and were watching. She took a step back and held her hand in front of her, palm up. "I need some of my money."

He burst out laughing. "You do?"

"Yes, sir! I've got a wedding to get ready for."

He dug into his pocket and handed her several coins. "Think that'll be enough?"

She examined her palm, put the coins in her skirt pocket, then hugged him again. "Yes, yes, yes! I love you so much!"

Becky hugged him and her mother. "Me, too! I love both of you!"

"HOW ABOUT YOU AND BLUE going on aboard? Becky and I need to find a few things before we sail."

Rebecca tugged on her mother's hand. "Why can't Daddy and Blue go with us?"

"Dogs usually aren't welcome in ladies' shops, sweetheart."

The girl screwed her face. "Well, I don't see why. He's such a good boy." She kneeled and gave the animal a kiss. "I'll be back, Blue. You stay with Daddy."

Henry handed Sue two tickets. "The ship will ring three warning bells before it sails."

"We won't be long."

Henry located his and Levi's room. The boy sat on the bed; the trunks and furs filled one corner. "Thank you, son. Did the steward give you a key?"

The boy held it out. "Yes, sir."

Henry took it, then flipped him a silver dollar. "We've got some time. Go see what you can find."

The boy caught it midair. "Yes, sir."

Henry held up a finger. "When you hear the boat's bell ringing, don't dillydally. She'll sail whether you're aboard or not."

"I'll keep an ear out. Thanks."

Henry busied himself unpacking, then took to working on the big honey jar. Without too much of a mess, he retrieved its contents. Once the coins were washed, he laid everything on the dresser. He spread out his inheritance, pieces from his mother, until it covered the surface. Looked like a jewelry store.

He studied it. She'd always loved the sparkle of gold and jewels and invested every extra coin; left him a fortune, but he'd trade it all to have her back.

She would have loved Susannah, but even more she would have loved to see him finally saved. He let himself follow that train of thought for a minute, then came to a conundrum. Would he have ever come with Sue if his mother had still been alive, if she was still sick and bedfast? She'd be so surprised to see him in Heaven. He smiled. Had it taken her death for him to finally come to salvation?

Before a solid answer presented itself, the first warning bell rang. He scooped everything off the dresser, raised his shirt, and tucked the valuables into the new money belt that the captain had found for him. He tossed his saddlebags under the bed and pointed at Blue. "Stay."

The dog turned a tight circle, then lay down. A louder second bell clanged as he reached the lower railing. Sue and Rebecca stood on the wharf behind a short line of well-dressed folks. Both of his ladies held wrapped, string-tied packages.

SUE AND BECKY BOARDED and searched the wharf with Henry, but there was no sign of Levi. The deckhands went to throwing off the mooring lines and preparing to shove off just as the boy showed. He jumped on, waving up at her. "Whew! Sorry, didn't mean to worry you."

"I'm proud you made it. I'd hate to leave my favorite nephew behind in New Orleans."

Henry offered his arm again, which she simply loved. If he only knew how much! She looped her near arm through his and placed her other hand on top.

"Wait till you see it, Aunt Sue!" Levi held his hands out. "Come on, Bitty Beck. You can ride on my shoulders."

His cousin put her hands on her hips. "I'm getting much too big for that." She grinned, then softened her tone. "I would be pleased to take your arm, though."

Henry beamed, showing Sue and Becky the grand steamboat. Its two fancy-topped chimneys that climbed high into the sky belched white smoke that curled away from the wharf.

Rebecca pointed at the little gingerbread wood-and-glass house perched in the middle at the very top. "Is that where the captain steers the boat? Way up there?"

"Yes, ma'am. Either him or the first mate."

Sue's gaze climbed the three decks, each fenced with pristine white railings. Her assessment ended at the rear of the boat with its huge paddle. Then she turned back to him.

He grinned. "You like those flags there on the jack staff?"

She loved it when he acted playful with her. "Oh yes, very gallant those pennants."

The deck and everything inside the big vessel overwhelmed her. Beautifully carved wooden arches, one after another after another, lined both sides of the grand hall. Elegant crystal chandeliers hung in the center from the entry all the way to the far end of the magnificent room. Overstuffed chairs invited seating; and musicians played harps, flutes, and violins.

"Mama, it's so—it's so fancy!"

"Come this way. We're on the second deck across the hall from each other." Henry led her up the wide stairs, then down to room 68. He opened the door.

"Oh, Henry!" Sue grinned and twirled into the room, falling across the bed laughing.

Becky followed suit and jumped on the soft mattress beside her. "Mama! I am surprised at you! Don't you know we do not treat other people's furniture that way?" She fell into a pile of giggles as Sue tickled her relentlessly.

"I can't breathe. Stop it, please! Stop, Mama!"

Henry tipped his hat. "We'll let you ladies get unpacked and see you a bit later."

"That sounds lovely. If not before, at dinnertime?"

"There's a calliope on the upper deck that announces the noonday meal. I'll call for you, and we can go down together."

Sue closed the door and locked it, then ran to the steamer trunk where she had packed her material. She removed the bolt and laid it on the bed next to the packages.

Becky started unwrapping them. "What's a cuhlopie?"

"Calliope, Rebecca. It's an organ—a little like a piano—that's run by steam."

"Like this boat?"

"Yes, ma'am. Just like that."

The girl unwrapped the two yards of lace and held it to her face. "Do you know how you're going to make your dress, Mama? I want puffy sleeves on mine and a high collar with lace under my chin. Straight down to the floor and more lace on the bottom."

"Well, sounds like you've done a powerful lot of thinking on this." Sue smiled in front of the full-length mirror and held several turns of material off the bolt in front of her. "I haven't really decided."

"You're going to be a beautiful bride, Mama."

The days on the steamboat passed in a flurry of fabric and lace and crystal baubles. Every time her father and his blessing came to mind, Sue refused to dwell on it or even consider he might refuse. Henry had promised, and God was on the throne and in control. She had great confidence in His love for her and trusted that He had sent Henry into her life.

By the end of their way up the Mississippi, two new, beautiful dresses hung sparkling and finished in the water closet, hidden from male eyes. Sue and Becky flanked Henry on the deck as the grand ship pulled into the harbor at Memphis. Two bellmen and Levi waited beside the trunks.

Sue could hardly believe how the city had grown. New buildings rose toward the sky in every direction. The ship's captain rang the bell from his gingerbread tower announcing its arrival, and the walkway was lowered to the dock. People clamored to get off and greet families and businessmen. In no hurry, Sue waited for the crowd to disperse somewhat, then strolled to the walkway holding Becky's hand.

Suddenly, a dark cloud settled over her heart. Would her joy be turned to mourning? How could she face another day if her father said no?

Certain she could find her childhood home, Sue wondered for the thousandth time if her daddy still lived there. Her stomach rolled, and her breath came hard. Ten years—a full decade—had passed, and today—this day—she might face him again.

CHAPTER

THIRTY-TWO

SUE STEPPED UP TO THE FRONT DOOR holding Henry's hand. Becky stood at her side. A rock the size of Gibraltar rolled in her stomach. Her breath caught, and her knees threatened failure. She made a fist, lifted it to the door, and knocked with great trepidation. Her heart pounded. Seconds seemed like hours. Her mouth went dry, and dizziness jeopardized her consciousness.

She turned to Henry. "What if he doesn't live here anymore?"

"Then we'll find him." He squeezed her hand softly.

At last, she heard footsteps making their way to the door on the hardwood floor inside. It opened, and a kind-looking lady peered out. "Good morning. May I help you?"

"Yes, I'm—" Sue's voice cracked. She stopped and cleared her throat. Had her father remarried? She smiled at the woman and began again. "My name is Susannah Abbott Baylor, and I'm trying—"

The lady's face lit up like the full moon over the prairie. Her eyes widened. "You're Miss Susannah?" She opened the door wider and hollered back inside. "Judge! Judge! It's Miss Susannah! She's come home!" She wrapped her arm around

Sue's shoulder and guided her inside. "I keep house for your father, dear."

Becky took Sue's hand, and Henry fell back.

"Hurry, Judge! It's Susannah! Your Susannah! She's here!"

A step tap step tap sounded in rapid succession. Her daddy appeared in the doorway of his study with a cane in his hand. Tears filled her eyes. He looked so much older. His hair had thinned and grayed, and his once broad shoulders seemed frail compared to what she remembered. She froze.

The lady stepped back and spoke softly, with great compassion in her voice. "See, Judge? I told you. God has answered our prayers. She's come home."

Her father dropped his cane and ran to her, embraced her, and Sue hugged him back. "Daddy, oh, Daddy, it's been so long! I'm sorry, Daddy. I'm so sorry. Can you ever forgive me?" She broke into sobs and held him tighter.

He squeezed, then held her back. "Shhh. I want to look at your face, Susannah. My dear Susannah, how my heart has yearned to see you again. I didn't know if you were even alive. But now you're home. Of course you are forgiven, Daughter." He turned to the woman and held up his hand. "Bring a robe and sandals, kill the fatted calf! My daughter was dead, and now she lives!" He filled his lungs, then exhaled slowly. "It's time to celebrate."

The lady hurried in one direction, then turned and went in another. "Oh, my goodness! Which way am I going? I'll prepare a grand homecoming dinner, sir." She turned to Susannah. "Welcome home, miss! Welcome home."

Her daddy looked past her for the first time and glared at Henry. "And who has brought you home to me, Susannah? This man isn't Andrew, unless I've gone senile."

"Daddy, I want you to meet Patrick Henry Buckmeyer. He wants to marry me." She turned to her daughter. "And this. This is your granddaughter, Rebecca Ruth. We call her Becky."

Becky stepped up. "So proud to make your acquaintance, Grandfather!" She giggled. "I'm so glad Daddy brought us to see you!" She hugged him tight, then turned and looked up at Sue. "And, Mama, you are the only one who calls me Becky. Daddy always calls me Rebecca."

The declaration took Sue by surprise. "Well, which do you prefer, sweetheart?"

"I like Rebecca." She smiled, which softened her tone. "It is the name you gave me."

Her father looked sternly at Sue. "Well, well." He patted the little girl's back. "So Patrick here is her father, and he finally wants to marry you?"

Henry stepped forward with his hand extended. "I go by Henry, sir. Rebecca's father, Andrew, passed before she was born, but she's been praying for a daddy and adopted me." He smiled and extended his hand.

The judge shook it, but not heartily. "Well, well." He looked to Sue again. "Sounds to me like there's a long story I need to hear. Come into the study and catch me up."

Rebecca held her grandfather's hand, and he led her to his study. Henry brought up the rear. Sue wished Levi had come, but understood why he'd elected to stay at the hotel since the man was no kin of his.

"I sent three separate letters, Daddy, but never heard back. I didn't know—I guess you never—"

"Letters?" He stopped and turned to face her. "I never got any letters, Susannah. Not one word in ten years from you—my only daughter."

Her eyes filled with tears, but she did her best not to let them fall. "Oh, Daddy, I'm so sorry. There's no mail service out there; I sent them with travelers. One, a man name of Winston, said he was an old friend of yours. I'd hoped he'd be faithful."

He closed his eyes, obviously thinking. "Cheney Winston, had to be. Heard he met an ill fate on the Mississippi. Steamboat fire." He threw his free hand in the air. "It is good to know you wrote, and now you're here. All is well with my soul." He looked down at his granddaughter. "How about you, young lady? All well with you?"

"Yes, sir, Grandfather."

"Then let's hear what your mother has to say for herself. What do you say?"

"I say let's!"

Sue started the story before she even took a seat. "Anyway, after Andrew and I married, we went to the Sulphur Fork Prairie in the Texas territory, where his brother worked a steam-powered sawmill. He had invited Andy to be his partner in a logging business."

She shared much of the past decade, with Becky interjecting and embellishing Sue's version. "In Jefferson, Henry bought our neighbors' cotton and a flatboat that we took to New Orleans." Sue glanced over at her fiancé. "From there, he brought us here on a steamboat. I've missed you so much, Daddy. I'm sorry for leaving the way I did. All these years, I've wanted to see you again, face you, and ask your forgiveness."

He nodded deeply one time. "You've made my heart glad once again, Susannah. I have suffered over your impetuousness and absence these ten years gone by, but, yes, Daughter, I certainly do forgive you and love you every bit as much as I ever have."

Henry stood. "Sir, Judge Abbott, I love your daughter, too. More than life. I brought her here to Memphis for the opportunity of asking you, sir, for her hand in marriage."

A sudden rush of love overwhelmed Sue, and her eyes filled with humble tears that God had made her to be this man's wife.

Her father looked taken aback. Shocking the great Judge Abbott had never been an easy thing to do. He stood, with a slight gesture toward Henry. "Ladies, if you'll grant us leave of your most pleasurable company; we men have matters to discuss."

Sue glanced at Henry, a bit shaken herself. He gave her a little nod as though saying, "I'm fine," but she didn't want to leave him in there alone. Why would her daddy ask such a thing? Nonetheless, she rose and took Rebecca's hand. "You'll excuse us then, Daddy. Henry."

THE JUDGE SAT BEHIND HIS DESK and gestured toward the wingback chair that rested in front of it where Sue had been sitting before. "Please sit."

"Thank you, sir."

"If I heard right, you've known my daughter for a month now?"

Henry smiled. "Yes, sir. But though we weren't formally introduced before, I've been smitten with Susannah for four years."

"So, you used her misfortune to worm your way into her life?"

"No, not at all, sir; she came to me asking for help. Actually, it quite surprised me, but I do understand that you might see it that way. I do not."

"What's your trade, son?"

"I don't have just one exactly."

"Jack-of-all-trades, master of none?"

Henry looked past the man to the bookcase that covered the wall behind his desk and then met his eyes again. "I wouldn't say that, exactly. Although I do make a good living through trade. And I hunt."

"Been married before?"

"No, sir."

"Engaged?"

"No, sir, I never asked a woman to wed, not until now."

"Fathered any children?"

Henry shook his head; this was one tough old man. "No, sir. None."

"Well, to your credit, you are here asking for my blessing. Why'd it take you so long if you've been smitten with her for four years now?"

"I wanted to have more to offer. I've been working hard, saving, and, of course, the vow."

"The what?"

Henry explained Sue's promise to God, and her reasons for making it, then about the long line of suitors she'd rebuffed over the years. "I never should've waited so long to get to know her, but my mother took ill, and . . . plans change." He grinned. "I knew one thing for sure, your daughter's vow would not be broken, and so, here I am."

The judge looked away, then nodded ever so slightly. He faced Henry again. "Your mother, is she better now?"

"No, sir. She went home to her reward."

"And are you a believer, Mister Buckmeyer?"

"Yes, sir."

"Your father, is he alive?"

"Last I heard."

The judge held his hand out. "You've seen my house; the one Susannah grew up in. I do not want to think of her out there living in that wild Texas territory in some drafty sod cabin. Of course, it's only natural that I want what is best for my daughter and for her to be happy." He stood and held his hands out, palms up, as though showing Henry the opulence of his estate. "Can you build my Susannah such a house as she grew up in?"

He lifted a finger that silenced Henry, then paced. "Excuse me for speculating, but it appears that you're not of her station, Mister Buckmeyer. Even without my help, it seems that she's done well for herself financially, and now, as I see it, you might wish to capitalize on her hard-won success. What do you say to that?"

Henry stood, raised his shirt enough to undo his money belt, then went to pulling the gold coins out. "This is what I sold my bois d'arc seeds for this year, less what I spent on the way here." After he'd stacked the money on the judge's desk, he retrieved the jewelry and jewels he'd acquired over the years and inherited, and laid those down as well. "My mother lived frugally, and I was her only heir. Some of these pieces I bought for her because she loved the sparkle, but I could hardly get her to wear any of it, though she did enjoy fingering them." He smiled.

The judge looked at the pile of gold chains, rings, lockets, and sparkling pins. "Very impressive."

"Sir, I want to give Sue and Rebecca the best of everything."

"Commendable."

"And you should know, even though she hired me to accompany her on the Jefferson Trace, I've not taken one cent from your daughter, sir." He held his hands behind his back and nodded to the wealth. "And this doesn't even include our cotton money. That's in the safe back at the hotel." He smiled. "Sir, I give you my word that I will build your daughter a home befitting the lady she is."

The judge stared at him for many minutes.

Henry's heart beat against his chest, but he didn't say more.

The man walked over and flung his study's door open. "Susannah!"

SHE HEARD HIS CALL from her room upstairs and immediately rose.

"Can I bring your dolly, Mama?"

"Of course, but hurry along." Sue ran down the stairs, then slowed and caught her breath before rounding the corner. "Yes, Daddy?"

"Come in here, please."

She walked into his study and sat down. A tall, fairly wide stack of gold coins sat on her father's desk flanked by an assortment of jewels. None of that had been there when she'd left, and their cotton money she knew to be in the safe at the hotel. Had her father bought Henry off? Or tried to? Henry wouldn't accept, would he?

The judge did seem in a better mood, and she certainly never expected that. Had the talk gone well? She glanced at Henry to discern any speck of an answer from his countenance. He stood beside her and only slightly grinned when she looked his way. Rebecca walked straight past to her grandfather and climbed onto his knee. He lifted her and sat her back a bit, smiling broadly.

She laid her face on his chest. "I can hear your heart beating."

"Well, that's a good thing. I see you have one of your mother's dolls there. Did you know I bought that for her when she was about your age?"

"No, sir. I never imagined that she grew up in such a fine house with so many dolls." Rebecca played with a brass button on his vest. "Are you rich, Granddaddy?"

Sue cleared her throat. "Excuse me. I appreciate that you two need to get to know one another, but I'm a bit anxious here, Daddy." She stared at her father. "Won't you please tell me what you had to say to my Henry?"

The judge raised one eyebrow and turned to Rebecca. "Her Henry?"

The girl smiled. "Actually, truth be known, sir, he was my Henry first. Did he tell you that he's a friend of President Jackson?"

The judge looked at Henry with raised eyebrows, then stuck out his bottom lip. "No, he did not."

"Well, he is. And did he tell you he was a hero at the Battle of New Orleans with Old Hickory himself?"

Her grandfather smiled now. "Didn't mention that either."

Sue cleared her throat again.

"Oh, Susannah, you were always too impatient. I've heard your mother tell you a hundred times that patience was a virtue."

"Daddy!"

"I need to know something." He leaned toward her. "Do you truly love this man, Daughter?"

She turned and looked into Henry's face. "Yes, I do, Daddy,

with all my heart and soul and mind. I know I said I loved Andrew all those years ago, and I did, but I also wanted to show you, prove that I was grown. That love doesn't even compare to the love I hold in my heart for this man. Daddy, I know that God made me to be his wife, and him to be my husband."

Rebecca took her grandfather's face in her hands. "And I love him, too, and the sweet Lord sent him to be my daddy. I want him to stay with us forever and ever, so please, Granddaddy, tell me and tell me now that you are going to give us your blessing!"

He burst out laughing. "You are so much like your mother when she was your age, young lady." He looked to Susannah and studied her face, then to Henry, and, last, back to his granddaughter. He nodded. "All right then, yes. I will give my blessing on this union. But on one condition."

Sue held her breath. "Condition? But, Daddy—"

"Wait, Susannah." He held up his hand with his palm toward her. "My stipulation is that you'll allow me the honor of marrying you while you're here. You don't have to leave right away, do you?"

Sue jumped up and hugged Henry's neck, then ran around and hugged her daddy and Rebecca together. "Of course! Of course, you can marry us! I'd love that! How soon can you get to it?"

"My goodness, were you thinking to get married before supper, Susannah?"

She laughed and ran back around to Henry. "Could we?"

"Mama! We didn't bring our dresses!"

She looked at her daughter. "I was only teasing, silly. Would tomorrow night be too soon?"

Her daddy laughed the way Sue remembered him laughing

before her mother passed. "Tomorrow evening works for me. I'd like to book you and Henry a suite at the fanciest place I can find for your honeymoon weekend. Consider it a wedding gift." He lifted Rebecca and sat her on his desk. It made Sue smile. He used to sit her up on that very same desk. "And that way, my granddaughter and I can have a little time as well. We'll get to know one another better."

Henry dropped to one knee, and the room stilled. He retrieved the special gold and emerald ring from his vest pocket—the one Rebecca had chosen at Titus's Trading Post—then held it up toward her. "Susannah, now that your father has given his blessing."

She held out her left hand, and he took it.

"I love you and pledge all that I am and all that is mine to you. I promise to protect you and love you all the days of my life before God, your father, and our daughter. Will you make me the happiest man in the world? Will you be my wife?"

"Yes! Yes! Yes!" He stood, and she threw her arms around his neck. "I love you, Henry Buckmeyer!" She lifted her shoulders and shivered with delight, smiling so big she could hardly talk through it. "And this means we get Blue Dog, too!"

Rebecca clapped. "Yay! And for free!"

ACKNOWLEDGMENTS

For this book, I prayed; starting with chapter one and throughout the writing to typing "The End," then mailing it off, and I continue praying for God's anointing on it. For the gifts He has given—my dear husband Ron, fifteen years at the DFW Writers' Workshop where mentors took newbie writers and patiently taught and advised; for a creative vein, a way with—and love for—words, I first acknowledge and give all the glory to He who sits on the throne. I love and adore You, Abba. Thank You for setting the story of *Vow Unbroken* on course and for every blessing!

Among those blessings, besides my four children and fourteen grandsugars, I count my family and so many friends who He's given me to love and polish my life. Some old, some new, but to each one who offered an encouraging word along my writing way, I thank you.

Then the Lord crossed my path with the perfect agent, Mary Sue Seymour of The Seymour Agency. I'll never forget her stepping off the elevator in Mount Pleasant, Texas, and hugging my neck. "You're the first McAdoo I've met who wasn't family!"

Doesn't our Father have such a wonderful sense of humor?

Mary Sue's maiden name was McAdoo! I have no idea what the odds are, but with God, all things are possible. He definitely got our attention. No one can say He didn't orchestrate this wonderful journey every step of the way!

After that North East Texas Writers' Conference in April, on the trip back to DFW Airport, Mary Sue said, "Write me a historical Christian romance set in the 1800s, and I'll sell it." I did, and she did. Sent it to her in July, contracted for representation in August, then on October 10, shy of six months since meeting, she forwarded the offer from Howard Books. It's a joy to work with a woman who so loves the Lord. Thank you, Mary Sue!

Knowing she was sending the manuscript out to editors, again, I prayed, this time for God's divine choice, who turned out to be Beth Adams. God touched her heart with *Vow Unbroken* and called her to be a part of this Kingdom project. She found my story worthy, and so honored me when Howard Books, a division of Simon & Schuster, became my publisher. Beth's insightful suggestions truly improved Sue and Henry's story and helped make it even more of a tool in the Carpenter's hand to draw folks unto Him and His great love. Beth, you are a Texas-size blessing, and I thank you! How great it is to work with all the folks at Howard Books; that they all love Christ makes it an absolutely amazing experience.

Last, but oh so important, I want to acknowledge you, my reader. I pray *Vow Unbroken* makes you laugh and cry and that the Father sends His favor and personally speaks to you through these pages. I'd love to hear your testimony! If it blesses you, please tell your friends or buy an extra copy to give them! I'm grateful for each and every one of you. A big Texas thank-you for reading my novel.

READING GROUP GUIDE

INTRODUCTION

Widowed and a single parent to her daughter and nephew, Susannah Baylor refused to be swindled out of a fair price for her cotton harvest. She also refused to entertain the thought of marrying another man without the blessing of her estranged father. With the wise counsel of her best friend and relentless grit and determination, Susannah embarks on a journey across dangerous terrain that transforms her heart and changes her life forever.

TOPICS AND QUESTIONS FOR DISCUSSION

1. Which character in the story do you identify with or enjoy the most? What were some of the character's strengths? How did the character change or grow throughout the story? Was there a fatal flaw?

2. As chapter one opens, Susannah Baylor is talking with the man she had made an agreement with to purchase her cotton, and the conversation doesn't go as she expected. If you had been in her shoes, what would you have done? What words would you use to describe her in this first scene?

3. Why do you think Sue gets so irritated when Henry assumes leadership for deciding where to stop for the day or when to unhitch the animals on the initial leg of their journey on the trace? Have you ever been in a similar situation where you didn't fully know the best options, but you wanted to maintain control? How did you respond?

4. What role does Blue Dog play in the story? How is the story enriched by his presence? Are you a dog lover?

5. What were the assumptions Sue made about Henry before she knew him? How did her assumptions compare with the reality of her experience with him? What does her experience with Henry reveal about her own heart? Have you ever marginalized someone based on hearsay or your own prejudgments?

6. Describe the transformation that happens in Levi throughout the book. What do you think were some of the key factors that affected the change in his attitude and actions?

7. Have you known children like Rebecca Ruth? Describe the ways that she actually sees people and situations more clearly than her mother throughout the story. How is she a picture of Christ?

8. What prompted Susannah Baylor to make her vow? How do you feel about making vows like that? Read Matthew 5:33-37. What does Jesus say about oaths/vows in this passage? What do you think verse 37 means?

9. Sue blamed herself for her husband's death and for depriving her daughter of her father. What was her reason for blaming herself? If you had the chance to talk with her, what would you say to her about her self-contempt? How was Henry a messenger of the gospel to her?

10. When she started the journey on the trace, what was Sue's single-minded purpose? How did her determination help and how did it get in the way of progress? Have you ever wanted something so much that you lost sight of everything else? What does scripture call that kind of devotion to something or someone other than God?

11. At the Titus Trading Post, Henry spent "a month's worth of gathering and cleaning seeds" on gifts for Sue and her children. How does his generosity and lavish giving impact you? Have you had someone in your life who delighted in giving good things to you? Read Ephesians 1:3-14. What do these verses say about God's giving to us?

12. What qualities do Sue and her father share? What was your impression of her father?

13. In what ways does Henry reflect the image of God throughout the story? Read Genesis 1:27. Who does this passage say God made in his image? What does it mean to be made in God's image? How does this impact your assumptions and perspective about people who are not Christians?

14. How did Henry describe the impact of "being saved"? What is the difference between salvation and "being a good person"?

15. What was your favorite scene or chapter in the book?

ENHANCE YOUR BOOK CLUB

1. Read Proverbs 31. At your next book club, discuss how your perspective about being a woman compares with the picture painted in Proverbs 31. Discuss the tension of inhabiting both the strength and tenderness in a woman's heart. How have you responded to this tension in your life?

2. Read *Lost Women of the Bible* by Carolyn Custis James. At your next book club, discuss the first chapter on Eve and how Sue's character in *Vow Unbroken* reflects God's design for women (*ezer*).

3. Watch *Pride and Prejudice*, BBC version (5 hours). Discuss the themes of pride and prejudice illustrated throughout the movie and compare and contrast with the same themes in *Vow Unbroken*.

A CONVERSATION WITH CARYL McADOO

1. **What was the inspiration for writing *Vow Unbroken*?**

"Caryl," one of my mentors once said, "pick a genre."

But I never had. Then at a writers' conference, I met my agent, Mary Sue Seymour, (Can you believe her maiden name was McAdoo?) and she told me that historical Christian romances had a growing readership. Historical . . . hmm. That reminded me of a piece written then read for critique by Marion Butts, a teacher, historian, and colleague at the Red River Writer's Workshop. He told of yesteryear farmers from this history-rich area forming wagon trains to haul their cotton to market on the Jefferson Trace back in the 1800s.

Sounded like a great story setting and challenging journey. I loved the idea of writing a love story that would glorify God and minister to my readers. So, let's see—what if my heroine, Susannah Baylor, missed going with her neighbors and had to get her harvest to market by herself?

2. **What intrigues you about life in the 1800s on the prairie?**

What an exciting era that was in Texas, with plenty of hard work for its inhabitants. Most every aspect of my state history has fascinated me since I visited the Alamo as a little girl. Once I decided to write a historical, I dove into it anew, especially the history of my new home, Red River County, known since the 1800s as the Gateway to Texas.

The simplicity of prairie life and that razor's edge the early settlers' lives balanced on are what drew me to the time period. One bad crop, one wrong decision, or any number of natural disasters could wipe them out, and yet they headed west and overcame.

I hope my Sue's determination and grit well represents the spirit of those early pioneers.

3. What character was the most enjoyable to develop and why?

That's hard because I do love my Henry and young Rebecca—and Levi, too—but if I have to pick, I must say Susannah. I'd never choose to live her life and experience all the horrible obstacles she faced after marrying young and moving west, but I like to think that with God's help, I would overcome just like she did. I love her faith, her obedience, and how she trusts in the Lord to work everything out no matter how bad things get.

And that Blue Dog! Wasn't he just special?

4. Would you have enjoyed traveling by wagon across the country? Are you a camper?

I would! There'd be no hesitation to climb aboard. I'd jump at the chance so long as my own "Henry," my husband Ron, went along, and he'd be game for sure! I'd definitely enjoy traveling in a covered wagon. At that slower pace, you can really see the countryside and have the opportunity to meet folks along the way.

I am an adventurer, but not so much a camper at heart. I'm more of a twentieth-century lady, spoiled to life's luxuries like running water and flushing potties, appliances like stoves and refrigerators, and—especially in Texas—air-conditioning.

5. **Who have been your mentors on your journey to becoming an author?**

Oh, this is an easy question. The Lord led me to the DFW Writers Workshop back in the early '90s. I had always loved English and fancied myself a writer, and joined the group with completed, hand-written Biblical fiction. I learned there that I'd made every mistake possible!

But this awesome group of successful authors took me under their wings and spoon-fed me the craft. Writing creative fiction is a specialty, and without published authors like John McCord, Jack Ballas, and Don Whittington sharing their knowledge and time every week, fifty-two weeks a year; without their patient guidance, I'm not certain I ever would have been published.

God knew just what I needed.

6. **What is your strategy on days when you have writer's block?**

Well, pray always, of course. I've found that when the writing stops flowing freely, and the story refuses to go forward, I need to crawfish. Travel back to the place where my characters were last comfortable, then let them go where they want to, instead of where I was trying to take them. Works every time.

7. **What was the most challenging part of writing this story?**

Getting my dear Henry saved. He was such a good man and so confident. Because of his strength and self-assurance, I had to take him to the end of himself before it was believable that he would cry out to God for salvation. I pray that others who are good, moral people of honor and integrity will see themselves in Henry and realize they, too, need a Savior.

8. What kind of books do you enjoy reading for leisure?

If I'm reading, I'm not writing. But when I allow myself the luxury, I enjoy historical fiction, and mostly stick to Christian books to avoid foul language. I hate having to "say" those words in my head! I especially love reading stories set in Israel, so Bodie Thoene is a favorite author of mine. I love all her Zion series and one day hope to personally visit the Holy Lands she takes me to in her stories.

I love reading colleagues' books, too. Talia Carner's *Jerusalem Maiden* and Ann Everett's *Laid Out and Candle Lit* are a couple of great examples, although those stories wouldn't be classified as Christian. When you know the author, it just makes for some special reading.

9. Blue Dog plays a significant role in the story. Are you a dog lover?

I am! When we first moved to Red River County, this dog showed up. We're rearing four grandsons, and they all begged to keep him. We made him a warm place to sleep, fed him, and named him Franklin Doganor "Roo"sevelt. After about a week, a neighbor came on his four-wheeler and said, "That's my dog."

"Okay." The boys were crushed. "We're sorry. We thought he was a stray."

So the man tried to load him up (he said the dog loved

riding the four-wheeler), but Roo wouldn't get aboard. The owner lifted him onto the ATV and took him home. In no time, Roo came right back. The neighbor came three or four times to retrieve him, and we'd hear Roo barking and howling. Once he came back dragging a chewed-off rope dangling from a new collar.

The man finally gave him to us. We offered to pay, but he said no. Roo chose us of his own accord, and that's who I fashioned Blue Dog after. As a matter of fact, that's our Roo on the front cover of *Vow Unbroken*! How much fun is that?!

Presently, twice a day, we feed five dogs; three medium-to-big outside hounds and two small inside lap puppies. You can add to that three horses, two donkeys, a small herd of Nigerian dwarf dairy goats, several barn cats, and some free-range, egg-laying hens, and Roscoe, their rooster.

I love all animals! I've raised hedgehogs and hamsters and love aquariums, too. I told Ron once, that at any gift-giving occasion, he'd always get a gold star if my present was breathing! How easy am I?

10. *Vow Unbroken* is written very much in the vernacular of the 1800s. How did you prepare yourself to write so clearly in that time period?

Where else to go but the World Wide Web? I absolutely can't imagine how authors prior to the computer revolution did it. Every time I think of that, I'm reminded of Daniel 12:4, "But thou, O Daniel, shut up the words, and seal the book, even to the time of the end: many shall run to and fro, and knowledge shall be increased." What time in history has ever seen such an increase of knowledge as our own? Any bit of information is available right in our homes—even in our cars on our phones! It's amazing, and I am blessed to write with such resources a mere click away.

My characters' dialogue and introspection had to sound right, so a part of my research focused on the words and phrases used back then. It proved fascinating to find how so much of their slang had made it through the centuries, and that we're still saying the same things today. Others fell from grace, and those were fun to bring back to life in *Vow Unbroken*.

And as I'd be writing, if I had a question about a modern word, I'd go to the internet and ask when it came into use. For instance, "okay" was a WWII word, so I had to be very careful not to use it. Even after several edits, I still came across one and changed it to "alright."

Then my copy editor at Howard Books changed that to "all right." Speaking of Susan, she was awesome as was her attention to detail. She caught several common words used today that slipped by me, words and phrases like "glitch," "welcher," and "even keeled," which all came into popular use after 1832. So I cannot take all the credit that the vernacular in my story puts my readers right into that great past era. I'm thankful for the great help Simon & Schuster's Howard Books provided to make *Vow Unbroken* the best it could be—at every junction! They are totally impressive.

11. Have you ever lived on a farm?

Oh yes! But I guess more a ranch than a farm—although my husband Ron has grown wheat and soybeans on some of the 882 McAdoo acres here in Red River County, Sue's block in *Vow Unbroken*. Country living has always been a desire of our hearts.

Way back in the early '70s when our children were young, we rented a little farm house between Dallas and Tarrant counties (County Line Road, as a matter of fact) and had horses, a sheep, chickens, dogs, and cats, and a big garden.

Then, before we moved to Northeast Texas in '08, though a city girl, I still had all the same animals I do now—and even more—at our River Bottom Ranch in Grand Prairie. Irving, our lifelong home, was across the street. God miraculously provided the one hundred thirteen acres in the heart of the DFW Metroplex for us to keep the dozen quarter horses we inherited from my husband's father.

I still have that website with information about that ranch, and we still lease the land, though I'm a bona fide Red River County–lovin' lady through and through now. And isn't it interesting we live on another "county line" road? We're on the Red River side and Bowie County is across the street. Guess I'm going to need a Word from the Lord to ever move back to a big city.

12. Do you have plans to write another novel?

Why, yes; yes, I do. I have so many stories to share. I've written another novel titled *Heart Stolen,* set in 1844 with Levi, Sue's teenage nephew in *Vow Unbroken*, as my Texas Ranger hero. He rescues a Red River Valley girl, Sassy, from a band of Comanche and gets her home in time for Aunt Sue and Uncle Henry's Thanksgiving dinner.

And I'm already working on a new story in my Red River Chronicles called *Hope Reborn* with all these characters I've come to love and a few new ones—including a female

New York novelist! But she decides to go to Texas in Chapter One. My stories will always have a Texas setting. Like most Texans, I do love this great Lone Star State! When Beth, my editor, asked the cover designer to produce a logo for *Vow*, I was so excited and loved "A Lone Star Novel!"

I'm also thinking about other storylines, some contemporary, with entirely different characters. But all these players in my stories become my friends—well, the good guys. And I always want to find out what's happening with them as time marches on. I hope my readers feel the same way about everyone.